MARCHING THROUGH THE 'STANS

Trying not to wince, Belisarius studied the young—the *very* young—officer Calopodius standing in front of him. Belisarius thought—perhaps—to detect a slight trace of humor lurking somewhere in the back of his eyes. *I hope so*, he thought, rather grimly, *He'll need a sense of humor for this assignment.*

Aide, the sentient jewel from the future, tried to reassure him. **It worked for Magruder on the peninsula.**

Belisarius managed his own version of a mental snort. *Magruder was facing McClennan, Aide. McClellan! You think that vaudeville trickery would have worked against Grant or Sherman? Or Sheridan?*

He swiveled his head, looking toward the Malwa across the river. The enemy commander didn't *have* to be particularly talented to make Belisarius' scheme come apart at the seams. He simply had to be . . . determined, stubborn, and willing to rack up a butcher's bill. If anything, in fact, lack of imagination would work in his favor. If McClellan hadn't been such an intelligent man, he wouldn't have been spooked by shadows and mirages.

All right, I admit it's a stunt. But if it doesn't work, all that happens is that Calopodius and his men retreat. There's no disaster involved, since you're not depending on him to protect your supply lines.

Belisarius almost laughed. *Because I won't have any supply lines*, he finished. *Because I'm going to be trying a stunt of my own. Marching through two hundred miles of enemy territory, living off the land as I go.*

It worked for—

I know it worked for Grant in the Vicksburg campaign, interrupted Belisarius, a bit impatiently. This time he did laugh aloud, albeit softly. *Even Grant and Sherman would have called me a lunatic. Even Sheridan!*

Apparently realizing the futility of reassurance, Aide got into the mood of the moment. Brightly, cheerily: **Custer would have approved.**

THE BELISARIUS SERIES

An Oblique Approach

In the Heart of Darkness

Destiny's Shield

Fortune's Stroke

The Tide of Victory

The Dance of Time
(upcoming)

THE TIDE OF
VICTORY

ERIC FLINT
DAVID DRAKE

THE TIDE OF VICTORY

Copyright © 2001 Eric Flint & David Drake

A Baen Books Original

Baen Publishing Enterprises
P.O. Box 1403
Riverdale, NY 10471
www.baen.com

ISBN: 0-7434-3565-6

Cover art by Gary Ruddell

First paperback printing, October 2002

Cataloging-In-Publication Number 2001025729

Distributed by Simon & Schuster
1230 Avenue of the Americas
New York, NY 10020

Typeset by Brilliant Press
Printed in the United States of America

ACKNOWLEDGEMENTS

As this series has progressed, a number of people have provided us with assistance in one manner or another. It's time to thank them:

Conrad Chu
Judith Lasker
Joe Nefflen
Pam "Pogo" Poggiani
Richard Roach
Mike Spehar
Ralph and Marilyn Tacoma
Detlef Zander

...and probably several others I've forgotten to mention, for which my apologies in advance.

I'd also like to take the opportunity to thank Janet Dailey for the many ways in which she's helped me out over the past year or so. I can't remember if that assistance involved my work on the Belisarius series, but it probably did—and even if it didn't, she's way overdue for my public appreciation anyway.

Eric Flint
January, 2001

To Dick and Dolores

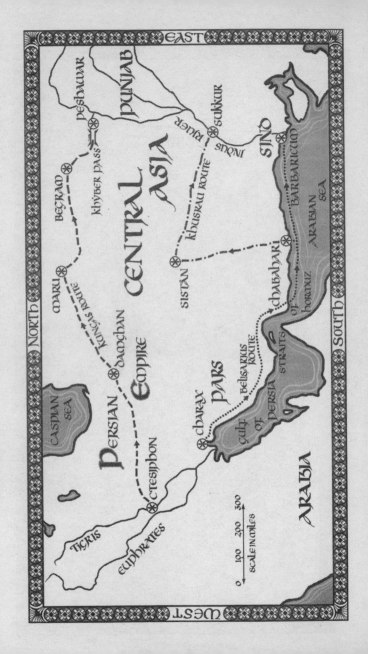

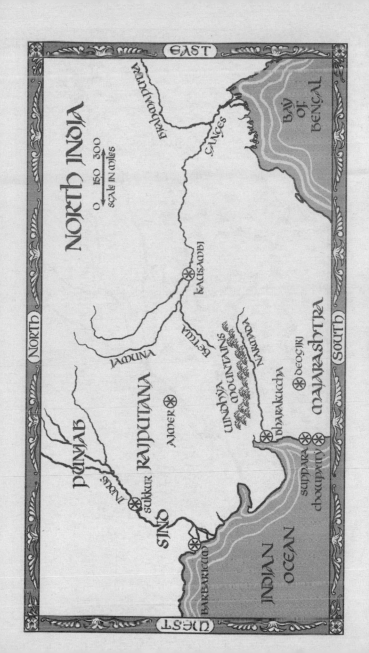

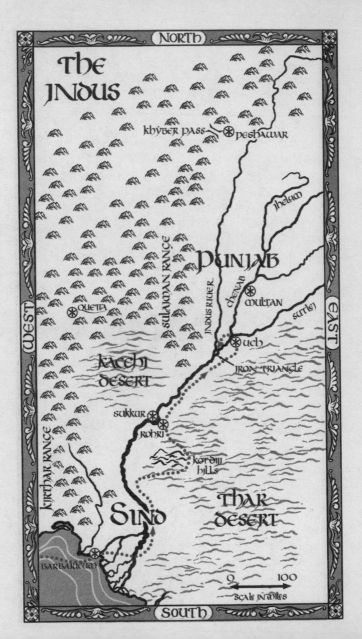

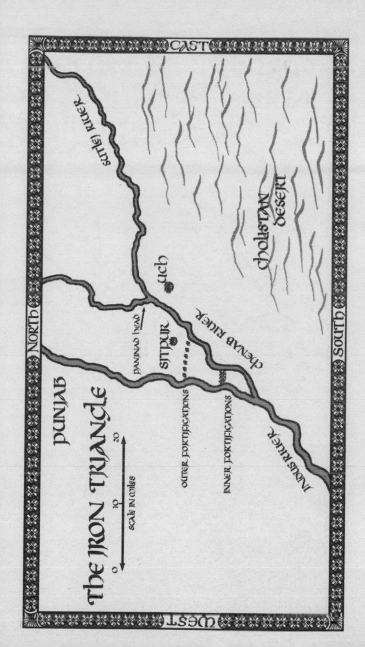

PROLOGUE

Knowing what to expect, the two sisters had already disrobed by the time their new owner returned to his tent. The older sister's infant was asleep on the pallet. The sisters were a bit concerned that the ensuing activities would awaken him—the pallet was small and thin, oddly so for such an obviously wealthy man—but not much. The baby was accustomed to the noise, after all, having spent the first year of his life in a brothel crib.

Unless, of course, their new owner was given to bizarre tastes and habits . . .

That was the real source of the sisters' anxiety. For all its foulness, the brothel had at least been fairly predictable. Now, for the first time since their enslavement, they faced an entirely new situation. New—and unsettling. Their new owner had said nothing to them, other than commanding them into his tent after his caravan stopped for the night.

But, as they waited, they took solace in the fact that they were still together. Against all odds, they had managed to keep from being separated during the long years of their captivity. Apparently, it tickled their new owner's fancy to have sisters for his concubines. They would see to it that he was satisfied with the result.

In that manner, they might preserve the remaining fragment of their family.

So it was, when their new owner pushed back the flap and entered the tent, that he found the sisters reclining nude on the pallet. The fact that they were holding hands was the only indication that any uneasiness lurked beneath their sensual poses.

Standing still and straight a few feet from the pallet, he studied them for a moment. The sisters found the scrutiny unsettling. They could detect nothing of lust in that gaze. For all the natural warmth of the man's dark brown eyes, there seemed to be little if any warmth in the eyes themselves. And not a trace of animal heat.

That was odd. Odder, even, than the austerity of the pallet and the tent's furnishings. Their new owner was obviously as healthy as he was rich. He was not especially tall, but his broad shoulders and lean hips were those of a physically active man. And there was something almost feline about the way he moved. Very poised, very balanced, very quick.

"Stand up," he commanded abruptly.

The sisters obeyed instantly. They were accustomed to inspection by prospective customers. As soon as they were on their feet, both of them assumed familiar poses. Languid, sensual, inviting. But they were still holding hands.

"Not like that," he said softly. "Just stand straight. And turn around slowly." His thin lips curved into a smile. "I'm afraid you'll have to stop holding hands for a bit."

Flushing slightly, the sisters obeyed.

"Slower," he commanded. "And lift up your arms so I can see your entire bodies."

This was *not* customary. The uneasiness of the sisters mounted. The last characteristic that slave prostitutes wanted to see in a new customer was *different*. But, of course, they obeyed.

In the long minutes which followed, the sisters found it increasingly difficult to keep the worry out of their faces. Their new owner seemed to be subjecting every inch of their bodies to a detailed and exhaustive scrutiny. As if he were trying to commit them to memory.

"Which of these scars are from your childhood?" he asked. His voice was soft and low-pitched. But the sisters took no comfort in that mild tone. This was a man, clearly enough, who had no need to raise his voice for the simple reason that command came easily to him. He would not be denied, whatever he wanted. Which, again, was not a characteristic which slave prostitutes treasured in their customers. Especially new and unknown ones.

They were so startled by the unexpected question that they did not respond immediately. Instead, they exchanged a quick and half-frightened glance.

Seeing the glance, their new owner's face broke into another smile. But this one was not thin at all, and seemed to have some actual humor in it.

"Be at ease. I have no intention of adding any new scars to the collection. It is simply information which I must have."

The smile disappeared and the question was asked again. This time, with firm command. "Which scars?"

Hesitantly, the younger sister lifted her left leg and pointed to a scar on her knee. "I got this one falling out of a tree. My father was furious with me."

Their owner nodded. "He would know of it, then? Good. Are there any other such? Did he beat you afterward? And, if so, are there any marks?"

The sisters looked at each other. Then, back at their owner.

"He never beat us," whispered the older. "Not once."

"Our mother did," added the younger sister. She was beginning to relax a bit. Enough that she managed a little chuckle. "Very often. But not very hard. I can't remember even being bruised."

The man shook his head. "What kind of silly way is that to raise children? Especially girls?" But the question was obviously rhetorical. The smile was back on his face, and for the first time the sisters detected the whimsical humor which seemed to reside somewhere inside the soul of their new owner.

He stepped up to the older sister and touched her cheek with his forefinger. "That is the worst scar. It almost disfigures your face. How did you get it?"

"From the brothel-keeper."

The man's eyes widened slightly. "Stupid," he mused. "Bad for business."

"He was very angry with me. I—" She shuddered, remembering. "The new customer had—unusual demands. I refused—"

"Ah." With a light finger, he traced the scar from the ear to the corner of her mouth.

"I think he forgot he was wearing that huge ring when he slapped me."

"Ah. Yes, I remember the ring. Probably the same one he was wearing when we conducted our transaction. A large ruby, set in silver?"

She nodded.

"Excellent," he said. "Easy for you to remember, then."

He turned to the younger sister. Placing one hand on her shoulder, he rotated her partway around. With the forefinger of his other hand, he traced the faint lines across her back.

"These are your worst. How?"

She explained. It was a similar story, except the individual involved had been the chief pimp instead of the brothel-keeper, and the instrument had been a whip rather than a ring.

"Ah. Yes, I believe I met him also. Rather short, squat. The little finger of his left hand is missing?"

The two sisters nodded. He returned the nods with a curt one of his own. "Excellent, also."

He stepped back a pace or two. "Can either of you write?"

The sisters were now utterly confused. This man was the *weirdest* customer they had ever encountered. But—

So far, at least, he did not seem dangerous. The younger sister spoke first. "Not very well."

"Our father taught us a bit," added the older sister. "But it's been a long time. Several years."

Both of the sisters, for the first time, found it almost impossible to maintain their poise. Memories of their father were flooding back. Their eyes were moist.

The man averted his gaze, for a moment. The sisters took advantage of the opportunity to quickly pinch the tears away. It would not do to offend their new owner.

They heard him snort softly. "Taught his daughters! Scandalous, what it is." Another soft snort. Again, the sisters thought to detect that strange whimsical humor. "But what else would you expect from—"

He broke off abruptly and looked back at them.

"In a few days, you will write a letter. As best you can." Seeing the uncertainty in their faces, he waved his hand idly. "I am not concerned if the handwriting is poor. All the better, in fact."

His eyes moved to the pallet, and then to the baby asleep to one side. "It will be crowded, with the four of us." Again, the thin smile. "But there's no help for it, I'm afraid. Appearances must be maintained."

Moving with that unsettling ease and speed, he

glided past them and reclined on the pallet. He was lying on the opposite side from the infant. He patted the middle of the pallet with his hand.

"Come, girls. Sleep. It has been a long day, and tomorrow will be longer. And the days after, as well. We have a considerable distance to travel."

Quickly, the sisters did as they were told. After the confusion of the preceding minutes, they almost found comfort in this familiar process. Not quite.

The younger sister lay next to him. The gesture of protection for the older came automatically to her. The two of them had protected each other for years, as best they could. If she exhausted him, he might be satisfied. Her sister's infant would not be disturbed.

Their new owner was still fully clothed. She began to stroke his chest, her fingers working at the laces.

Her hand was immobilized by his own. The man's grip was gentle enough, but she could sense the iron muscles and sinews in his hand.

"No," he said softly. "That is all finished. Just sleep." He moved her hand away.

Uncertainly, she obeyed. She stared at his profile. He was not a handsome man, not in the least. His face was lean and tightly drawn. High cheekbones, a sharply curved nose, thin lips below a thin mustache, clean-shaven cheeks so taut they seemed more like leather than flesh. Except for the mustache, he reminded her more of a bird of prey than a man.

But she found herself relaxing, despite his fearsome appearance. His voice was soft, after all. And she had never been abused by a bird.

His eyes were closed. "Finished," he repeated. "There will be no more scars."

Two days later, at daybreak, he arose from the pallet with his usual energy. The sisters had become accustomed to his way of moving. They no longer even found it frightening.

"Enough time has elapsed," he announced. "I will be gone for a few days. Three, perhaps four."

His words brought instant fear. The younger sister's eyes moved immediately to the tent flap. The older sister, suckling her infant at her breast, did not look up. But her sudden indrawn breath was quite audible.

Their new owner shook his head. "Have no fear. The soldiers in my escort will not molest you. I have given them clear instructions."

He turned away and began to push back the flap of the tent. "They will obey those instructions. You can be quite certain of it."

Then, he was gone. The sisters stared at each other. After a few seconds, their tension eased. They still did not know their new owner's name, since he had not provided it. But they were coming to know him. Well enough, at least.

Yes. *His* instructions would be obeyed. Even by soldiers.

He returned at midmorning, three days later. When he entered the tent, he was carrying a leather sack in one hand and a roll of leather in the other. Once flattened on the floor of the tent, the leather roll measured perhaps eighteen inches square.

"Should be big enough to prevent a mess," he murmured. He jerked his head, motioning the sisters toward him, while he untied the sack.

When they were squatting next to him, their new owner spilled the sack's contents onto the piece of flat leather.

He had gauged correctly, and grunted his satisfaction. Even with the addition of the fluid pooled at the bottom of the sack, the two objects did not leak blood onto the floor.

Both hands had been severed at the wrist, as if by a razor. Or—

The sisters glanced at the dagger scabbarded to their owner's waist. They had seen him shave with it, every day. He shaved with the quick and sure motions with which he did everything—except honing the blade. That, he seemed to enjoy lingering over.

One hand was plump. The middle finger sported a large silver ring, with a great ruby set at its center. The other hand was thick and stubby. The little finger was missing.

He rose and moved to one of the chests against the side of the tent. Opening it, he withdrew a small piece of vellum and writing equipment.

"And now, the letter."

Long before the sisters had finished, they were sobbing fiercely. Their new owner did not chide them for it. Indeed, he seemed obscurely satisfied. As if the tears staining the words and causing the letters to run added something valuable to the message.

When they were done, he began to roll up the vellum. But the younger sister stopped him.

"Wait. There is something we can put in it." She hurried to the far side of the pallet and began plucking apart the threads along the seam. Her older sister opened her mouth, as if to protest. But whatever protest she might have made went unspoken. Indeed, by the time her sister had extracted the object hidden within the pallet, she was smiling. "Yes," she whispered. "*Yes.*"

The younger sister came back to their owner and, shyly, extended her hand. Nestled in the palm was a bright golden coin.

"It's all we have," she said. "He won't recognize it, of course, because we got it after—" She fell silent, fighting back further tears. "But still—"

The man plucked the coin out of her hand and held it up for inspection. Within seconds, he was chuckling softly.

"Freshly minted Malwa imperial coin. I wonder—"

Smiling, he tucked the coin into the vellum and rolled it up. Then, quickly folding it further, he began tying it up with cord. As he worked, he spoke softly, as if to himself.

"I wonder . . . Ha! Probably not, of course. But wouldn't that be a delicious irony?"

The work done, he transferred the smile to the sisters. They had no difficulty, any longer, recognizing the humor in it. "I'm a man who appreciates such things, you know."

They nodded, smiling themselves.

His own smile faded. "I am not your friend, girls. Never think so. But, perhaps, I am not your enemy either."

He lifted the package and hefted it slightly. "We will discover which, one of these days."

The older sister sighed. "It's not finished, then?"

Their owner's smile returned, this time with more of bright cheer than whimsy. "Finished? I think not!"

He was actually laughing, now. For the first time since they had entered his possession.

"I think not! The game has just begun!"

In the days, weeks and months to come, that package—and the ones which went with it—would cause consternation, three times over. And glee, once.

The consternation came in ascending degrees. The least concerned were the soldiers who investigated the murder and mutilation of a brothel-keeper and his chief pimp.

"Who cares who did it?" yawned the officer in charge of the squad. "Plenty more where they came from."

He turned away from the bed where the brothel-keeper's body had been found. The linen was still soaked with blood from a throat slit to the bone. "Maybe a competitor. Or it could have been a pissed-off customer." It was apparent, from the bored tone of his voice, that he had no intention of pursuing the matter further.

The pimp who had succeeded to the brothel's uncertain ownership sighed. "No problem, then?" He fought very hard to keep satisfaction out of his own voice. He was quite innocent of the murders, as it happened, but as the obvious suspect . . .

"Not that I can see," stated the officer firmly. Just as firmly, he stared at the new brothel-keeper.

"On the house!" that worthy announced promptly. "You and all your men! For a full day!"

The officer grinned. "Case closed."

There was more consternation, a few days later, when the murderer reported to his master.

"You idiot," growled Narses. "Why in the name of God did you kill them? We don't need any attention being drawn. A simple slave purchase, all it was. Happens every day."

"So do brothel killings," came the retort. Ajatasutra shrugged. "Three reasons. First, I thought the hands would lend a nice touch to the package. Proof of good intentions, so to speak."

Narses snorted. "God help us. You're pretending to *think*." He displayed his inimitable sneer. "His daughters have been hopelessly polluted. What difference does it make—you're Indian yourself, you know how it works—that a couple of the polluters are dead? How many hundreds are still alive?"

"You might be surprised. Purity is one thing, the satisfaction of vengeance is another. Even we heathen Hindus are not immune to that. *Even* a philosopher like him will feel a twitch, as much harm as he knows that will do to his karma."

Ajatasutra leaned forward in his chair, stretching his arms and arching his back. He seemed to take as much pleasure in the supple movements as a cat. "Secondly, I've gotten out of practice." Half-growling: "Your methods are too damned subtle to keep an assassin's skills properly honed."

Again, Narses snorted. *"Pimps."*

Ajatasutra's lips twisted into a wry grin. "Best I could find." The grin faded. When it was completely gone, his still and expressionless face seemed more like that of a hawk on a limb than a man in a chair.

"And, finally. I felt like it."

Narses said nothing. He neither snorted nor sneered.

Weeks later, the package caused immense consternation. It struck the palace at Deogiri like a tornado, leaving a peshwa and his wife weeping tears of joy, an empress confused and uncertain, her advisers divided and torn.

"It's a trap!" insisted the imperial consort. Raghunath Rao sprang to his feet and practically pounced his way over to the open window in the imperial audience chamber. There, planting his hands on the wide ledge, he glared fiercely to the north. The broken hill country of Majarashtra stretched to the horizon. Beyond, invisible in the distance, lay the Narmada river and the Vindhya mountains. And, beyond that, the great Gangetic plain where the Malwa beast straddled the Indian subcontinent.

"A trap," he repeated.

Empress Shakuntala moved her uncertain gaze to the commander of her personal bodyguard. Former commander, rather. As of the previous day, Kungas was no longer her *mahadandanayaka;* no longer her *bhatasvapati.* Officially, the man once known as "great commandant" and "lord of army and cavalry" had no title at all in the empire of Andhra. He had been relieved of all responsibilities, since he and his own consort were soon to be founding their own empire.

Officially.

Kungas' shoulders made the little twitch which served him for a shrug. "Probably so." His gaze moved to the other woman in the room. Shakuntala's eyes followed.

Irene cleared her throat. "Actually, Your Majesty"— she gave an apologetic glance at the figure in the window—"I find myself in a rare moment of disagreement with Rao."

Rao barked a laugh. He turned back into the room. "'Rare moment!' Such a diplomat."

Irene smiled. "But disagree I must. This maneuver has to be Narses' work. A simple trap is not his style."

Everyone in the room eyed her skeptically. Irene's shrug was as expressive as her future husband's had been terse. "I'm sorry. I realize that must sound hopelessly vague. Even naive. But—"

Her own frown was simply one of concentration. "But I'm really quite sure that I'm right. I can detect Narses' mind at work here. He's up to something, be sure of it. Something—" Her hands groped a bit. "Something *complex.* Something *convoluted.*"

She glanced at Kungas and Rao. Her frown was instantly replaced by a wicked smile. "The problem with these two, Your Majesty, is that they think like *men.* You know—crude. Simple."

Shakuntala's laugh filled the large chamber like a bell. She and Irene exchanged a grin. Rao scowled. Kungas' face, as usual, had no expression at all.

"You must remember, Empress," continued Irene, "that Narses is a eunuch. He thinks more like a woman than a man. Subtle, tricky. *Shrewd.*"

Grin. Grin. Scowl. Nothing.

"Not a trap," she insisted. "Or, at least, not the obvious trap. What would he have to gain, beyond inflicting a minor wound on Belisarius?"

"And a major one on our peshwa," growled Rao. He jerked his head angrily at the door. "Dadaji should be here, to give us his wisdom in counsel. He is absent simply because he too overcome with—with—"

"Joy?" suggested Irene. "Relief?"

"For the moment. But what of later? If it *is* a trap, once it is sprung? When he realizes that his daughters are lost forever."

Kungas spoke. "That's foolish, Rao. And you know it. Dadaji would not be incapacitated for long. He would do the rites—just as he did months ago when the news of his son's death in battle came—and continue onward. More fiercely than ever, now that Malwa added a new wound to his soul."

Rao took a deep breath. He nodded abruptly, indicating his acceptance of Kungas' point. But, still, he was scowling. "I don't *trust* this thing!"

"Trust?" exclaimed Irene. "What has that got to do with it?" Her own laugh had none of the young empress' pealing quality. It was more like the caw of a crow.

"I don't trust *Narses*, Rao. What I trust is simply his *craftsmanship.*"

She pointed a stiff finger at the opened parcel on the low table near the door. The shriveled hands and the message for the empress lay exposed. The shakily written message for Holkar, and the coin, were absent. Dadaji and his wife had those in their own chambers, clutching them as fiercely as they did each other. Adding their own tears of joy to the long-dried ones which had smeared the ink.

"He's *up* to something, I tell you!"

The empress ended the discussion, in her usual decisive manner. She clapped her hands, once. "Enough! It is not for us to decide, in any event. We are simply the conduit. If there is a trap, it is aimed at Belisarius. He must make the decision."

She pointed her own imperious finger at the parcel. "Take it with you tomorrow, Irene. Kungas. Take it with you on your journey to Persia, and put it into Belisarius' hands. Let him decide."

Mention of that journey, even more than the empress' command, ended the discussion. With not much less in the way of sorrow than Shakuntala, Rao gazed at the two people who would, within a day, be gone from their company. Probably forever. Two people who had done as much as any in the world to bring one empire back from the grave, where Malwa had thought Andhra safely planted. And now proposed to do the same yet again, in Malwa's very heartland.

"God be with you," he murmured. His usual wry smile emerged. "He is rumored to have good vision, you know. Even in the Hindu Kush, I am certain he will notice you."

The glee came as Irene and Kungas were walking through the halls of the palace, back toward their own chambers.

"I hope you're right," muttered Kungas.

Irene's eyes widened. "Are you *kidding*? Of course I'm right! He's *up* to something. And since—I know

I've told you this—he's probably the only spymaster in the world as good as me, that means—"

She seized Kungas' muscular arm in both hands and began spinning her lover around her, whirling down the corridor like a top.

"Oh, Kungas! We're going to have so much *fun!*"

Chapter 1
CTESIPHON
Spring, 533 A.D.

Are you sure of this? asked Aide. The crystalline thought in Belisarius' mind shivered with uncertainty. **They have protected you for so long.**

Belisarius made the mental equivalent of a shrug. *This coming campaign is different, Aide. I will be commanding—*

He broke off for a moment, scanning the imperial audience chamber. The crooked smile that came so naturally to him made its reappearance. There was enough of royalty, nobility, officers and advisers crowded about to fill even that huge and splendiferous room. The costumes and uniforms worn by that mob were as varied as the mob itself. Roman, Persian, Ethiopian, Arab—only the Kushans were absent, for reasons of secrecy.

No one in the West has assembled such a gigantic force since the days of Xerxes and Darius and Alexander the Great. I will be leading well over a hundred thousand men into India, Aide. So there's no way I'll be at the forefront of any more cavalry charges.

The crystal being from the future flashed an image in Belisarius' mind. For just an instant, the Roman general saw a Homeric figure storming a rampart, sword in hand.

Aide's voice came sour, sour. **Alexander the Great did.**

Belisarius snorted. *Alexander was a lunatic as well as a genius. Thought he was Achilles come back to life. I have no such pretensions, myself. And if I ever did—*

He winced, remembering the way Rana Sanga, Rajputana's greatest king as well as champion, had hammered Belisarius into a bleeding pulp on a battlefield in the Zagros mountains. Would have killed him, in fact, if Valentinian hadn't come to his rescue.

You should not send Valentinian away! Especially not when you're sending Anastasius also!

Belisarius ignored Aide's last remark, for the moment. The raging argument between Sittas and Kurush which had filled the audience chamber for several minutes seemed to be coming to a head, and he thought it was about time that he intervened. It wouldn't do to allow two of his top commanders to come to actual blows, after all.

Loudly, he cleared his throat. Both Sittas and Kurush stopped bellowing, although they did not leave off their ferocious mutual glares.

"Kurush will command the left," pronounced Belisarius. Sittas made a choking sound and transferred his glare from his Persian equivalent to the top commander of the joint expedition. Beneath the indignation and outrage in his expression lurked something of the small boy—*betrayed!*—by his trusted older brother.

Belisarius shook his head. "Don't be stupid, Sittas. The left wing will be responsible for protecting the entire expedition against Malwa cavalry raids. Rajputs and Pathans, most like. The Aryans are far more experienced cavalrymen than Roman cataphracts in that kind of mountainous terrain."

The words did not seem to mollify Sittas at all. To the contrary—Belisarius' huge friend was giving him the enraged boar's glare that was one of Sittas' trademarks.

Belisarius found it hard not to smile. On one level, of course, he could hardly blame Sittas. The official justification which Belisarius had just given for allowing the Persian dehgans to take the prestigious position on the expedition's left flank was absurd. By the time Belisarius' huge army was nearing the Indus valley, the Malwa would certainly have detected the northern expedition of Kungas and his Kushans. Any Rajput or Pathan raiders available to the Malwa after their crushing defeat the previous year at Charax would be busy trying to protect the Hindu Kush. They certainly wouldn't be wasting their time in futile cavalry raids against Belisarius' army far to the south in Baluchistan.

But—

The Kushan expedition was still a secret, so Sittas—choking with indignation all the while—could not argue the point. He was forced, grudgingly and angrily, to cede the argument and resume his seat. Kurush did likewise. Fortunately, the young Persian general had enough tact to keep his face expressionless rather than indulge in open gloating.

Good enough, thought Belisarius. He would make it a point to discuss the matter with Sittas privately after the council meeting. In truth, he should have discussed it with him prior to the meeting. But in the press of his responsibilities, he simply hadn't thought of it. Belisarius had been away from the imperial court at Constantinople for so long that he'd forgotten the touchy pride of the capital city's elite cataphracts. He should have realized that Sittas would find a point of honor in the issue of whether the left flank was under the command of Persians or Romans.

Stupid, he thought sourly. *Sittas should have the sense to understand that I* must *keep the Persians satisfied. And their pride is even touchier!*

His eyes met those of Agathius. Belisarius' chief of staff was sitting at a large table across the room, with the campaign maps and logistics records spread out in front of him. Seeing the easy manner in which Agathius handled that mass of written material, no one would have guessed that he had been effectively illiterate until a year ago. Beneath Agathius' brawler's appearance, the chief of staff was as intelligent and capable as any man Belisarius had ever met.

There seemed to be a little twinkle in Agathius' eyes. Belisarius gave him the faint hint of a smile, as a man does when he is sharing a subtle unspoken secret with another.

Stupid noblemen . . .

Until the injuries which had crippled him at the Battle of the Nehar Malka, Agathius had been a cataphract himself—and a great one. But the lowborn baker's son had never approached war with any attitude beyond plebeian practicality.

Agathius now cleared his own throat. "If we can move on to the logistics . . ."

Belisarius nodded his assent. As Agathius began running through the state of the logistical preparations for the coming campaign, Belisarius let his thoughts go inward again.

It is too important an opportunity to pass up, Aide. If Irene is right—

She's guessing! Nobody knows what that cryptic message means!

Belisarius made the mental equivalent of a shrug.

She's a very good guesser, you know. And I think she's right. The thing has all the earmarks of a Narses maneuver.

He's a traitor.

No, Aide. He was *a traitor. Now he is in the service of another. And, unless I miss my own guess, I suspect that he is serving Damodara very faithfully indeed. Not*—there came a momentary silent chuckle—*that I think Damodara has any idea what his chief of espionage is doing.*

Aide said nothing for a moment, though his uneasiness was still evident. Then: **But why Valentinian and Anastasius?** He complained. **They aren't spies and intriguers. They—**

—are the deadliest soldiers in my army, Belisarius completed the thought. *And they both speak the language—well enough, at least—and they are both familiar with India. I don't think Narses wants spies, Aide. He has plenty of his own. I think—*

You're guessing!

Belisarius sighed. *Yes, I am. And I am also a good guesser. And can I finish my thought without interruptions?*

He could sense the "jewel" sulking. But Aide kept his peace.

As I was saying, Belisarius continued, *I suspect that what Narses needs are people who can get someone out of India in a very big hurry. Or protect them. And who better for that than Valentinian and Anastasius and Kujulo?*

Aide was silent, but Belisarius could sense the unspoken disagreement.

Oh, stop sulking! Say what you were going to say.

The thoughts came in a rush. **And that's another thing—those three are well known to the Malwa! They will be spotted!**

By whom? The only ones who would recognize them are Chandragupta's imperial entourage—which there's no chance at all of encountering, as tightly sequestered as Skandagupta keeps himself—and—

The Rajputs! Rana Sanga fought Valentinian in single combat for hours! You think—

Belisarius drove over the protest. *And Damodara's Rajputs—who, by all accounts, have been stationed in Bihar and Bengal since they returned to India. Half a continent away from where Valentinian and—*

Things change, pouted Aide. **You say that yourself, all the time.**

Again, Belisarius made that mental shrug. *Yes, they do—and probably will again. Judging from what Irene told us of the Maratha rebellion's progress, I imagine that Damodara and Rana Sanga will soon be ordered into the Great Country. Which—*

He could sense Aide's growing surly *pout*, and had to fight down another smile. *Which is also half a continent away.*

Belisarius broke off the exchange. In his usual terse and efficient manner, Agathius was completing his logistics report. Belisarius braced himself for another round of bellowing and bickering.

Kurush was already on his feet. "What is this nonsense?" he roared. "Not more than *four* servants—even for Aryan nobility? Absurd! Impossible!"

Belisarius gave Sittas a quick, sharp glance. The Roman general's returning glare faded instantly into a look of suppressed glee and cunning.

Sittas shoved his great powerful form out of his chair. "Nonsense," he rumbled. "Any Roman cataphract can make do with two servants, easily. But if the noble sahrdaran thinks maintaining a lean baggage train is a problem, perhaps we could reconsider the assignment—"

Bellow, roar, rumble. Sound and fury.

Ah, the joy of command, thought Belisarius sourly.

You will keep Isaac and Priscus? Came Aide's timid, fearful thought.

Yes. No point in sending them *into the Malwa maw.* He began to add some jocular remark, but then, sensing the genuine anguish lurking in Aide's mind, he shifted immediately.

They are almost as good as Valentinian and Anastasius, Aide. I will be safe enough.

There came a crystalline equivalent of a sigh. Then: **It is just— I love you dearly.**

The roar and bellow of outraged and bickering dehgans and cataphracts continued to fill the chamber, as a gigantic army continued to take form and shape. But the commander of that army himself was oblivious to it all, for a time, as he communed with the strangest form and shape which had ever come into the world. And if others might have found something strange in the love and affection which passed between man and crystal, neither the man himself nor the crystal gave it a moment's thought.

They had been together for years now, since the monk and prophet Michael of Macedonia had brought Aide and his warning of a terrible future to Belisarius' door. Over the course of those years of battle and campaign, they had come to know each other as well as father and son, or brother and brother. What they thought—hoped—was the final campaign of the long war against Malwa was now upon them. They would survive, or not, as fate decreed. But they would go into that furnace united in heart and soul. And that, more than anything—so *they* thought, at least—was the surest guarantee of future triumph.

❖   ❖   ❖

A sharp sound echoing in the audience chamber brought Belisarius' mind back to the present. A brisk handclap, he realized. Belisarius saw Khusrau Anushirvan rising from his throne perched at the opposite side of the chamber.

"Enough!" The Persian emperor clapped his hands again. Beneath the thick, square-cut beard, his youthful face was stern. "Enough, I say. At least for the moment. It is past noon, and we have an imperial wedding to attend."

He turned his head to Belisarius. The sternness of his expression seemed to ease a bit. "A wedding which, I'm sure the illustrious Roman general will agree, is more important than the details of marching order and logistics."

Belisarius nodded and rose to his own feet. "Indeed so, Emperor. Far more."

Chapter 2

When Tahmina's father brought her dowry down the central thoroughfare in Ctesiphon, the huge crowd of Persian onlookers began murmuring with excitement. Excitement—and deep approval. Even the street urchins knew that the dowry for an imperial wedding was the product of endless negotiations. The dowry which Baresmanas was bringing to the palace was so bizarre that it could only have resulted from the suggestion of the Romans themselves.

The approval of the crowd was profound. Many began chanting the name of the Roman emperor Photius, to whom Tahmina was about to be wed. Here and there, even a few haughty dehgan knights were seen to join in the plaudits.

They had been expecting a caravan, laden with treasure. Enough in the way of gold and silver and gems and jewelry and precious linens to bankrupt the Persian empire. A bitter price to pay for the security of a Roman alliance against the Malwa, but a price that could not be avoided. Not much more than a year before, the Malwa who had devastated Mesopotamia had only been driven off by the efforts and cunning of the Roman general Belisarius. Today, that same Belisarius would demand Persia's fortune in payment.

Instead—

Baresmanas of the Suren, the greatest of the seven great sahrdaran families who constituted Persia's highest nobility, was walking slowly down the thoroughfare. Dressed in his finest regalia, he was simply leading a horse.

Not any horse, of course. Even the street urchins realized that the magnificent black steed which pranced behind its master was the finest in all of Persia—a land which was renowned for its horses. But not even such a horse would bankrupt their empire.

The horse bore three things only.

The first was a saddle. No ceremonial saddle, this, glittering with gems and gold inlay. Instead, it was a heavy lancer's saddle, equipped with the new stirrups which the Romans had recently introduced into cavalry warfare. The finest such saddle imaginable, of course. No village dehgan could have afforded it. But, again, nothing to cause their emperor to raise the taxes.

The second was a bow, held in the small hand of the horse's rider. The finest that Persia's greatest bowyer could construct, of course. But, still, just a bow—to anyone but Persians.

The crowd's approval swelled and swelled, as the meaning of that horse and bow penetrated. *Photius! Photius!* By the time Baresmanas neared the great aivan in the center of the imperial palace where the wedding was to be held, the great throng was positively roaring. Precious few Persian emperors, in the long history of the land of the Aryans, had ever received such public acclaim.

A lowborn mongrel, the Roman emperor was said to be. So the crowd had heard. A bastard at birth, it was even whispered. But now, seeing the horse and the bow, they understood the truth.

Photius! Photius!

✧   ✧   ✧

At the entrance to the aivan, Baresmanas assisted the third of the horse's burdens in her descent. The task was a bit difficult, not because his daughter Tahmina was a weakling, but simply because her wedding costume was heavy and cumbersome.

When she was securely planted on her feet, Baresmanas leaned over and whispered. "So. Who was right? I, or your mother?"

Tahmina's smile was faintly discernable through the veil. "I never doubted you, father. Even before I read the book you gave me."

Baresmanas started slightly. "Already? All of it? *Herodotus?*"

As Baresmanas handed the reins of the horse to one of his chief dehgans, Tahmina straightened. "All of it," she insisted. "My Greek has become almost perfect."

A moment's hesitation, before the girl's innate honesty surfaced. "Well . . . For reading, anyway. I think my accent's still pretty horrible."

Side by side, father and daughter walked slowly toward the aivan. The entrance to the aivan was lined with soldiers. Persian dehgans on the left, Roman cataphracts on the right.

"Then you understand," said Baresmanas. He did not have to gesture at the chanting crowd to make his meaning clear.

"Yes, father."

Baresmanas nodded solemnly. "Learn from this, daughter. Whatever prejudices you may still have about Romans, abandon them now. You will be their empress, before the day is done, and they are a great people worthy of you. Never doubt that for a moment. Greater than us, in many ways."

He studied the soldiers standing at their posts of honor alongside the aivan's entrance. To the Persians, he gave merely a glance. Baresmanas' dehgans were led by Merena, the most honorable of their number.

But it was the leader of the Roman contingent which was the focus of the sahrdaran's attention. An odd-looking soldier, in truth. Unable to even stand without the aid of crutches. The man's name was Agathius, and he had lost his legs at the battle of the Nehar Malka where Belisarius destroyed a Malwa army.

Agathius was a lowborn man, even by Roman standards. But he was counted a duke, now, by Persians and Romans alike. Merena's own daughter had become his spouse.

"*A thousand years ago,*" Baresmanas said harshly, "a time that we ourselves have half-forgotten, daughter, but they have not. A thousand years ago, one of their finest historians explained to his people the Aryan way of raising a manchild."

"*Teach him horsemanship, and archery,*" murmured Tahmina. "*And teach him to despise all lies.*"

"That is the Emperor of Rome's pledge to you, daughter, and to all of the Aryans," said Baresmanas. "A boy not yet eleven years old. Do you understand?"

His daughter nodded. She turned her head slightly, studying the cheering crowd. *Photius! Photius!* "I am so astonished," she whispered.

Baresmanas chuckled. "Why? That a half-Greek, half-Egyptian bastard whoreson would understand us so well?"

She shook her head, rippling the veil.

"No, father. I am just surprised—"

Photius! Photius! They were entering the blessed coolness of the aivan, the huge open-air entrance hall so distinctive of Persian architecture. The soldiers began closing in behind them.

A whisper:

"It had never occurred to me before this moment. Not once. That I might be able to love my husband."

Inside the huge aivan, the Roman empress regent was scowling. Of course, there was nothing new about that. Theodora had been scowling since she arrived in Persia. For any number of reasons.

One. She hated to travel.

Two. She *especially* hated to travel in the desert.

Three. She didn't much like Persians. (A minor point, this. Theodora, as a rule, didn't much like anybody.)

Four. She had now been standing in her heavy official robes for well over an hour. Hadn't these stupid Persians ever heard of *chairs*? Idiots! Even the Aryan Emperor Khusrau was standing.

Five . . .

"I *hate* being proved wrong," she hissed.

"Shhh," hissed Antonina in return. "This is supposed to be a solemn occasion. And your scowl is showing, even through the veil."

"And that's another thing," grumbled Theodora. "How is a woman supposed to breathe with this monstrous thing covering her face? Especially in the heat of late afternoon?"

The veil rippled slightly as she turned her head. "At least they have enough sense to hold public ceremonies in this—this—what's it called, anyway?"

Belisarius, standing on Theodora's other side, leaned over and whispered. "It's known as an *aivan*. Clever, isn't it? Of course, it'd never work in our climate. Not in the winter, anyway."

For all its majestic size—the aivan was a hundred and forty feet long and eighty feet wide; at its highest, the arching vault was a hundred feet above the floor—the structure was open to the elements. The entrance through which Baresmanas and Tahmina were proceeding served as an enormous doorway. The style of architecture was unique to the Persians, and produced a chamber which was much cooler than either the outdoors or an enclosed room.

Theodora was now scowling at Belisarius. "Oh, all right. Go ahead and say it. You were right and I was wrong."

Belisarius said nothing. He knew better than to gloat at Theodora's expense. Not even the insects perched on the walls were *that* stupid.

His diplomacy did not seem to assuage the empress regent's temper. "I *hate* being wrong," she repeated sourly. "And I still would have preferred taking the treasure. I can *see* gold. Can even count it with my own fingers."

Belisarius decided that a response would not qualify, precisely, as "gloating." True, Theodora wasn't fond of disagreement, either. But the woman was more than shrewd enough to have learned—long since—to accept contrary advice without punishing the adviser. Listen to it, at least.

"We'd have wound up losing the treasure anyway, soon enough," he murmured. "Bankrupt Persia, and then what? The Persians go looking for treasure to replace it. The nearest of which is in Roman territory."

He paused, listening to the chants of the huge crowd outside the palace. *Photius! Photius!* Then: "Better this way."

Theodora made no reply, beyond the inevitable refrain. "I *hate* being proved wrong."

Photius was standing alone at the center of the aivan, as befitted his manly status. And that he *was* a man, no one could deny, even if he was only ten years old. He was getting married, wasn't he?

The Emperor of Rome was not pleased at that new found status. He had been perfectly content being a mere boy.

Well . . .

His eyes moved to the cluster of Roman scholars standing amidst the small mob of Persian priests packed against the far wall of the aivan. His tutors, those. Even at the distance, Photius thought their expressions could curdle milk. Greek philosophers, grammarians, rhetoricians and pedants did not appreciate being forced to mingle with Persian *mobads* and *herbads*. Bunch of heathen witch doctors. Traffickers in superstition and magic. Peddlers of—

The emperor's eyes moved away. The first trace of a smile came to his face since he'd awakened that morning. As an official "man," maybe he wouldn't have to put up with *quite* as much nattering from his tutors.

When his eyes fell on the small group of his bodyguards, the smile widened a bit. Then, seeing the vulgar grin on the face of Julian, the chief of his bodyguards, Photius found himself struggling not to grin himself.

He would have preferred it, of course, if his longtime nanny Hypatia could have been present also. Damn the implied questioning of his manly state!

Sigh. But the only women which the stiff Aryans would allow at such a public gathering were the bride and her immediate female relatives. Darkly, Photius suspected the Aryans would have dispensed with them also, if it weren't for the simple fact that—push come to shove—females were sadly necessary for the rite of marriage.

Now, catching the first hint of motion at the aivan entrance, Photius' eyes were drawn thither. His about-to-be-bride was finally entering.

Tahmina's mother, he knew, would not be coming. Her presence was customary at such events, but the woman claimed to have contracted some mysterious and incapacitating disease. Baresmanas had made fulsome apologies for her absence in advance, which the Roman delegation had accepted graciously. Even though not one of those Romans— nor, for that matter, any member of the Persian nobility—doubted for an instant the real nature of the disease. Incapacitating, yes; mysterious, no. Such is the nature of the ancient illness called bigotry.

Her daughter? Of the *Suren*, the purest blood of the Aryans short of the emperor himself! Married to—to—

The mongrel Roman whoreson bastard sighed. *Great. Just great. My wife will hold her nose whenever I'm in the same room with her.*

Tahmina was much nearer, now. Despite himself, Photius was fascinated to see her move. Even under the heavy Persian robes, he could sense the lithe and athletic figure. Tahmina was fifteen years old. Just old enough—quite unlike Photius himself—that she was beginning to bring her body under control. There was no gawkiness at all in that easy, gliding progress.

Maurice, his father's cataphract, had seen the girl before. Maurice had told him that she was extraordinarily beautiful. For a moment, Photius was cheered by the thought.

Only for a moment. *Great. Just great. I'll have the most beautiful wife in the world. And she'll still be holding her nose whenever I'm around.*

Then, finally, his eyes met those of his approaching bride. Between the heavy veil and the headdress, Tahmina's dark eyes and the bridge of her nose were all that Photius could see of her face.

The Emperor of Rome froze.

Tahmina's own eyes were fixed upon him. They never moved once, in the time it took for her to finally take her place next to him.

Beautiful eyes, of course. As clear and bright as moonshine, for all their darkness. Brown eyes, technically, but of such a deep hue they almost seemed black. So much, Photius had expected. But he had not expected the warmth he saw in them. Like embers, glowing.

And he *certainly* hadn't expected to hear the whisper, just as the ceremony finally began. In heavily accented but perfect Greek.

"Relax, husband. You will like me. I promise."

And he did relax, even if the ceremony itself was long, and tedious, and required him to follow a labyrinth of carefully rehearsed gestures and words. Photius, too, had read Herodotus. And so he knew the creed of the Aryans.

Teach them horsemanship, and archery.
And teach them to despise all lies.

Hours later, in the midst of the great festivities which were spilling all through the public areas of the palace—all through the entire city, in fact—Emperor Khusrau Anushirvan sidled up to Belisarius.

"That went supremely well, I thought."

Belisarius nodded. For once, his smile was not crooked at all. It was every bit as wide and open as the emperor's own.

"I thought so, too." They were still standing in the aivan. Through the great opening, the last colors of sunset could be seen. Belisarius glanced at the small door which led to the private quarters of the imperial entourage. Photius and Tahmina had been provided with a suite in those quarters, for their use until the imperial Roman delegation returned to Constantinople some days hence. The new husband and bride had just passed through that door, not more than ten minutes earlier.

Belisarius' smile now assumed its more familiar, crooked shape. "Of course, I'm not sure Photius is still of that opinion. He seemed cheerful enough earlier. But now—" The Roman general chuckled. "He looked for all the world like a man being led to his own execution."

Khusrau grinned. "Nonsense. I raised the girl, you know, as much as Baresmanas did. She is every bit as intelligent as she is comely. I assure you that your stepson will soon be at ease."

The Emperor of Iran and non-Iran paused. "Well . . . Not at *ease*, precisely."

Belisarius' eyes widened a bit. "He's only ten years old, Your Majesty."

Khusrau's face bore an expression of supreme smugness. "Romans. Such a primitive folk."

After his servants dressed him in his bedclothes, Photius nervously entered the sleeping chamber and found Tahmina already waiting for him. She was lazing on the bed, wearing her own nightgown. As soon as Photius entered, she smiled and patted the bed next to her. "Come, husband," she said softly.

"I'm only ten years old," Photius managed to choke out.

"Relax, I say," murmured his wife. She arose and led him gently to the bed. "Lie down."

Photius did as he was commanded. He could not imagine doing otherwise. For all of Tahmina's poise and demure demeanor—*how does she manage that, wearing nothing but a silk gown?*—her hands upon him were strong and firm. She was bigger than he was, true. But it was more the certainty of her intentions, and the sheer beauty of her person—Maurice had been right, been right, been right that drove him to obey.

It seemed but an instant before she had him

stretched out on the bed, herself alongside, and was gently caressing his little body. Slowly, Photius felt the rigidity leaving his muscles.

"I'm only ten years old," he repeated. This time, more by way of an apology than an expression of terror.

"Of course you are," murmured Tahmina. Gently, she kissed his forehead. "Relax, husband." She raised her head and smiled serenely down upon him, while her hands continued their caresses.

"You will age. Soon enough, be sure of it. And when the time comes, you will not be anxious at all. You will know everything. About me. About you. It will be so easy."

Photius thought she had the most beautiful voice he had ever heard. He felt like he was drowning in the darkness of her eyes.

The rest of the night, until they fell asleep, was a time of wonder for him. Wonder of the body, partly. Ten years old is not too young for everything, after all, and Tahmina was as sensuous as she was beautiful. Her caresses felt more wonderful than anything Photius could imagine.

But, mostly, it was wonder of the mind. He had never imagined it. Not once. That he might come to love his wife.

Within an hour after awakening the next morning, wonder turned to certainty. Ten years old was not, after all, too young for a man to understand that pleasures of the mind outweigh pleasures of the body.

His wife turned out to be a genius, too. Such, at least, was Photius' firm conviction. Who else would know so many ways to thwart officious tutors?

"And another thing," she explained, nestling his head into her shoulder. "When they start nattering about your grammar—"

For the first time, Photius assumed the proper mantle of husbandly authority.

"Hush, wife!" he commanded. He lifted his head, summoned his courage—Emperor of Rome!—and planted a kiss on his wife's cheek. After the evening and night, all those *hours*, it came almost easily to him.

Tahmina laughed. "See? Not long!"

Some time later, again, Tahmina was gazing down upon him serenely.

"You will have concubines," she said softly, "but I intend to see to it that you do not spend much time with them."

Photius cleared his throat. "Uh, actually, concubines are not permitted under Christian law." A bit guiltily: "Not supposed to be, anyway."

Tahmina's eyes grew very round. "*Really?* How odd!" The beautiful eyes narrowed a bit. "I will be converting, of course, since a Christian empire must have a Christian empress." Narrowed further. "I foresee myself a devoted convert." Slits. "A religious fanatic, in fact."

Photius gurgled like a babe. "S'okay with me!"

"It better be," growled his wife. A moment later, she was giving him a foretaste of the punishment which awaited Christian sinners.

And so the servants found them. The servants, and Julian.

The prim and proper servants frowned, needless to say. *Such unseemly conduct for royalty!* But Julian, scarred veteran of many battlefields, was immensely pleased. A Persian empress tickling a Roman emperor, he thought, boded well for the future. Perhaps Belisarius was right, and the thousand year war was finally over.

That still left the Malwa, of course. But that thought brought nothing but a sneer to the cataphract's face. *Anything* was child's play, compared to Persian dehgans on the field of battle.

Chapter 3

That same morning, while Photius and Tahmina began laying the foundation for their marriage, another wedding took place. This wedding was private, not public. Indeed, not to put too fine a point on it, it was a state secret—unauthorized knowledge of which would earn the headsman's sword.

Another foundation was being laid with this wedding. A new empire was being forged, destined to rise up out of the ruins of Malwa. Or rather, destined to play a great part in Malwa's ruination.

The ceremony was Christian, as was the bride, and as simple a rite as that faith allowed. The bride herself had so stipulated, in defiance of all natural law—had insisted, in fact. She had claimed she wanted a brief and unembellished ceremony purely in the interests of security and secrecy. Given that the bride was acknowledged to be a supreme mistress in the arts of espionage and intrigue, the claim was accepted readily enough. Most people probably even believed it.

But Antonina, watching her best friend Irene kneeling at the altar, was a bit hard-pressed to restrain a smile. She knew the truth.

First thing that scheming woman's going to do, after she gets to Peshawar, is hold the biggest and most splendiferous Buddhist wedding in the history of the world. Last for a month, I bet.

Her eyes moved to the man kneeling next to Irene. Kungas was droning his way through the phrases required of a Christian groom with perfect ease and aplomb.

Any Christian objects, of course, she'll claim her husband made her do it.

Kungas was destined to be the new ruler of a new Kushan empire. The Kushans, in their great majority, adhered to the Buddhist faith. In secret, for the most part, since their Malwa overlords had decreed their grotesque Mahaveda version of Hinduism the established religion and forbade all others. But the secrecy, and the frequent martyrdoms which went with it, had simply welded the Kushans that much more closely to their creed.

Naturally, their new ruler would insist that his wife the empress espouse that faith herself. Naturally. He was a strong-willed man, everyone knew it.

Ha!

Belisarius glanced down at her, and Antonina fiercely stifled her giggle.

Ha! It was her idea, the schemer! Never would have occurred to Kungas.

Kungas was the closest thing Antonina had ever met to a fabled atheist. Agnostic, for a certainty. He was prepared to accept—as a tentative hypothesis—the existence of a "soul." Tentatively, he was even willing to accept the logic that a "soul" required a "soul-maker." *Grudgingly*, he would allow that such a "soul-maker" of necessity possessed superhuman powers.

That he—or she—or it—was a *god*, however . . . *The* God?

"Rampant speculation," Kungas called it. In private, of course, and in the company of close friends. Kungas was literate, now, in both Greek and Kushan. But he was no intellectual and never would be. "Rampant speculation" was his lover Irene's serene way of translating his grunted opinion. "Pure guesswork!" was the way Antonina had heard it.

But if Kungas was no intellectual, there was nothing at all wrong with his mind. That mind had been shaped since childhood in the cauldron of battle and destruction. And if, against all logic, the man who had emerged from that fiery furnace was in his own way a rather gentle man—using the term "gentle" very loosely—he had a mind as bright and hard as a diamond.

His people were Buddhists, whatever Kungas thought. So would he be, then. And his empress, too, now that she mentioned it to him.

Ha! Pity the poor Malwa!

In the brief reception which followed the wedding, the Emperor of Iran and non-Iran advanced to present his congratulations along with his wife. So did Theodora, the Empress Regent of Rome. So too did Eon, the *negusa nagast* of Ethiopia and Arabia, accompanied by his own wife Rukaiya. The man and woman destined to be the rulers of a realm which still existed only in the imagination were being given the official nod of recognition by three of the four most powerful empires in the world.

The most powerful empire, of course, was absent. Which was hardly surprising, since even if that empire had known of this wedding it would hardly have approved. The new realm would be torn from Malwa's own bleeding flank.

Belisarius and Antonina saw no need to join the

crowd pressing around Kungas and Irene. Neither did Ousanas.

"Silly business," muttered Ethiopia's *aqabe tsentsen*— vizier, in effect, although the title actually translated as "keeper of the fly-whisks." The quaint and modest title was in keeping with Ethiopian political custom.

"Silly," he repeated. He glanced at Antonina. "Don't lie, woman. You know as well as I do that she'll be a Buddhist soon enough." He snorted. "And God knows what else. All those mountains are full of pagans. She'll be getting remarried every week, swearing eternal devotion to whatever prancing goat-god happens to be the local fancy."

Antonina maintained an aloof smile. "I think that's absolute nonsense. I can't believe you could be so cynical." She bestowed the serene expression upon Belisarius. He responded with his own smile, more crooked than ever, but said nothing.

Antonina's smile now went to the small group of soldiers standing just behind her husband. All three of the top Kushan commanders of Belisarius' army—former commanders, as of this moment—were gathered there. Vasudeva was in the center, flanked by Vima and Huvishka.

"Surely you don't agree with him," stated Antonina.

Vasudeva's smile, as always, was a thin and economic affair. "Wouldn't surprise me," he said. "Not a bad idea, in fact. Pagans are a silly superstitious lot, of course, but they're not the least bit inclined toward exclusivity." He stroked his wispy goatee. "Maybe."

"*Et tu, Brute?*" muttered Antonina.

Vasudeva's smile widened. "Antonina, be serious." He nodded toward the wedding couple and the small crowd gathered about them. "Have I not myself—me and my officers—been the subject of just such a pre-meditated marital display this very morning?"

Antonina was a bit disconcerted by the Kushan general's perspicacity. Belisarius had told her, but she was not very familiar with the man herself.

Shrewd indeed!

All three of the Kushan generals were now smiling. "And quite well done it was, too," murmured Vima approvingly. "What ambitious general, daydreaming of his own possible lineage, would risk bringing the wrath of such empires down on his head? Wouldn't do at all to overthrow the *established* dynasty, in the face of such universal approval."

Belisarius was studying the faces of the three men. For once, there was no smile at all on his face.

"It's been done, and often enough," he said softly. His gaze came to rest on Vasudeva. Vasudeva's smile was still in place.

"Not here," said the Kushan. He glanced at Kungas. "All of us have spent time with him, Belisarius, since he arrived. We are satisfied. He will make a good emperor." His two subordinates grunted their agreement. Vima added: "And where else could you find such a scheming empress?"

Vima studied Irene. "I suppose you could marry the widow, over the body of her dead husband. But—"

Huvishka shuddered. "Talk about sleeping with both eyes open!"

A little laugh swept the group. Belisarius nodded. In truth, he was not surprised at the easy way in which the Kushan generals had accepted Kungas as their new monarch-to-be. Belisarius had come to know all three Kushan soldiers well, in the past two years. They approached life with hard-headed practicality, and were not given in the least to idle fancies.

Still—

Kungas and Irene had brought fewer than three thousand Kushan soldiers with them from Majarashtra.

There were over ten thousand serving under Vasudeva's command in Belisarius' army. Two thousand of those had been with Vasudeva when Belisarius defeated them at the battle of Anatha. The rest had come over after the Malwa disaster at Charax. When the Malwa commanders started their defeated army marching back to India, their Kushan troops had mutinied. The march would be a death march, and they knew it. And knew, as well, that Kushans would do a disproportionate share of the dying. The Ye-tai, not they, would receive what little extra rations could be smuggled off boats along the coast.

It was an awkward situation, thus. All of the Kushans serving under Belisarius had been released for service in their own cause. On the one hand, that gave Kungas a small but by no means laughable army. On the other, it meant Kungas and Irene would be marching across the Persian plateau in order to rebuild the shattered empire of the Kushans accompanied by an army most of whose soldiers owed them no allegiance at all. Everything would depend on the attitude of the officers those soldiers did know and trust. First and foremost, Vasudeva and Vima and Huvishka.

Just as Vasudeva had shrewdly surmised, the main purpose of the wedding which had just been held was to make the attitude of Rome and Persia and Ethiopia as clear as crystal. *This man—and this woman—have our official seal of approval. So don't get any wild ideas.*

"Good enough," murmured Belisarius. "Good enough."

Later that morning, Irene and Kungas went to the Roman emperor's chambers to receive his own official seal of approval. Which they got, needless to say, with considerably less reserve than from his elders and nominal subordinates. Irene was eventually forced to pry him loose.

Photius was struggling with unmanly tears. "I'll miss you," he whispered.

Irene chucked him under the chin. "So come and visit. And we'll do the same."

Photius managed a smile. "I'd like that! Theodora hates to travel, but I think it's exciting." He hesitated; a trace of apprehension came to his face, as he glanced quickly at the taller girl standing next to him.

Tahmina had his little arm firmly held in her hands. "Whatever my lord and husband desires," she crooned.

Irene grinned. "Well said! My own philosophy exactly."

Kungas grunted. Irene ignored the uncouth sound. A very stern expression came to her face, and now she was wagging her finger in front of Photius' nose.

"And remember! Every new book that comes out! I'll expect it sent to me immediately! Or there'll be war!"

Photius nodded. "Every one, as soon as it comes out. I'll get the very first copy and sent it to you right off, by fast courier." He stood straight. "I can do that, you know. I'm the Emperor of Rome."

"Quite so," crooned Tahmina.

That evening, in the suite of the imperial palace which had been set aside for the use of Kungas and Irene, a different ceremony took place. At sundown, Antonina bustled into the room. Behind her came a servant, carrying a large and heavy crate.

Antonina planted her hands on hips and gave the men sitting on the various divans scattered about the large salon a ferocious glare. The glare spared no one—not her husband, not his chief commanders Maurice and Sittas and Agathius, not Ousanas and

Ezana, not Kungas nor his chief officers, not the Persian general Kurush. If they were male, they were dead meat.

"*Out!*" She hooked her thumb at the door. "All of you, at once! Take this military folderol somewhere else. This room is hereby dedicated to a solemn ritual."

Maurice was the first to rise. "Got to respect hallowed tradition," he agreed solemnly. "Let's go, gentlemen. We're pretty much done with everything except"—he sighed heavily—"the logistics. And Agathius and I can do that with Belisarius in his own chambers." He gave Antonina a grin. "It'll take us hours, of course, but so what? This one won't be coming back tonight."

As he moved toward the door: "Not on her own two feet, anyway."

Antonina growled. Maurice hastened his pace. Antonina's growl deepened. A small tigress, displeased. The rest of the men followed Maurice with considerable alacrity.

When they were gone, Antonina ordered the servant to place the crate on a nearby table. He did so, and then departed at once. With a regal gesture, Antonina swept the lid off the crate. More regally still, she withdrew the first bottle of wine.

"Soldiers," she sneered. "What do they know about massacre and mayhem?"

Irene was already bringing the goblets. "Nothing." She extended them both. "Start the slaughter."

Chapter 4

"I wish you'd stop doing this," grumbled Agathius. "It's embarrassing." The powerful hands draped on the arms of the wheelchair twitched, as if Agathius were about to seize the wheel rims and propel himself forward. Then he had to hastily snatch the maps and logistics records before they slid off his lap onto the tiled floor.

Seeing the motion, Maurice snorted. "Are you crazy?" The grizzled veteran, striding alongside the wheelchair, glanced back at the young general pushing it. "It's good for him, doing some honest work for a change instead of plotting and scheming."

Belisarius grinned. "Certainly is! Besides, Justinian insisted on a full and detailed report—from me personally. How can I do that without operating the gadget myself?"

Agathius grumbled inarticulately. The wheelchair and its accompanying companions swept into one of the vaulted and frescoed chambers of the imperial palace. A cluster of Persian officers and courtiers scrambled aside. By now, many days into the ongoing strategy sessions at Ctesiphon, they had all learned not to gawk in place. Belisarius did *not* maneuver a wheelchair with the same cunning with which he maneuvered armies in the field. *Charge!*

When they reached the stairs at the opposite side of the chamber, leading to the residential quarters above, Belisarius and Maurice positioned themselves on either side of the wheelchair. As Agathius continued his grumbling, Belisarius and Maurice seized the handles which Justinian had designed for the purpose and began hauling Agathius and his wheelchair up the stairs by main force, grunting with the effort. Even with his withered half-legs, Agathius was still a muscular and heavy burden.

Below, the knot of Persian notables watched the operation with slack jaws and open eyes. They had seen it done before, of course—many times—but still . . .

Unseemly! Servants' work! The top commander of the greatest army since Darius should not—

At the first landing, Belisarius and Maurice set the contraption down and took a few deep breaths. Agathius looked from one to the other, scowling fiercely. "I *can* climb stairs myself, you know. I do it at home all the time."

Belisarius managed a grin. "*Justinian*, remember? You think the Roman Empire's Grand Justiciar—not to mention Theodora's husband—is going to settle for a secondhand account?"

"He's way off in Adulis," protested Agathius. "And he's completely preoccupied with getting his beloved new steam-powered warships ready." But it was weak, weak.

Belisarius shrugged. "Yes—and he's blind, to boot. So what? You think he doesn't have spies?"

Maurice snorted sarcastically. "And besides, Agathius, you know how much Justinian loves designing his gadgets. So just shut up and resign yourself to the inevitable." Sourly: "At least *you* don't have to lift this blasted thing. With an overgrown, over-muscled ex-cataphract in it."

They'd rested enough. With a heave and a grunt, Belisarius and Maurice lifted Agathius and the wheelchair and staggered their way upward. When they reached the top of the stairs and were in the corridor leading to Agathius' private chambers, they set the wheelchair down.

"All . . . right," puffed Belisarius. "You're on your own again. Justinian wants to know how the hand grips work also."

"They work just fine," snapped Agathius. To prove the point, he set off down the corridor at a pace which had Belisarius and Maurice hurrying to catch up—puffing all the while. Agathius seemed to take a malicious glee in the sound.

At the entrance to his chambers, Agathius paused. He glanced up at Belisarius, wincing a bit and clearing his throat.

"Uh—"

"I'll speak to her," assured Belisarius. "I'm sure she'll listen to reason once—"

The door was suddenly jerked open. Agathius' young wife Sudaba was standing there, glaring.

"*What is this insane business?*" she demanded furiously. "*I insist on accompanying my husband!*" An instant later, she was planted in front of Belisarius, shaking her little fist under his nose. "*Roman tyrant! Monstrous despot!*"

Hastily, Maurice seized the wheelchair and maneuvered Agathius into the room, leaving Belisarius—Rome's *magister militum per orientem*, Great Commander of the Allied Army, honorary *vurzurgan* in the land of Aryans—to deal alone with Agathius' infuriated teenage wife.

"A command responsibility if I ever saw one," Maurice muttered.

Agathius nodded eagerly. "Just so!" Piously: "After

all, it was *his* decision to keep the baggage train and camp followers to a minimum. It's not as if *we* insisted that the top officers had to set a personal example."

"*Autocrat! Beast! Despoiler! I won't stand for it!*"

"Must be nice," mused Maurice, "to have one of those meek and timid Persian girls for a wife."

But Agathius did not hear the remark. His two-year-old son had arrived, toddling proudly on his own feet, and had been swept up into his father's arms.

"Daddy go bye-bye?" the boy asked uncertainly.

"Yes," replied Agathius. "But I'll be back. I promise."

The boy gurgled happily as Agathius started tickling him. "Daddy beat the Malwa!" he proclaimed proudly.

"Beat 'em flat!" his father agreed. His eyes moved to the great open window, staring toward the east. The Zagros mountains were there; and then, the Persian plateau; and then—the Indus valley, where the final accounts would be settled.

"They'll give me my legs back," he growled. "The price of them, at least. Which I figure is Emperor Skandagupta's blood in the dust."

Maurice clucked. "Such an intemperate man you are, Agathius. I'd think a baker's son would settle for a mere satrap."

"Skandagupta, and nothing less," came the firm reply. "I'll see his empty eyes staring at the sky. I swear I will."

When Belisarius rejoined them, some time later, the Roman general's expression was a bit peculiar. Bemused, perhaps—like a stunned ox. Quite unlike his usual imperturbable self.

Agathius cleared his throat. "It's not as if I didn't give you fair warning."

Belisarius shook his head. The ox, trying to shake away the confusion.

"How in the name of God did she get me to agree?" he wondered. Then, sighing: "And *now* I'll have Antonina to deal with! She'll break my head when I tell her she's got another problem to handle on shipboard."

Maurice grinned. "I imagine Ousanas will have a few choice words, too. Sarcasm, you may recall, is not entirely foreign to his nature. And he *is* the military commander of the naval expedition. Will be, at least, once the Ethiopians finish putting their fleet together."

Belisarius winced. His eyes moved to the huge table at the center of the chamber. Agathius had already spread out the map and the logistics papers which he had brought with him to the conference. They seemed a mere outcrop in the mountain of maps, scrolls, codices and loose sheets of vellum which practically spilled from every side of the table.

"That's the whole business?" he asked.

Agathius nodded. "Yes—and it's just as much of a mess as it looks. Pure chaos!" He glowered at the gigantic pile. "Who was that philosopher who claimed everything originated from atoms? Have to ask Anastasius. Whoever it was, he was a simpleminded optimist, let me tell you. If he'd ever tried to organize the logistics for a combined land and sea campaign that involved a hundred and twenty thousand men—and that's just the soldiers!—he would've realized that everything turns *into* atoms also."

"Thank God," muttered Belisarius, eyeing the mess with pleasure. "Something simple and straightforward to deal with!"

In the event, Antonina was not furious. She dismissed the entire matter with an insouciant shrug, as she poured herself a new goblet of pomegranate-flavored water. Belisarius had introduced her to the

Persian beverage, and Antonina found it a blessed relief from the ever-present wine of the Roman liquid diet. Especially when she was suffering from a hangover.

The goblet full, she took it in hand and leaned back into her divan. "Sudaba and I get along. It'll be a bit crowded, of course, with her sharing my cabin along with Koutina." For a moment, suspicion came into her eyes. "You *didn't* agree to letting her bring the boy?"

Belisarius straightened proudly. "There I held the line!"

Aide flashed an image into his mind. *Hector on the walls of Troy.* Belisarius found himself half-choking from amusement combined with chagrin.

Antonina eyed her husband quizzically. Belisarius waved a weak hand. "Nothing. Just Aide. He's being sarcastic and impertinent again."

"Blessed jewel!" exclaimed a voice. Sitting on another divan in his favored lotus position, Ousanas cast baleful eyes on Belisarius. "I shudder to think what would become of us," he growled, "without the Talisman of God to keep you sane."

Antonina sniffed. "My husband does *not* suffer from delusions of grandeur."

"Certainly not!" agreed Ousanas. "How could he, with a mysterious creature from the future always present in his mind? Ready—blessed jewel!—to puncture inflated notions at a moment's notice."

Ousanas took a sip from his own goblet. Good red wine, this—no silly child's drink for him. "Not that he has any reason for such grandiosity, of course, when you think about it. What has Belisarius actually accomplished, these past few years?"

The aqabe tsentsen of the kingdom of Axum— empire, now, since the Ethiopians had incorporated southern Arabia into their realm—waved his own hand. But there was nothing weak about that gesture. It combined the certainty of the sage with the authority of the despot.

"Not much," he answered his own question. "The odd Malwa army defeated here and there, entirely through the use of low-minded stratagems. The occasional rebellion incited within the Malwa empire itself." His sniff was more flamboyant than Antonina's, nostrils fleering in contempt. "A treasure stolen from Malwa and then given away to Maratha rebels—a foolish gesture, that!—and a princess smuggled out of captivity. Bah! There's hardly a village headman in my native land between the great lakes who could not claim as much."

Antonina grinned. As a rule, disrespect toward her husband was guaranteed to bring a hot response. But from Ousanas—

Axum's aqabe tsentsen was not Ethiopian himself. Ousanas had been born and bred in the heartland of Africa far to the south of the highlands. But he had spent years as the dawazz to Prince Eon, a post whose principal duty was to nip royal self-aggrandizement in the bud. Eon was now the *negusa nagast* of Axum, the "King of Kings," and Ousanas had become the most powerful official in his realm. But the former hunter and former slave still had his old habits.

And, besides, they were close friends. So close, in fact, that Ousanas was the most frequently cited "lover" of the huge male harem which Antonina was reputed to maintain. By now, of course—after Antonina had played a central role in crushing the Malwa-instigated Nika rebellion in Constantinople, reestablished imperial authority in Egypt and the Levant, and led the naval expedition which had rescued Belisarius and his army after their destruction of the Malwa logistics base at Charax—not even the scandal-mongering Greek aristocracy gave more than token respect to the slanders.

The Malwa espionage service had long since realized that the rumors had been fostered by Antonina herself, in order to divert their attention from her key role in her husband's strategy.

So, knowing Ousanas, Antonina responded in kind. "Yes, surely. But what Bantu headman can claim to have put his stepson on the throne of the Roman Empire?"

Ousanas snorted. "Rome? Bah!" He leaned forward, gesticulating eagerly. "A realm of peddlers and peasants! No, no, Antonina—for true grandeur you must visit the great and mysterious empires in central Africa! The cities are paved with silver and jade, the palaces cut from pure crystals. The emperors—every one of them a former headman from my native region, you understand—are borne to the gold-inlaid toilets on elephants draped with—"

"And the elephants shit diamonds themselves," interrupted Ezana. The Axumite naval commander—he *was* a native-born Ethiopian—gave Ousanas a sour glance. "It's odd how these marvelous African empires of his keep moving further south as we Axumites extend our rule." Another sniff was added. "So far, though, all we seem to encounter are illiterate heathen savages scrabbling in the dirt."

Ousanas began some retort, but Ezana drove over it. "The Persian girl does not concern me, Belisarius. Not by herself. As young as she is, Sudaba is not a stranger to campaigns. She was with Agathius at the Nehar Malka, after all. Any Persian noblewoman who could manage on board one of those miserable river barges"—the inevitable Axumite pride in their naval expertise surfaced—"can *surely* manage aboard one of our craft."

That contented thought gave way to a scowl: "But if this starts a mudslide of women demanding to accompany their men—" Ezana swiveled his head and brought another occupant of the salon under his cold scrutiny. "My own half-sister, soon enough!"

Under that hard gaze, the pale face of young Menander turned pink with embarrassment. The Roman officer knew that Ezana was aware of his intimate relationship with Deborah, but he still found the casual manner in which Ethiopians handled such things unsettling. Menander was too close to the Thracian village of his upbringing not to be a bit edgy. In *his* village, the half-brother of a seduced sister would have blood in his eye. And no Thracian villager was half as skilled and experienced in mayhem and slaughter as Ezana!

"I've already spoken to her about it," he muttered. "She agreed to stay behind." Guiltily: "Well . . . in Charax, anyway."

"Marvelous," grunted Ezana. "Our precious naval base is about to become as populous as Bharakuccha. The women will be bad enough." His next words caused Menander to turn beet red. "The inevitable squalling brats which follow will practically carpet the city. Our stevedores will be tripping all over them trying to load our warships. Our soldiers will have to fight their way to the docks."

Belisarius sighed and spread his hands. "Yes, Ezana—I know. But I can't accomplish miracles. As it is, we'll still manage to keep the camp followers to a bare minimum." He tried to rally his pride. "In proportion, we'll have the smallest baggage train since Xenophon's march to the sea."

"Marvelous," grunted Ousanas. "Perhaps we should follow his lead then. Strand ourselves in the middle of the Malwa empire and try to fight our way *out*."

Menander recovered his aplomb. Young and sometimes bashful he might be, but no one had ever accused him of cowardice. "We already did that," he pointed out cheerfully. "Only a handful of us, of course, not Xenophon's fabled ten thousand. I much prefer the current prospect. Marching *into* Malwa, with over a hundred thousand!"

"*You* won't be in that number," retorted Ezana. "No, boy. You're for the cut and thrust of boarding parties."

"Me?" Menander's eyes widened in mock astonishment. "Nonsense. *I'm* the gunnery specialist. *I* am required to stay back while Axumite marines storm across the decks. *My* duties—"

The last occupant of the salon now spoke. "Bullshit, boy!" John of Rhodes rose from his divan and planted his arms akimbo. "The *real* gunnery specialist is Eusebius—who's too nearsighted to storm a latrine, anyway. And since *I'm* the commander of the gunship fleet, that leaves you as the top Roman officer in the armada to show these haughty black fellows"—he and the two Africans exchanged grins—"how to wield hand weapons properly in the close quarters of a desperate boarding operation."

"That's nonsense, also," said Antonina. She drained the rest of her goblet. "If all goes as planned, there won't *be* any boarding operations. Just the dazzling maneuvers of warships firing cannons at long range, destroying the Malwa with precision and style."

And that, of course, brought a storm of criticism and outrage.

Idiot! Have you learned nothing?

The First Law of Battle!

Every battle plan in history—

"—gets fucked up as soon as the enemy arrives," she finished. "Men. Such slobs. Everything always has to be messy and untidy." Serenely: "Fortunately, *this* expedition will have a woman's hand on the rudder."

Five pairs of male eyes, ranging in color from bright

blue to deepest brown, joined in condemnation of such folly.

Antonina poured herself another goblet. "Trust me," she said, still with absolute serenity. "You'll see."

Belisarius' final meeting of the day took place late that night, in the back room of a small tavern to which he had come cloaked in secrecy.

"There's nothing more I can tell you," he concluded. "If we hear anything further, of course, I'll let you know. But since you'll be off as soon as Ezana can finish assembling his small fleet, I don't imagine there'll be anything else."

Anastasius grunted. "Not if you're right, and Narses is behind it all." He shrugged his massive shoulders. "Speaking for myself, I hope he is. Information's valuable, but I'd rather trust my life to Narses' fine and subtle hand."

Valentinian glared at him. Clearly enough, the weasel-thin cataphract did not share his giant companion's equanimity.

"Speak for yourself," he snarled. "I'd rather trust a scorpion than Narses." The glare shifted to Belisarius. "And *don't* repeat Irene's fancy phrases to me. Fine for her to talk about trusting Narses' so-called 'craftsmanship.' *She'll* be on the other side of the Hindu Kush from the bastard, with thirteen thousand Kushan bodyguards."

The last occupant of the room spoke up. "Ah, but you forget. She'll be without *me*. And since I'll be coming with *you*, I think that fairly evens the odds."

Valentinian was now glaring at Kujulo. But, even for Valentinian, the glare was hard to maintain. After Belisarius' rescue of then-princess Shakuntala from her captivity at Venandakatra's palace in Gwalior, Valentinian had fought his way out of India with Kushans at his side—Kujulo among them. He had then spent two years fighting against Kushans and, after Vasudeva and his men took service with Belisarius, with them at his side. There were perhaps no soldiers in the world, beyond the general's own Thracian bucellarii to whom Valentinian belonged, that he respected and trusted more than he did Kushans. And, of them, more than Kujulo himself.

Still—

"I'm not complaining," he complained. He took his own quaff of wine, and then squinted bitterly at the Persian vintage as if all the sourness of the universe were contained therein. "If it can be done, we'll get the girls out. Although I *still* don't understand why Narses would go to all this trouble—not to mention huge risks for himself—just to get Dadaji's daughters back to their father."

Belisarius shrugged. "That part doesn't make sense to any of us, Valentinian. Irene no more than me. But—"

His crooked smile made its appearance. "That's all the more reason to investigate. There's *got* to be more involved."

"What do you think?" asked Anastasius.

Belisarius scratched his chin. "I have no idea." He glanced at Valentinian. "But I can't help remembering the last words Lord Damodara said to you, before he released you from captivity."

Valentinian scowled. "That silly business about you having a proper respect for grammar?"

Belisarius nodded. "Yes, that." His chin-scratching went into high gear. "I can't help but wondering if what we're seeing here isn't a master grammarian at work. Parsing a very long sentence, so to speak."

Valentinian threw up his hands with exasperation. "I still say it's silly!" He planted his hands firmly on the table and leaned forward.

"We'll do it, General. If it can be done at all. But I'm giving you fair warning—"

He pushed himself back and took a deep breath. "If we run into Rana Sanga, I'm surrendering right off! No way in hell am I going to fight *that* monster again!"

Chapter 5
BIHAR
Spring, 533 A.D.

The knuckles on Rana Sanga's right hand, gripping the tent pole, were as white as bone. For a moment, Lord Damodara wondered if the pole would snap. The thought was only half-whimsical. The Malwa commander had once seen the leader of his Rajput troops cut an armored man in half—*vertically*. Sanga's sword had come down through the shoulder, split the sternum and the ribs, and only come to a halt when the sword broke against the baldric's buckle.

True, his opponent had been a lightly armored rebel, and as small as Bengalis usually were. Still—

"I'm glad I'm using bamboo to hold up my tent," he remarked casually.

Startled, Rana Sanga's eyes came to his master. Then, moved to his hand. Slowly, with an obvious effort, the tall Rajput king released his grip.

The hand became a fist and the fist slammed into his left palm. Damodara winced at the noise. That punch would have broken the hands of most men. Sanga didn't even seem to notice. There were times when Damodara wondered if the Rajput was entirely human.

For all Sanga's courtesy and stiff honor, there was something about the Rajput king—something that went beyond his towering stature and tigerish frame—that made the Malwa general think of the asuras of the ancient chronicles and legends. Demons . . .

Lord Damodara shook the thought away, as he had so often before. The asuras had been evil creatures. However ferocious in combat, Rana Sanga could not be accused of the same. Not by any sane man, at least; and whatever else Damodara was, he was most certainly sane.

The Malwa general heaved a very faint, very controlled sigh. *And that is perhaps all I am. Sane.* He turned away from the sight of his silent, seething, enraged subordinate and studied the new maps which had been brought to the command tent. Damodara's keen mind found comfort in those maps. The lines drawn upon them were clean and precise. Quite unlike the human territory which they so glibly claimed to represent.

Honor. Morality. Those are for others. For me, there is only sanity.

"There is no leeway in the orders, Rana Sanga," he said harshly. "None whatsoever."

Sanga was now glaring at an idol perched on a small pedestal next to the tent's entrance. The very expensive ivory carving was a miniature statue of the four-armed, three-headed and three-eyed god called Virabhadra. In each of his hands, the god bore a bow, an arrow, a shield and a sword. The weapons were all made of pure gold. A necklace of sapphire skulls adorned his bare chest, and each cyclops eye was a ruby. The scarlet color of the gems seemed to reflect Sanga's rage with blithe indifference.

Virabhadra had once been a minor god, one of Siva's variations. But the Mahaveda cult which dominated the

Malwa empire's new version of Hinduism had elevated him to much higher status. Damodara rather loathed the statue, himself, despite its value. But it helped to keep the ever-suspicious priests of Malwa from prying too closely into his affairs.

"I have already come under criticism for my methods of suppressing rebellion here in eastern India," he added softly. He gestured at one of the scrolls on his large desk. "I received that from Nanda Lal just two days ago. The emperor's spymaster is wondering why we have made such infrequent use of impalement."

Sanga tore his eyes away from the statue. "That idiot," he snarled, utterly oblivious to the fact that he was insulting one of the emperor's close kinsmen in front of another. For some reason—or, rather, a reason he chose not to examine closely—Damodara found that unthinking trust something of a small treasure in its own right.

Sanga began pacing back and forth in the command tent. His steps, as always, were as light and powerful as a tiger's. And his voice carried the rumbling undertones of the same predator of the forest.

"We have spilled a river of blood across this land," he growled. "Here, and in half of Bengal also. Stacked heads in small piles at the center of a hundred villages. And then burned the villages. And for what?"

He paused, for a moment, and glared at the closed flap of the tent as if he could see the ravaged countryside beyond. "To be sure, the rebellion is suppressed. But it will flare up again, soon enough, once we are gone. Does that—that—" Teeth clenched: "—*spymaster* really think that impaling a rebel instead of decapitating him will serve us for magic?"

Damodara shrugged. "In a word: *yes*. Nanda Lal has always been a firm believer in the value of terror. As much as Venandakatra, the truth be told, even if he does not take Venandakatra's personal pleasure in the doing."

Mention of Venandakatra's name, inevitably, stoked the Rajput's rage. But Damodara did not regret the doing of it. Rana Sanga, in the privacy of Damodara's tent, could afford to rage. Lord Damodara had no such luxury himself. There was no superior in front of whom *he* could pace like a tiger, snarling his fury at bestial cruelty. Damodara had no superiors, beyond Nanda Lal and the emperor himself. And the being from the future called Link which ruled them in turn. Nanda Lal and Emperor Skandagupta would—at best—immediately remove Damodara from command were he to express such sentiments to them. The *thing* would almost certainly do worse.

"My family is in Kausambi now, you know," he said softly. "All of them. I just got a letter from my wife yesterday. She is not pleased with the climate in the capital—it's particularly hard on my parents—but she says the emperor has provided them with a very fine mansion. Plenty of room, even with three children."

The quiet words seemed to drain Sanga's anger away, as quickly as water pouring out of a broken basin.

"So soon?" he murmured.

Damodara shrugged and spread his hands widely. The lithe gesture brought a peculiar little pleasure to him. After the past two years of arduous campaigning—first in Persia, and then in eastern India—the formerly rotund little Malwa general was almost as fit as any of his Rajput soldiers.

"Did you expect anything else, King of Rajputana?" Damodara chuckled harshly. "*Of course* the emperor insists on taking my family hostage, in all but name. Except for his Ye-tai bodyguard troops—arrogant bastards—everybody admits that we possess his empire's finest army."

"Small army," grunted Sanga.

Again, Damodara shrugged. "Only by Malwa

standards. Anywhere else in the world, forty thousand men—half of them Rajputs, and all the rest adopting Rajput ways—would be considered a mighty host. And our numbers are growing."

He turned back to the table with its clean and simple maps. When he spoke again, his voice was as harsh as Sanga's. "But—yes, by Malwa standards, a small army. So let us put all else aside and concentrate on what we must do. *Must*—do."

He waited until Sanga was at his side. Then, tracing the line of the Ganges with a finger: "Venandakatra can squawk all he wants about immediate reinforcement in the Deccan. Nanda Lal, at least, understands logistics. We will have to follow the Ganges to the Jamuna; then, upstream to the Chambal."

The two men had spent years fighting and leading side by side. Sanga immediately grasped the logic. "Yes. Then—" His own long finger touched the map. "We make our portage here and come south into the Gulf of Khambat following the Mahi river."

Damodara nodded. "It's a roundabout way. But, in the end, we will approach Bharakuccha from the north, shielded from Rao's—ah, I believe the term Lord Venandakatra prefers is 'brigands'—by the Vindhya mountains."

"Not much of a shield," murmured Sanga. "Not from Rao and his—" The Rajput's lips pursed, as if tasting a lemon. "Brigands."

"Enough, I think. Until we reach Bharakuccha and can get reliable local intelligence, I *don't* want to be blundering about in the Great Country. Not with the Panther roaming loose."

The two men stared at the map in silence for a bit longer. Then, heaving a sigh, Rana Sanga spoke almost in a whisper.

"I used to dream, sometimes—long ago, when I was

still young and foolish—of meeting him again in single combat on the field of honor."

Damodara tried to salvage something out of the ruins. "And so you shall!"

Heavily, Sanga shook his head. "No, Lord. As you say, the orders carried no leeway. Once we cross the Narmada, we will be under Lord Venandakatra's command. Politically, at least, since he is the Goptri of the Deccan. You know as well as I do that he is not called the Vile One for no reason."

Again, the heavy sigh. "There will be no honor for us in the Great Country, Lord Damodara. Not a shred."

Damodara said nothing. There was nothing to say.

Shortly thereafter, Rana Sanga left the tent and returned to his own. There, for two hours, he paced back and forth in silence. His Rajput officers stayed well clear of the tent. Sanga spoke not a word, but black anger emanated from him like an asura in captive fury.

Even the guards standing outside the entrance moved as far away from it as possible. Their presence at the tent was a formality, in any event. Rana Sanga was universally—by friend and foe alike—considered the greatest living Rajput warrior as well as Rajputana's finest general. "Guarding" him was a bit on the order of setting cubs to guard a tiger.

Late in the afternoon, a Ye-tai appeared before the tent and requested permission to pass. Toramana, that was, an officer whom Damodara had recently promoted to the status of general. Of the thousands of Ye-tai soldiers in Damodara's army, Toramana was now ranked the highest.

The Rajput guards eyed him uncertainly.

They did so, in part, because Toramana was the kind of man who, armed and armored as he was, would cause any soldier to pause. Toramana was himself considered a mighty warrior, as well as a canny general. He was big, even for a Ye-tai, and not yet thirty years old. His taut and well-muscled body was evidence of the rigorous regimen he had maintained since boyhood—a boyhood which had itself been spent in the harsh environment of the Hindu Kush. His face, bony and angular in the Ye-tai way, was quite unreadable—which was not common in that breed of men.

For the most part, however, the Rajput guards hesitated because they knew the purpose of Toramana's visit. He had come to receive the answer to a question, a question which all the Rajputs in Damodara's army had been discussing and debating privately for days. And, for most, had settled on the same answer as the two guards standing in front of Rana Sanga's tent.

"It is not a good time, General Toramana," said one of the guards quietly. "Rana Sanga is in a rage. Best you return tomorrow, when the answer is more likely to be the one you desire."

The big Ye-tai officer studied the guard, for a moment. Then, shrugging: "If the answer is the one I desire, then I will have to deal with Rana Sanga for years to come. Do you think this is the last day Rajputana's greatest king will have cause for fury? Best I get the answer in his worst moment. That alone will be a promise greater than any words."

The guards returned his calm gaze by looking away. The truth of the statement could not, after all, be denied.

"Enter then, General," said one.

"Our wishes go with you," murmured the other.

Toramana nodded. "My thanks. Things will be as they will be." He pushed aside the tent flap and entered.

❖   ❖   ❖

Hearing someone come into his pavilion, Sunga ceased his restless pacing and spun around. His hand did not fly to the sword belted at his waist, but his mouth opened, ready to hurl words of angry dismissal. Then, seeing who it was, he froze.

For a moment, the two big men stared at each other. The light shed by the lamps in the tent caused both of their faces to be highlighted, making them seem ever harder than usual. Warrior faces, as if cast in bronze. Sanga was taller than Toramana—the Rajput king was taller than almost anyone—and even broader in the shoulders. But the smaller Ye-tai did not seem in the least intimidated.

Which was one of the things Sanga liked about him, when all was said and done. That . . . and much else. It was odd, really. Sanga had never been fond of Ye-tai, as a rule. Rather the contrary.

"I forgot," he said quietly, his rage beginning to ebb. Sanga gestured at a nearby table. The simple piece of furniture was set very low, with cushions on either side resting on the carpets. "Please sit."

When they were seated, Sanga did not pause for more than a moment before speaking.

"First, a question of my own. Why did you protect Holkar's woman and child?" Before Toramana could answer, Sanga added: "And do not tell me it was because of any strategic acumen. You had no way of knowing, in the chaos of the final assault, that the man you had cut down was the son of Dadaji Holkar. We did not discover that until the following day."

Toramana began to speak, but Sanga pressed on over the words.

"Nor do I wish to hear that you intended to keep the woman for your own concubine. You have two already, both of them more attractive than that woman. And neither one of them came with child, though the

Bengali has now borne one of your own. So—why? According to reports, you even had to threaten several of your own soldiers who sought to use the woman."

"It did not take much of a threat," said Toramana. He chuckled softly. "They were subdued with a scowl and a few words. It was more in the way of old habit on their part, than any real urgency. The army, after all, has plenty of camp followers. I think they were simply feeling an urge to break free of Rajput discipline. The men who overran the rebel camp were all Ye-tai, after all."

He shrugged. "The woman was wailing, clutching her man's dead body. The baby, cast aside, was wailing louder still. What man not ridden by a demon can feel lust in such circumstances? There were only two courses of action. Kill them both, or keep them safe from harm."

Silence. The two men matched gazes. The younger Ye-tai was the first to look away. "We do what we must, Rana Sanga. Such is the nature of the world. But there is no reason to do more. A man ends at the limit of his duty. The beast continues beyond. I am a man, not a beast."

The answer seemed to satisfy the Rajput. He planted his large hands on the table and rose to his feet in a single easy movement. Then, began pacing again. This time, however, the pacing was that of a man engrossed in thoughtful consideration, not one working off a rage.

"I have a half-sister named Indira," he said quietly. "You suggested a cousin, but if we are to do this it would be best to do it properly." Teeth flashed in his beard, as much of a snarl as a smile. "If nothing else, it will bring the full weight of Malwa down upon us— you more than me—and if a man is to take on a challenge he may as well do it in the spirit of legend.

I find the thought of Malwa's outrage soothing, at the momont."

Toramana's eyes were wide open, now. His body was no longer relaxed in the least. Very stiff, he was. Clearly, he had not been expecting to hear *this*—not from Rana Sanga!

The Rajput's teeth flashed again, but there was more of real humor in the expression now. "Did you really believe all the tales? *The ultimate Rajput?*" Sanga snorted. "I have given much thought, over the years, to the relation of truth to illusion. It is a simple fact—deny it who will—that the Rajputs themselves are not so many generations removed from barbarism. And came, I am quite certain, from the same mountains that produced you."

He resumed his pacing, very slowly now. "Besides, Indira is a vigorous girl. Very prone to bending custom and tradition in her own right, much to the displeasure of my family. But I am fond of her, despite the difference in our ages. I was more of an uncle to her than a brother, in years past. I can think of no cousin who would be as suitable. Most of them would wail in horror at the very thought. Indira, on the other hand—"

He paused, then chuckled. "Knowing her, she is likely to find the thing a challenge and an adventure."

The pausing stopped abruptly. All traces of humor vanished. The Rajput king stood straight and tall. Without looking at Toramana, he murmured: "Very fond of her, I say. If I discovered she has been abused, I will challenge you and kill you. Do not doubt it for a moment. Neither the challenge nor the killing."

He swiveled his head and brought the Ye-tai under his stony gaze. Then, to his satisfaction, discovered that the young warrior was not bridling at the threat. For all Toramana's own great skill at war, he was more than intelligent enough, despite his relative youth, to understand that he was no match for Sanga.

"I am not abusive to women," said Toramana. Quietly, but perhaps a bit . . . not angrily, no, but sternly for all that.

"Yes, I know." Sanga's lips tightened, as if he were tasting something a bit sour. "I asked Lord Damodara to have Narses spy upon you." His eyes moved away. "My apologies. But I needed to know. Narses says that both your concubines seem in good health, and satisfied with their position. The Bengali even dotes on you, he says, now that you have produced a child."

"I will not disown the boy," said Toramana, the words coming curt and abrupt.

Sanga made a small, dismissive gesture with his hand. "That will not be required. Nor, for that matter, that you put aside the concubines. You are a warrior, after all, bringing your blood to that of a warrior race. Let the old women chatter as they will."

Suddenly, a grin appeared on Sanga's face. His earlier rage seemed to have vanished completely.

"Ha! Let the Malwa priests and spies scurry like insects. Let Nanda Lal squirm in *his* soul, for a change."

Moving with the speed and grace which was his trademark, Sanga resumed his seat at the table. Then, leaning over, he bestowed his grin on Toramana.

"Besides, Indira is very comely. And, as I said, a spirited girl. I do not think there is much danger that you will be overly distracted by concubines."

He gestured to a bowl containing fruit and pastries. "Let us eat, Toramana. I will have my servants bring tea, as well. After the campaign in the Deccan—or as soon as there seems to be an opportunity—it will be done. Perhaps in Rajputana, which would be my preference so long as I can attend. If not, I will send for Indira and you will be wed within the bosom of the army.

"Which," he continued, reaching for an apricot, "would perhaps be best in any event. The marriage, after all, was created in the army. Only that forge was hot enough to do such difficult work."

That night, long after Sanga had departed, Lord Damodara's spymaster entered the command tent. The Malwa commander, engrossed in his study of the maps, gave the old Roman eunuch no more than a glance. Then, using his head as a pointer, he nodded toward a small package resting on his nearby field cot.

"There," he said. "Make sure my wife receives it. Send it off tonight, if possible."

"You are not planning to visit her yourself?" asked Narses. "The army will be passing Kausambi on our way to the Deccan."

Damodara's headshake was curt and abrupt. "I cannot. Nanda Lal's instructions on that matter were as clear and precise as all the rest. I am not to leave the army under any circumstances."

"Ah." Narses nodded. "I understand."

The eunuch moved over to the cot and picked up the package. By the weight and feel of it, there was nothing inside the silk wrapping beyond a few message scrolls and some trinkets for Damodara's three children. Narses began to leave the tent. Then, at the flap, he paused as if an idle thought had come to him.

"I've obtained some more slaves for your wife's household," he said. "They came cheaply. Two whores a bit too well-used to turn a profit any longer. But the brothel-keeper said they were obedient creatures, and capable enough in the kitchen."

Damodara shrugged, as a bull might twitch off annoying and meaningless insects. His finger was busy tracing a route for his Pathan trackers through the

Vindhyas, where they might serve to give advance warning of any Maratha ambush.

"As you command, my lord." A moment later the eunuch was gone. Damodara was only vaguely aware of his departure.

As soon as he entered his own tent, Narses gave Ajatasutra the "thumbs up" and extended the package. The assassin rose with his usual lazy grace and took it in hand.

"I *still* say that's an obscene gesture," he murmured. But he was through the tent flap before Narses could do more than begin his baleful glare.

Outside, Ajatasutra paced through the darkness enshrouding the army's camp with quick and sure feet. The flames of the various campfires provided little in the way of illumination, but that bothered him not in the least. Ajatasutra was quite fond of darkness, the truth be told.

The soldiers clustered about the campfire in one of the more distant groves never saw him coming until he was standing in their midst. Startled, the six men rose to their feet. All of them were experienced mercenaries. Two of them were Biharis, but the others were Ye-tai. In their cups, those four would have boasted that no man could catch them unawares.

They were not in their cups now, however. Ajatasutra had left clear instructions on that matter also. They stood still, awaiting their orders.

"Tonight," said Ajatasutra. "Immediately." He handed the package to one of the Bihari soldiers. "See to it—personally—that Lady Damodara receives this."

As the mercenaries hurriedly began making ready for departure, Ajatasutra stepped over to the small tent pitched nearby. He swept back the flap and peered inside.

The two sisters were wide awake, staring at him with apprehension. The light shed by a small oil lamp made their faces seem especially taut and hollow. The older sister was clutching the baby to her chest.

"No trouble?" he asked. The two girls shook their heads.

"Get ready," he said softly. "You're leaving tonight. For your new owner. The journey will be long, I'm afraid."

"Are you coming?" asked the younger.

Ajatasutra shook his head. "Can't. I have duties elsewhere." Then, seeing the sisters' apprehension turn to outright fear, Ajatasutra chuckled dryly. "Your new owner is reputed to be quite a nice *lady*."

His slight emphasis on the last word seemed to relieve their tension a bit. But only for a moment. Now, the sisters were staring past his figure, at the dimly seen shapes of the soldiers gearing up for travel.

Ajatasutra chuckled again. "There'll be no problem on the trip, other than days of heat and dust. I will leave clear instructions."

The stiffness in the sisters' posture eased. The older cleared her throat. "Will we see you again?"

Ajatasutra tossed his head in an abrupt, almost minute gesture. "Who knows? The world's a fickle place, and God is prone to whimsy."

He dropped the tent flap and turned away. In the minutes which followed, he simply stood in place at the center of the grove, watching the soldiers make their preparations. The Ye-tai were ready within minutes, their horses soon thereafter. What little delay occurred came from the two Bihari mercenaries and the small elephant in their care. Both men were experienced in the work. They would alternate as mahout and guard riding in the howdah.

But Ajatasutra's attention was not on the Biharis. He

was not concerned about them. His careful study was given, first, to the howdah itself. Then, when he was satisfied that his instructions had been followed—the cloths serving as the howdah's curtains were cheap and utilitarian, but did an adequate job of shielding the occupants from external view—he turned his scrutiny upon the Ye-tai who would serve as the howdah's escort.

As was usually the case with Ye-tai, the semi-barbarians were big men. Big, and obviously fit. They were standing just a few feet away, their mounts not far behind them. If the heavy armor and weapons draped upon their muscular bodies caused them any discomfort, there was no sign of it.

Ajatasutra drifted toward them. At that moment, out of the corner of his eye, he saw the tent flap move aside. The sisters emerged and began walking slowly and timidly toward the elephant, the older one still clutching her infant. Ajatasutra had long since provided the sisters with more modest saris than the costumes they had worn as prostitutes. But, even in the poor lighting provided by the dying campfires, their young and lithesome figures were quite evident.

The eyes of the Ye-tai followed their progress, as did Ajatasutra's.

"Pretty little bitches, aren't they?" he mused. His voice, as usual, carried an undertone of whimsy and humor.

The Ye-tai in the center, the leader of the little group, grunted. "That they are. The older one's a bit off-putting, what with that scar on her face, but the young—"

His next grunt was not soft at all. More like an explosive breath—a man kicked by a mule. But the eruption ended almost as soon as it began. As the Ye-tai's head came down, Ajatasutra's dagger plunged into his eye. Halfway to the hilt, before a quick and practiced twist removed the blade before it could become jammed in the skull.

As the Ye-tai slumped to the ground, Ajatasutra stepped aside.

"Wrong answer," he said mildly. His eyes were on the three survivors.

For perhaps two seconds, the Ye-tai seemed frozen in place. The youngest and least experienced of them began moving his hand toward his sword, but one of his companions slapped the hand away.

"Uglier than sin, the both of them," the man rasped. "Rather fuck a crocodile, myself."

Ajatasutra's lips might have quirked a bit. It was difficult to tell, in the darkness. The same darkness, perhaps, explained the ghostly ease with which he now crowded the three mercenaries.

"I can find you anywhere in India," he murmured. "Anywhere in the world. Don't doubt it for a moment."

"A crocodile," husked the young Ye-tai.

Now, even in the darkness, Ajatasutra's smile was plain to see. "Splendid," he said agreeably. His hand—his left hand—dipped into his cloak and emerged holding a small pouch.

"A bonus," he explained. Then, nodding to the corpse: "For seeing to the quiet disposal of the body."

Feeling the weight of the pouch, the newly-promoted mercenary leader grinned. "Crocodile food. River's full of them."

"See to it." Ajatasutra gave a last glance at the elephant. The younger sister was already in the howdah and the older was handing up the baby. A moment later, the two mahouts were assisting her aboard the great creature.

The Ye-tai began to watch the procedure. Then, struck by a very recent memory, tore their eyes away and moved them back to their master.

But he was gone. Vanished into the night, like a demon from the ancient fables.

That very moment, in the far-distant Malwa capital of Kausambi, a demon from the fabled future came to its decision.

"NO CHOICE," it pronounced. "THE KUSHANS GROW MORE UNRELIABLE BY THE DAY. AND THE YE-TAI ARE NOT ENOUGH TO BOLSTER THE REGIME. WE MUST WELD THE RAJPUTS TO OUR SIDE."

The Emperor of Malwa made a last, feeble attempt to safeguard the exclusivity of his dynasty. "They are bound to us by solemn oaths as it is. You know how maniacally the Rajputs hold their honor. Surely—"

"THAT IS NOT ENOUGH. NOT WITH BELISARIUS COMING. THE PRESSURE WILL BECOME INTENSE. NOT EVEN RAJPUT HONOR CAN BE RELIED UPON TO WITHSTAND THOSE HAMMER BLOWS. THEY MUST ALSO BE WELDED BY TIES OF BLOOD. DYNASTIC TIES."

Skandagupta's corpulent little body began to swell like a toad. His mouth opened, ready to utter a final protest. But the sharp glance of Nanda Lal held him silent. That, and the frozen immobility of the four Khmer assassins standing against the nearby wall of the royal chamber. The assassins were all members of Link's special cult, as were the six enormous tulwar-bearing slaves kneeling against the opposite wall. The emperor had seen those knives and tulwars flash before, more than once. They would not hesitate for an instant to spill the life of Malwa's own ruler.

Ruler, in name only. The true power behind Malwa's throne resided in the body of the young woman who sat in the chair next to him. Lady Sati, she was called, one of Skandagupta's first cousins. But the name was as much of a shell as the body itself. Within that comely female form lurked the being called Link, the emissary and satrap of the new gods who were reshaping humanity into their own mold.

"IT WILL BE DONE," decreed the thing from the future. The slender hands draped loosely over the carved armrests made a slight gesture, as if to indicate the body within which Link dwelled. "THIS SHEATH IS PERFECTLY FUNCTIONAL. MUCH HEALTHIER THAN AVERAGE. IT WILL SERVE RANA SANGA AS WIFE AND MOTHER OF HIS CHILDREN. THE DYNASTY WILL THEN BE RAJPUT AS WELL AS MALWA. THE SWORDS AND LANCES OF RAJPUTANA WILL BE WELDED TO US WITH IRON BARS. TIES OF BLOOD."

Nanda Lal cleared his throat. "There is the matter of Sanga's existing wife. And his three existing children."

The thing inside Lady Sati swiveled her head. "A DETAIL. BY ALL ACCOUNTS, HIS WIFE IS PLAIN AND PLUMP." Again, the shapely hands made that little gesture. "THIS FORM IS BEAUTIFUL, AS MEN COUNT SUCH THINGS. AND, AS I SAID, PERFECTLY FUNCTIONAL. RAJPUTANA'S KING WILL HAVE NEW CHILDREN SOON ENOUGH. HE WILL BE RECONCILED TO THE LOSS."

The Malwa spymaster hesitated. This was dangerous ground. "Yes, of course. But my spies report that Sanga dotes on his family. He will still be upset—suspicious, even—if—"

"BY ROMAN HANDS. SEE TO IT, SPYMASTER. USE NARSES. HE WILL KNOW HOW TO MANAGE THE THING IN SUCH A WAY AS TO DIVERT SUSPICION ONTO THE ENEMY. SANGA WILL BLAME BELISARIUS FOR THE MURDER OF HIS FAMILY."

Very dangerous ground. But, whatever else he was, Nanda Lal was no coward. And, in his own cold way, as devoted to the Malwa purpose as any man alive.

"Narses cannot possibly be trusted," he growled. "He was a traitor to the Romans. He can betray us as well."

For the first time, the creature from the future seemed to hesitate. Watching, Skandagupta and Nanda Lal could only wonder at the exact thought processes which went on behind that cold, beautiful exterior. Lightning calculation, of course—that much was obvious from the years they had spent in Link's service. But not even the icy spymaster could imagine such an emptiness of all emotion. Try as he might.

"TRUE, NANDA LAL. BUT STILL NOT AN INSU-PERABLE PROBLEM. BRING NARSES BEFORE ME. IN PERSON. I WILL DISCOVER THE TRUTH OF HIS LOYALTIES AND INTENTIONS."

"As you will, Lady Sati," stated Nanda Lal. He bowed his head obediently. An instant later, the Emperor of Malwa followed suit. The thing was settled, beyond any further discussion and dispute. And if neither man—especially Skandagupta—faced the prospect of a future half-Rajput dynasty with any pleasure, neither did they concern themselves over the possibility of Narses' treachery. Not with Link itself to ferret out the eunuch's soul. No man alive—no woman or child—could hide its true nature from that scrutiny. Not even their great enemy Belisarius had been able to accomplish *that*.

Chapter 6
MESOPOTAMIA
Spring, 533 A.D.

"What's the matter, large one? Are you sick?" asked Belisarius. "You haven't complained once since we left Ctesiphon."

Sittas smiled cheerfully. Planting his feet firmly in the stirrups, he raised himself off the saddle and heaved his huge body around to study the army following in their tracks.

"Complain?" he demanded. "Why should I complain? God in Heaven, would you look at the *size* of that thing!"

Belisarius copied Sittas' maneuver, albeit with considerably more ease and grace. The army following them seemed to cover the entire flood plain. To inexperienced eyes—such as those of the peasants who stared at it from the relative safety of their huts—it would have seemed like a swarm of locusts. And, for the peasants, just about as welcome. True, Emperor Khusrau had promised to pay for any damage done by the army in its passage. Mesopotamian peasants, from the experience of millennia, viewed imperial promises with a skepticism that would have shamed the most rigorous Greek philosopher.

Belisarius had no difficulty finding the underlying order in the seeming chaos.

Kurush's Persian dehgans, fifteen thousand strong, maintained their position on the prestigious left flank. They had done so since the moment the army's core passed through the gates of Ctesiphon and began collecting the units gathered outside the city. The gesture was a bit pointless, since there was no danger of a flank attack here in Mesopotamia. But the Persian aristocracy treasured its little points of honor.

Sittas' own units, the ten thousand heavy cataphracts from Constantinople and Anatolia, were assuming the equivalent position on the army's right wing. Whatever disgruntlement they might still be feeling at the implied slight was being exercised by their vigilance in keeping raiders from the desert at bay. Not that any Arab freebooter in his right mind would attack such an army, even if Belisarius didn't have his own Arab camel contingents riding on the flank of the cataphracts.

Belisarius smiled at the sight, but his study was soon concentrated on the army's center. The cataphracts and dehgans were familiar things. They had dominated warfare in the eastern Mediterranean for centuries. It was the units marching in the army's center which were new. *Very* new.

Sittas' own scrutiny had also reached the army's center. But, unlike Belisarius, his gaze was not one of pleasure and satisfaction.

"Silliest damned thing I've ever seen," he grumbled.

"Thank God," sighed Belisarius, apparently with great relief. "A complaint! I was beginning to wonder seriously about your health."

Sittas snorted. "I just hope you're right about this—this—what's his name?"

"Gustavus Adolphus." Belisarius turned back around and faced forward. He'd seen enough, and the position was awkward to maintain even with stirrups.

"Gustavus Adolphus," he repeated. "With an army more or less designed like this one, he defeated almost every opponent he ever faced. Most of whom had armies which, more or less, resembled the Malwa forces."

Sittas snorted again. " 'More or less, more or less,' " he echoed in a sing-song. "That does not *precisely* fill me with confidence. And didn't he get himself killed in the end?"

Belisarius shrugged. "Leading one of his insanely reckless cavalry charges in his last battle—which his army won, by the way, even with their king dead on the field."

Belisarius smiled crookedly. For a moment, he was tempted to turn around in the saddle and look at his bodyguards. He was quite certain that the faces of Isaac and Priscus, that very moment, were filled with solemn satisfaction at hearing such antics on the part of commanding generals described as "insane."

But he resisted the impulse. For all that he enjoyed teasing Sittas for his inveterate conservatism—

Damned dinosaur, came Aide's sarcastic thought.

—Belisarius also needed to have Sittas' confidence. So:

"You've already agreed, Sittas—or do we have to go through *this* argument again—that armored cavalry can't face unbroken gun-wielding infantry in the field."

"I know I did. Doesn't mean I have to like it." He raised a thick hand, as a man forestalls an unwanted lecture. "And *please* don't jabber at me again about Morgarten and Laupen and Morat and all those other heathen-sounding places where your precious Swiss pikemen of the future stood their ground against cavalry. I'm sick of hearing about it."

Sittas' voice slipped into an imitation of Belisarius' baritone. " 'As long as the gunmen are braced with solid infantry to protect them while they reload, they'll butcher any cavalry that comes against them.' Fine, fine, fine. I won't argue the point. Although I will point out"—here Sittas' tone grew considerably more enthusiastic—"that's only true as long as the infantry doesn't break and run. Which damn few infantry don't, when they see cataphracts thundering down on them."

Aide's voice came again. **Stubborn as a mule. Best give him a stroke or two. Or he'll sulk for the rest of the day.**

Belisarius had reached the same conclusion. His next words were spoken perhaps a bit hastily. "I'm certainly not arguing that cavalry isn't irreplaceable. Nothing like it for routing the enemy and completing their destruction—*after* their formations have been broken."

So did Belisarius pass the next hour or so, with Aide grousing in his mind and Sittas grumbling in his ear, extolling the virtues of cavalry under the right circumstances. By the time Maurice and Agathius arrived with a supply problem which needed Belisarius' immediate attention, Sittas seemed to be reasonably content.

Have to do it all over again tomorrow, concluded Aide sourly.

Sittas rode off less than a minute after Agathius began explaining the problem. The big Greek nobleman's enthusiasm for logistics paralleled his enthusiasm for infantry tactics.

How did he ever win any campaigns, anyway? demanded Aide.

Belisarius was about to reply. But Maurice, as if he'd somehow been privy to the private mental exchange, did it for him.

The Thracian cataphract, born a peasant, gazed after

the departing aristocratic general. Perhaps oddly, his face was filled with nothing more than approval. "Still trying to make him happy? Waste of time, lad, until Sittas has had a battle or two under his belt. But at least we won't have to worry about him breaking under the lesson. Not Sittas. If there's a more belligerent and ferocious general in the world, I don't know who it is. Besides, who really knows the future anyway? Maybe Sittas will lead one of his beloved cavalry charges yet."

By midafternoon, Agathius' problem was well on the way to solution. Agathius had only brought the problem to Belisarius because the difficulty was purely social, rather than technical, and he felt the commanding general needed to take charge. Some of the Persian dehgans were becoming vociferously indignant. Their mules, laden with burdens which were far too heavy for them, were becoming indignant themselves. Mules, unlike horses, cannot be driven beyond a certain point. The Persian mules reached that point as soon as the sun reached the zenith, and had promptly gone on what a future world would have called a *general strike*. And done so, moreover, with a solidarity which would have won the unadulterated approval of the most doctrinaire anarcho-syndicalist.

Even Persian dehgans knew that beating mules was pointless. So, turning upon less redoubtable opponents, they were demanding that room be made for their necessities in the supply barges which were streaming down the Tigris. The Mesopotamian and Greek sailors who manned those craft—no fools, they—steadfastly ignored the shouted demands of the dehgans on the banks and kept their barges a safe distance from the shore. So—

"They've been hollering at me for two hours, now," grumbled Agathius. "I'm getting tired of it."

Dehgans! grumbled Aide. **Only thing in the world that can make Greek noble cataphracts seem like sentient creatures.**

Belisarius turned to one of his couriers. For a moment, he hesitated. In campaigns past, Belisarius had always used veteran professionals for his dispatch riders. But on this campaign, he had felt it necessary to use young Greek nobles. Partly, to mollify the sentiments of the Roman empire's aristocracy, which was slowly becoming reconciled to the Justinian dynasty. But, mostly, to mollify the Persian aristocracy, which would take umbrage at orders transmitted to them by a commoner.

This particular dispatch rider was named Calopodius. He was no older than seventeen, and came from one of the Roman empire's most notable families. Belisarius had, tentatively, formed a good opinion of the boy's wits and tact. Both of which would be needed here.

Calopodius immediately confirmed the assessment. The boy's face showed no expression at all beyond calm alertness. But his words carried a certain dry humor, under the aristocratic drawl.

"I received excellent marks from both my rhetorician and grammarian, sir."

Belisarius grinned. "Splendid! In that case, you should have no difficulty whatsoever telling Kurush to get down to the river *immediately* and put a stop to this nonsense."

Calopodius nodded solemnly. "I don't see any difficulty, sir. Be much like the time my mother sent me to instruct my father's sister to quit pestering the stable boys." A moment later, he was gone, spurring his horse into a canter.

"I wonder if Alexander the Great had to put up with this kind of crap," mused Maurice.

"Of course not!" derided Belisarius. "The man was

Achilles reborn. Who's going to give Achilles an argument?"

But the retort failed of its purpose. Lowborn or not, Maurice and Agathius were every bit as familiar with the Greek epics as any senator.

"Agamemnon," they chorused in unison.

Chapter 7

Antonina viewed the gadget with some disfavor. Ousanas, with considerably more.

"Romans are madmen," he growled. "Lunatics, pure and simple." He swiveled his head, bringing Ezana under his gaze.

"You are the admiral, Ezana. A seaman, where I am a simple hunter. Explain to this supposedly nautical-minded Roman"—here a fierce glare at John of Rhodes—"the simple truths which even a simpleminded hunter can understand." He flipped his hand toward the gadget, peremptorily, the way a man dismisses an annoying servant. "Like trying to use a lioness for a hunting dog. More likely to bite the master than the prey."

Ezana, like Ousanas, was scowling. But the Ethiopian naval commander's scowl was simply one of thoughtfulness.

"Stick to hunting and statesmanship, aqabe tsentsen," he grumbled. "You're supreme at the first and not an outright embarrassment at the second." He studied the gadget for another few seconds. "Hunting lioness . . ." he murmured. "Not a bad comparison, actually."

Ezana's scowl was suddenly replaced by a cheerful

grin. "Not bad! But tell me, Ousanas—what if the lioness were genuinely tame? Or, at least, not quite feral?"

Presented with this outrageous possibility—*a tame lioness?*—Ousanas practically gurgled with outrage. His usual insouciant wit seemed to have completely deserted him.

"Never seen the man in such a state," commented Antonina slyly. She cocked her head at her companion. "You, Menander?"

But Menander was not about to enter *this* fray. The expression on his face was that of a man invited to enter a den of lions and argue the fine points of dining etiquette with its denizens. Clearly enough, the young Roman naval officer intended to champion the only safe and logical course. *Silence.*

Antonina smiled. Sweetly, at Menander; jeeringly, at Ousanas.

"Tame lioness! Not bad!" she exclaimed.

John of Rhodes, the designer of the gadget in question, finally entered the fray himself. His preceding silence, while one of his beloved contraptions was subjected to ridicule, was quite unlike the man. John of Rhodes had once been Rome's most acclaimed naval officer. Forced out of the navy because of his inveterate womanizing—which, alas, included seducing wives of several of his superior officers and visiting senatorial delegates—John had been plucked out of premature retirement by Belisarius and Antonina and put to work designing the new weapons which Aide had brought from the future. Then, as he showed as much energy and ability in that work as he had in his former career, John had found himself once again elevated to high naval rank. Higher, in substance if not in form, than any rank he had previously held. Officially, he was still a captain; in reality, he was the admiral of the

Roman Empire's new fleet of gunpowder-armed warships. Its smallest fleet, true, but the only one which was growing by leaps and bounds.

Throughout the course of his checkered career, however, two things about John of Rhodes had remained constant. He was still a womanizer, although—under Antonina's blood-curdling threats—he had managed to keep his attentions away from the wives of Roman officers and Persian notables. And he was perhaps the most dyspeptic man Antonina had ever encountered. His preceding silence, while Ousanas scowled and sneered, was the surest indication that even John of Rhodes was a bit leery of his new invention.

Finally, however, he rallied. "The thing is perfectly safe!" he bellowed. John began stumping about the deck of the warship, gesticulating madly. "I got the idea from Belisarius himself! And none other than *Aide* gave *him* the design!" Stump; stump. "For your information, O great hunter from Africa"—here, he and Ousanas matched magnificent sneers—"this device insured the supremacy of Rome at sea for centuries in—in—"

His right hand groped, trying to point to that unknown and unseen future which would have been, if the "new gods" of the future had not intervened in human history. The gesture was vague and uncertain. John had tried to seduce Irene Macrembolitissa on several occasions. The attempts had been quite futile, of course. Irene was not in the least susceptible to the charms of seducers. But, in her own lioness way, she had enjoyed toying with a would-be predator. So, on one occasion, she had fended off John's advances by a learned explanation of the logical complexities involved in changing the past by intervening from the future. Notions like the "river of time" had mingled freely with "paradox" and "conundrum." By the time she was done. John was exhausted, utterly confused, and resigned to a night of celibacy.

"—in that other history," he concluded lamely.

He rallied again, pointing with a stiff finger to the gadget. " *'Greek fire'* they'll call it! The scourge of Rome's enemies at sea."

Ousanas' thundering rejoinder was cut short by Ezana. "Why don't we try the thing out," he suggested mildly. "After all, what's the harm?"

The Ethiopian admiral's eyes scanned the Roman ship in whose bow the "gadget" was positioned. Christened the *Theodora Victrix*—whatever else he was, John of Rhodes was no fool—she was the latest warship to join the Roman fleet in the Erythrean Sea. And, though the ship had been built in Adulis by Ethiopian shipwrights, she was not an Axumite vessel. So—

"Worst that happens," Ezana concluded serenely, "is that the ship burns up."

John glared at him, but remained silent.

"That's it, then," decided Antonina. She headed for the gangway connecting the ship to the dock. She fluttered her hand toward Ousanas. "No doubt the aqabe tsentsen will wish to remain on board during the trial, scrutinizing every step of the operation with his keen hunter's eye."

Ousanas refrained from trampling Antonina in his hurry to get off the ship. But he only did so by the simple expedient of picking her up and carrying her off in his arms.

Ezana, oddly enough, decided to remain. Afterward, of course, he would claim he did so to maintain the reputation of Axum's seamen. Bold, valiant—fearless as lions. But, in truth, the Ethiopian naval officer was simply curious. And he was not enough of a hunter himself to understand the absurdity of a tame lioness.

❖   ❖   ❖

In the end, the trial was a roaring success. Quite literally. Once the *Theodora Victrix* and her two accompanying ships were completely out of sight of land, the cargo vessel being towed by the Axumite galley on which Antonina and Ousanas were safely perched was cut loose. Wallowing in the gentle waves of the Persian Gulf, while John made his final approach, the hulk seemed like a witless calf at the mercy of a lioness.

As soon as the *Theodora Victrix* was within range, John ordered his chief gunner Eusebius to activate the Greek fire cannon. This took a bit of work, since the "cannon" was more in the nature of a primitive pump than anything else. The gadget was temperamental as well as dangerous. But, soon enough, a satisfying gush of roaring flames spouted from the barrel and fell upon the target vessel.

Within seconds, the cargo hulk was a raging inferno. John of Rhodes began capering about on the deck of the *Victrix*, making gleeful—and, from the distance, suspiciously obscene-looking—gestures at Ousanas on the observer ship. Within minutes, he was helping Eusebius and the other gunners to pour amphorae full of sand on those portions of the warship's bow which had been set aflame by the last dribbles of the Greek fire cannon.

"We'll call it a roaring success," Antonina pronounced. She pursed her lips, studying the frantic activities of the men on the *Victrix*'s bow. Then, cocking her head at Menander, added: "But make sure that we put in another requisition for amphorae. And you'd better tell John to start experimenting with different kinds of sand."

Menander sighed. "Telling John" anything was akin to giving orders to a temperamental predator. Best done from a distance—best of all, by somebody else.

Ousanas snorted. "Tame lioness!"

❖   ❖   ❖

But Menander's qualms proved unfounded. By the time the two ships arrived back at the docks in Charax, John of Rhodes was in splendid spirits. The minor mishap at the end, clearly enough, was beneath contempt. Indeed, he even pranced off the ship proclaiming himself the need to find *slightly* more suitable chemicals for extinguishing fires at sea than simple desert sand.

"Chalk, maybe," he opined cheerfully. Standing on the docks, arms akimbo, John surveyed the landscape surrounding Charax with great serenity. "Got to be some, out there. For that matter, sea salt might do the trick. Plenty of that. And who knows? Maybe dried camel dung. *Plenty* of that stuff!"

Antonina left the matter to him. She was already surrounded by a small horde of Roman officers and Persian officials, each of whom was clamoring for her attention on some other matter of pressing concern. Throughout, Antonina maintained her composure, and issued the necessary orders. By now, she was an accomplished general in her own right, and had long since learned one of the basic axioms of war. *Amateurs study tactics; professionals study logistics.*

By sundown, she was able to relax in the comfort of the small villa she had obtained in Charax's best quarter. More or less.

"Do we *have* to settle the question of the camel provender?" she demanded crossly, pausing in the act of pouring herself a goblet of wine. "*Tonight?*"

A sheepish expression came upon Menander's face. "Well . . . No, actually. It can wait. Not as if there's any shortage of Arabs eager and willing to provide it for us." Perched on a chair across from the divan where Antonina lounged, Menander scowled. "It's just— Damned hagglers! Always got to allow extra time dickering with Arabs."

The Thracian villager surfaced: "Bad as Greeks!"

Antonina smiled. Then, after savoring the first sip of wine and cocking an eye at Ezana and Ousanas—also lounging on nearby divans; no alert chair-perching for *them*—she murmured: "Don't you have another pressing engagement yourself tonight, Menander?"

The Roman officer flushed. His eyes were riveted on Antonina, as if by sheer force of will he would keep them from flitting to the fearsome figure of his paramour's half-brother.

Thankfully, Ezana was in a good mood. So he eased Menander over the hurdle.

"Best run, boy. Keep my eager sister waiting and she'll likely take up with some passing stray Arab." Smugly: "Who will *not*—given the way Deborah looks—waste any time at all in *haggling*."

Seeing the look of sudden alarm which now flitted across Menander's face, Antonina could not stop herself from giggling. "Go!" she choked, waving her hand. A moment later, Menander did as he was commanded.

When he was gone, Antonina looked at Ezana. "She wouldn't really, would she?"

Ezana shrugged. "Probably not. The silly girl's quite infatuated with the lad."

Antonina's head now swiveled to bring Ousanas under her gaze. The humor left her eyes entirely.

"Speaking of infatuation."

Glaring at Ousanas, in the scale of "waste of effort," ranked somewhere in the vicinity of the labors of Sisyphus. Ethiopia's aqabe tsentsen responded with the same grin with which the former slave dawazz had greeted similar scowls from Axumite royalty.

"I fail to see the problem," he said. "True, the girl was a virgin. But—"

He waved his own hand. Ousanas, like Belisarius'

cataphract Anastasius, was a devotee of Greek philosophy. The gesture carried all the certainty of Plato pro-
nouncing on a small problem of ontology. "That is by
the nature of things a temporary state of affairs.
Certainly with a girl as lively and pretty as Koutina.
Who better than me to have assisted her through that
necessary passage?"

Antonina maintained the glare, even in the face of
that peerless grin.

"Besides, Antonina, you know perfectly well that
having the secure loyalty of your personal maid is
essential to the success of our enterprise. Koutina will
be at the top of the list for every enterprising Malwa
spy here in Charax. Of which there are probably several hundred by now, at least half of which are superb
seducers—and just as good once they get the girl in
bed as they were getting her there in the first place."

Again, Ousanas made that philosophical gesture. "So
I view my activities as a necessary concomitant of my
diplomatic duties. So to speak. Foiling the machina-
tions of the wicked enemy with my own incomparable
stroke of statecraft. So to speak."

Antonina hissed: "If she gets pregnant—"

Finally, the grin faded. For once, there was nothing
of the brazen jester in Ousanas' expression. "I have
already asked her to become my concubine, Antonina,"
he said softly. "Once the war is over. And she has agreed."

He did not add any further promise. There was no
need. Of many things, people might wonder about the
strange man named Ousanas. Of his honesty, no one
had any doubt at all.

Certainly not Antonina. Indeed, she was quite taken
aback by the aqabe tsentsen's statement. She had simply
intended to obtain a promise from Ousanas to see to
it that her maid was taken care of properly, once the
dalliance was over. She had never expected—

"Concubine," in Axum's elite, was a prestigious position. The position of wife, of course, was reserved for diplomatic and political necessities. But an officially recognized concubine was assured a life of security and comfort—even wealth and power, in the case of the aqabe tsentsen's concubine.

Koutina was a peasant girl from the Fayum, born into the great mass of Egypt's poor. Her own children would now enter directly into the world of status, with not even the slight blemish which Roman society attached to such offspring.

Ousanas' grin made its triumphant reentry. "So? Are there any other concerns you wish to raise?"

Antonina cleared her throat. From long experience, she knew it was *essential* to rally in the face of Ousanas' grin.

"Yes!" she piped. Sternly: "We must see to the final preparations for the landing at Barbaricum. Belisarius, you know, *insists* on accompanying Valentinian and the others up to the very moment when they are set ashore in India. Even—so he told me in his last message—if he has to leave his army before they finish the march to Charax."

Ezana groaned. "Antonina, that's *already* the best-planned and best-prepared military expedition in the history of the world." Scowling: "The only uncertainty—you said so yourself, just this morning!—was the reliability of the Greek fire weapon. Which we just tested this very day!"

Rally. "There are still some minor logistical matters to be settled!" Antonina insisted.

Ezana groaned again. Ousanas clapped his hands.

"Ridiculous!" he stated. "Petty stuff which can be well enough handled by your host of underlings." The aqabe tsentsen drained his goblet and placed it on the small side table nearby.

"We have *much* more important matters to discuss. I got into an argument with Irene, just the day before she and Kungas set off on that harebrained expedition of theirs. Can you believe that the crazed woman has been studying these idiot Buddhist philosophers lately? Mark my words! Give it a year and she'll be babbling the same nonsense as that Raghunath Rao fellow. *Maya*, the so-called 'veil of illusion.' All that rot!"

Ousanas leaned forward on his divan, hands planted firmly on knees. "Our duty is clear. We must arm ourselves in advance—*re-arm* ourselves, I should say—with the principles of Greek philosophy. I propose to begin with a survey of the dialectic, beginning with Socrates."

Antonina and Ezana stared at each other. Even the black Ethiopian's face seemed pale.

"Logistics," choked Ezana. "Critical to any successful military enterprise." Hastily he rose and began pacing about. "Can't afford to overlook even the slightest detail. The matter of the brass fittings for the stays is particularly critical. Can't ever have enough! And the metalsmiths here in Charax are already overworked."

He slammed hard fist into firm palm. "So! I propose the following—"

Chapter 8
BARBARICUM
Spring, 533 A.D.

The first rocket was a flare, one of the newly designed ones with a small parachute. After it burst over the ramparts at Barbaricum, it drifted down slowly, lighting the area with an eerie glow. Within seconds, several other flares came to add their own demonic illumination.

"Open fire!" roared John of Rhodes.

Immediately, the small fleet of Roman warships under John's command began firing their cannons into the shipping anchored in the harbor. Under cover of night, John had sailed his flotilla into gunnery range without being spotted by the sentries on the walls of the city. The larger fleet of Ethiopian warships following in his wake began adding their own gunfire to the brew.

John's ships, pure sailing craft, would be limited to one pass at the Malwa shipping. The Axumite vessels, with their oared capability, would wind up doing most of the damage even though none of those galleys carried the same weight of cannon. Without the necessity of tacking back upwind in order to escape—*not* something John wanted to do once the huge siege cannons on Barbaricum's walls began firing—the Ethiopians would be able to take the time to launch the fireships.

For that reason, John was all the more determined to wreak as much havoc as he could in the short time available. In particular, he was determined to strike at the Malwa warships—which, unfortunately, were moored behind a screening row of merchant vessels. Now that the flares were burning brightly, he could see those war galleys moored against the piers.

"Closer!" he bellowed, leaving it to his sailing master to translate the command into nautical terms.

Standing on the deck at John's side, Eusebius winced. Through his thick spectacles—another of the many new inventions which Aide's counsel had brought into the Roman world—the gunnery officer could see the mouths of the siege cannons overlooking the harbor, illuminated by the cannon fire and the flares. Once they came into action, those guns would be firing stone balls weighing more than two hundred pounds. True, the siege cannons were as awkward to load and fire as they were gigantic, and the weapons were wildly inaccurate. Unlike smaller cannons, whose bores could be hand-worked into relative uniformity and for which marble or iron cannon balls could be polished to a close fit, the giant siege guns and their stone missiles were the essence of crudity. But if one of those balls *did* hit a ship . . .

Eusebius winced again.

"Closer, damn you!" bellowed John.

A few miles further south along the Indus delta, Belisarius had a dazzling view of the battle which was taking shape in Barbaricum's harbor. At the distance, of course, he couldn't see any of the details. Not even with his telescope. But the visual and auditory display was truly magnificent. Which, when all was said and done, was the whole point of the exercise. Whatever damage John and the Ethiopians succeeded in inflicting on the Malwa at Barbaricum, the true purpose of that bombardment was to divert attention from Belisarius' doings.

"All right, General," growled Valentinian. "You can stop smiling so damned crookedly. I admit that you were right and I was wrong." Sourly: "Again."

In the darkness, there was no way Valentinian could have spotted that smile on Belisarius' face, not even standing next to him. Still, the general removed the smile. He reflected, a bit ruefully, that Valentinian knew him more than well enough to know Belisarius' characteristics.

So did Aide, for that matter. **Damned stupid crooked smile,** came his own surly thought.

There was no moon that night. There was not even a starblaze. India's monsoon season had begun, and the sky was heavily overcast. Except for the distant glare of the flares and cannon fire, the nearby coast was shrouded in darkness.

In that same darkness, Valentinian and Anastasius and Kujulo began lowering themselves into the river barge which had pulled alongside their vessel. The barge had been towed all the way from Charax. It was one of the Indian vessels which had been captured after the Malwa invasion of Persia was defeated the year before. Belisarius had chosen it because it would be indistinguishable from the other barges plying their trade along the Indus river.

Lowering themselves slowly and carefully—falling into the sea laden with armor and weapons was the fastest way to drown that the human race had ever discovered—the three leaders of the expedition eventually found the security of the barge's deck. As their accompanying party of Kushan soldiers followed, Anastasius' voice came up out of the darkness.

"Any last instructions?" the giant Thracian cataphract asked.

"No. Just be careful."

That statement was met by the sound of muttering. Valentinian's last words, Belisarius was quite certain, consisted of pure profanity.

Don't blame him, said Aide. The thought was almost a mutter itself. Aide had reconciled himself to Belisarius losing his best bodyguards, but he was still not happy with the situation.

Belisarius made no reply to either voice. In truth, he was not feeling any of the usual surety which accompanied his decisions. This expedition—everything about it—was dictated by the logic of spycraft, not warcraft. That was not a realm of human endeavor in which the Roman general felt completely at ease. He was relying heavily on Irene's advice, coupled with his own estimate of an old eunuch. A traitor, to boot.

The lines holding the barge to the warship were cast off. Belisarius could hear the barge's oars begin to dip into the water, moving the craft toward the unseen mouth of one of the delta's outlets.

"I hope you know what you're doing, Narses," he whispered.

The uneasy thought of Narses' former treason brought a sudden whimsy to his mind. For a moment, he hesitated, gauging the noise. Then, satisfied that the roar of the distant battle would disguise any sound, he shouted a few words toward the receding barge.

"Anastasius! You're a philosopher! What do you think of the veil of illusion?"

Anastasius' rumbling voice came back out of the darkness. "You mean that Hindu business about 'Maya'?

Bunch of silly heathen rot. No, General—things are what they are. Sure, Plato says they're only a shadow of their own reality, but that's not the same—"

The rest was lost in gunroar and distance. But Belisarius' crooked smile was back.

"This'll work," he said confidently.

Mutter mutter mutter, was Aide's only comment.

"I think maybe we should—"

Eusebius fell silent. Even after his years of close association with John, Eusebius knew better than to prod the Rhodian. Right at the top of John's multitude of character traits, admirable or otherwise, *stubbornness* took pride of place.

But even John, it seemed, was satisfied at the destruction which his flotilla had inflicted on the Malwa vessels anchored in the harbor. His cannonade, combined with the guns of the Ethiopians, had pounded much of the shipping into mastless and unmaneuverable wrecks. True, he hadn't been able to strike very hard at the war galleys moored to the piers. The merchant vessels—just as the Malwa no doubt intended—had served as a protective screen.

The issue was moot. John had no doubt at all that every seaman on those merchant ships had long since abandoned their vessels and fled to the safety of the shore on whatever lifeboats had been available. There would be no one left to prevent—

"That's the first one," said Eusebius with satisfaction.

John looked to the north. The Axumites had lit the first of the fireships and were pushing it off. Within seconds, John could see the other three fireships burst into sudden flames.

He moved his cold eyes back to the harbor. "That's so much kindling, now," he grunted with satisfaction. With the prevailing winds as they were, the fireships would inexorably drift into the tangled mass of battered merchant shipping. Given the speed with which fire spread across wooden ships, all of the vessels in Barbaricum's harbor would be destroyed soon enough.

"Time to go," he stated. He turned and issued the orders to the sailing master.

No sooner was he done than a huge roar filled the harbor. The ramparts of the city were suddenly illuminated by their own cannon fire. The huge siege guns had finally gone into action.

Eusebius flinched, a little, under the sound. John grinned like a wolf.

"Relax, boy. A first salvo—fired in the darkness? They'll be lucky if they even manage to hit the ocean."

Realizing the truth of the Rhodian's words, Eusebius relaxed. His shoulders, tense from the past minutes of action, began to slump.

A moment later, not knowing how he got there, Eusebius was lying on the deck of the ship. The entire vessel was rolling, as if it had collided with something.

There are no reefs in this harbor, he thought dazedly. *Every shipmaster we talked to swore as much.*

The area of the ship where he had been standing was half-illuminated by the flames of the fireships drifting into Barbaricum's harbor. Eusebius could see that a section of the rail had vanished, along with a piece of the deck itself. In front of him, lying on the shattered wooden planks, was an object which Eusebius thought he recognized. By the time he crawled over and picked it up, the helmsman was shouting at him.

Still half-dazed, Eusebius realized the man was demanding instructions. The sailing master had apparently also vanished.

There was no need, really, for the steersman to be given orders. Their course was obvious enough, after all. *Get the hell out of here.* The steersman was simply seeking reassurance that leadership still existed.

Shakily, Eusebius rose to his feet and shouted something back at the steersman. Anything. He didn't even think of the words themselves. He simply imitated, as best he could, the assured authority with which John of Rhodes issued all his commands.

Apparently the tone was enough. Broken planks falling into the sea from the splintered deck and rail, the ship sailed out of Barbaricum's harbor. On what remained of that portion of the deck, Eusebius studied the object in his hands, as if it were a talisman.

An hour later, the barge on which Valentinian and his expedition was making its way up the Indus was part of a small fleet of river craft, all of them fleeing from the battle at Barbaricum.

"Worked like a charm," grunted Kujulo. The Kushan gazed at the small horde of vessels with satisfaction. The vessels were easy to spot, fortunately. All of them—just as was true of their own barge—had a lookout in the bow holding a lamp aloft. For all the urgency with which the river craft were making their escape from the holocaust in Barbaricum, the oarsmen were maintaining a slow and steady stroke. Except for the meager illumination thrown out by the lamps, the night was pitch dark. No merchant—and these were all merchant vessels—wanted to escape ruin in a besieged harbor only to find it by running his ship aground.

"Worked like a charm," Kujulo repeated. "Nobody will ever notice us in this mob. Just another batch of worthless traders scurrying for cover."

As usual, Valentinian looked on the dark side of things. "They'll turn into so many pirates in a heartbeat, they learn what cargo we're carrying."

Kujulo's grin was wolfish. "Two chests full of Red Sea coral? A small fortune, true enough. I tremble to think of our fate, should these brave river men discover the truth."

Anastasius snorted sarcastically. After a moment's glower, Valentinian's own grin appeared. Very weaselish, it was.

"Probably not the worst of our problems, is it?" he mused, fingering the hilt of his sword. But it was only a momentary lightening of his gloom. Soon enough, he was back to muttering.

"Oh, will you stop it?" demanded Anastasius crossly. "Things *could* be worse, you know."

"Sure they could," hissed Valentinian. "We could be floating down the Nile, bound hand and foot, fighting crocodiles with our teeth. We could be hanging upside down by our heels in the Pit, fending off archdevils with spit. We could—"

Mutter, mutter, mutter.

By the time Belisarius and his ship made the rendezvous with the Roman/Ethiopian fleet which had savaged Barbaricum, the sun was rising. So, as he climbed the rope ladder onto John of Rhodes' flagship, he got a good view of the damage done to it amidships. One of the huge stone cannon balls, clearly enough, had made a lucky hit in the darkness. Fortunately, the ship was still intact below the water line, and the masts had remained unscathed.

Eusebius met him at the railing.

"Where's John?" demanded Belisarius.

The nearsighted gunnery officer made a face. Silently, he led Belisarius over to a folded, blood-stained piece of canvas lying on the center of the deck. Then, squatting, he flipped back the canvas covering and exposed the object contained within.

Belisarius hissed. The canvas contained a human arm, which appeared to have been ripped off at the shoulder as if by a giant. Then, spotting the ring on the square, strong-fingered hand, he sighed.

Antonina had given John that ring, years ago, as part of the subterfuge by which she had convinced Malwa's spies that the Rhodian was one of her many lovers. Once the subterfuge had served its purpose, John had offered to return it. But he had immediately added his wish to keep the thing, with her permission. His "lucky ring," he called it, which had kept him intact through the many disastrous early experiments with gunpowder.

"May God have mercy on his soul," Belisarius murmured.

Next to him, a voice spoke. The bitterness in the tone went poorly with its youthful timber.

"Stupid," growled Menander. "Pure blind fucking bad luck. A first salvo, fired at night? They should have been lucky to even hit the damned ocean."

Belisarius straightened, and sighed again. "That's the way war works. It's worth reminding ourselves, now and again, so we don't get too enamored of our own cleverness. There's a lot of just pure luck in this trade."

The general planted a hand on Menander's shoulder. "When did you come aboard?" Menander, he knew, had been in command of one of the other ships in the flotilla.

"Just a few minutes ago. As soon as there was enough light to see what had happened, I—" The young officer fell silent, cursing under his breath.

Belisarius now squeezed the shoulder. "You realize that you've succeeded to the command of John's fleet?"

Menander nodded. There was no satisfaction at all in that gesture. But neither, Belisarius was pleased to see, was there any hesitation.

"So it is," stated the general. "That will include those

two new steam-powered ships Justinian's building, once they get here from Adulis. You're more familiar with them than anyone except Justinian anyway, as much time as you've spent with the old emperor since he got to Adulis."

Menander smiled wryly. When Justinian had been Emperor of Rome, before his blinding by Malwa traitors had disqualified him under Roman law and custom, he had been an enthusiastic gadget-maker. Since he relinquished the throne in favor of his adopted son Photius, Justinian's hobby had become practically an obsession. Along with John of Rhodes, Justinian had become the chief new weapons designer for the Roman empire. And he loved nothing so much as the steam engines he had designed with Aide's advice and whose construction he had personally overseen. Even to the extent of accompanying the engines to the Ethiopian capital of Adulis and supervising their installation in ships specially designed for the purpose.

Throughout that work, Menander had been the officer assigned to work with Justinian. The experience had been . . . "Contradictory," was Menander's diplomatic way of putting it. On the one hand, he had been able to spend a lot of time with Deborah also. On the other hand . . .

He sighed. "I could usually manage an entire day in Justinian's company without losing my temper. Barely. John of Rhodes couldn't last ten minutes." He stared down at the severed arm. "Damn, I'll miss him. So will Justinian, don't think he won't."

Belisarius stooped and flipped the covering back over its grisly contents. "We'll send this to Constantinople. I'll include instructions—'recommendations,' I suppose I should say—to my son. Photius will see to it that John of Rhodes gets a solemn state funeral, by God. With all the pomp and splendor."

Even in the sorrow of the moment, that statement caused a little chuckle to emerge from the crowd of Roman officers standing nearby.

"I'd love to be there," murmured one of them. "Be worth it just to see the sour faces on all those senators John cuckolded."

Belisarius smiled, very crookedly. "John will answer to God for his failings." The smile vanished, and the next words rang like iron hammered on an anvil. "But there will be no man to say that he failed in his duty to the Empire. *None.*"

Chapter 9
INDIA
Spring, 533 A.D.

"I've had enough," snarled Raghunath Rao. "Enough!"

He spent another few seconds glaring at the corpses impaled in the village square, before turning away and moving toward the horses. Some of the Maratha cavalrymen in Rao's company began removing the bodies from the stakes and preparing a funeral pyre.

Around them, scurrying to gather up their few possessions, the villagers made ready to join Rao's men in their march back to Deogiri. None would be foolish enough to remain behind, not after the Wind of the Great Country had scoured another Malwa garrison from the face of the earth. Malwa repercussions would be sure to follow. Lord Venandakatra, the Goptri of the Deccan, had long ago pronounced a simple policy. Any villagers found anywhere in the area where the Maratha rebellion struck a blow would pay the penalty. The Vile One's penalties *began* with impalement. "Ringleaders" would be taken to Bharakuccha for more severe measures.

Other soldiers in Rao's company had already finished

executing the survivors of the little Malwa garrison they had overrun. Unlike the villagers who had been impaled—"rebels," by Malwa decree; and many of them were—Rao's men had satisfied themselves with quick decapitations. Some of the cavalrymen were piling the heads in a small mound at the center of the village. There would be no honorable funeral pyre for *that* carrion. Others were readying the horses for the march.

"Enough, Maloji," Rao murmured to his lieutenant. For all the softness of his tone, the sound of it was a panther's growl. "The time has come. Lord Venandakatra has outlived his welcome in this turn of the wheel."

Maloji eyed him skeptically. "The empress is already unhappy enough with you for participating in these raids. Do you seriously expect—"

"I am her husband!" barked Rao. But, a moment later, the stiffness in his face dissolved. Rao was too much the philosopher to place much credence in customary notions of a wife's proper place in the world. Any wife, much less *his*. Trying to browbeat the empress Shakuntala—wifely status be damned; age difference be damned—was as futile a project as he could imagine.

"I made her a promise," he said softly. "But once that promise is fulfilled, I am free. To *that*, she agreed. Soon, now."

Maloji was still skeptical. Or, perhaps, simply stoic. "It's a first pregnancy, old friend. There are often complications."

Finally, Rao's usual good humor came back. "With *her*? Be serious!" He gathered up the reins of his horse with one hand while making an imperious gesture with the other. "She will simply decree the thing: *Child, be born—and don't give me any crap about it.*"

❖   ❖   ❖

In her palace at Deogiri, Shakuntala was filled with quite a different sentiment. Staring down at her swollen belly, her face was full of apprehension.

"It will hurt, some," said Gautami. Dadaji Holkar's wife smiled reassuringly and placed a gentle hand on the empress' shoulder. "But even as small as you are, your hips are well-shaped. I really don't think—"

Shakuntala brushed the matter aside. "I'm not worried about that. It's these ugly stretch marks. Will they go away?"

Abruptly, with a heavy sigh, Shakuntala folded the robe back around herself. Gautami studied her carefully. She did not think the empress was really concerned about the matter of the stretch marks. If nothing else, Shakuntala was too supremely self-confident to worry much over such simple female vanities. And she *certainly* wasn't concerned about losing Rao's affections.

That left—

Shakuntala confirmed the suspicion. "Soon," she whispered, stroking her belly. "Soon the child will be born, and the dynasty assured. And Rao will demand his release. As I promised."

Gautami hesitated. Her husband was the peshwa of the empire of Andhra, reborn out of the ashes which Malwa had thought to leave it. As such, Gautami was privy to almost every imperial secret. But, still, she was the same woman who had been born and raised in a humble town in Majarashtra. She did not feel comfortable in these waters.

Shakuntala perhaps sensed her unease. The empress turned her head and smiled. "Nothing you can do, Gautami. Or say. I simply want your companionship, for the moment." She sighed again. "I will need it, I fear, in the future. There will be no keeping Rao. Not once the child is born."

Gautami said nothing. Her unease aside, there was nothing to say.

Once the dynasty was assured, the Panther of Majarashtra would slip his leash. As surely as the sun rises, or the moon sets. No more to be stopped than the tide. Or the wind.

Yet, while Gautami understood and sympathized with her empress' unhappiness, she did not share it herself. When all was said and done, Gautami *was* of humble birth. One of the great mass of the Maratha poor, who had suffered for so long—and so horribly—under the lash of the Vile One.

Her eyes moved to the great window in the north wall of the empress' bedchamber. As always, in the hot and dry climate of the Deccan, the window was open to the breeze. From high atop the hill which was the center of Andhra's new capital city of Deogiri—the *permanent* capital, so Shakuntala had already decreed; in this, as in her marriage, she had welded Andhra to the Marathas—Gautami could see the rocky stretches of the Great Country.

Beyond that, she could not see. But, in her mind's eye, Gautami could picture the great seaport of Bharakuccha. She had been there, twice. Once, as a young wife, visiting the fabled metropolis in the company of her educated husband. The second time, as a slave captured in Malwa's conquest of the Deccan. She could still remember those squalid slave pens; still remember the terrified faces of her young daughters as they were hauled off by the brothel-keeper who had purchased them.

And, too, she could remember the sight of the great palace which loomed above the slave pens. The same palace where, for three years now, Lord Venandakatra had made his residence and headquarters.

"Soon," she murmured.

✧   ✧   ✧

Near the headwaters of the Chambal, Lord Venandakatra's lieutenant was haranguing Lord Damodara and Rana Sanga. Chandasena, his name was, and he was much impressed by his august status in the Malwa scheme of things.

It was a very short harangue. Though Chandasena was of noble Malwa brahmin stock—a Mahaveda priest, in fact—Lord Damodara was a member of the *anvaya-prapta sachivya*, as the Malwa called the hereditary caste who dominated their empire. Blood kin to Emperor Skandagupta himself.

Perhaps more to the point, Rana Sanga was Rajputana's greatest king.

Fortunately, Sanga was no more than moderately annoyed. So the backhanded cuff which sent Chandasena sprawling in the dirt did no worse than split his lip and leave him stunned and confused. When he recovered his wits sufficiently to understand human speech, Lord Damodara furthered his education.

"My army has marched to Mesopotamia and back again, and across half of India in the bargain, and defeated every foe which came against us. Including even Belisarius himself. And Lord Venandakatra—*and you*—presume to instruct me on the proper pace of a march?"

The short Malwa lord paused, staring at the hills about him with hands placed on hips. The hips, like the lord's belly, no longer retained the regal fat which had once adorned them. But his little hands were still as plump as ever.

"Venandakatra?" he mused softly. "Who has not marched out of his palace since Rao penned him in Bharakuccha? Whose concept of logistics is to whip his slaves when they fail to feed him appropriate viands for his delicate palate?"

Damodara brought his eyes down to the figure sprawled on the ground. Normally mild-mannered, Malwa's finest military commander was clearly fighting to restrain his temper.

"*You?*" he demanded. The hands on hips tightened. "Rana Sanga!" he barked. "Do me the favor of instructing this dog again on the subject of military travel."

"My pleasure, Lord." Rajputana's mightiest hand reached down, seized the Vile One's envoy by his finery, and hauled him to his feet as easily as he might pluck a fruit.

"In order to get from one place to another," Sanga said softly, "an army must get from one place to another. Much like"—a large finger poked the envoy's nose—"this face gets to the dirt of the road." And so saying, he illustrated the point with another cuff.

Sometime later, a less-assured envoy listened in silence as Lord Damodara gave him the reply to Lord Venandakatra.

"Tell the Vile—*him*—that I will arrive in the Deccan as soon as possible. Of which I will be the judge, not he. And tell him that the next insolent envoy he sends will be instructed with a sword, not a hand."

After Chandasena had made his precipitous departure, Rana Sanga sighed. "Venandakatra *is* the emperor's first cousin," he pointed out. "And we *will* be under his authority once we enter the Deccan."

Lord Damodara did not seem notably abashed. "True, and true," he replied. Again, he surveyed the scene around him, with hands on hips. But his stance was relaxed, now, and his eyes were no longer on the hills.

His round face broke into a cheery smile. "Authority, Rana Sanga, is a much more elusive concept than people realize. On the one hand, there is consanguinity to royal blood and official post and status. On the other—"

A stubby forefinger pointed to the mass of soldiers streaming by. "On the other, there is the *reality* of twenty thousand Rajputs, and ten thousand Ye-tai and kshatriyas who have been welded to them through battles, sieges and victories. And, now, some ten thousand new Bihari and Bengali recruits who are quickly learning their place."

Sanga followed the finger. His experienced eye picked out at once what Damodara was indicating. In every other Malwa army but this one, the component forces formed separate detachments. The Ye-tai served as security battalions; the Malwa kshatriya as privileged artillery troops. Rajputs, of course, were elite cavalry. And the great mass of infantrymen enrolled in the army—peasants from one or another of the many subject nations of the Gangetic plain—formed huge but poorly-equipped and trained levies.

Not here. Damodara's army was a Rajput army, at its core, though the Rajputs no longer formed a majority of the troops. But the Ye-tai—whose courage was admired and respected, if not their semi-barbarous character—were intermingled with the Rajputs. As were the kshatriyas, and, increasingly—and quite to their surprise—the new Bengali and Bihari recruits.

"The veil of illusion," mused Sanga. "Philosophers speak of it."

"So they do," concurred Damodara. His air seemed one of detachment and serenity. "The *best* philosophers."

That night, in Lord Damodara's headquarters tent, philosophical detachment and serenity were entirely absent.

For all that he was an old man, and a eunuch, Narses was as courageous as any man alive. But now, reading again the summons from the Grand Palace, he had to fight to keep his hands from trembling.

"It arrived today?" he asked. For the second time, which was enough in itself to indicate how shaken he was.

Damodara nodded somberly. He made a vague gesture with his hand toward the entrance flap of the tent. "You would have passed by the courier on your way in. I told him to wait outside until I had spoken to you."

Narses' eyes flitted around the interior of the large tent. Clearly enough, Damodara had instructed *everyone* to wait outside. None of his officers were present, not even Rana Sanga. And there were no servants in the tent. That, in its own way, indicated just how uneasily Damodara himself was taking the news.

Narses brought himself under control, with the iron habit of a lifetime spent as an intriguer and spymaster. He gave Lord Damodara a quick, shrewd glance.

First things first. Reassure my employer.

"Of course," he said harshly, "I will report to Great Lady Sati that you have never given me permission to do anything other than my officially specified duties. Which is the plain and simple truth, as it happens."

Lord Damodara's tension seemed to ease a bit. "Of course," he murmured. He studied his spymaster carefully.

"You have met Great Lady Sati, I believe?"

Narses shook his head. "Not exactly. She was present, yes, when I had my one interview with Great Lady Holi. After my defection from Rome, and before Great Lady Holi departed for Mesopotamia. Where she met her death at Belisarius' hands."

He left unspoken the remainder: *and was— replaced?—by Great Lady Sati.*

"But Lady Sati—she was not Great Lady, then—said nothing in the interview."

Damodara nodded and began pacing slowly back and forth. His hands were pressed together as if in prayer, which was the lord's habit when he was engaged in deep thought.

Abruptly, he stopped his pacing and turned to face Narses squarely.

"How much do you *know*, Roman?"

Narses understood the meaning. "Malwa is ruled by a hidden—something. A *being*, let us call it. I do not know its true name. Once, it inhabited the body of Great Lady Holi. Today, it resides in Great Lady Sati. Whatever it is, the being has supernatural powers. It is not of this earth. I believe, judging from what I have learned, that it claims to come from the future."

After a moment's hesitation, he added: "A divine being, Malwa believes it to be."

Damodara smiled thinly. "And you?"

Narses spread his hands. "What is divinity, Lord? For Hindus, the word *deva* refers to a divine creature. For Zoroastrians, it is the word assigned to demons. What, in the end, is really the difference—to the men who stand under its power?"

"What, indeed?" mused Damodara. He resumed his pacing. Again, his hands were pressed together. "Whatever the being may be, Narses—divine or not, from the future or not—have no doubt of one thing. It is truly superhuman."

He stopped and, again, turned to face the eunuch. "One thing in particular you must understand. A human being *cannot* lie to Li—the being—and keep the lie from being detected."

Narses' eyes did not widen in the least. The spymaster had already deduced as much, from his own investigations.

"It *cannot* be done," the Malwa lord reiterated forcefully. "Do not even imagine the possibility."

Narses reached up and stroked his jaw. "The truth only, you say?" Then, seeing Damodara's nod, he asked: "But tell me this, Lord. Can this being truly read a man's thoughts?"

Damodara hesitated. For a moment, he seemed about to resume his pacing, but instead he simply slumped a bit.

"I am not certain, Narses."

"Your *estimate*, then." The words were spoken in the tone of command. But the lord gave no sign of umbrage at this unwarranted change of relationship. At the moment, his own life hung by as slender a thread as the eunuch's.

Whatever his doubts and uncertainties, Damodara was an experienced as well as a brilliant military commander. Decisiveness came naturally to him, and that nature had been honed by his life.

"No," he said firmly. "In the end, I do not believe so. I think it is simply that the being is—is—" He groped for the words.

Narses' little exhalation of breath seemed filled with satisfaction. "A superhuman spymaster. Which can study the same things any spymaster learns to examine—posture, tone of voice, the look in the eyes—to gauge whether a man speaks true or false."

Damodara's head nod was more in the way of a jerk. "Yes. So I believe."

For the first time since he read the message summoning him to the Grand Palace, Narses smiled. It was a very, very thin smile. But a smile nonetheless.

"The truth only, then. That should be no problem."

Damodara studied him for a moment. But he could read nothing whatever in the old eunuch's face. Nothing in his eyes, his tone of voice, his posture. Nothing but—a lifetime of intrigue and subterfuge.

"Go, then," he commanded.

Narses bowed, but did not make to leave.

Damodara cocked his head. "There is something you wish, before you go?"

"Yes," murmured Narses. "The fastest courier in the army. I need to send new instructions to Ajatasutra."

"Certainly. I shall have him report to your tent immediately." He cleared his throat. "Where is Ajatasutra, by the way? I haven't noticed him about lately."

Narses stared at him coldly. Damodara broke into sudden, subdued laughter.

"Never mind! Sometimes, it's best not to know the truth."

Narses met the laughter with a chuckle. "So, I am told, say the very best philosophers."

Ajatasutra himself might not have agreed with that sentiment. But there was no question at all that he was being philosophical about his own situation.

He had not much choice, after all. His needs required that he stay at one of the worst and poorest hostels in Ajmer, the greatest city of Rajputana. And, so far as Ajatasutra was concerned—he who had lived in Constantinople as well as Kausambi—the *best* hostel in that hot and dusty city was barely fit for cattle.

He slew another insect on his pallet, with the same sure stroke with which he slew anything.

"I am *not* a Jain," he growled at the tiny corpse. His cold eyes surveyed the horde of other insects taking formation in his squalid little room. "So don't any of you think you'll get any tenderhearted philosophy from *me*."

If the insects were abashed by that grisly threat, they gave no sign of it. Another legion, having dressed its lines, advanced fearlessly to the fray.

"This won't be so bad," said the older sister. "The lady even says she'll give me a crib for the baby."

The younger sister surveyed their room in the great mansion where Lord Damodara's family resided in the capital. The room was small and unadorned, but it was spotlessly clean.

True, the kitchen-master was a foul-mouthed and ill-tempered man, as men who hold such thankless posts generally are. And his wife was even worse. But her own foul mouth and ill temper seemed focused, for the most part, on seeing to it that her husband did not take advantage of his position to molest the kitchen slaves.

In her humble manner, the sister had become quite a philosopher in her own right. "Are you kidding? This is *great*."

Below them, in the depths of the mansion's great cellar, others were also being philosophical.

"Start digging," commanded the mercenary leader. "You've got a long way to go."

The small group of Bihari miners did not even think to argue the matter. Indeed, they set to work with a will. An odd attitude, perhaps, in slaves. But they too had seen the way Ajatasutra gave *instructions*. And, like the two sisters whom they did not know, had reached an identical conclusion. The assassin was deadly, deadly. But, in his own way, a man who could be trusted. Do the work, he had told them, and you will be manumitted—and given gold besides.

There was no logic to it, of course. For whatever purpose they had been brought here, to dig a mysterious tunnel to an unknown destination, the purpose had been kept secret for a reason. The slaves knew, as well as any man, that the best way to keep a secret is to kill those who know it. But, somehow, they did not fear for their lives.

"Oddest damned assassin I've ever seen," muttered one of the mercenaries.

"For what he's paying us," said the leader, "he can sprout feathers like a chicken for all I care." Seeing that the tunnel work was well underway, he turned to face his two subordinates. His finger pointed stiffly at the casks of wine against one of the stone walls of the cellar.

"Do I have to repeat *his* instructions?"

The other Ye-tai shook their heads vigorously. Their eyes shied away from the wine.

"Good," he grunted. "Just do as we're told, that's it. And we'll walk away from this as rich men."

One of the mercenaries cleared his throat, and pointed his own finger up at the stone ceiling. "Won't anyone wonder? There'll be a bit of noise. And, after a while, we'll have to start hauling the dirt out."

Again, the captain shrugged. "He told me he left *instructions* up there also. We stay down here, and food and water will be brought to us. By the majordomo and a few others. They'll see to the disposal of the dirt."

"Shouldn't be hard," grunted one of the other mercenaries. His head jerked toward the far wall. "The Ganges is just the other side of the mansion. I saw as we arrived. Who's going to notice if *that* river gets a bit muddier?"

A little laugh greeted the remark. If the Ye-tai mercenaries retained much of their respect for Malwa's splendor, they had lost their awe for Malwa's power and destiny. All of them were veterans of the Persian campaign, and had seen—fortunately, from a distance—the hand of Belisarius at work.

None of them, in any event, had ever had much use for the fine points of Hindu ritual.

"Fuck the Ganges," muttered another. "Bunch of stupid peasants bathing in elephant piss. Best place I can think of for the dirt that's going to make us rich men."

And so, another philosopher.

Chapter 10
THE PERSIAN GULF
Summer, 533 A.D.

"So how many, Dryopus?" asked Antonina. Wearily, she wiped her face with a cloth that was already damp with sweat. "For certain."

Her secretary hesitated. Other than being personally honest, Dryopus was typical of high officials in the Roman Empire's vast and elaborate hierarchy. For all his relative youth—he was still shy of forty—and his apparent physical vigor, he was the sort of man who personified the term: *bureaucrat*. His natural response to any direct question was: first, cover your ass; second, hedge; third, cover your ass again.

But Antonina didn't even have to glare at him. By now, months after arriving in Persia to take up his new duties, Dryopus had learned that "covering your ass" with Antonina meant giving her straight and direct answers. He was the fourth official who had served her in this post, and the only one who had not been shipped back to Constantinople within a week.

"I can't tell you, for certain. At least ninety ships.

Probably be closer to a hundred, when all the dust settles."

Seeing the gathering frown on Antonina's face, Dryopus hurriedly added: "I'm only counting those in the true seagoing class, mind. There'll be plenty of river barges that can be pressed into coastline service."

Antonina rose from her desk and walked over to the window, shaking her head. "The river barges won't be any use, Dryopus. Not once the army's marched past the Persian Gulf ports. No way they could survive the monsoon, once they get out of sheltered waters. Not the heart of it, at least. By the tail end of the season, we could probably use them—but who really knows where Belisarius will be then?"

At the window, she planted her hands on the wide ledge and leaned her face into the breeze. The window in the villa which doubled as Antonina's headquarters faced to the south, overlooking Charax's great harbor. The slight breeze coming in from the sea helped alleviate the blistering summer heat of southern Mesopotamia.

But the respite was brief. Within seconds, she turned back to Dryopus.

"Who's the most obstreperous of the hold-outs?" she demanded.

"Those two brothers who own the *Circe*." This time, Dryopus' answer came with no hesitation at all. "Aco and Numenius."

As Antonina moved back to her desk, her frown returned in full force. "Egyptians, aren't they? Normally operate out of Myos Hormos?"

"Yes. That's one of the things they're squealing about. They claim they can't take on military provisions until they've unloaded their cargo in Myos Hormos, or they'll go bankrupt." Dryopus scowled. "They say they're carrying specialty items which are in exclusive demand in Egypt. Can't sell them here in Mesopotamia."

"Oh—that's nonsense!" Antonina plumped down in her chair and almost slapped the desk with her hands. "They're bringing cargo from Bharakuccha, right?" With a snarl: "That means spices and cosmetics. Mostly pepper. Stuff that'll sell just as well in Persia as anywhere."

Dryopus, sitting on his own chair across from her, spread his hands in a little gesture of agreement. "They're just making excuses to try to avoid being pressed into service as part of the supply fleet for the army. By all accounts, those two brothers are among the worst chiselers in the trade—which is saying something, given the standards of merchant seamen. There's even been accusations that they burned one of their own ships a few years ago, to collect the insurance on the cargo."

He shrugged. "I don't really understand why they're being so resistant. It's true that the profit margin they'll make from military shipping is lower. But, on the other hand, they're guaranteed steady work for at least a year—which they're certainly not in the regular India trade!—and the risk is minimal. Lower, really, than the risk in trading with India. In fact, the reason the *Circe* came into port later than any of the other ships from Bharakuccha—according to Aco and Numenius, at least—is that they were detained in the harbor for a month by Malwa officials trying to shake them down."

Antonina nodded. It was the custom of the day for trade between belligerent realms to continue unchecked during wartime. Roman merchant vessels, of course, were not allowed to sail directly into Bharakuccha's harbor—any more than the Persians allowed Malwa shipping into their own ports. But the ships themselves were usually not molested. They simply had to add the extra expense of unloading their cargo with lighters.

Still . . . It was a perilous enough business. Custom be damned, there were plenty of instances where greedy officials and military officers extorted merchant vessels from enemy nations. Sometimes, even, plundered them outright. The Malwa were especially notorious for the practice.

"Nonsense," repeated Antonina. "It's a *lot* safer. They'll be under the protection of Axumite warships the whole time. And nobody has ever accused the Ethiopians of illegally sequestering cargoes." A rueful little smile came to her face. "Of course, the Axumites don't need to, after all. They take an automatic cut of anything which passes through the Red Sea."

She straightened her back, having come to a decision.

"Enough! I've got to get this thing settled, so we can firm up our numbers. If we crack down on Aco and Numenius, that'll send a clear message to the other malingerers. I want a team of inspectors crawling all over the *Circe* by the end of the day, Dryopus. They're to inspect the cargo and report back. If it's nothing but the usual stuff, we unload that ship tomorrow—by force if necessary—and start stocking it with military supplies."

Dryopus jotted a quick note, nodding. "Done."

"What's next?"

Again, Dryopus hesitated. But the hesitation, this time, was not that of a bureaucrat. In his own distant manner, Dryopus had become something of a friend for Antonina over the past months of joint work, as well as simply a subordinate. The next item of business . . .

Antonina sighed. "John?"

Dryopus nodded. "Yes. We've got to make provisions for transporting his—what remains of his body—back to Constantinople."

A flicker of pain crossed Antonina's face, but only

briefly. Belisarius had brought the news back over a week ago, and she had already finished most of her grieving.

"What are the alternatives?" she asked.

"Well . . . we could dispatch one of the smaller cargo vessels—"

"No. The war comes first."

Dryopus shrugged. "In that case, I'd suggest hiring one of the Arab caravans. We could use the barge traffic on the Euphrates, of course, but the Arabs have been complaining that they're not getting their fair share of the war trade."

Antonina nodded. "Yes. They'll take it as an honor, too. But make sure you hire one of the Beni Ghassan caravans. They've been Rome's allies for centuries. They'll be offended if the job is given to anyone else. Especially the Lakhmids."

Dryopus made a note. "Done."

"What's next?"

"There's the matter of the livestock provisions. Camels, specifically."

"Again?" groaned Antonina. She wiped her face with the cloth. Again. In that heat, of course, the cloth was already dry. Still . . .

She stared down at it, scowling. "I should go into business for myself," she said glumly. "Selling salt."

She fluttered the scrap of linen. "There's enough right here—" Then, seeing the look on Dryopus' face, she choked off the words.

"What?" she demanded, half-wailing. "We're running low on salt? *Again?*"

Chapter 11

Under the best of conditions, giant armies on the march throw up enormous clouds of dust. And these were not the best of conditions.

Belisarius was leading a hundred and twenty thousand men into India against the Malwa, along with as many horses, camels and mules. His army had now left the flood plains of Khuzistan province, and had entered the narrow strip of lowlands bordering the Persian Gulf.

Technically, they were marching through Pars province, the historic homeland of the ancient Achaemenid dynasty as well as the Sassanids. But this was not the Pars province that most people thought of, with its ancient cities of Persepolis and Shiraz and the irrigated regions around them.

Partly, Belisarius had chosen the southern route to avoid the inevitable destruction of farmland which a marching army produces, even if the army is under discipline. But, mostly, he had done so because of overriding logistical concerns. There was no way that an army that size could be provisioned by farmers along their route. Until they reached the Indus valley, Belisarius and his army would be entirely dependent on seaborne supplies. So, whatever other problems that route created, they would be forced to hug the coast of the Persian Gulf and the Arabian Sea.

A coast which, sad to say, was one of the bleakest coasts in the world: as arid as a desert, with little in the way of vegetation beyond an occasional palm grove.

Kurush reined in his horse next to Belisarius. The Roman general was sitting on his own mount atop a small rise, observing the army marching past. Sittas was alongside him; his bodyguards, Isaac and Priscus, were a few yards away.

"Did I mention the roses and nightingales of Shiraz?" asked Kurush. "And the marvelous vineyards?"

Sittas scowled. Belisarius simply smiled.

"Several times," he replied. "Each day of our march."

The Persian general grimaced. "Can't help it, I'm afraid." He reached up a hand and wiped dust from his face, leaving little streaks behind in the veil of sweat. Then, scowling himself: "Wouldn't be quite as bad if we weren't doing this in summertime."

Belisarius shrugged. "We've got no choice, Kurush. Without the monsoon blowing to the east this time of year, this whole expedition would be impossible."

The statement was about as pointless as Kurush's remark about roses and nightingales. The Persian general was just as familiar with the logistical facts of life as Belisarius.

"So I've heard you say," muttered Kurush sourly. "Several times, in fact—each day of our march."

Belisarius' lips quirked, but he made no response. He was busy studying the marching order, trying to determine if there was any possible improvement to be made.

"Forget it," said Sittas, as if he'd read Belisarius' mind. He waved a large and thick-fingered hand at the troops. "Sure you could tidy it up—theoretically. But it'd take you three days to do it, with the army standing still. And then within another three days it'd be a mess all over again."

Belisarius sighed. He had already reached the same conclusion. The army marching past him was far larger than any army he had ever led in the past. Than *any* Roman general had led in centuries, in fact. It had not taken Belisarius long to realize that, at a certain point, quantity doesn't transform into quality. The kind of tight and precise marching order he had always managed to maintain in the past was simply an impossibility here.

"Given, at least," he murmured, "that we're under such a tight time schedule."

Kurush and Sittas said nothing. Again, the statement was pointless. They, along with all the other top commanders of the allied army, had planned this expedition for months. They knew just as well as Belisarius that the march to the Indus valley *had* to be completed before the monsoon season ended in November. Or the army would die of thirst and starvation.

It might die anyway, even if they kept to the schedule. The Indus valley was fertile, true, but Belisarius was quite certain that Link would order a scorched earth campaign in the valley once the Romans and Persians arrived at Barbaricum and began their march upriver to the Malwa heartland.

That is what he would do, after all. The Malwa had no real chance of holding Barbaricum and the coast, once Belisarius arrived at the Indus delta. The shocking and unexpected destruction of their great army in Mesopotamia the year before had forced the Malwa to concentrate on fortifying their own homeland, and to shelve—at least for a time—any plans for conquest.

But fortifications strong enough to withstand the forces Belisarius was bringing to India simply could not be erected quickly, not even with the manpower

available to the Malwa. So, according to Belisarius'
spies, Link had done exactly what he would do: concentrate on fortifying the upper Indus valley, the region
called the Punjab. So long as the Malwa controlled the
Punjab, they controlled the entrances to the Ganges.
Losing the lower valley would be painful, but not fatal.

All the more so because of the geography of the
region. The Indus "valley" was really two valleys,
which—at least from a military point of view—were
shaped somewhat like an hourglass. The lower valley,
the Sind, was broad at the coast and the Indus delta
but narrowed as it extended north toward the city of
Sukkur and the gorge beyond. Past the Sukkur gorge,
the upper valley widened again. The name "Punjab"
itself meant "land of five rivers." The upper valley was
shaped much like a fan, with the Indus and its main
tributaries forming the blades.

If Belisarius could break into the Punjab, where he
would have room to maneuver again . . .

That would truly press the Malwa against the wall.
So, just as Belisarius would have done, Link would
fortify the Punjab and the Sukkur "bottleneck"—but
leave the Sind to its own devices. The monster would
station soldiers there, to be sure. But their main task
was not to prevent Belisarius from taking the lower
valley, but to delay him long enough to allow Link to
transform the Punjab and Sukkur into an impregnable
stronghold. Those Malwa forces would retreat slowly
northward, burning and destroying everything in the
valley as they went. "Scorched earth" tactics with a
vengeance.

Conceivably, if the Malwa could wrest control of the
sea from the Romans and the Ethiopians, they could
even turn the Sind into a death trap. Do to Belisarius'
great army the same thing he had done to them at
Charax.

Belisarius knew that unless he could break Link's plans before they came to fruition, he was faced with years of fighting a brutal, slogging campaign which had more in the nature of siege warfare than battles in the open field. A war of attrition, not maneuver, which would charge Rome with a price in blood and treasure which it could probably not afford. He had bloodied Malwa badly, over the past two years, and the Maratha rebellion in the Deccan which he had helped set into motion was bleeding it further still. But the fact remained that the Malwa empire could still draw on greater resources than Rome and Persia and Ethiopia combined. A long war of attrition was far more likely to work in favor of the Malwa than Belisarius.

Link would certainly do its best to make it so. The cybernetic organism was just as familiar with human history as Aide. The Malwa empire was now on the defensive, and they would adopt the methods and tactics which would be used in a future world by the Dutch rebels against the Spanish.

And those tactics worked for almost a century, came Aide's voice. **Until the Spanish finally gave up.**

Belisarius made the mental equivalent of a shrug. *True. But the Spanish were never able to outflank the Dutch defenses, because the Dutch backs were protected by the sea. Malwa is not. I know Link's plans. I also believe I can foil them, when the time comes. Don't ask me how, because I don't know yet. But war is a thing of chaos, not order, and I think my understanding of that is far superior to Link's. "Superhuman intelligence" be damned. War is not a chess game. It is, in the end, more a thing of the soul than the mind. And that thing has no soul. It will try to control the chaos, where I will revel in it.*

Belisarius could sense the hesitation in Aide's mind.

But the only thoughts which finally came were simply: **I trust your judgement.**

Belisarius chuckled. Hearing the soft sound, Sittas cocked an inquisitive eye at him.

"Aide was just expressing his confidence in my judgement," murmured Belisarius. "I wish I felt as much."

He expected to hear Sittas make one of his usual quips—at Belisarius' expense—but his large friend simply chuckled himself. "As it happens, I agree with the cute little fellow. I think your strategy for this campaign is damned near brilliant. Hell, not even 'damned near,' when I think about it."

Belisarius scowled. "It's too complicated. Too intricate by half. Too much step one, step two, step three. Maurice hasn't stopped nattering at me about it for a single day. And I don't disagree with him, either. It's going to start coming apart at the seams, soon enough, and I'll be back to making strategic decisions on a saddle." The scowl faded, replaced by a slight, crooked smile. "Which, I admit, seems to be something I have a certain aptitude for. More than Link does, I'm willing to bet. *Am* betting."

Sittas lifted his great bulk up on the stirrups for a moment, his eyes scanning the huge army. "Where is the old grouch, anyway?"

After a moment, he eased back in the saddle. The task of spotting a single man in that great horde of soldiers and moving equipment, even a top officer with his banners and entourage, was essentially hopeless.

"Of course he's grumbling," grumbled Sittas. "What would life be for the morose old bastard, without the pleasure of grousing to fill it up? But the fact is—this time—he's just plain wrong."

Almost angrily, Sittas gestured at the arid landscape ahead of them. "That's what it's going to be like, Belisarius, from here on. I'm not even sure the Malwa will bother to contest the delta, when we finally arrive at Barbaricum. Just cede it and let us get well established. Then, when the monsoon shifts, watch us starve beneath the walls of their fortifications upstream. By the time we get there, you know they'll have stripped the delta clean."

"Easier said than done."

Sittas shrugged. "Sure, I know." He barked a little laugh. "Easy for historians to say: 'they ravaged the countryside.' Never catch one of those languid fellows trying to destroy croplands. Hard work, that is—harder than growing stuff, that's for sure. Wouldn't wish it on a peasant."

Belisarius smiled. He doubted if Sittas had actually ever read any of those historians he was denouncing. But Belisarius knew that Sittas had once gotten embroiled in a loud argument with three historians at an imperial feast. In the end, Theodora had sent her personal guards to quell the large and outraged general.

Belisarius *had* read many of those historians, on the other hand. And while he felt none of Sittas' sputtering fury at the stupidities of over-educated and over-sheltered intellectuals, he understood it perfectly well. Aristocratic scribblers suffered from the inevitable habit of turning prosaic and complex reality into simple metaphors. Almost poetry, really, which they blithely assumed was an accurate representation of reality.

Destroy the countryside. Ravage the land.

As it happened, Belisarius had given those very orders himself over the years. Especially in his earliest years as an officer, campaigning against barbarians in the trans-Danube and Persians in the Mesopotamian borderlands. But both he and his men had understood the prose between the poetry, the unspoken qualifiers attached to the muscular verbs and nouns:

As best you can—in the time allowed. To the extent

*possible—given the number of men available. Whatever
you can do—with military equipment instead of agricultural implements, and teams of mules instead of oxen.*

He could remember hearing his men cursing bitterly, wrestling with the endless and exhausting work
of trying to destroy the tough vines and wood of grape
fields and olive groves. Or the backbreaking work of
cutting and assembling grain in piles suitable for burning. Not to mention the well-nigh hopeless task of
finding all the food caches hidden away, by peasants
who were far more experienced than soldiers at hiding such things—and had a far greater incentive to do
the job properly.

It could almost never be done really successfully. Time
after time, throughout the future history which Aide had
shown him, Belisarius recognized the same pattern. An
army marching through a region, "devastating the land,"
and then—not a year later—everything was back again.
Half of it, at least. "Mother Nature," especially when
assisted by poor and industrious peasants, was far
tougher than any army of soldiers.

In truth, the most successful method was the most
ruthless. The method the Mongols would use in Central
Asia: *kill everyone.* Don't just destroy the irrigation
works and the infrastructure, but kill all the people
living there as well. Eliminate the labor force which
could rebuild what was destroyed.

Those were methods Belisarius would never use.
Precious few armies in history ever had. But he had
no doubt at all the Malwa would use them in the delta
of the Indus. The last order Link would give, after its
soldiery destroyed everything they could, was to kill
all the peasants living there. The multitude of that poor
and humble folk, whose calloused hands were so much
better at rebuilding than the sinewy hands of soldiers
ever were at destroying. And then heap their corpses

atop their own ravaged land, so that their putrefaction could finish the work of destruction.

Malwa's *own* peasants. Who would not even be given the one mercy which peasants throughout time had usually been able to expect from their rulers, no matter how tyrannical: to be left alive, that they might be exploited further.

He found his own eyes searching the passing horde, looking for Maurice. A humble fellow himself, Maurice, in his own way. Born into the Thracian peasantry, and, despite his now exalted rank, not given to pretensions. The thought filled Belisarius with a strange, grim satisfaction. The first of the many blows he intended to rain on Malwa would be to send *that* man to rescue the enemy's own people.

He had thought Maurice would grumble at the order. Not because of its content, but because of the intricacy of the maneuvers involved. But, for once, the old veteran had not complained. Had not, even, ritually intoned his precious "First Law of Battle."

"Makes sense," he had grunted. "We'll need them for a labor force." The smile which followed had been almost seraphic. "War's a stupid, silly business, anyway. So why not turn it completely upside down?"

Oddly enough, Belisarius *did* spot Maurice in the horde. And did so in the oddest place.

"Look!" he barked, pointing an accusing finger. "He's finally going soft on us!"

Sittas' eyes followed Belisarius' finger. When he spotted Maurice himself, he burst into laughter. So did Kurush.

"He'll claim he had to work over some logistics with Agathius," chortled the Persian general. "You watch! Swear, he will, that only dire necessity forced him into it."

When Maurice finally came alongside the little rise where Belisarius and Sittas and Kurush were positioned, he glared up at them. Almost down at them, actually, perched as he was in the spacious comfort of Agathius' howdah atop a great war elephant.

"Had some logistical problems to sort out," he claimed loudly.

Agathius looked up from the papers he was studying and spotted Belisarius and the others. Then, heaving his crippled but still powerful body erect with a muscular arm on the edge of the open howdah, he grinned. "He's lying through his teeth," he shouted. "We've spent the whole morning playing with artillery positions, against these different sketches."

Even without being able to see into the howdah, Belisarius understood what Agathius was talking about. Among the many tasks he had set himself, in the months spent in Ctesiphon planning the Indus expedition, was overseeing the work of a dozen artists-become-draftsmen. Transcribing, onto parchment, Aide's descriptions of the fortifications of a future world. The designs of fortresses created in Renaissance Italy and Holland, as engineers and architects of the future grappled with the challenge of gunpowder artillery used in sieges.

Engineers and architects—and artists. Michelangelo, who would become famous to later generations as a painter and sculptor, had been famous in his own day as well; primarily, however, as one of Renaissance Italy's best military architects. He had been the city of Florence's Commissary General of Fortifications. He had lavished, over many months, as much care and attention on the critical hill of San Miniato as he would the Sistine Chapel, diverting the Mugnone and guiding the stream into a moat, as he would guide a brush; and bestowing San Miniato with as many intricate details—bastions and fascines—as he would a fresco depicting creation.

Then, having given Agathius the wherewithal to study the siege methods of the future, Belisarius had set him to work on designing, with the vast knowledge Agathius had gained from his long work as Belisarius' chief of logistics, the best methods to counter those fortresses.

Belisarius had no doubt at all that Link would distill the wisdom of Europe's best military architects in the first centuries of gunpowder warfare as it created Malwa's fortresses in the Indus valley. Of course, Belisarius would counter that with his own knowledge of history, given to him by Aide. Most of all, though, he would counter it with the keen brain of Agathius. As canny and meticulous a man as Belisarius had ever met in his life. And one whose own origins were as humble as Maurice's. Which, for Belisarius at least, added a certain zest to the whole affair.

"And how does that work go, then?" he demanded.

Agathius fluttered his hand vaguely. "Well enough. Given, at least, that Maurice picks holes in all my finest schemes. Pessimistic grouch, he is. 'If anything can go wrong, it will.' The usual."

Maurice was still half glaring at Belisarius. "Hate riding in this thing, myself. Give me a horse any day."

Kurush and Sittas immediately responded to that disclaimer with a variety of scoffing jests. Belisarius smiled, but said nothing.

As it happened, he didn't really doubt Maurice's claim. But even Maurice, as conservative as he was, had bowed to the inevitable.

The Roman army, throughout the centuries, had never favored the war elephants which so many of their opponents had treasured. True, the monsters could be ferocious in battle. But they could often wreak as much havoc in their own army as in the enemy's. Still, Belisarius had brought a number of the great beasts with him on this expedition. He had no intention of actually using them in combat. But the elephants could bear officers in howdahs, after all, along with the maps and charts and documents needed for the huge army's staff. Why waste the mind of a man like Agathius by perching him on a saddle for weeks? When the same man, even though crippled, could spend those weeks of marching engaged in the same crucial work he had overseen for months?

So, Belisarius did not join in the badinage. After a few seconds, he blocked it out of his mind entirely and returned to his study of the army passing before him.

What a hodge-podge! he thought, half-ruefully and half-cheerfully. *War elephants from ancient armies, plodding alongside men armed with our version of the Sharps rifle of the American Civil War. And look over there, Aide—a mitrailleuse in a chariot! I swear they found that relic in some Sumerian vault.*

It'll work, came the serene thought in reply. **You'll make it work.**

Chapter 12
AJMER
Summer, 533 A.D.

"Be careful," murmured Kujulo. "This city has changed."

Valentinian and Anastasius swept the streets of Ajmer with their eyes, shielded under lowered helmets. Neither of them had ever been in the largest city in Rajputana, so they had no basis for comparison.

"What's different?" asked Valentinian softly. He reached up his hand and scratched the back of his neck idly. The casual gesture exuded the weariness of a caravan guard finally reaching his destination after a long and arduous trek. Meanwhile, not casually at all, his eyes kept scouring the vicinity.

"This is not a Rajput city any longer," replied Kujulo. "Not really. Look there, for instance—down the street, to the left."

Without moving their heads, Valentinian and Anastasius looked in that direction. Valentinian couldn't really see much, since he was riding at the head of the caravan to Kujulo's right. But Anastasius, riding to the Kushan's left, had a clear view into the street in question—which was really more in the way of an alley.

"Mangy pack of dogs," he muttered. "But a big pack, too." A moment later, yawning, he added: "And you're right about that much. If any of those sorry bastards are Rajputs, I'd be astonished. I don't think I've ever seen a Rajput with as much filth all over him—not even after a battle—as any of that lot have on their feet alone."

The slowly moving caravan was now passing the mouth of the alley, and Valentinian was finally able to get a good look.

" 'Dogs' is an insult to dogs. But—" He paused, until the alley was behind them. "They're hungry-looking, I give you that."

Anastasius and Valentinian now both looked to Kujulo. The "leadership structure" of their peculiar expedition was a fluid thing. Sometimes one, then another, of the three men in command had taken the lead over the weeks since they landed in the delta and made their slow way into Rajputana. Usually either Valentinian or Anastasius. But now that they had arrived at Ajmer, both of the Roman cataphracts were clearly willing to let Kujulo guide them.

This unfamiliar and exotic city was *terra incognita* to them. So too, of course, had been the Thar desert and the Aravalli mountains. But rough terrain, whatever its specific features, is much the same in many places—and both Anastasius and Valentinian were veterans of marches across such. Usually as part of an army, true, rather than a merchant caravan. But the experience had not been especially foreign. Neither, certainly, had been the two brief skirmishes with bandits.

Ajmer, however, was a different matter. Here, the "terrain" was not so much geographic as human. And neither of them knew anything about the customs and habits which characterized the city.

Kujulo immediately made clear that he was something of a novice, also. Or, it might be better to say, a man who returns to a place he had known years earlier, and finds it has been completely transformed.

"In the old days," he growled, "no gang like that would have dared lounge openly in the streets of Ajmer. Rajput women would have driven them off, sent them scampering back into their hovels."

"I'm pretty sure there's another pack in that alley up ahead," murmured Valentinian. "A more lively bunch, seems like. At least judging from the way their lookout ducked back into the alley when I spotted him."

The only sign of Kujulo's tension was a slight shift in the way he rode his saddle. The Kushan seemed slightly discomfited by the fact that he had no stirrups.

They all were, in truth. By now, of course, stirrups had become adopted by almost all Malwa cavalry units. But the devices were still rare in civilian use, and they had decided from the beginning that they couldn't afford to risk drawing attention to themselves. To all outward appearances, the two Roman cataphracts and the seventeen Kushans who accompanied them were nothing more than the guards and drivers of a merchant caravan. A relatively small one, at that.

"There's no order in this city any more," continued Kujulo. "All the Rajput soldiers, by now, must have been drawn into the Malwa army. Probably have a small unit of common soldiers policing the city, with maybe a handful of Ye-tai to stiffen them up. But their idea of 'policing' will be either lounging in the barracks or—more likely—doing their own extortions."

There was a little stir in the alley still some distance away, coming up on their right. Three men were leaning out of it, studying the oncoming caravan like so many predators in ambush. Small and mangy predators, to be sure, but . . .

As Valentinian had rightly said, *hungry-looking*.

"Hell and damn," rumbled Anastasius. Moving slowly, casually, he loosened the mace belted to his thick waist. As he did so, moving his head with the same casual ease, he glanced back over his shoulder. "Hell and damn," he repeated. "That first bunch is peeking at us from behind."

Facing forward again, his basso rumble deepened. "It's an ambush, sure. In broad daylight on a busy street."

"Let's take it to 'em, then," said Valentinian. His narrow weasel face showed not a trace of emotion. His hand loosened his own weapon, the spatha he favored, and his left leg began to rise.

Kujulo eyed him sharply. Valentinian could dismount from a horse faster than any man he had ever seen. Just as he could do anything faster than any man he had ever seen. Within seconds, he knew, the lightly armored cataphract would be plunging his whipcord body into that alley up ahead.

Of the outcome, Kujulo had no doubt at all. Even had he been faced with real soldiers, Valentinian would transform that narrow alley into a creek of blood. Dealing with dacoits, the alley would erupt like a burst dam, spilling blood and limbs and heads and intestines everywhere.

"*No*," he hissed. "The city is full of spies."

Valentinian's leg froze. His shoulder twitched irritation. "So? A caravan defending itself."

They were not more than fifteen yards from the mouth of the alley. Kujulo hissed again. "No caravan defends itself the way you will. Or Anastasius." The grunt that followed combined grim humor with exasperation. "Or me, for that matter, or my Kushans."

Ten yards, now. "What else do you suggest?" snarled Valentinian softly. "Let them kill half of us, to show Malwa spies we are nothing but merchant sheep?"

His shoulders twitched irritation again. The leg began to rise. "Damn that. Let's take it to them."

Suddenly, a little chorus of shrieks erupted from the mouth of the alley. An instant later, spewing forth like so many pieces of a bad fig from a man's mouth, six dacoits burst into the street. Two were shrieking, one was staggering. The other three, silent, simply raced off.

Raced off *away* from the caravan, not toward it. Followed, within a second or two, by the shriekers. The last dacoit staggered another step or two, then sprawled on his face and lay still. Blood was beginning to stain his filthy clothing.

Kujulo raised his hand, as any caravan leader would when faced with similar circumstances. "*Halt!*"

The caravan stopped. All the Kushans further back drew their weapons, as did Kujulo and the Roman cataphracts. The street was suddenly empty of all life, except for the group of dacoits who had begun emerging from the alley behind. But they too, seeing the new circumstances, hastily scampered out of sight.

Kujulo studied the alley. He held his own sword a bit awkwardly. Not too demonstratively, just enough to make him seem like a caravan master instead of an experienced soldier. From the corner of his eye, he saw that Valentinian's grip was expert—just as, out of that same corner, he had seen the blinding speed with which the cataphract had drawn the blade.

"Can you just *try* not to seem like the perfect killer," he muttered sourly.

Valentinian ignored him. His dark eyes were riveted on the alley mouth.

Again, motion. A dacoit emerged, slowly, clutching his throat. His eyes were gaping wide and his face was pale. Blood was pouring through his fingers. He took two steps into the street before his knees collapsed and he toppled onto his face.

Another dacoit came, this one like a limp rag being slapped against the mudbrick wall of the nearest building which formed the alley's corner. The front of his clothing was a red blotch and his head was sagging. He was being held by the scruff of the neck by another man.

"Rob me, will you?" snarled the man who held him. A knife flashed into the dacoit's back, flashed again. Then, contemptuously, the man tossed the would-be robber's body onto that of his fellow.

Valentinian studied him carefully. The man was average in height, but very wide-shouldered. His hawk face was sharp and angry. He strode into the street, stooped like a raptor, and wiped the gore off his dagger on the clothing of his last victim.

Then, straightening and sheathing the weapon, he glared at Kujulo and the Romans.

"And you?" he demanded.

Kujulo sheathed his sword and raised his other hand in a placating gesture. "We are merchants, lord. No more."

The man's glare did not fade in the least. His clothing, though clean, was utilitarian and plain. "No lord, I!" he barked. Then, sneering: "But neither am I one to be troubled by dacoits. Nor any man."

Despite his belligerence, the man stepped aside and waved his hand.

"Pass by, pass by!"

Kujulo set the caravan back into motion. As they drew alongside the alley, the glaring man snorted contemptuously. "A caravan, is it? Hauling what—sheep dung?"

He shook his head sarcastically. "You'll be lucky if any stable will put up as sorry a lot as you. But I suppose the low-caste inn two streets up might do so." And with that, he was gone, vanishing back into the alley like a wraith. Neither Valentinian nor Kujulo could hear his footsteps.

"Well," mused Anastasius, "that's one way to arrange a meeting. I don't remember Antonina describing him as being quite so broad-shouldered, though. You, Valentinian?"

Valentinian seemed lost in thought. He said nothing for a few seconds. Then, softly: "I don't remember her saying he could move that quickly, either." The words seemed filled more with interest than concern. One raptor gauging another.

"Splendid," growled Kujulo. "You *will* remember that we didn't come all this way to fight a duel on a mountainside?"

Valentinian's narrow smile made an appearance. "No danger of that. I don't believe he's any more taken by dramatic public duels than I am."

The words did not seem to bring much reassurance. The sour expression was still on Kujulo's face when the caravan pulled up before the inn. Nor was his displeasure primarily caused by the obvious dilapidation of the establishment.

One raptor gauging another.

"Splendid," he growled.

Chapter 13

MARV

Summer, 533 A.D.

"How are you feeling?" asked Kungas, smiling down at Irene. The expression was broader than the usual faint crack in the mask which normally did Kungas for a smile. Suspicious souls, in fact, might even take it for a . . .

"Stop grinning at me," grumbled Irene. Painfully, she levered herself up from the pallet where she had been resting. "I ache all over, that's how I'm feeling."

Now sitting up, she studied Kungas' face. Seeing that the smile showed no sign of vanishing—might even be widening, in fact!—she scowled ferociously.

"Feeling superior, are we? Enjoying the sight of the too-clever-by-half female puddled in exhaustion and fatigue? Undone by the frailty of her flesh?"

Still smiling, Kungas squatted next to her and stroked Irene's cheek. "Such a suspicious woman! Actually, no. All things considered, you are doing extremely well. The army thinks so, too."

He chuckled. "In fact, the bets are being settled right now. Most of the soldiers were wagering that you wouldn't make it as far as Damghan—much less all the

142

way to Marv. And the ones who thought you might weren't willing to place much of a stake on it."

Irene cocked her head and listened to the gleeful sounds coming through the walls of the small tent. She had wondered—a bit, not much; as preoccupied as she had been with her own misery—why so many people seemed full of good cheer. Kushans were addicted to gambling. Those were the sounds of a *major* bet being settled, at long odds and with a big payoff.

"So who's collecting, then?" she demanded crossly.

"The camp followers, who else? The women are getting rich."

That news lightened Irene's mood immensely. She had discovered, in the long and arduous weeks of their trek across all of Persia, that she got along very well with the Kushan women. Much to her surprise, in fact. She had assumed from the outset, without really thinking about it, that the mostly illiterate and tough women who had become the camp followers of the none-too-literate and *very* tough army of Kungas would have nothing in common with her.

In many ways, of course, they didn't. Irene was sophisticated and cosmopolitan in a way that those women never would be, any more than the soldiers to whom they were attached. But women in Kushan society enjoyed far greater freedom than Irene would have expected in a society forged in the mountains and deserts of central Asia.

Perhaps that was because of the practical needs of the Kushan dispersal after the Ye-tai conquest of their homeland, and the later policies of their Malwa overlords. But Irene liked to think it was the legacy of the Sarmatians who had once, in the days of Alexander, ruled the area that would eventually become the Kushan empire. The Scythians whom the Sarmatians displaced had kept women in a strictly subordinate position. But every Sarmatian girl, according to ancient accounts, was taught to ride a horse. And—so legend had it, at least—was expected to fight alongside the men, armed and armored, and was even forbidden to marry until she had slain an enemy in battle.

Perhaps that was all idle fancy. The Kushan women, for all their undoubted toughness, were not expected to fight except under extreme circumstances. But, for whatever reason, Irene had found that the Kushan women took a certain sly pleasure in her own ability to discomfit, time after time, the self-confident men who marched under Kungas' banner.

Even the banner itself was Irene's, after all. None of the Kushans, not even Kungas, had given much thought to a symbol. They had simply assumed they would, as was custom, use some sort of simple device—a colored strip of cloth, perhaps, wound about their helmets.

Irene, guided by her own intelligence and many hours spent in discussion with Belisarius and Aide, had decreed otherwise. And so, as the Kushan army made its trek across Asia, its progress was marked by the great fluttering banners which Irene had designed. She had stolen her designs from the ancient Sarmatians and the Mongols of what would have been the future: a bronze dragon's head with a wind sock trailing behind, and the horsetail banners below it. Very flashy and dramatic, it was.

"If you are able to move," said Kungas softly, "I could use your help. Things are coming to a head."

Irene winced. At the moment, *moving* was the last thing she wanted to do. Accustomed all her life to the soft existence of a wealthy Greek noblewoman, the grueling trek had taxed her severely. Her brain understood well enough that exercising her aching muscles was the best remedy for what ailed her. But her body practically shrieked in protest.

Still, she understood immediately the nature of Kungas' problem. And knew, as well, that she was the best person to solve it. Partly because of her skill at diplomacy. And partly—

She sniffed disdainfully. "And once again! Allow stubborn men to compromise because all of them can blame their soft-headedness on a feeble and fearful woman. There's no justice in the world, Kungas."

Her husband's smile had faded back into the familiar crack-in-the-casting. "True enough," he murmured. "But it's such an *effective* tactic."

"Help me up," she hissed. "And you'll probably have to carry me."

In the event, Irene managed the task on her own two feet. Mincing through the marketplace in Marv, she even had the energy to stop along the way and banter with the Kushan women who had set up their impromptu stalls everywhere. She ignored resolutely all of Kungas' little signs of impatience and unease. First, she needed the periodic rest. Second—and more important—the attitude of the women would influence the army. Having found that secret weapon, she intended to use it to maximum advantage.

Eventually, she and Kungas made their way into the small palace which had served the former commander of the Malwa garrison for his headquarters. It was an ancient edifice. The Kushans had built it originally, centuries earlier, as a regional palace. Before the Malwa came, it had served the same purpose for the Sassanids after they conquered the western half of the Kushan empire. The Persian conquerors had decreed the former Kushan land to be one of their *shahrs*—the equivalent of a royal province—and, most significantly, had included it within the land of Iran proper.

Which was the source of the current controversy,

of course. Now that Kungas had retaken Marv, with the help of Baresmanas and some two thousand Persian dehgans assigned by Emperor Khusrau to accompany the Kushan expedition (that far, and no farther), the question which had once been abstract was posed in the concrete.

Who was to be the new ruler of the region?

The Kushans, naturally enough, inclined to the opinion that Marv, originally theirs to begin with, should be theirs again. The more so since they had done the actual work of driving the Malwa garrison out of the walled city. The Persians had done nothing more than pursue and harry already broken troops trying to flee through the oasis which surrounded Marv.

The Persians, on the other hand . . .

As Irene passed through the entrance, she heaved a small sigh. Relief from the sun's heat, to some extent; mostly, exasperation at the typical haughtiness of Persians. Even Baresmanas was being stiff over the matter. Although Irene suspected that was due more to stiff instructions from Khusrau than his own sentiments.

Moving slowly and painfully, Kungas at her side ready to lend a hand if need be, Irene made her way through the narrow corridors of the palace. The walls of the palace were thick, due as much to the need for insulation from summer's heat and winter's cold as the crude nature of the original design. Narrow corridors made for a gloomy walk, and Irene took the time to steel herself for the coming fray. She let the darkness of the corridor feed her soul, swelling the stark message that she bore with her to the people who had adopted her as their queen.

By the time she and Kungas reached the chamber where the quarrel was raging, Macrembolitissa the spymaster had vanished. Queen Irene of the Kushans was the woman who made her entrance.

"Silence," she decreed. Then, gratefully easing herself into a chair immediately presented by one of the Kushan officers, she nodded at Baresmanas and the three Persian officers standing by him.

"I agree with you, Baresmanas, and will see it done. Now please leave. We Kushans must discuss this matter in private."

Baresmanas bowed and complied immediately. Within seconds, he and the other Persians had left the room. Immediately, the stunned silence into which Irene's pronouncement had cast the half dozen Kushans in the room—not Kungas; he was silent but not stunned in the least—began to erupt in a quickly-growing murmur of protest.

"Silence!" she decreed again. Then, after sweeping them with a cold gaze, she snorted sarcastically. "Boys! Stupid boys! Quarreling over toys and trinkets because you cannot see an adult horizon."

She leaned forward in the chair—not allowing any trace of the spike of pain that movement caused to show in her face—and pointed an imperious finger to the narrow window which looked to the northeast. "In *that* direction lies our destiny, not this miserable region of dust and heat."

Kungas smiled, very faintly. Knowing Irene's purpose, and supporting it, he still felt it necessary to maintain his own dignity. He *was* the king, after all, not she. He *was* what Romans would have called the man of the house, after all, not she.

"It is one of the most fertile oases in central Asia, wife. A fertility only made possible by our own irrigation works. Which we—not Persians nor Ye-tai nor Malwa—constructed long ago."

Irene shrugged. "True. And so what? The center of Kushan strength will lie, as it always did, in our control of the great mountains to the east. The Hindu

Kush—that must be the heart of our new realm. That, and the Pamirs."

The last sentence brought a stillness to the room. The Pamirs were even harsher mountains than the Hindu Kush. No one had ever really tried to rule them, in anything but name.

Irene smiled. The expression was serene, self-confident; erasing all traces of her former sarcasm and derision.

"You are thinking too small," she said quietly. "Much too small. Thinking only of the immediate task of reconquering our ancient homeland, and holding it from the Malwa. But what of our future? What of the *centuries* which will come thereafter?"

Vasudeva, who had become the military commander of Kungas' army, began tugging gently at the point of his goatee. Now that his initial outrage was fading, the canny general was remembering the fundamental reason that all of the Kushans had greeted Kungas' marriage with enthusiasm.

The damned Greek woman was *smart*.

"Explain." Then, remembering protocol: "If you would be so kind, Your Majesty."

Irene grinned, and with that cheerful expression came a sudden relaxation spreading through the room. The hard-bitten Kushan soldiers, for all that Irene's ways often puzzled and bemused them, had also come to feel a genuine fondness for the woman as well as respect for her intelligence. Irene, grinning, was a thing they both liked and trusted. They too, when all was said and done, had a sense of humor.

"We are too small to hold Marv, Vasudeva. That is the simple truth. Today, yes—with the Persians forced into an alliance with us. If we drive the issue, Baresmanas will accede. But what of the time *after* Malwa has fallen, when the Persians will seek to lick their wounds by new triumphs, new additions to their realm?"

The Kushans stared at her. Then, slowly, one by one, they pulled up chairs and took their seats. It did not occur to any of them, at the time, to ask permission of their king and queen to do so. And, remembering the omission later, they would be pleased at the fact that neither of their monarchs—for this *was* a dual monarchy, in all but name—took the least umbrage at their casual informality.

It did not even occur to Irene to do so, actually. She was at heart a thinker, and had always enjoyed thoughtful conversation. Seated on a proper chair—not a damned saddle.

"Think, for once," she continued, after all were seated. "Think of the *future*, not the past. What we can control militarily—can hold against anyone, once we have built the needed fortifications—are the mountains. But those mountains cannot provide the wealth we need for a prosperous kingdom. That, in a nutshell, is the problem we face."

She paused. Quickly, all the Kushans nodded their heads. Once she was sure they were following her logic, she went on.

"Only two avenues are open to us, to overcome that quandary. The first is to seize fertile areas in the lowlands, such as Marv . . ." She waited, just a moment, before adding: "And the Punjab, which I know many of you are assuming we will."

Again, the Kushans began to stiffen. And, again, Irene's lips twisted into an expression of scorn.

"Spare me! I know Peshawar is in the Punjab—just at the edge of it, at least. And one of the holiest cities of the Buddhist faith." She pressed herself back into the chair, using her hands on the armrests as a brace. The motion brought some relief to the ache in her lower spine. "The Vale of Peshawar we can claim, easily enough. So long as we make no claims to the Punjab itself."

She hesitated, thinking. "I am fairly certain that we can claim Mardan and its plain as well, with the Buddhist holy sites at Takht-i-Bahi and Jamal Garhi. Unless I am badly mistaken, Belisarius will allow the Persians to take the Sind. Once Malwa has fallen, therefore, it will be the Rajputs and—I suspect, at least—the Persians who will be our principal competitors for the wealth of the Punjab. *Let them have it*—so long as we control Peshawar and Mardan."

"And the Kohat pass!" chimed in Kungas. Very energetically, the way a proper husband corrects a minor lapse on the part of his wife.

Irene nodded. Very demurely, the way a proper wife accepts her husband's correction. "And the pass." Then, with a sniff: "Let others squabble over the town of Kohat itself. A Pathan town! More grief than anything else."

Vima, another of the top officers of the Kushan army, now spoke up. "In essence, what you propose is that we take just enough of the Punjab to protect the Khyber pass. Base our claim to Peshawar and Mardan on religious grounds, but make clear that we will not contest the Punjab itself. While, at the same time, locking our grip on the Hindu Kush."

"Yes."

Vima shook his head. "From a military point of view, Your Majesty, the logic is impeccable. But that small portion of the Punjab cannot possibly provide enough food for our kingdom. Not unless we are prepared to live like semi-barbarians, which I for one am not. A *civilized* nation needs agricultural area, and lots of it." Semi-apologetically: "Such as the oasis of Marv would provide us."

Irene sniffed. "Have no fear, Vima! I can assure you that I am even less inclined than you to live like a semi-barbarian." She shuddered. "God, can you imagine it! *Me?* Spending half my life in a saddle?"

The Kushans all laughed. But Irene was pleased to see that the laughter contained not a trace of derision. She *had* made her way to Marv in a saddle, after all. Resolutely spurning each and every suggestion that she ride in a palanquin, or even one of the carts which the camp followers used.

A warrior nation, the more so when it was striking a lightning blow at their hated enemy, needed a warrior queen who would not delay them with her frailties. Her illustrious Roman pedigree had pleased the Kushans, for it brought a certain glamor and aura of legitimacy to their cause. But they did not need the reality of the weak flesh it came in. So, using her intelligence and iron will to stifle that flesh, Irene had submitted to the pain. And for all that they might jest about it, the Kushan soldiers understood and respected her for it.

Once the humor of the moment had settled in, Irene shook her head. "I said there were *two* alternatives, Vima. You have overlooked the other. A kingdom—a rich kingdom—can also base itself on trade. And, over time, the expansion which trade brings in its wake."

Again, she pointed to the northeast, in a gesture which was even more imperious. Then, regally, swept it slowly to the west—until half the northland had been encompassed by her finger.

"*The north.* From the Tien Shan mountains to the Aral Sea. We will not dispute the Punjab with the Rajputs, nor the oases and badlands of Khorasan with the Persians. Let *them* toil in the fields. Let *them* maintain the dikes and canals. We will control all the passes which connect the land of the Aryans to India, and both of them to distant China. We—with our military power rooted in the Hindu Kush and the Pamirs—will reap the benefits from those ancient trade routes. Which, with Malwa gone and ourselves to maintain order, will spring back like giant trees."

Kungas chimed in again. This time, not as a husband correcting his wife, but as a king allied with his queen. "Yes. And under our rule, all of Transoxiana will flourish anew. Bukhara, Samakhand, Tashkent—*our* cities, they will be, reborn from the ashes. And great metropolises they will become, to rival Constantinople or Ctesiphon or Kausambi."

All the Kushan generals, as was their custom, were now tugging the tips of their goatees. Vima and Huvishka were even fondling their topknots, the sure sign of a Kushan warrior lost deep in thought.

"Difficult," murmured Vasudeva. "Difficult." His goatee-tugging became vigorous. "Beyond Transoxiana lie the great steppes. Time after time, fierce tribes have come sweeping down from that vastness, burning and pillaging all in their wake. No one has ever managed to stymie them, for more than a century or two. We ourselves came from that place, and were in turn overrun by the Ye-tai after civilization made us soft. Why would it not happen again?"

Irene laughed. With delight, not sarcasm. As was true of any enthusiast trained in the dialectic of Socrates, nothing pleased her more than a well-posed question. Like a fat lamb it was, stretched bleating on the altar.

"Guns, Vasudeva! Guns! Those steppe nomads have never been numerous. You know as well as I that the accounts of 'hordes' are preposterous. It was always their mounted mobility combined with archery which made them so formidable. But firearms are superior to bows, and no primitive nomads can make the things.

Once civilization became armed with guns, the threat from the steppes vanished soon enough."

She leaned forward. This time, her enthusiasm was so great that she barely noticed the pain that movement caused her. "I spent many hours, with Belisarius, speaking with the Talisman of God. Let me now pass on to you what the Talisman told me of the future. Of a great nation that would someday have been called Russia, and how it conquered the steppes."

And so, until long after nightfall, Irene told her Kushans of the great realm they would create. The realm that she called by the odd name of *Siberia*. A realm which would be created slowly, not overnight. More by traders and explorers and missionaries than armies of conquest—though armies would also come, when needed, from the secure fastnesses of the great mountains which bred them. Slowly, but surely for all that.

Let the Kushans avoid entanglements with Indians and Persians, and there was no power to stymie their purpose in Siberia. The distant Chinese, as ever, were preoccupied with their own affairs. The other power that might contest the area, the nation that would have been called Russia in a different future, was still centuries from birth. Whether it would be born in this new future was not something which Irene could foresee. But, even if it were, it would remain forever on the far side of the Urals. Siberia, with all the great wealth in its vast expanse, would be *Kushan*.

And so, while the Kushans built the foundation of their own future, they would also shield the rest of civilization from the ravages of barbarism. Having no cause for quarrel over territory, the Romans and the Persians and the Indians would acquiesce in the Kushan control of the great trade routes through central Asia. Might even, when called upon, send money to defray the costs of holding back the barbarians.

In the end, the queen's soldiers were satisfied. The queen's plan appealed to their military caution in the present as much as to their political ambitions for the future. They were small and weak, still. By planting their roots in the protected mountains, not exposing them to the peril of the oases and the plains of the Indus, they would lay the basis for the great Buddhist empire which would eventually spread throughout half of Asia. *To the north!*

As they made their way back to their tent, Irene still mincing her steps, Kungas allowed the smile to spread across his face. In the darkness, illuminated only by the cookfires and the few lanterns in the market, there was no one to see that unusually open expression on the king's face.

"That went marvelously well. Tomorrow, of course, you will twist the screw on Baresmanas."

Irene grimaced. Not at the thought of the next day's negotiations, but simply because her back now seemed like a sea of fire. "He'll shriek with agony," she predicted. "But he'll still give me the guns."

As it happened, Baresmanas did *not* squeal with pain, because he put up no more than a token resistance.

"Please! Please! I can't bear the thought of spending so many hours locked in combat." For a moment, his patrician Aryan face took on a severity which the most rigid Roman paterfamilias would have envied. "Not for myself, of course! Perish the thought. But you are a frail woman, in much pain because of the rigors of the journey. So my chivalrous instincts seem to have overwhelmed me. The guns are yours, Irene. The cannons, at any rate. Khusrau insisted that I hang onto the hand-held firearms."

"I want half of *them* as well," snapped Irene. The pain was making her grouchy. "And three-fourths of the powder and bullets. Your damned dehgans can't use the things properly anyway—and you know it as well as I do!"

Baresmanas shifted uncomfortably in his chair. "I foresaw this. Even warned the emperor!" He sighed again, and shook his head ruefully. "Ah, well. We Aryans have always been noted for our chivalry. I am a pawn in your hands."

Irene eased herself back into her own chair, again using the pressure of her hands on the armrests to stifle the pain in her spine. Then, smiled cheerfully. "Oh, don't be so gloomy. Khusrau can hardly punish you very severely, after all. Not with your own daughter being the new Empress of Rome! That might start a new war."

Three days later, the entire Kushan army departed Marv, leaving Baresmanas and his Persians in sole possession of the fertile oasis. With them went all of the Kushan artisans whom Lord Damodara had resettled in Marv the year before, in the course of his own campaign in the Persian plateau. The Kushan artisans wanted no part of Aryan rule. The Persians were notorious for their haughty ways.

But, still more, they were fired with enthusiasm for the Kushan cause. Most of them, after all, had come from Begram in the first place. And that city—the largest Kushan city in the world, and the center of Kushan industry and craftsmanship—was where Kungas proposed to march next. March upon it—and take it.

So, as Irene minced her way toward her horse, the Kushan camp followers and the new artisan families which had joined them cheered her on her way. Even more loudly than the Kushan soldiers, who were themselves cheering.

Before she reached the horse, several Kushan soldiers trotted up bearing a palanquin. They urged her to avail herself of the device—even offered, against all custom, to bear it themselves instead of putting slaves to the purpose.

Irene simply shook her head and minced past them. Behind her back, she could hear the gleeful sounds of the wagers being settled.

"The next time I see Antonina," she muttered bitterly, under her breath, "I'm going to have some harsh words to say to *her* on the subject of staring at a horse."

Three hours into the march, a party of Kushan women trotted their horses up to ride alongside her. Five of them, there were, all quite young. The oldest was no more than twenty, the youngest perhaps fifteen.

Irene was surprised. Not by the sight of Kushan women on horseback, which was uncommon but by no means considered outlandish. But by the fact that all five of them had swords belted to their waists, had bows and quivers attached to their saddles, and held lances in their hands.

"We're your new bodyguard," announced the oldest proudly. "Don't let anyone tell you otherwise!"

"The king said it was suitable," said the youngest. Very stiffly, as if she expected contradiction and argument.

The oldest, apparently fearing the same, rushed further words to the fore. "We checked with the oldsters. Every one of us—every one!—has Sarmatian ancestors." A bit uncertainly: "Some ancestors, anyway. All Kushans do, after all."

Irene grinned. "Splendid! I couldn't have asked for a better bodyguard. I feel better already."

The queen's sarcastic wit had already become famous among her Kushan subjects. So, still uncertain, the young women stared at her anxiously.

Irene erased whatever trace of humor might have been on her face. "I'm quite serious," she said serenely. "I'm sure you'll do well enough, if I'm ever attacked. But what's even more important is that you'll guard me against the *real* enemy."

The oldest girl laughed. "Boredom! Men never know what to talk about, on a march. Except their stupid wagers."

At the mention of wagers, all the girls looked smug. Irene was quite certain that every one of them had just gained a significant increase in their wealth.

"Do any of you know how to read?" she asked.

Seeing the five girls shake their heads, Irene's sarcasm returned in full force.

"Typical! Well, there'll be none of that, my fine young ladies. If you expect to be *my* bodyguard, you'll damned well learn how to read! I can teach you from saddleback—you watch and see if I can't."

Serene calm returned. "That way we'll *really* have some fine conversations, in the weeks and months ahead. Not even women, when you get right down to it, are superhuman. Ha! I sometimes wonder what those stupid illiterate goddesses talked about, other than sewing and seduction."

Chapter 14
CHARAX
Summer, 533 A.D.

Antonina surveyed the large crowd piled into the reception chamber of Emperor Khusrau's palace. *Whatever else changes,* she thought ruefully, *Persians will always insist on their pomp and ceremony.*

The palace had once belonged to the imperial official in charge of overseeing Charax. After they seized the city, the Malwa had made the building their military headquarters. Then, once Belisarius had retaken the city, the palace had been returned to the Persians. But since Khusrau had decided to plant himself in Charax for the duration of the war, the building had assumed full imperial trappings. True, the Persians had not insisted on reconstructing the entire edifice. Not with the dynamic and practical Khusrau as their emperor. But they had patched up the war damage, repainted every surface, hauled every conceivable manner of statuary and decoration from the imperial capital of Ctesiphon. And, most of all—or so it seemed to Antonina, scanning the scene—packed it with every grandee in the far-flung Persian empire.

God, will you look at that crowd! Like sardines in an amphora.

She spotted Ousanas and a handful of Axumite officers in a nearby alcove off the main audience chamber. The Ethiopians had brought some of their beloved stools, and were ensconced upon them circling a small table piled high with goblets and wine jugs. The table was obviously Persian in design, and Antonina wondered idly how the Axumites had managed to obtain the thing. There was not a single table to be seen anywhere else in the jam-packed audience hall, or any of the other alcoves she could see.

Probably by threatening mayhem on the majordomo. She emitted a faint chuckle. *Which also explains the relative population scarcity in that alcove. Even Persian grandees get nervous around testy Axumites.*

The Axumites, like the Romans, were now allies of the Persian empire. But the Ethiopians had very little of the Roman patience with imperial protocol and the elaborate social finery which went with it. There had been any number of minor clashes between the Axumites and the Persians. None of those clashes had been violent, other than a handful of brawls in the dock area between sailors, but the Persian grandees generally avoided the company of Ethiopians except when it was absolutely necessary. An attitude which the Axumites reciprocated in full.

Ousanas spotted her and waved a hand, inviting her to join them. Antonina smiled, shook her head, and wiggled her fingers. Understanding the meaning of the gesture, Ousanas grinned at her and went back to his carousing.

Antonina sighed. "*Somebody,*" she grumbled under her breath, "has to maintain diplomatic appearances."

Glumly, she eyed the mob between her and the emperor. Khusrau, perched on a throne atop a dais at the far end of the audience hall, was the only person sitting in the entire chamber. Antonina estimated that it would take her ten minutes to squeeze her way up to Khusrau's august presence in order to tender her official Roman diplomatic regards.

And twice that long to squeeze my way out, battling against the flow. I'll be mashed like a grape by the time it's over.

She had forgotten about her bodyguards.

"Allow us," murmured Matthew's voice, coming from behind her. Behind her, and well *above* her, for Matthew was practically a giant.

A moment later, Matthew and Leo were plowing a path for Antonina through the crowd. Following in their wake, she was almost amazed at the speed they were making. The more so, since the two bodyguards were actually being quite gentle in their methods. Neither Matthew nor Leo was carrying any weapons, for such were forbidden in the presence of the emperor. They didn't even use their hands, just the inexorable forward movement of their immense bodies. But the combination of their size, stolidity—and Leo's truly hideous-ugly features—worked like a charm. Within two minutes, Antonina had arrived at the foot of the emperor's throne.

Seeing her, Khusrau smiled and leaned over.

"You really don't have to do this," he murmured. "It's all a pure formality, since I'll be seeing you tomorrow at our usual planning session."

"Yes, I do," hissed Antonina in reply. "Or else half your grandees will be whispering in your ear by the end of the night, predicting imminent Roman treachery. And you and I would have to waste all our time tomorrow figuring out ways to counteract the rumors instead of planning the campaign."

Khusrau chuckled. "And as many of your own officials, I'll wager."

Antonina shook her head firmly. "Only a third of them. Romans aren't as touchy as Aryans, Emperor." She scowled. "Which, I admit, probably comes to the same fraction of *active* officials. Since about one-third of my officials are so corrupt they don't pay attention to anything except counting their bribes."

Khusrau laughed aloud, this time. Hearing the sound, practically everyone in the great chamber froze for an instant. A hush fell over the room. Hundreds of eyes were riveted on the sight of the emperor laughing at a jest made by the wife of Belisarius.

In some completely indefinable manner, a certain tension seemed to ease from the room. A moment later, everyone was back to their jabbering conversation.

"And another successful maneuver," said Khusrau quietly. "Begone, Antonina. It looks far more comfortable in that alcove with those disrespectful black savages. And if I know Ousanas, the wine's even better than what my servants are dispensing."

A vague look of longing came over the emperor's face, as if he felt a certain envy at the prospect. Khusrau was an energetic and active man, and Antonina had no doubt at all he would have much preferred to squat on a stool around a convivial table of Axumite officers himself than spend hours on a massive throne in an audience chamber.

But the moment was brief, and the emperor's expression resumed its normal air of serenity. Khusrau Anushirvan was the Emperor of Iran and non-Iran, after all. And, truth to tell, he much enjoyed that status, despite its occasional drawbacks.

Antonina nodded and turned away. Three minutes later, following easily in the path cleared for her by Matthew and Leo, she was perched on a stool at the table in the alcove. Reaching, with no little eagerness, for the goblet full of wine handed to her by Ousanas.

Alas. She had barely managed to sip from the goblet when she heard someone clearing his throat behind her. Another official of some kind, demanding some small decision from her.

She was in a shorter temper than usual. "Can't this wait—" she began to snarl, turning her head. Then, seeing that it was Dryopus standing behind her, she fell silent. One of the many things she liked about Dryopus was that he did not, unlike most Roman officials, insist on passing along to his superior every petty decision to be made.

Dryopus was frowning slightly. "My apologies for disturbing you, Antonina. But I am a little concerned by the situation with the *Circe.* More than a little, actually."

"Why? What did the inspectors report?"

"They *haven't* reported, Antonina. I've not seen or heard from them since we sent them off this morning to inspect the ship."

Antonina stiffened and set the goblet down on the table. "That was hours ago!"

The cheerful conviviality had left the faces of the Axumites also. "What is wrong, Antonina?" asked Ousanas.

Quickly, Antonina sketched the situation. The stubborn reluctance—odd, under the circumstances—of the brothers Aco and Numenius to allow their ship to be used for hauling military supplies; her decision to send inspectors this morning.

"Malwa," stated Ousanas firmly. "The *Circe* is loaded with gunpowder, and packed with Malwa soldiery. That's a fireship, aimed at the shipping in the harbor."

His quick conclusion summed up the worst of Antonina's fears. She rose abruptly and began heading toward the entrance to the palace. Behind her, she heard the scrape of stools as the Axumites followed suit.

"That ship *has* been kept out of the harbor itself,

hasn't it?" she asked Dryopus, who was scurrying next to her.

"Oh, yes," he assured Antonina. "Until they've been inspected, no ship is allowed past the screen of galleys into the harbor. Those were your orders from the very beginning, and I've seen to it they've been scrupulously adhered to."

Ousanas had drawn alongside her and heard Dryopus' last words.

"Won't matter," he said curtly. "The Malwa are canny, and their spies are excellent. By now, those procedures of yours have become routine. The Malwa waited until enough time had elapsed for everyone to become lackadaisical."

"The procedures *have* been followed," insisted Dryopus stubbornly. "Not a single ship has ever entered the actual harbor without being inspected. Not one!"

Antonina felt compelled to defend her subordinate. "He's right, Ousanas. And while I have no doubt many ships have come in carrying contraband, that's not the same thing as sabotage. No inspector, no matter how corrupt, is crazy enough to accept a bribe from a Malwa ship loaded with soldiers and weapons."

Ousanas shook his head. "The problem is not with the inspectors. It's with the galleys. By now, those soldiers and sailors are so bored with guard duty they won't be paying attention to anything."

They had reached the palace's aivan, which was doubling for the evening as a weapons repository for the nobility enjoying Khusrau's hospitality. The Axumite weaponry was as distinctive as the Ethiopians themselves, so by the time Antonina and Ousanas came up the Persian soldiers guarding the weapons had sorted them from the rest.

Ousanas himself had brought nothing but his great spear. He waited impatiently while the other Axumite officers donned their armor and attached the baldrics holding their swords. That done, the officers took up their own spears and the entire party began hurrying through the aivan.

Antonina had brought no weapons of any kind herself, and was now regretting the loss. But when she murmured something to that effect, Ousanas smiled grimly.

"Not to worry," he said. "Your maidservant was smart and efficient even before she obtained me for a paramour."

At that moment, they passed through the entrance vault of the aivan and debouched onto the street beyond. Antonina immediately spotted Koutina, squatting among a small horde of servants waiting for their masters and mistresses to emerge from the imperial soiree.

Actually, Koutina was the only one of the servants who was *not* squatting. She was perched comfortably on a piece of luggage standing on end. The handcrafted leather-and-brass valise was something which Koutina was in the habit of carrying with her every time she and Antonina went anywhere beyond the immediate vicinity of the small mansion Antonina had appropriated for her activities. Weeks earlier, she had requested enough money from Antonina to pay for the rather expensive item. Which Antonina had given her readily enough, of course. She had long since come to have complete confidence in Koutina's ability to manage all of Antonina's household affairs.

Antonina *had* wondered about that valise. The thing was rather large, and heavy enough that Koutina had had straps attached to it by which she could hoist the thing onto her shoulders. But the one time Antonina had inquired, Koutina had simply smiled and said it contained the odd necessities which might be required by some unlikely eventuality.

Koutina had spotted them even more quickly than
Antonina had spotted her, and was already hurrying
toward them. Koutina had clearly realized something was
wrong, judging by the frown on her face. And instead
of hoisting the valise onto her shoulders, she was beginning to undo the buckles holding the valise shut.

A sudden suspicion came to Antonina. "Has that
thing got—?"

Ousanas snorted. "A smart and efficient woman, I
said." Scowling, he eyed the western horizon and, then,
the harbor area to the south. "The sun has already set.
And it will be dark tonight, with a new moon. The
Malwa planned this well."

Antonina was still not quite as certain of the situation as Ousanas, but she was relieved to see the
contents of the valise, once Koutina opened it up and
set it before her. Inside the case was Antonina's gun
and her cleaver, along with the cleaver's scabbard.

"I tried to figure out a way to carry your cuirass,"
said Koutina apologetically, "but the leather-maker said
it would require something almost the size of a trunk.
And be very heavy to carry."

"Tell me about it," grumbled Antonina, buckling on
the scabbard. Then, more cheerfully: "It doesn't matter,
Koutina. That damned cuirass is more of a hazard than
a help at sea, anyway. Which is where I'm sure we're
headed. I'm just glad you were foresighted enough to
bring my weapons. Thank you for that."

Koutina reacted to the praise with a simultaneous
smile and frown. Smiling: "You're welcome." Frowning: "You shouldn't be using them at all!" Koutina
pointed an accusing finger at Matthew and Leo: "That's
what they're here for!"

Matthew looked embarrassed. Leo might have
scowled, but it was hard to tell. Leo *always* looked like
he was scowling.

For a moment, Antonina considered summoning a palanquin. But she dismissed the idea immediately. It would take at least three palanquins to carry her bodyguards and the Axumites, along with herself. By the time they were assembled, they could have walked halfway to the harbor. The imperial palace was less than a mile from the docks.

The Axumites had already reached the same conclusion and were starting into a dogtrot. Antonina hurried to keep up with them. That pace was one which Ethiopian soldiers could keep up for hours. Antonina couldn't, but she was sure she could maintain it long enough to reach the harbor.

"I have no intention of mixing myself into the fray." The effort of trotting made the words came out very firmly indeed.

"You always say that," came Koutina's equally firm rejoinder. "And look what happens! At the battle with the Arabs! And you joined the assault on Lady Holi's ship!"

"Not ladylike," insisted Antonina. She was beginning to pant a little.

So was Koutina, but the maidservant wasn't about to let the issue slide. "Promises!" She gazed ahead at the darkness looming over the gulf beyond the harbor. "Are you sure we're going to have to go out on boats?" Gloomily: "I don't swim very well."

"You can stay on the docks."

"Where you go, I go. But are you sure?"

Antonina was about to reply that she wasn't really sure of anything. But, at that moment, the darkness over the waters of the gulf was suddenly streaked by flashes. A bit like horizontal lightning, perhaps.

"I'm sure," she said. "That's Malwa rocket fire. The attack has started."

Chapter 15

They reached the docks just a few minutes later. By the time they got there, Roman officers had already organized at least eight galleys to set out into the harbor. The first of the galleys, in fact, was just beginning to cast off.

"Impressive," stated Ousanas. "The galleys guarding the harbor may have been caught napping, but the rest of your naval forces were alert."

One of the other Axumite officers laughed harshly. "It helps to have a battle erupt, to wake up dozing seamen." He studied the gulf beyond the harbor—what could be seen of it, in the darkness, which was not much—and pronounced: "The three galleys on guard have been badly hammered, I think. I haven't seen a rocket flare in over a minute, and that was only the one."

"Out of action now," agreed Ousanas. "Let's hope the survivors can row their ships ashore. But it doesn't matter." He pointed to the galleys getting ready to leave the docks. "They won't be caught by surprise. That Malwa ship will never make it into the harbor."

Antonina studied the galleys. Each one held upward of two hundred and fifty men, between the rowers and the marines. Like any war galley setting into battle, each ship was crammed with as many men as could possibly fit into it. And, except for the ram bracing at the bow, each galley was built like a cockleshell. With war galleys, almost everything was sacrificed for speed.

Then, her gaze moved further down the docks and came to rest on the *Theodora Victrix*. That ship, a small sailing vessel built primarily to use its fire cannon, used only a small crew. And it was very sturdily built, with a well-designed rocket shield over the bow. The principal "maneuver" of the *Theodora Victrix* in battle was simply to sail directly at the enemy, shrugging off missiles, until it got close enough to bathe them in a gout of hellfire.

The *Victrix* was also ready to cast off. Even though harbor defense was none of its normal duties, the officers and sailors of the ship had also responded to the emergency. Antonina could see Eusebius standing on the dock next to the ship, staring out to sea. The dock area was very well lit, even at night, and Antonina could recognize him easily.

"No," she said decisively. "We'll keep the galleys back, as a last defense, and use the *Victrix*."

She was already starting to hurry toward the *Victrix*, issuing orders as she went to the various naval officers on the docks. Fortunately, the commander of the harbor patrol came up to her at that moment, and she was able to delegate the task of holding back the galleys to him.

"And what about the cannons?" he asked. He pointed at the darkness which was all that could be seen of the gulf beyond the immediate harbor area. "I've had them holding their fire, because there's nothing to see and I was afraid they'd hit our own galleys."

Antonina glanced up at the fortifications above the harbor area. The snouts of a dozen huge cannons glimmered in the lantern-light.

"Keep them loaded and ready," she commanded. "When the time comes for them to start firing, I'll send up a signal rocket. Green flare."

"What'll they shoot at?" asked the commander.

Antonina grinned. "They won't have any trouble spotting the target. Trust me."

The commander nodded and left. Antonina's brief exchange with him had enabled Ousanas and the other Axumites to catch up with her. "Are you mad?" demanded Ousanas. "Why use the *Victrix*? The galleys can handle the matter. Quite easily, I can assure you." One of the other Ethiopians grunted his agreement.

Stubbornly, Antonina shook her head. "I don't doubt it, Ousanas. And then what?"

Seeing the look of incomprehension on his face, she sighed with exasperation. "*Think*, Ousanas." She jerked her head toward the still-unseen Malwa ship. "That ship—this is your own theory, man!—is packed with explosives. Enough to rupture the whole harbor. It's got to be crewed by Mahaveda. Fanatic priests. No one else could be trusted for such a suicidal mission."

Ousanas jerked a little, startled into a sudden understanding of her point. "Once the Mahaveda see they've no chance of reaching the harbor—"

"They'll wait until the galleys are surrounding them and blow the ship," Antonina finished, grimly. Again, she started hurrying toward the *Victrix*. "I doubt if even one of those galleys would stay afloat. Two thousand men—more than that!—would be spilled into the sea at least a mile from shore. Half of them would be dead before they hit the water. Of the rest, we'd lose half in the darkness before they could be rescued."

"At least half," muttered Ousanas, keeping pace with her. Sourly: "Why is it that Roman sailors refuse to learn how to swim? No Axumite soldier is allowed aboard a ship until he can prove—"

His comparison of the relative merits of Roman and Ethiopian sailors was broken off by Eusebius' shout of recognition.

"We're heading out!" Antonina shouted back. Under her breath: "Or whatever the proper damned nautical expression is."

"Don't sneer at proper nautical terms, woman," chuckled Ousanas. "They're all that's going to make this crazy scheme of yours work. Or hadn't you noticed that we'll be sailing before the wind?"

Guiltily, Antonina realized that she hadn't given any thought at all to the matter. She must have made a little start of surprise herself, because Ousanas immediately laughed.

"I thought not!"

They were almost at the *Victrix*. By now, Antonina was starting to pant with the exertion of their race from the palace. But she managed to gasp out: "Will we be able to do it?"

Ousanas grimaced. "The wind's right. And the current will be with us. So we'll be able to sail down on them quickly, while they're struggling to row up into the harbor. But once the contact's made—"

They were at the *Victrix* now. Antonina answered Eusebius' babbled questions by simply grabbing him and marching him ahead of her across the gangplank. By the time she and Ousanas were aboard, Eusebius was clear on his duties and was beginning to issue the needed commands.

Antonina hurried forward and entered the enclosed section of the bow. Inside the heavy and well-built rocket shield, the light cast by the lanterns on the docks and the few on the ship was blocked completely. She groped her way to the vision slits and stared into the distance. Everything in the gulf was pitch-black now. Belatedly, she realized she hadn't given any thought at all to the most basic problem: *how will we spot the enemy?*

Fortunately, Ousanas had thought about it. She heard him entering the shield a few seconds later. "I just checked with Eusebius, Antonina. The *Victrix* carries twenty rockets equipped with flares, for night operations. In addition to the usual signal rockets. We should be able to spot the Malwa ship once we get out of the harbor."

The *Victrix* was getting underway. Antonina could feel the motion of the ship, as well as hear the sounds of the sailors hurrying about their tasks. Eusebius' shrill voice periodically rose above everything else.

Some part of her was saddened to recognize John of Rhodes' training in the confidence with which Eusebius issued his commands. Antonina remembered the first time she met Eusebius, years before, at her estate in Daras. John had employed him to assist in the work of designing the new gunpowder weapons. For all his brilliance as an artificer, young Eusebius had been as shy and socially awkward a man as she had ever met in her life.

No longer. Eusebius would never have more than a portion of John's casual ease of command, true, but he had come very far from where he started. That was only one of the many legacies which John of Rhodes had left behind him, and Antonina took a moment again to grieve his loss.

Only a moment, however. There was a battle to be fought and won.

She turned away from the view-slit and began groping in the darkness. "Help me find the igniters, Ousanas, so we can light the lanterns. They should be in a cabinet around here somewh—never mind."

She'd found the cabinet, and quickly pried it open. Feeling her way, she found one of the ignition devices she was seeking. A few seconds later, the first of the lanterns located inside the shelter was lit, and she was finally able to see something.

The first thing she saw was Koutina, squeezed into the shelter alongside Matthew and Leo.

"What are you doing here?" she demanded.

Koutina smiled shyly, and held up the valise. "You didn't take your gun. Only the cleaver. So I thought I should bring it along. Just in case."

Antonina sighed, half with exasperation and half with affection. "You shouldn't be here at all. But it's too late to do anything about it now. So leave the valise here and get below decks." She looked to Matthew. "See to it, please."

Koutina started to squawk some kind of protest, but Matthew had her ushered out of the shelter before she could finish the first sentence.

The next thing Antonina saw, in the lantern-light, was Ousanas' big grin.

"And what are *you* doing here?" he demanded. "You've got no more business here than she does."

Antonina shook her head irritably. "I could ask the same of you, Ousanas! This is a Roman ship, not an Axumite one."

"I've gotten accustomed to watching out for you," he replied, as he finished lighting the rest of the lanterns. He placed the igniter back in the cabinet and shrugged.

"But I told my officers to stay back on the docks. There's no good reason to risk them on this expedition." He eyed the large, complicated-looking gadget which filled the center of the shelter. "What they know about using Greek fire cannons would fill the world's smallest book."

That comment drew Antonina's own eyes to the fire cannon. With the lanterns lit, the true nature of the "bow shelter" was apparent. She was reminded, forcefully, that the shelter could more accurately be called a "turret." An unmoving one, true. But a turret nonetheless.

For the first time since the crisis started, she felt a trace of hesitation and unease. In truth, although she understood the basic workings of the device, Antonina had no real idea how to operate it under combat conditions. Under any conditions, actually.

At that moment, Eusebius came into the bow shelter. The relaxed and casual glance he gave the fire cannon reassured Antonina. However awkward Eusebius might still be in social situations, he was as adept an artificer and mechanic as any in the world.

"You'll have to operate the cannon," she pronounced.

Eusebius' eyes widened. *Who else?* was the obvious thought behind that startled expression. Antonina found herself forcing down a giggle.

"Good," she pronounced. "That's settled. What do you want me and Ousanas to do?"

Eusebius looked back and forth from each to the other. "You, I mostly just want to stay out of the way, Antonina. Except for telling me what you want done." He eyed Ousanas' spear. "Him, I'd just as soon keep around. Never know. The *Victrix* isn't designed for boarding operations. But—you never know."

"We're *not* going to be doing any boarding, Eusebius. In fact, I want to stay as far away from that oncoming Malwa ship as possible. It's bound to be crammed with gunpowder and every incendiary device known to man."

Eusebius nodded. He'd obviously figured that much out himself. "You just want to torch it, and get as far away as possible before it blows. But the Malwa may have their own plans, and so I can't say I'm sorry to see Ousanas and that spear of his in the area. We only have a handful of marines to fend *off* any boarding attempt."

He came forward, edging his way around Antonina—the fire cannon in the center made the turret a cramped place—and peered through the viewing slit. "Can't see a damn thing. I've got the crew ready to start sending up flares. Probably ought to send up the first one very soon. We've got no idea how close that enemy ship has gotten by now."

"Go ahead and fire it off, then. But not the green one; that's my signal to the battery," said Antonina.

Eusebius worked his way past her again. Just as he reached the open space at the rear of the turret, leading to the deck beyond, a sudden thought came to Antonina.

"Eusebius! I'm puzzled by something. If *we* have flare rockets, why doesn't the battery guarding the harbor? I'd think they could handle bigger ones, in fact."

Again, Eusebius' eyes widened. If anything, he seemed more startled than before. "They could, actually. Much bigger ones. Big enough to reach several miles out to sea and light up the whole area enough for the battery to have a target even at night."

He cleared his throat. "As to why—? Well, the basic reason is that nobody ever thought of it." He ducked his head and scuttled out of the turret.

Ousanas chuckled. "War is too serious a business to leave in the hands of men, Antonina."

"My thoughts exactly!" She turned back to the viewing slit and peered into the darkness. "Mind you, they're handy to have around. When the crude muscular stuff actually happens."

Chapter 16

A few minutes later, the first flare went off. Her face pressed against one of the viewing slits in the shield, Antonina scanned the dark sea looking for any sign of the approaching Malwa suicide ship.

She didn't have very long to spot anything. When the flare erupted, about three hundred feet above the sea, it cast a very satisfactory light over a large area. But the parachute failed to deploy, and the spent rocket plunged into the water after providing only a short moment of illumination.

"Damn the thing!" She turned her head and glared at Eusebius. "What went wrong?"

Eusebius didn't seem greatly perturbed. "What usually happens." He straightened up from his own viewing slit and shrugged. "Those flare rockets are pretty crude, Antonina. Not much more sophisticated, except for the venturi, than the simplest Malwa rockets. Well over half the time, the propellant fires too unevenly—or too hot, or both—and burns through the parachute rigging before the flare goes off."

"Why don't we fix the problem?" she grumbled.

"Not worth it. That'd make for very expensive rockets. The way it is, we can carry plenty of them."

He turned his head and bellowed—shrilled, more precisely—an order for another flare to the seamen waiting at the rocket trough just behind the bow shield. They were obviously expecting the order, and the next flare went up seconds later.

"The trick," said Eusebius softly, as he pressed his eyes back to the slit, "is not to try to scan the whole area. I always assume the rocket is going to malfunction, so I always start by scanning the area just ahead. Then, for the next one, the area to my left. Then—"

He broke off. The second flare erupted—and, again, plunged almost immediately into the sea.

Antonina slapped the side of the shield in frustration. "Couldn't see anything!"

Eusebius was already shrilling another order. Then, turned back again to the viewslit. "Nothing in front of us or to the left. Now we'll see what it looks like to starboard."

Antonina held her breath. Then, erupted in more cursing. Louder, this time. The parachute for the third flare had deployed satisfactorily. But the flare itself failed to ignite, and the only light shed was the faint glow of a still-smoldering rocket fuselage as it drifted gently down to the waves.

"*Another!*" shrilled Eusebius.

But that flare became almost a moot point. Just before Eusebius issued the command, Antonina suddenly saw the enemy vessel. It was well illuminated by the back flash of a rocket volley sent their way by the Malwa. Clearly enough, the three rockets sent up by the Romans had provided the enemy with a target.

"Stupid," muttered Eusebius. "They're still three hundred yards off. They should have waited."

Antonina held her breath. But Eusebius' confidence proved justified. Five of the six rockets fired by the Malwa missed the Roman vessel by a good fifty-yard margin—one of them even exploding in midair almost as soon as it left the enemy ship. The Malwa too, clearly enough, were plagued with malfunctioning missiles.

The last missile caromed off the sea surface and skipped past the *Victrix*, missing the stern by not more than ten feet.

Antonina turned her head and saw Ousanas pressing himself into the entrance of the bow shield. There wasn't much room, with the three-man crew staffing the fire cannon. The Ethiopian aqabe tsentsen grinned at her.

"Getting hot now," he said. "Much cooler in here, behind these splendid shields."

Ironically, the fourth Roman flare went off perfectly. Looking back through her viewslit, Antonina could see that the Malwa ship was now perfectly illuminated.

"You should get back now also, Antonina," muttered Eusebius. His tone was half-apologetic, but firm for all that. "There's really nothing more for you to do. Everything's clear enough from here on. They're struggling against the wind and the current, and we're sailing right for them. Everything works for us now. They have to use oars, which means they can't fire too many more broadsides without losing way completely. And pretty soon we'll be coming at them bow-on anyway. I doubt they'll be able to fire more than two rockets at a time."

Reluctantly, Antonina backed away from the viewslit and began edging her way to the rear. Between the cramped space and her own voluptuous figure, getting past the two fire-cannon handlers on her side was a bit of a chore.

"Good thing you aren't wearing that obscene breastplate of yours," said Ousanas. "Or those men are crippled. Instead of enflamed with passion."

Antonina burst out laughing. The two cannon men

tried to restrain their own laughter, but not with any great success. One of them shook his head ruefully, as he made a last minute adjustment to the complicated machinery of the flamethrower.

Some cool, calculating part of Antonina's mind recognized that their easy humor was a subtle indication of the respect and affection in which she was held by the soldiers and sailors under her command. Whatever resentment they might once have felt, being led by a woman—even if she was the wife of Belisarius—seemed to have vanished over the course of the two years since she had set sail from Constantinople.

And the same part of her mind, as she finally reached the rear of the shelter and squatted next to Ousanas, also finally understood something about her husband. She had often heard Maurice and Belisarius' bodyguards grumble at the general's stubborn insistence on exposing himself to danger. A characteristic which she, also, had always considered nothing more than childishness—even stupidity. But now, examining her own reluctance to leave the viewslit for the relative safety of the rear of the shield, she finally understood. Over the last two years, she too had internalized her own position of power and authority. And found the same profound distaste for ordering other people into danger if she was not prepared to share it herself.

Ousanas seemed to read her thoughts. "It's still stupid," he murmured. "Eusebius is perfectly correct—there's nothing further you can do now."

She stared up at him. Even squatting as they both were, the tall African hunter towered above her.

"You are a truly magnificent man, Ousanas of the lakes," she said softly. "I don't think I've ever told you that. If I weren't in love with Belisarius, I would set my sights on you."

He stared back at her. In another man, the dark eyes would have had a speculative gleam in them. Wondering if her words were a subtle invitation. But Antonina would not have spoken those words to another man. And so the eyes of Ousanas contained nothing but a soft glow of warmth and affection.

"I dare say you'd succeed, too," he chuckled. "You are quite magnificent yourself."

He shook his head, slightly. "But it probably wouldn't work, anyway. I fear with my new-found august status that my eventual marriage will be a thing of state. And I can't really see you as a concubine. A wife or a courtesan, but never a concubine."

"True," she nodded. For a moment, she paused, gauging the sounds of another oncoming Malwa volley. But her now-experienced ear recognized another miss, even before the sailor who had taken her place at the viewslit exclaimed: "Stupid bastards! They're still two hundred yards off. Waste of rockets."

"True," she repeated. Her curiosity was now aroused, and she found a welcome relief in it from the tension of simply waiting for battle to erupt. She cocked her head, smiling.

"But why wouldn't you select a high-placed Roman wife?" she asked. "Not me, of course, but someone else. It would seem a natural choice, given the new realities. I would think—certainly hope—that Axum intends to retain its alliance with Rome even after the Malwa are broken. And I'm quite sure Theodora would be delighted to round up three dozen senators' daughters for you to select from."

She spread her hands, palms up, as if weighing two things in the balance. "Granted that empires and kingdoms are fickle creatures, and not given much to sentiment. But I still can't see where the future holds any serious reason for conflict between Rome and

Ethiopia. We'd gotten along well for two centuries, after all, even before the Malwa drove us into close alliance."

"I agree," said Ousanas. The abrupt forcefulness of the statement, Antonina suspected, was a reflection of Ousanas' own tension at being forced to remain idle while others prepared to fight. "But that's part of the reason why I won't. The truth is, Antonina, there's no real reason for closer ties between Rome and Axum. The same distance that keeps us from being enemies, also makes close friendship unnecessary."

Ousanas paused for a moment, staring at the fire cannon in front of him. Something in the deadly shape of the device seemed to concentrate his thoughts. His expression became sternly thoughtful.

"Eon and I have discussed this at length, many times now. And twice—I'm not sure you even know about this—I spent hours with Belisarius, questioning Aide through him."

Antonina *hadn't* known of those sessions, as it happened, but she wasn't particularly surprised. Ousanas was one of the few people in the world, beyond Belisarius himself, who had "communed" directly with Aide. And so he understood, in a way that almost no one else would, just how encyclopedic was the crystal's knowledge of human history—including the vast centuries and millennia that would have unfolded, had the "new gods" not brought Malwa into existence. Antonina realized that Ousanas, canny as always, would have taken advantage of that opportunity to provide himself with the knowledge he would need as the aqabe tsentsen of Axum.

Translated literally, the term meant "keeper of the fly whisks." But the position was the highest in the Axumite realm, second only to that of the negusa nagast himself. His responsibility, in essence, was to guide the

Ethiopian King of Kings in shaping the destiny of his people.

"Africa is the future of Ethiopia, Antonina. Not Rome, or any other realm of the Mediterranean or Asia."

He spread his own hands, palms down, as if cupping the head of a child. "A vast continent, full of riches. Populated only—except for Ethiopia and the Mediterranean coast—with tribes of hunters and farmers. Many of whom, however, are also skilled iron-workers and miners. Organized and shaped by Ethiopian statecraft, there's a great empire there to be built."

Antonina's eyes widened. "I've never pictured you— or Eon—as conquerors. Neither of you seems to have the, ah, temperament—"

"Not bloodthirsty enough?" he demanded, grinning. Then, with a chuckle: "*Statecraft*, I said."

He shrugged. "I'm quite sure we will have our share of battles with barbarian tribes. But not all that many, truth to tell, and more in the nature of short wars and skirmishes than great campaigns of conquest and slaughter. Keep in mind, Antonina—I am Bantu myself—that Africa is not heavily populated. And there is no great Asian hinterland producing Huns and such to drive the other tribes forward. We expect most of the task to be one for missionaries and traders, not soldiers. Peaceful work, in the main."

He broke off. Another Malwa volley was coming— and would strike home or come close, judging from the sound.

"Two rockets!" shouted the sailor at the viewslit. "One of them—"

An instant later, the shield shook under the impact of a missile. Antonina was a bit startled. Unconsciously, she had been expecting the same deep *booming* sound which she remembered from her experience in the battle outside Charax's harbor the year before. But the *Victrix*'s bow shield was no primitive, jury-rigged thing of leather stretched over poles. This warship was not a hastily converted galley. The *Victrix* had been designed from the keel up for this kind of battle, and the shield was a solid thing of timber clad with metal sheathing. It shrugged off the rocket as easily as a warrior's shield might shrug off a pebble thrown by a child.

"Ha!" shrilled Eusebius. "John was right! They need cannons—big ones, too, not piddly field guns—to break through this thing. And they don't have any!"

The sailor at the viewslit next to him shook his head. Antonina couldn't actually see the grin splitting his face, but she had no doubt it was there. "Not on this miserable priest-ship, anyway. Probably be a different story when we come up against the Malwa main fleet."

He turned his head toward Eusebius, showing his profile to Antonina. He *was* grinning. "But that's for a later day."

The sailor's grin faded. "Captain, I can handle this from here on. We're only a hundred yards off. Better see to the cannon. You're still the only one who can really use it very well."

Eusebius nodded. Watching, Antonina was struck by the little exchange. A different commander might have taken umbrage at such a semi-order coming from a subordinate. But although Eusebius had, more or less, become comfortable in his new role as a ship captain, he still had the basic habits and instincts of an artisan accustomed to working with others.

She didn't think John would have approved, really. But John was gone, and Antonina herself was not much concerned over the matter. She suspected that Eusebius' methods would probably work just as well.

And it was not her business, anyway. She forced her eyes away from Eusebius and looked at Ousanas. "Continue," she said. She spoke the word so forcefully that she was reminded, again, of her own tension.

"Not much else to say, Antonina. Axum has slowly been extending its rule to the south anyway, over the past two centuries. But heretofore the process was basically unplanned and uncoordinated. Most of our attention was focused on the Red Sea and southern Arabia. We will retain those, of course. But we will seek no further expansion in that direction. The Arab farmers and townsmen and merchants of Yemen and the Hijaz are content enough with our rule. But if we press further, we would simply embroil ourselves in endless conflicts with the bedouin of the interior—not to mention the certainty of an eventual clash with Persia. No point to any of it!"

He broke off. Another rocket volley. Both rockets, this time, struck the shield. And both were deflected just as easily and harmlessly.

"So after the war with Malwa," Ousanas resumed, "we will concentrate on the African interior—and do it properly. We will start by sending an expedition, led by myself, to incorporate the land between the great lakes which is my own homeland. That is the first step—along with seizing and settling the east African coast. At least as far south as the Pangani river. We will also seize the island of Zanzibar and build a fortress there. And we will found a new city on the coast, which will be destined to become a great seaport."

He smiled whimsically. "There are definite advantages, you understand, to Aide's knowledge of the future. Eon has even decreed that we will give that city the name it would have had, centuries from now. Mombasa."

He paused for a moment, his eyes becoming slightly

unfocused. "The thing is, Eon and I are also thinking far into the future. We will not live to see it, of course—neither us nor our great-grandchildren—but we think our plans will eventually produce a very different Africa than the one which existed in the old future. In that future, Axum became isolated very soon by the Moslem conquests. And so, instead of being the conduit into Africa for that Mediterranean civilization of which we are becoming a part, Ethiopia retreated into the highlands. And there it remained, century after century, still more or less intact—but playing no further role in the history of the world or even Africa."

He cocked his head, gauging the sounds of the next Malwa volley. They were very close now, and both rockets missed entirely. Clearly enough, the priests manning the rocket troughs were getting rattled.

Eusebius and one of the sailors were now wrestling with the fire cannon's barrel, swiveling it to starboard. Unlike the rigid, single-piece construction of a normal cannon, the flamethrower was designed in such a way that the barrel could be positioned in any one of five locations, covering an arc of ninety degrees, without moving the main body of the device. One of the other sailors was removing the shield covering the rearmost firing slit on the starboard side. Eusebius, following Antonina's earlier terse instructions, intended to sail the *Victrix* right down the length of the Malwa galley, bathing it in hellfire as it passed. Hopefully, by the time the ship exploded, the *Victrix* would have sailed past far enough to avoid any catastrophic damage. Unless—

Again, Ousanas seemed to read Antonina's thoughts. "Let's hope one of those damned priests doesn't decide to blow the ship while we're alongside," he muttered. Then, a bit more brightly: "But probably not, since we're only one ship—and they'll have no way of knowing you are aboard."

"Or you," she retorted. "You *are* Axum's aqabe tsentsen. A Mahaveda might decide that was a satisfactory prize to take to hell with him."

Ousanas chuckled. "In the dark of night? Just another heathen black savage, that's all." He took Antonina's hand in his own and squeezed it. Then, gently, turned her wrist over and opened his palm. Her small hand, dusky-Egyptian though it was, was pale across the breadth of his own hand, black with African color.

"It means little to us, in our day," he mused, staring down at the contrast. "But a day will come—would have, at least—when that will not be so. A day when milk-white north Europeans, barbarians no longer but in some ways even more barbarous, will enslave Africans and claim that the difference in race is justification enough. A claim which they will be able to make because, for over a millennium, Africa remained isolated from world civilization."

He shook his head, smiling slightly. "Isolation is a bad thing, for a people as much as a person. So Eon and I, as best we can, will see to it that it never happens. Ethiopia's new destiny is to mother a different Africa. And I— "

His smile spread into a grin. "I am destined, I fear, to marry some half-savage creature who is even now squatting by the edge of one of the great lakes. But whose father can claim to be the 'great chief' of the land." He sighed. "Hopefully, I will be able to convince the creature to learn how to read. Or, at least, not to use my books for kindling."

"*Get ready!*" shrilled Eusebius. One of the sailors began frenziedly working the lever which filled the fire cannon's chamber. From beyond the shield, Antonina could hear the indistinct shrieks of Mahaveda priests shouting their own orders. She thought she hoped— to detect confusion in those sounds.

But, for the moment, she blocked all of that from her mind. She would give that moment to the man named Ousanas, for whom, over the years, she had come to feel a great loving friendship.

"You will do well," she whispered. "And I have no doubt the girl will find you just as magnificent as I do."

He grinned, gave her hand a last little squeeze, and rose to his feet. Then, reaching over and grasping the great spear which he had left propped securely against the wall of the shield, he turned toward the entrance facing aft.

"First, we must survive this battle. And I suspect the Malwa priests will be pouring over the side onto our decks." His lip curled. "Screaming refugees, pretending to be fierce boarders."

Antonina said nothing. She just basked, for a few seconds, in her enjoyment at watching Ousanas move. Antonina had always had a purely sensuous side, which reveled in the sight of handsome and athletic men. And, in the case of her husband, who was one himself, the feel of such a male body.

But no man, in her life, had ever displayed such pure masculine grace and power as Ousanas. Watching him move reminded her of nothing so much as the Greek legends of Achilles and Ajax. So, for those few seconds, Antonina was able to forget all her tension in the simple pleasure of admiration.

"*Now!*" shrilled Eusebius. The sailor pumping the lever ceased; another turned a valve; Eusebius himself—this was the most dangerous task—ignited the deathspew gouting from the barrel.

"Just as I said," Antonina murmured to herself, "they're so handy to have around when the crude stuff starts happening."

Chapter 17

The interior of the bow shield, despite its small apertures, was suddenly filled with the reflected light of the fire cannon's effects. Antonina realized, even before she heard Eusebius' shout of triumph, that the very first blast must have struck the target perfectly.

"Like painting with fire!" shrieked Eusebius gleefully. "Look at it burn!"

Before his last words were even spoken, the sound of screams came through the shield, piercing Antonina's ears.

Mahaveda priests who had been positioned at the bow, she realized. *Suddenly turned into so many human torches.*

For all the horror in the thought, Antonina felt not even a twinge of remorse. Truth be told, with a few exceptions such as Bishop Anthony Cassian—Patriarch Anthony, he was now—Antonina had never been fond of any kind of priest, even Christian ones. She had been denounced by such too many times, in her reprobate youth.

Mahaveda priests had all the vices of any clerics, and none of their virtues. Their cult was a bastard and barbaric offshoot of Hinduism, more savage than that of any pagan tribe, and with the added evil which the sophistication of civilized India provided.

Burn in hell, then. As far as Antonina was concerned, the Mahaveda priests were finding their just reward.

During the few seconds which had elapsed, Eusebius and his cannon crew had been working feverishly. The cannon's fire-chamber was refilled; the sailor pumping the lever ceased abruptly; the valve was reopened by his mate. In those few seconds, Antonina realized, the *Victrix* must have carried alongside the *Circe*'s beam.

"Again!" cried Eusebius. *Ignition.*

Another flare filled the interior of the bow shield, brighter this time. Antonina knew in the instant that the hideous weapon had struck true yet again. More screaming filtered through the shield. Less distant.

She heard Ousanas mutter: "They'll be coming now. No choice." The aqabe tsentsen, still standing in the rear entrance of the shield, hefted his great spear.

Antonina's gaze was torn away from Eusebius and his men working at the cannon. For the first time, through the opening in the rear, she was able to see the destruction wreaked by the fire cannon. The *Circe* slid into view. The bow of the Greek merchant vessel seized by the Malwa was wreathed in flames. Even as she watched, a Mahaveda priest—she assumed it was a priest; hard to tell, from the way he was burning—stumbled on the railing and plunged into the sea.

"Again!" *Ignition.* Another flare. Most of the starboard side of the enemy vessel, Antonina realized, was now a raging inferno. More of the *Circe* slid into her view.

She hissed. Whether through deliberate effort or simply accident, the two ships were almost touching. Not more than five or six feet separated them—close enough to pose the danger of fire spreading.

A slight motion caught her eye. Antonina saw that Ousanas was shifting his stance. Clearly enough, the African was getting ready to fight.

For a moment, Antonina was puzzled. Granted, the deck of the *Circe* was level with that of the *Victrix*. Granted, also, the two ships were close enough for boarders to leap across. But—

What enemy could possibly hurl their bodies through that inferno?

The answer came almost as soon as the question. Mahaveda priests.

Fanatics. This was a suicide mission in the first place.

Antonina scrambled to her knees and began opening the valise. Before she even managed to lay hands on her gun, she caught sight in the corner of her eye of the first priest leaping onto the *Victrix*.

The sight froze her, for an instant. The Mahaveda was like a demon—screaming and waving a sword—burning from head to foot. His garments were afire, and his face was already blackened and peeling away. She realized he must have been almost blind by now.

The priest managed to land on his feet. He stood for perhaps a second, before Ousanas leapt forward and decapitated him with a great sweep of his spear. The aqabe tsentsen was such a powerful man that he was quite capable of using that spear like a Goth barbarian would use a two-handed sword. The more so since the blade of the spear was a huge leaf, fully eighteen inches in length and as sharp as a razor.

Antonina started to rise, the gun in her hands, but Matthew shoved her back down with a hand on her shoulder.

"Stay here," he hissed. Then, as if realizing the pointlessness of that advice, the cataphract shook his head and added: "Just stay behind us, will you? Back us up if it's needed—but stay *behind* us."

That said, Matthew surged out of the bow shield. Leo had already charged onto the deck and was swinging his mace at another priest hurling himself through the flames. The heavy weapon, driven by Leo's great strength, swatted the priest back against the hull of the *Circe*. The Mahaveda seemed to stick there for a moment, before his body dropped into the small gap between the ships. Antonina could hear the simultaneous sound of a splash and a hiss. That priest's clothing had also been afire.

By the time Antonina got to her feet and came out of the bow shield, holding her double-barreled firearm, the battle on the deck was in full fury. What seemed like a horde of priests was pouring over the side, matched only by Ousanas and her two bodyguards. *Only . . .*

Antonina almost burst into laughter. *Only . . .*

Three giants, great warriors one and all, matched against a tribe of troglodytes—all of whose experience at "combat" had been practiced in a torture chamber.

For a few seconds, she was mesmerized by the sight. Ousanas was in the middle, flanked by Leo and Matthew. His weapon flicked and stabbed like lightning, spearing one priest after another—half of them while still in midair. The aqabe tsentsen's skill was as great as his strength, too. Somehow he managed to land each strike without jamming the blade in bone or flesh. Most of the spear thrusts took the enemy in their throats, upending them into the sea while it spilled their lifeblood.

Matthew, with his spatha, and Leo, with his mace, made no attempt to match that precision. Nor had they any need to do so. Matthew's blade hacked bodies into pieces and Leo's warclub smashed them aside entirely.

Several of the *Victrix*'s sailors were now rushing up, swords in hand, prepared to support the three men fending off the boarders. Antonina shouted—"*Stay back! Stay back!*"—and fiercely waved them away. The sailors would be more of a hindrance than a help, she knew. In those close quarters, they would simply be an obstruction to the fighting room needed by Ousanas and Leo and Matthew.

The urgency of that task brought home to Antonina that she, also, was not thinking clearly. The three men fighting off the boarders did not need her help so much as they needed her to take charge of the situation.

Quickly, she scanned the scene. The Malwa ship was now engulfed in flames. Clearly enough, the few priests she could see frantically trying to quell the fires would not succeed. The *Circe* was doomed. No chance that the Malwa could reach the harbor and blow it up.

The danger which *did* remain was that the flames would reach the powderkegs which Antonina was certain filled every inch of the Malwa ship's hold. Unless the *Victrix* was well away by that time, she and everyone on her would join the Malwa in the ensuing destruction.

True, that would take some time. Most of the now-roaring inferno came from burning sails and rigging, not the *Circe*'s hull. By the time the fire burned through enough of the hull to reach the powderkegs, the *Victrix* could be a mile off.

Unless some priest realizes . . .

A vivid image flashed through her mind of a Mahaveda fanatic in the hold, bringing a torch to the powder. *Fanatics. And it was a suicide mission, anyway.*

She turned her head. Eusebius was no longer working at the fire cannon, but was staring at her. His face was as pale as Antonina suspected her own to be.

"Get us out of here!" she shouted.

Eusebius' face seemed to pale still further. He spread his hands in a helpless gesture.

Antonina cursed herself silently. She had forgotten that, taking charge of the fire cannon, Eusebius was no longer in control of the ship.

She turned back, facing the stern, her eyes seeking the helmsman. By now, the stern had drawn even with that of the *Circe*. Ousanas and the two cataphracts had kept moving aft down the side of the *Victrix*, fighting off the boarders doing the same on their own as the two ships passed each other. She saw two last boarders jump from stern to stern at the same instant that she spotted the helmsman of the *Victrix*.

The two priests went for the helmsman, but Ousanas intercepted them. A sweep and a thrust, and both Mahaveda were down. One dying on the deck, the other in the sea.

Antonina took no comfort at all from the sight. The fact that the priests had tried to kill the helmsman, while ignoring the onrushing Ousanas, suggested that the Mahaveda had already come to the same conclusion she had. No hope of accomplishing their original mission remained. That left . . . simply taking as many enemies with them as possible.

She started shouting at the helmsman, but broke off before uttering more than a few words. Clearly enough, the man understood the danger as well as she did. Nor, for that matter, was there much he could do that he wasn't doing already. The *Victrix* had been running before the wind as it was. No point in changing directions now.

She stared at the receding enemy ship. The *Circe* was no longer anything but a floating bonfire. There was not a chance that any man on her deck would still be alive within a minute or two. Nor, she thought— hoped—was there much chance that any of them would be able to fight their way across the deck to the hatchways leading to the hold.

That still left the possibility that at least one priest had stayed in the hold throughout the short battle, ready to ignite the powder if necessary.

Possibility?

Antonina winced. She was absolutely *certain* that a priest had been stationed there. Several of them, in fact—each one charged to make sure his fellows would not flinch at the very end when the time came to commit suicide. That had been the Mahaveda plan all along, after all. The only thing that had changed was that Antonina's intervention had prevented the *Circe* from reaching the harbor before they did so.

Ousanas trotted up to her, his spear trailing blood across the deck. "Only thing we can hope for is that they're still confused down there." Clearly enough, he had reached the same conclusion she had.

"One of the few times I've ever been glad those Mahaveda bastards are such fanatics," he said, grimly. "They'll be reluctant to blow it, not having reached their target. So until they're certain . . ."

She stared at him. Then, in a half-whisper: "They're *bound* to know that by now."

Ousanas shook his head. "Don't be too sure of that, Antonina. I got a better look at the conditions on the *Circe* than you did." He glanced at Eusebius, who had emerged from the bow shield and was charging back to the stern. The glance was very approving.

"That devil cannon of his must have hit them like a flood of fury. A tidal wave of fire and destruction. As confusing as it was horrible. I doubt the Malwa command structure survived more than a few seconds."

Again, he shook his head. "So . . . who knows? The priests in the hold may have been isolated from the beginning. And *still* don't know what's happening—and have no way of getting on deck to find out for themselves. Even Mahaveda fanatics will hesitate to kill themselves, when they're not sure what they'd be accomplishing by doing so."

Eusebius was shouting shrill orders. Some of the *Victrix's* sailors started dousing the stern of the ship with water kept in barrels. Others began dousing the rigging. That *should* have been done before the battle even started, Antonina realized. But everything had happened too quickly.

It was getting harder to see anything. The *Circe* was now two hundred yards away, and the fierce light cast by the burning ship was no longer enough to do more than vaguely illuminate the deck of her own ship. But there was still enough light for her to see that several of the sailors, apparently at Eusebius' command, were standing ready with hatchets and axes to cut away the *Victrix's* rigging.

"What are they doing?" she demanded. "The *last* thing we want is to lose our own sails."

Ousanas did not share her opinion. Instead, he growled satisfaction. "Smart man, Eusebius. He's figured out already that most of the explosives on board the *Circe* will be incendiaries." For a moment, he studied the ever more distant enemy ship. "We're far enough away, by now, that we can probably survive the actual shock of the explosion. But we'll soon be engulfed in fire ourselves. If we can cut away the rigging fast enough—that's what'll burn the worst—we might be able to keep the *Victrix* afloat. Maybe."

Something of Antonina's confusion must have shown in her face. Ousanas chuckled.

"Strange, really. You're normally so intelligent. *Think,* Antonina."

He pointed back at the *Circe.* The Malwa ship was no more than a bonfire in the distance, now. "Their plan was to blow it up in the harbor, right? In order to do what?"

She was still confused. Ousanas chuckled again.

"Think, woman! The Malwa aren't crazy, after all. Insanely fanatic, yes, but that's not the same thing as actual lunacy. The harbor *itself*—even the buildings surrounding it—is built far too solidly to be destroyed by any amount of gunpowder which could be stowed on a single ship. Which means that their real target was not the harbor but the ships in it. And the best way to destroy shipping is with flame."

Finally understanding his point, she heaved a small sigh of relief. She had been imagining the Malwa ship as a giant powderkeg, which, when it exploded, would produce a large enough concussion to shatter everything within half a mile at least. But if most of the explosives were designed as incendiaries . . .

Matthew and Leo came up, looming above her in the darkness. Ousanas placed his hands on Antonina's shoulders, turned her around—gently, but she could no more have resisted him than she could have a titan—and propelled her back into the bow shield.

"So *you*," he murmured cheerfully, "will ride out the coming firestorm in the safest place available."

Once they were inside the shelter, with Matthew and Leo crowding behind, he added even more cheerfully: "Me, too. The thought of losing Africa's future because of a damned Malwa plot is unbearable, don't you think?"

Antonina put her gun back in the valise and closed it. Then, still kneeling, she looked up at the aqabe tsentsen. As she expected, Ousanas was grinning from ear to ear.

She started to make some quip in response. Then Ousanas' figure was backlit by what seemed to be the end of the universe. Armageddon's fire and fury.

Fortunately, Ousanas was quick-thinking enough to kneel next to her and shelter her in his arms before the shock wave arrived. Matthew was quick-witted enough to start to do the same.

Leo, alas, had never been accused of quick-wittedness of any kind, save his animal reflexes in battle. So the concussion caught him standing, and sent him sprawling atop Ousanas and Matthew, with Antonina at the bottom of the pile.

But perhaps it was just as well. Antonina was too busy trying not to suffocate under the weight of three enormous men to feel any of the terror caused by the firestorm which followed.

The next morning, at daybreak, Roman galleys found the *Victrix*. The vessel was still afloat, but drifting helplessly in the sea. It had proved necessary to cut away all the rigging before the fire was finally brought under control. Most of the sailors had suffered bad burns—which two of them might not survive—but were otherwise unharmed.

The ship itself . . .

"It'll take us weeks to refit her," complained Eusebius, as he watched his sailors attach the tow rope thrown from one of the galleys.

"You don't have 'weeks,'" snarled Antonina. "Two weeks, the most."

Eusebius' eyes widened with surprise. "Two weeks? But our campaign's not supposed to start until—"

"Change of plans," snarled Antonina. She glared to the east. The direction of the Malwa enemy, of course. Also, the direction in which Belisarius' army was to be found, marching slowly toward the Indus.

"Assuming my husband listens to the voice of sweet wifely reason," she added. Still snarling.

Chapter 18
THE JAMUNA
Summer, 533 A.D.

Link awaited Narses on Great Lady Sati's luxury barge, moored just downstream from the fork of the Jamuna and Betwa rivers. The fact that the monster from the future had traveled to meet *him* made the already anxious eunuch more anxious still. Link rarely left the imperial capital of Kausambi. To the best of Narses' knowledge, it had never done so since it had become—resident, lodged, whatever grotesque term might be applied—within the body of the young woman who had once been Lady Sati.

As he was escorted up the ramp leading to the barge's interior by two of Link's special assassins, Narses forced himself to settle down. If he was to survive the coming hour, his nerves would have to be as cold as ice. Fortunately, a long lifetime of palace intrigue and maneuver had trained him in the methods of calmness.

So he paid little attention to his surroundings as the black-clad, silently pacing assassins guided him through the interior of the barge. A general impression of opulence, almost oppressive in its luxurious

197

weight, was all that registered. His mind and soul were preoccupied entirely with settling themselves within his heart.

A small, scarred, stony heart that was. With room in it for a single thought and purpose, no other.

The truth only. Narses is what I care about. Nothing more.

He entered a large chamber within the barge, somewhere deep in its bowels. At the far end, on a slightly elevated platform, sat Great Lady Sati. She was resting on an ornately carved chair made entirely of ivory. Her slender, aristocratic hands were draped loosely over the armrests. The veil was drawn back from her face, exposing the cold beauty of the young flesh.

In front of her, kneeling, were four immense men. They were naked from the waist up, holding equally naked swords in their huge hands. Great tulwars, those were. Two other such men were standing in the corners of the chamber, behind Great Lady Sati. Like the two assassins—and two others who were positioned in the corners of the room behind Narses himself—the giants were of Khmer stock. Nothing of India's flesh resided in those men.

But Narses paid them almost no attention at all. As soon as he entered the room, his eyes were drawn to the man sitting on a slightly less majestic chair directly to Great Lady Sati's right. Nanda Lal, that was. One of Emperor Skandagupta's first cousins, and the chief spymaster of the Malwa Empire.

The sight of Nanda Lal caused Narses' already-frigid soul to freeze completely. The sensation of relief was almost overwhelming.

Familiar ground, then. So be it.

A small stool was placed in the center of the floor, atop the rich carpet, perhaps ten feet from the elevated platform. Just close enough to Great Lady Sati and

Nanda Lal to enable easy conversation, but allowing the giant bodyguards the space needed to maintain a shield before Link's human sheath.

Narses did not wait for an invitation. He simply moved to the stool and took a seat. Then, hands placed on knees, waited in silence.

The silence went on for perhaps a minute, as Link and Nanda Lal scrutinized him. Then Great Lady Sati spoke.

"Are you loyal to Malwa, Narses?"

The eunuch found it interesting that Sati's voice had none of the eerie quality which his spies had reported to him, from indirect reports. It was simply the voice of a young woman. Pleasant, if chilly and aloof.

"No." He thought to elaborate and expand, but discarded the notion. *The truth only!* Elaboration—expansion even more so—always carried the risk of wandering into falsehood.

"Not at all?"

"Not in the least."

"Are you loyal only to yourself?"

"Of course." A trace of bitterness crept into his voice. "Why would it be otherwise?"

"We have treated you well," interjected Nanda Lal, a bit angrily. "Showered you with wealth and honors."

Narses shrugged. "You have made me the spymaster for your finest general, and sent me off into a life of hardship and danger. Traipsing across half of Asia—at my age!—with enemies on all sides. The wealth sits idle in small coffers, locked within the emperor's vaults, while I live in a tent."

Nanda Lal shifted his weight in the chair, clutching the arm rests. He was a heavy man, and muscular. The chair creaked slightly in protest.

"I'm sure you've managed to fill your own coffers with bribes and stolen treasure!" he snapped.

Narses rasped a harsh chuckle. "Of course. Quite a bit, too, if I say so myself."

Nanda Lal's dark face flushed with open anger at the sneering disrespect which lurked just beneath the eunuch's words. His heavy lips began to peel back from his teeth in a snarl. But before he could utter a word, Great Lady Sati spoke. And, this time, in *the voice*.

All thoughts of derision and banter fled from Narses, hearing that voice. It was sepulchral beyond any human grave or tomb. The words were still spoken with the tone produced by a young woman's throat and mouth; but the sound of them was somehow as vast and cavernous as eternity. This, Narses knew, was the true voice of the *thing* called Link.

"DESIST, NANDA LAL. YOUR ANGER IS POINTLESS AND STUPID."

Link's young-woman-shell kept its eyes on Narses, giving the Malwa spymaster not so much as a glance. The eyes, too, seemed as empty as a moonless, cloudcast night.

"YOUR SOLE LOYALTY IS TO YOURSELF, NARSES. YOUR HEART CANNOT BE WON BY ANY CAUSE, YOUR DEVOTION BY ANY HONOR OR SENTIMENT, YOUR MIND BY ANY TREASURE. YOU SEEK, NOW AS AT ALL TIMES, SIMPLY YOUR OWN ADVANTAGE."

There didn't seem to be anything to say in response. So Narses said nothing. Link studied him in silence for quite some time. Narses had never in his life felt so closely scrutinized.

"NO. I MISJUDGED. THERE IS SOMETHING MORE. SOMETHING YOU ARE HIDING."

Narses' hands did not so much as twitch, resting on his knees. He simply leaned forward slightly and replied:

"Yes. I enjoy the game itself. Perhaps even more,

I sometimes think, than the advantage it brings me.
I hide that from sight, because it gives me yet another
advantage. People assume me to be driven by ambition. Which is true enough, of course. But ambition
is ultimately nothing more than a tool itself."

Silence reigned, for a few seconds. Then:

"YES. YOU REVEL IN THAT SENSE OF
SUPREMACY. AN EMPTY MAN—NO MAN AT
ALL, BY HUMAN RECKONING—WHO FILLS
HIMSELF WITH HIS ABILITY TO SURPASS ALL
OTHERS."

Narses bowed his head slightly.

"WE CANNOT THEREFORE TRUST YOU IN
THE LEAST. NO MORE THAN WE COULD A
SWORD WHOSE HILT WAS SMEARED WITH
GREASE."

"Even less," snorted Narses. "A sword has neither
a brain nor a will. It will twist in your hand only from
mishap or accident, or carelessness. I can be counted
on to do it from my own volition."

"YES. TREASON WHICH REVELS IN TREA-
SON. NOT BECAUSE IT IS TREASON BUT
BECAUSE IT IS THE GREATEST GAMBIT IN
THE ULTIMATE GAME."

Again, Narses made that little bow of the head. A
master acknowledging another, and one perhaps greater
than he.

"SO BE IT. YOU THINK YOURSELF IMPERVI-
OUS, BECAUSE NOTHING CAN THREATEN YOU
EXCEPT PAIN AND DEATH. BUT I WILL HAVE
A HOSTAGE, NARSES."

Nothing in Narses' face or body—he would have
sworn it!—registered so much as a twitch. Though
somewhere through his icy, barren soul ran a sudden
hot spike of terror. *Ajatasutra. My son!*

"THERE IS SOMEONE CLOSE TO YOU,

THEN? YOU ARE NOT QUITE SO DETACHED FROM HUMANKIND AS YOU PRETEND."

Narses tried to speak, but found the words frozen in his throat. He could think of no truth, nor lie, which could shield him against that inhuman perception.

Nanda Lal spoke again. "We will find out who it is," he said, through tight teeth. "Then—rest assured—"

"BE SILENT. I WILL NOT SAY IT AGAIN. DO NOT SPEAK WITHOUT MY PERMISSION."

Nanda Lal's dark face seemed to pale. He pressed his heavy body back into the chair.

As before, the eyes of the shell called Great Lady Sati had never left Narses' face, even while uttering that apparently deadly threat. She spoke again, her words moving directly from the threat to Nanda Lal to the promise to Narses.

"SUCH A HOSTAGE WOULD BE MEANINGLESS. NARSES WAS CLOSE TO EMPRESS THEODORA ALSO. YET HE BETRAYED HER SOON ENOUGH. NO. I WILL HAVE THE ONLY HOSTAGE WHICH MEANS ANYTHING TO THIS MAN."

Her left hand lifted from the armrest and made a slight gesture. Narses could sense one of the assassins behind him coming forward, though he could not actually hear any footsteps on the heavy carpet.

A hand seized his neck. Not harshly, not with the intent to manhandle, simply to hold him still. A moment later, sharp pain lanced in the back of his head. A blade of some kind, he realized, had penetrated his flesh and cut out a small portion. He could feel blood slowly trickling down his back.

The assassin retreated. Narses stared at Link.

"HAVE YOU EVER HEARD OF A 'CLONE,' NARSES? NO? IT IS A HUMAN BEING MADE ENTIRELY FROM ANOTHER. A PERFECT COPY.

A MAN GROWN LIKE A BUD. YOU, A EUNUCH
WHO CAN HAVE NO CHILDREN, CAN STILL
SIRE YOURSELF. WITH NO WOMB OR WOMAN
NEEDED FOR THE PURPOSE."

The *thing's* eyes left Narses for a moment, looking
behind her.

"TAKE THE FLESH AND DEPOSIT IT IN THE
ICE CHEST. THEN RETURN." The young-woman/
empty-void eyes returned to Narses. "I WILL HAVE
IT GROWN, NARSES. WHILE YOU GO ABOUT
MY WORK, I WILL RAISE THE HOSTAGE YOU
HAVE GIVEN ME. BETRAY MALWA, AND YOU
WILL LOSE YOURSELF. YOU WILL BE, IN THE
END, AS EMPTY AS YOU HAVE ALWAYS
THOUGHT YOURSELF TO BE. CONSIDER THAT,
EUNUCH OF ROME. I—ONLY I—CAN GIVE YOU
ETERNITY."

Narses did not bow his head, this time, so much as
lower it. A gesture not of respect so much as defeat.

"WE UNDERSTAND EACH OTHER, THEN.
AND NOW, I HAVE A TASK FOR YOU."

The voice changed, in that instant, back to the voice
of Great Lady Sati. And in that voice it remained, for
the following minutes, as it explained to Narses the
nature of his new assignment.

After Great Lady Sati finished, Narses immediately
shook his head.

"It is a bad plan. Unworkable. Rana Sanga will not
believe it for a moment."

Nanda Lal began to speak, then glanced apprehen-
sively at Sati. She raised her hand in a stilling gesture.
But the motion conveyed no threat. Simply an admo-
nition to listen, before advancing an argument.

"Continue, Narses," she commanded.

"He has met Belisarius in person, Great Lady Sati.

Indeed, he has spent many hours in his company. No matter what evidence I leave, he will not believe for an instant that the Roman general ordered the death of his family. Instead, his suspicion will rest upon the Malwa dynasty. And become confirmed, the moment you advance the proposal of marriage. Trust me in this, if nothing else. The plan—*as conceived*—is unworkable."

Silence. Then:

"You have an alternative, I see. What is it?"

Narses shrugged. "For your purpose, there is no need to make Sanga suspect Belisarius directly. Simply to arouse his anger and rage at the chaos which the war has brought. India is in turmoil now, nowhere more so than the western borderlands. Summon Rana Sanga's family to Kausambi, at the emperor's command. Hostages themselves, to assure Sanga's loyalty along with Damodara's. Send a small force from the emperor's Ye-tai bodyguard battalions to escort them. Perhaps a dozen men. Then, along the route—while they are still in Rajputana—"

"Yes!" exclaimed Nanda Lal. His earlier anger at Narses vanished, in the excitement of the scheme. "Yes. That will be perfect. The caravan is attacked by brigands."

"Better, I think." Narses cocked his head, thinking. "*Kushan* brigands. As the loyalty of the Kushans unravels, due as much as anything to Belisarius' cunning, many of them have turned to banditry. And Kushan deserters make ferocious bandits. Far more believable that they would attack such a caravan than any common dacoits. Not to mention *succeed* in the attack. The treasure looted, Sanga's wife hideously abused, herself and the children slain afterward. Their bodies left for carrion eaters, mingled with the butchered corpses of their Ye-tai guards."

Narses shrugged. It was a small, modest gesture. "I imagine I can probably even find one or two deserters from the Roman army to include in the bandit force. Just enough—there will be eyewitnesses to the attack, of course—to weight Sanga's anger even further."

"He will be angry at us as well," opined Nanda Lal, pursing his lips. "After all, had *we* not summoned his family out of the safety of his palace . . ."

"That is meaningless," stated Great Lady Sati. "Sanga's resentment we can tolerate. So long as his rage remains unfocused, it will channel itself into the war and his oath. When the time comes, he will accept the marriage."

The slim young-woman's hands made a small curling gesture, indicating the entire body to which they belonged. "He will feel no sentiment toward this sheath. But we do not need his sentiment. The sheath is well-shaped, and has been well trained. It will arouse his lust, when the time comes. And when the children arrive, soon enough thereafter, his sentiment will have another place to become attached. That is sufficient for the purpose."

Great Lady Sati stared at Narses for a moment. Then: "Do it, traitor. And remember my hostage."

Narses arose and bowed deeply from the waist. After straightening, he looked at Nanda Lal.

"The Ye-tai general Toramana, as I'm sure you know, is the commander of the troop which escorted me here. I saw to that. I suggest this would be a good time for you to interview him. There are . . . excellent possibilities there, I think."

Nanda Lal nodded. Narses' lips twisted into a bitter little smile.

"You'll have spies on me also, of course. So let's save some time. I need to pay a visit on Lady Damodara in any event, to give her a parcel from her husband. Beyond that—"

He transferred his eyes to Great Lady Sati. "It would be best, in any event, if I set up my headquarters in Lady Damodara's palace. In order to organize this maneuver, I will need to see any number of people. Better to have such folk coming in and out of *her* palace than any other. Even if Sanga stumbles across any knowledge of my doings, he will simply assume I was acting on behalf of Damodara himself. And he will never suspect Damodara of such a cruel deed."

Great Lady Sati did not even pause. "I agree. Do it."

Nanda Lal chuckled. "It hardly matters, Narses. I don't have to bother to have you followed. You think I don't have spies inside Lady Damodara's palace?"

Narses regarded him calmly. "I'm sure you do. I am also sure that within three days of my arrival, those spies will be expelled from the house. Those who are not dead."

Nanda Lal froze, his eyes widening. Narses snorted—very faintly—and bowed to Malwa's overlord. "I'm sure you understand the logic, Great Lady Sati."

"It is obvious. There must be *no* suspicion. Your loyalty to Damodara must be unquestioned. Do not hesitate to kill all of Nanda Lal's spies, Narses. But do it shrewdly."

In the end, Narses did not kill all the spies. He saw no reason to kill the two cooks. Expulsion would serve as well, theft being the excuse—as it happened, a valid one. They *were* thieves.

He did not even bother to expel the two maids. He simply saw to it that their duties were restricted to the laundry, in a different wing of the palace than that where Lady Damodara and the children had their bedrooms. It was a large palace. There was no way the maids could find their way unobserved to the only other place in the palace which Narses needed to keep secret. The cellar deep below where a tunnel was being slowly extended.

He did have the two guards in Nanda Lal's employ assassinated, along with one of the majordomo's assistants. The guards simply had their throats slit while they slept, the night Ajatasutra arrived at the palace. The assistant, on the other hand, had been a retainer of Damodara's family since boyhood. So, before his own demise, Narses thought it was fitting to show the traitor the greatest of the secrets he had been trying—and failing—to ferret out for Nanda Lal. The secret he had never even suspected.

The assistant's body then vanished in the bowels of the earth, folded into a small niche which the Bihari miners dug in one side of the tunnel and then covered over. They did not even mind the additional work. Men of their class were not fond of majordomos and their assistants.

Although they did find a certain charm in the way the majordomo had pronounced many curses on his assistant's body as it was enfolded into its secret tomb. Quite inventive, those curses. And who would have thought such a stiff and proper old man would know so many?

If Lady Damodara noticed the disappearance of the guards and the assistant, or the reassignment of the maids, she gave no sign of it. Which, of course, was not surprising. The running of the household was entirely in the old majordomo's hands. Being also a man who had been a retainer of the family since boyhood—and one who was extraordinarily efficient—he was trusted to manage the household's affairs with little interference.

The daughters of Dadaji Holkar noticed, of course. They could hardly help notice, since they were assigned to replace the two maids—an assignment which they greeted with much trepidation.

"We don't know anything about how to take care of a great lady," protested the younger. "She'll have us beaten."

The majordomo shook his head. "Have no fear, child. The lady is not hot-tempered. A very kind lady, in fact. I have explained to her already that you are new to the task, and will need some time to learn your duties. She will be quite patient, I assure you."

Still hesitant, the girls looked at each other. Then the older spoke. "My infant will cry at night. The great lady will be disturbed in her sleep. She will be angry."

The old servant chuckled. "She has borne three children of her own. You think she has never heard such noises before?" He shook his head. "Be at ease, I tell you."

The girls were still hesitant. With most majordomos, they would not have dared to press the matter further. But this old man . . . he had been kind to them, oddly enough.

"Why?" asked the younger sister, almost in a whisper. "A great lady should have experienced maids, not . . . not kitchen drudges."

Kindly the old man might be, but the look he gave them now was not kind in the least. A hard gaze, it was. As if he were pondering the same question himself.

Whatever answer he might have given went unspoken. For a new voice echoed in the girls' little sleeping chamber.

"Because I say so."

The girls spun around. Behind them, standing in the doorway, was the man who had rescued them from the slave brothel so many months earlier.

They were so delighted to see him that they almost

squealed with pleasure. The youngest even began to move toward him, as if she were almost bold enough to clasp him in an embrace.

The man shook his head, although he was smiling. The headshake turned into a small gesture aimed at the majordomo. Making neither argument nor protest, the august head servant immediately left the room.

After he was gone, the man bestowed upon the girls that calm, hooded gaze which they remembered so well.

"Ask no questions," he said softly. "Just do as you are told. And say nothing to anyone. Do you understand?"

Both girls nodded instantly.

"Good," he murmured. "And now I must leave. I simply wanted to make sure all is well with you. It is, I trust?"

Both girls nodded again. The man began to turn away. The older sister had enough boldness left in her to ask a last question.

"Will we ever see our father again?"

The man paused in the doorway, his head turned to one side. He was not quite looking at them.

"Who is to say? God is prone to whimsy."

A little sob seemed to come from the younger sister's throat; almost instantly squelched. The man's broad shoulders seemed to slump a bit.

"I will do my best, children. More than that . . ." Whatever slump might have been in the shoulders vanished. They stood as square and rigid as ever.

"God is prone to whimsy," he repeated, and was gone.

"This is an unholy mess," grumbled Ajatasutra. "By the time I get back to Ajmer, Valentinian and Anastasius and the Kushans will have been festering for weeks in that miserable inn. When they hear about *this* little curlicue to your schemes, they will erupt in fury."

"All the better," snapped Narses. "Imperial Ye-tai troops aren't chosen for their timid ways, you know. And I can't have a smaller escort than ten—a dozen would be better—or the whole affair will ring completely false."

"Make it a dozen," chuckled Ajatasutra harshly. "Imperial Ye-tai be damned. Against *those* two Romans? Not to mention Kujulo and that pack of cutthroats he brought with him."

The assassin ran fingers through his beard. Then, smiled grimly. "You know what would be perfect? Have the escort led by some high Malwa mucky-muck. Nothing less than a member of the dynastic clan itself, *anvaya-prapta sachivya.* Some distant cousin of the emperor's. A young snot, arrogant as the sunrise and as sure as a rooster. He'll fuck up the assignment—probably insist on having himself and all the Ye-tai at the head of the convoy, leaving Rana Sanga's wife and kids to trail behind in the dust. Easy to separate them out and—"

As he spoke, Narses' eyes had widened and widened. "Why didn't *I* think of that?" he choked. "Of course!"

He eyed Ajatasutra oddly. "This is a little scary. I'm not sure I like the idea of you outthinking me."

Ajatasutra shrugged. "Don't get carried away with enthusiasm. Nanda Lal will have a fit, when you raise the idea."

"Not worried about that," retorted Narses, waving a casual hand. "If he gives me any argument, I'll just go right over his head. Great Lady Sati and I have an understanding."

Now it was Ajatasutra's turn to give Narses an odd look.

"S'true," insisted the old eunuch. "A very fine lady, she is, and an extraordinarily capable schemer." He paused. "For an amateur."

Chapter 19
CHARAX
Summer, 533 A.D.

By the time Belisarius got back to Charax, racing there in a swift war galley as soon as he got the news of the Malwa sabotage attempt, Antonina had her arguments marshaled and ready. And not just her arguments, either—in the few days which had elapsed, she had been working like a fiend to organize the "change of plans."

By the time the argument between them was just starting to heat up—

It's too early, Antonina! The army isn't ready! Neither is the Ethiopian fleet!

Get them ready, then! We can't wait any longer here!

Idiot woman! We have no way of knowing if Kungas has created a diversion yet!

I'll create one, you dimwit! A way, way bigger one than something happening in far-off Bactria! With or without the Ethiopians!

And that's another thing! I don't want you taking those kinds of chances!

Chances? Chances!? What do you think I'm facing

211

*here? There's no way to stop Malwa plots here in
Charax! The place is a menagerie! Chaos incarnate!*

—the argument got cut short by royal intervention.
Two royal interventions, in fact.

The first, by Khusrau Anushirvan. The Emperor of
Iran and non-Iran had known of Antonina's new plans,
of course. He had excellent spies. And he knew of
Belisarius' opposition within an hour after the argument between them erupted on the general's return
to Charax.

But it took him those few days, waiting for
Belisarius' return, to ponder his own course of action.
For all Khusrau's youth and energy, he was already
a canny monarch, one for whom statecraft and long-
term thinking was second nature. So he, unlike
Antonina herself, immediately saw all the possible
implications of her new proposal. And, for a variety
of reasons—not the least being the opposition he
expected to arouse among his Roman allies—he
needed to take some time to examine all aspects of
the problem.

A few days, no more. By midafternoon of the same
day that Belisarius returned in the morning and began
his raging quarrel with Antonina, Khusrau intervened.
Understanding the delicate nature of the business, he
even restrained his normal "Persian Emperor reflexes"
and came to the Roman headquarters accompanied by
no advisers and only a handful of Immortals for a
bodyguard.

When he was ushered into the chamber where the
dispute was taking place, Belisarius and Antonina broke
off immediately. Neither one of them was surprised to
see Khusrau appear, although they hadn't thought he
would show up this soon. For the moment, the argument was still largely an internal Roman affair.

Belisarius' face eased a bit. Antonina's jaws set more tightly still. Clearly enough, both of them expected Khusrau would be introducing yet another voice of masculine reason. Doing his best to aid Belisarius in calming down a somewhat hysterical female.

The emperor disabused both of them immediately. He saw no reason to dance around the issue. Nor, of course, was there any need to disguise the fact that he had spies in the Roman camp. That much was taken for granted—just as was the existence of Roman spies in Khusrau's own entourage.

"I agree with Antonina, Belisarius," Khusrau stated abruptly. With well-honed imperial reflexes, he headed for the largest and most luxurious chair in the chamber and eased into it.

Belisarius and Antonina were both staring at him, speechless. Neither of them, clearly enough, had expected to hear *those* words coming from the Emperor of Iran and non-Iran.

Khusrau wriggled his fingers. "My reasons are rather different from hers, however." He gave Antonina a very stern look. "Personally, I think her fears for the security of Charax are overstated. Certainly they are not sufficient to justify such a radical and ill-prepared change in the campaign."

That last statement, perhaps oddly, caused Belisarius' jaws to tighten—and almost brought a smile to Antonina's face. Both of them were experienced negotiators in their own right, and immediately recognized Khusrau's ploy for what it was. The emperor would side with Belisarius' *logic*, thus providing the Roman general with a face-saving gesture of male solidarity, while agreeing with the *substance* of Antonina's proposal.

Since Belisarius didn't require much, if anything, in the way of face-saving or male solidarity, and Antonina cared not a fig *why* her proposal was adopted . . .

Antonina, exuding feminine modesty and poise, eased herself into her own chair. Belisarius remained standing in the center of the chamber. "Get to it, Khusrau," he growled. Normally, the Roman general would not speak so abruptly to a Persian emperor, but his mood was getting fouler by the moment.

"Yes, do," murmured Antonina. The sound was practically a coo.

Khusrau's teeth flashed briefly through his beard. The smile, for all its brevity, was heartfelt and not a gesture. If there was anything the Emperor of Iran and non-Iran appreciated, it was negotiating partners who were smart enough not to require him to waste endless time in diplomatic folderol.

"Have either of you given much thought to the future?" he asked. "I am speaking of the more immediate political future after our triumph." He paused for a moment. "Not of the philosophical profundities regarding human destiny which are raised by the existence of the Talisman of God in our midst."

Again he paused, allowing Belisarius and Antonina time to absorb the fact that Khusrau was well aware of Aide's existence. He did not expect that either of them would be much surprised by that, but Aide's existence had only been revealed to a single Persian. And that one—

"Baresmanas said nothing to me," he added, "until I made clear to him that I already knew the secret. You may rest assured of that, Belisarius."

The Roman general nodded. "No, he wouldn't." Belisarius sighed and abruptly sat down on a chair next to him. "But there was no way to keep the Talisman a secret anyway. Nor, really, much reason to do so at this point."

None at all, agreed Aide.

Belisarius touched the pouch which lay on his chest

under the tunic. The pouch where, as always, Aide lay nestled. "Would you like to see him?"

Khusrau's eyes widened slightly. " 'Him'?" he asked. "A mystical jewel has a sex?" Under the thick, short, square-cut beard, the Persian emperor's teeth gleamed again. "Or is it simply—familiarity and ease? If so, I am a bit relieved."

He shook his head. "Not now, Belisarius. Later—yes, very much. But we have this to deal with first."

He waited. After a moment, Belisarius shrugged.

"You'll have to be more precise, Emperor. I have given quite a bit of thought to the political future after the fall of Malwa. But I suspect you have something very specific in mind."

Khusrau nodded. "At all costs, I wish to avoid a resumption of the ancient war between Rome and Persia. A war which, as things now stand, is almost certain to resume within a decade after Malwa is finished."

This time, both Belisarius and Antonina were genuinely startled. Over the past two years, since Rome had answered Persia's desperate plea for an alliance against the Malwa invaders, the relations between the two empires—for all that they had been frequently locked in warfare over a period measured in centuries—had been quite good.

Khusrau lifted his shoulders and spread his hands. "The problem lies with Iran, not Rome. Consider— which I think neither of you really has done—what the world will look like to the Aryans after this war is over. Especially to Iran's nobility."

He gave both of them a long, measured stare. "Rome emerges splendid and triumphant. Its lands untouched by the war, its populace unravaged, its military power and commercial might enlarged, its future bright and certain." After a brief pause: "And

Iran? A land half-ruined by the Malwa. And a land, moreover"—here his voice hardened—"whose emperor is bound and determined to transform its ancient customs. Specifically, is bound and determined to bridle the rambunctious Aryan nobility which is both the source of Iran's traditional military power and, always, the shackle to its forward progress."

He's right, said Aide unhappily. **I've been thinking about it myself, now and then. I didn't want to raise it with you, because you have enough to worry about. But . . . he's right. Persia will be a powderkeg after the war.**

"You fear rebellion," stated Belisarius. Seeing Khusrau's impassive face, the Roman general's lips quirked in a crooked smile. "No, not really. Not Khusrau Anushirvan. If it comes to it, you will lead that nobility into war against Rome in order to keep their allegiance."

"If need be. But there is a way to avoid the entire problem. Simply give my nobles a different field of conquest. Or, it might be better to say, a vast new realm in which to exercise their energies and ambitions." Khusrau shrugged. "Not even the Aryan *azadan*"—the term meant *men of noble birth*, and referred to the class of armored knights who formed the backbone of Persia's military strength—"are enamored of war for its own sake, after all. Give them new lands, new wealth, new areas in which to exercise their authority and their talents . . ."

He let the thought trail off, certain that the two other people in the room would see the point.

Antonina, for one, did not. She saw not a trailing thought, but a vast leap of logic.

"You can't be serious, Emperor! If you march into Central Asia, you will clash with the Kushans. Who, comes to it"—her jaws set—"are ultimately a more important ally for Rome than Persia. At least in the long run. And the same if you march into the Deccan against our Maratha allies. That leaves only the Ganges plain, and that would embroil you in an endless war with the Malwa successor state. In a land teeming with a multitude of people who have no reason—none!—to welcome another wave of conquerors from the west. The whole idea—"

"That's not what he's talking about, Antonina," interrupted Belisarius. The Roman general *had* followed the trailing thought to its logical end point. "He's talking about the Indus valley."

Belisarius scratched his chin. "Whose political future, now that the subject is raised, we have never really decided. I assumed some sort of military occupation, in the interim, followed by—"

"Lengthy negotiations!" barked Khusrau. "With me bidding against Shakuntala and Kungas, and Rome acting as an 'honest broker'!" He snorted. "And probably against someone else, too. As Antonina says, the Ganges will not remain unruled for long after Malwa's fall. Even leaving aside those damned Rajputs perched on the border."

He swept his hand in a firm gesture. "So let us forestall the whole process. The Indus will go to the Aryans. The delta, at the very least, and the valley itself to the edge of the Thar desert and as far north as the fork with the Chenab."

"Sukkur and the gorge," countered Antonina immediately. "Further north than that, you'll simply have endless trouble with the Rajputs and the Kushans." She smiled sweetly. "Let them bicker over control of the Punjab. You'll have the whole of the Sind, which is more than enough to keep the azadan busy. Besides—"

"Enough!" snapped Belisarius. He glared at Antonina, and then transferred the glare to Khusrau.

"We are *not* going to get into this. Neither Antonina nor I have the authority to negotiate such things for the Roman Empire. And you can be quite certain that Theodora is going to have a tighter fist than"—another glare—"my idiot wife. Whose only purpose in agreeing with you—"

"Is because it makes her proposal workable," concluded Khusrau forcefully. "It means your thrust into the central valley can be done by *me*, leading an army of dehgans, instead of requiring you to split your own forces. It simplifies your logistics enormously, and makes possible moving up the assault on Barbaricum and the seizure of the delta."

Belisarius' eyes almost bulged. "By *you*? That's impossible, Khusrau! You're needed here in Persia to—"

He broke off, choking a little.

Khusrau's teeth were gleaming in his beard, now. "To keep the Empire of Iran and non-Iran stable? To keep the always restive azadan from their endless plots and schemes? So that Mesopotamia can continue to serve as the stable entrepot for the campaign in the Indus?"

Antonina was unable to suppress a giggle. "That's one way to keep the azadan from being, ah, 'restive.' Take them off on a great plundering expedition. Like the Achaemenids of old!" Without rising from her chair, she gave Khusrau an exaggerated bow. "Hail, Cyrus reborn!"

Khusrau chuckled, and returned the bow with a nod. "Darius, at the very least." He moved his eyes back to Belisarius. "You *do* have wide-ranging authority on anything that concerns military affairs. You can always present the thing to Empress Theodora—excuse me, Empress *Regent* Theodora—as a necessity for the success of the campaign against the Malwa."

He bestowed another nod on Antonina. "In light of

the new circumstances uncovered by Antonina, Theodora's best and most trusted friend."

Belisarius started to snarl a reply, but forced it down. Then, growling: "I agree that it might work. With the emperor *personally* leading a campaign into the central valley . . ."

He fell silent, for a moment, his acute military mind working feverishly almost despite himself. " . . . staging itself in the little known fertile basin of the Sistân, as we'd already planned . . ."

There was a large campaign map lying on a nearby table. By the time Belisarius finished half-mumbling those last words he was leaning over it. Antonina and Khusrau both rose and came to his side.

The Roman general's finger traced the route. "It'd be a monster of a trek. Even if . . . assemble an army of dehgans in the Sistân—from where?"

"I'd start in Chabahar," stated Khusrau, pointing to a port on the coast of the Gulf of Oman. "Exactly as you were planning to do, anyway, with Maurice's expedition. Most of the dehgans are here in lower Mesopotamia already, so it would be easy to ship them to Chabahar. And from there—just as you've been planning—the expedition would march north to the Sistân. Shielded from any enemy view by the mountains to the east. Take—let us say—a week to refit and recuperate, and we'd begin the invasion of the middle Indus valley. Just as you were planning all along."

Belisarius' scowl was now ferocious. "*That* route? An entire army of Persian dehgans? Impossible, Khusrau! You'd have two deserts and a mountain range to cross, before you reach the Indus at Sukkur."

"Just below the Sukkur gorge, which separates the Sind from the Punjab," said Antonina brightly. "The natural northern frontier of the new Aryan province of Industan."

Both men glared at her. Then, glared at each other.

"Impossible!" repeated Belisarius. "I was only planning to send a small expedition. Six thousand men, most of them light Arab cavalry. Just enough to surprise the Malwa and drive the population south while we established a beachhead in the delta. How in creation do you expect to get a large army of *dehgans*—heavily armored horsemen—through that kind of terrain?"

Khusrau smiled beatifically. "You forget two things, Belisarius. First, you forget that village dehgans from the plateau and the northeast provinces—thousands upon thousands of whom are gathered here in lower Mesopotamia, grumbling about the absence of any prospect for glorious battle—are far more accustomed to traveling in arid terrain than you, ah, perhaps more civilized Romans."

He understood the sarcastic raise of the Roman general's eyebrow, and shook his head in response. "You are not really familiar with that breed, Belisarius. Most of your contact has been with the higher nobility of the Aryans. Most of whom, I admit, could be accused of loving their creature comforts. But the dehgans from the east . . .

"A crude lot!" he barked, half laughing. "But, for this campaign, the cruder the better."

Belisarius scratched his chin. He understood Khusrau's point, and was remembering various jests which high Persian noblemen like Kurush had made to him in the past concerning the rough, frontier nature of the eastern dehgans.

"And the other thing?"

Khusrau looked smug. "You forget, I think, that the Sistân is the home of the legendary Rustam. National hero of the Aryans."

Belisarius groped, for a moment, at the significance of this last statement. But Aide understood it at once.

The crystal's excited thoughts burst into Belisarius' mind.

He's right. He's right! The Sistân is just today's name for ancient Drangia. The Sistân—its population, I mean—will be awash in mythology. A sleepy, isolated province—but it's still fertile and densely inhabited, because Tamerlane hasn't wrecked it yet—won't ever, now, actually, because we've already changed history—

Aide was practically babbling with excitement.

Don't you see? How they'll react—when the Emperor of Iran and non-Iran himself comes? And demands their assistance in a great new feat of glory for the Aryans?

Belisarius' eyes widened.

It's perfect! It's perfect! The whole population will turn out! Men, women and children— oldsters!—cripples! You couldn't ask for a better logistics train! Not that those rubes would understand the word "logistics," of course. For them it'll just be a crusade. The one and only chance they've had in centuries to rekindle the old legends and bring them back to life.

Widened. Aide babbled on.

Perfect, I tell you! Everyone of them—most of the men, anyway—will be expert camel drivers. There's already food, and plenty of water. Before Tamerlane destroyed the area—in the future that would have been, I mean, and we need a new tense for that because that's such a stupid way of saying it—the Sistân was famous for its irrigation works—well, not exactly "famous," but it had them even if almost nobody knew about them—dams and qanats, everything!

Then, perhaps a bit aggrieved: *I already told you that, which is why you came up with your original*

plan. You must have forgotten the specifics, though, or you'd understand right off why Khusrau's scheme is so much better.

Belisarius made a wry smile. *Et tu, Aide?*

There came the image of a crystalline snort, as impossible as such a thing was to describe in words. Belisarius was reminded of a mirror, splintering in pieces and reforming in an instant.

Don't be petty. It's beneath your dignity. It *is* a better plan. All you hoped to do was drive some of the population south. Khusrau, with—with—

"How many dehgans, Emperor?" asked Belisarius, on behalf of Aide.

"I am confident I can marshal twenty thousand heavy cavalry. Not all of them dehgan lancers, of course. A third, perhaps—but the rest will be armored archers, and you of all people know how ferocious—"

Belisarius waved his hand. "Please! An army of twenty thousand Persian lancers and archers, with another ten thousand infantry, is heavy enough to punch through any Malwa force that will be available in the mid-Indus. Especially—"

More than enough! For a moment, Aide's enthusiasm waned a bit. **Of course, the Persians won't be able to besiege any real citadels or fortifications . . .**

"Don't need to," said Belisarius aloud, forgetting in the excitement of the moment that neither Khusrau nor Antonina could have followed his mental exchange with Aide. Then, remembering, he began to explain—but Khusrau interrupted him.

"No need to," he concurred. "With twenty thousand heavy cavalry I can break any Malwa force in the field. So what if they retreat into their fortresses along the river? I can quickly establish military rule and bring almost the entire population under my control. Keep them working in the fields, providing us with food and billeting while we protect them against Malwa sallies."

"You'll wind up saving the lives of a lot more peasants this way," added Antonina quietly. She understood fully, even if Khusrau did not, how heavily the thought of those peasants slaughtered at Malwa hands had weighed upon her husband. Belisarius had hoped to save perhaps a few tens of thousands with his light cavalry expedition. No more than that.

But now—with such a powerful force in the mid-valley . . .

"We could save almost all of them," he murmured. Then, giving Khusrau a somewhat stony eye: "Not that their lives will be all that splendid, under Aryan martial law."

"Better than being butchered," retorted Khusrau. "As for the rest . . ." He shrugged. "I can keep the dehgans from committing any real atrocities. The first few days will be rough, of course. No way to keep such soldiers from pilfering what little treasure there might be and pestering the local women."

" 'Pestering'!" snorted Antonina.

Again, Khusrau shrugged. "And so a number of Indian peasants find themselves with bastards soon thereafter. Not even many of those, truth to tell, because my dehgans will be looking for concubines anyway. So they will formalize the relationships, more often than not, and see to the well-being of their new offspring."

"The peasant men won't like that much," pointed out Belisarius. He cut off Khusrau's rebuttal with his own. "But that's neither here nor there. They've doubtless been suffering worse under the Malwa as it is. They'll adjust, soon enough. Especially since Indian peasants are even less inclined than most of the world's peasantry to care two figs who happens to rule their area. As long as their new masters don't tax them dry—you *will* extend your new tax system to the Indus, yes?—"

Khusrau nodded. "I'll do more than that. I'll use the Indus as the testing ground. Along with much else." The emperor began pacing about slowly. "I'm sure, by now, you have deduced my plans for transforming Aryan society. I've had enough of these damned squabbling noblemen. As much as possible, I intend to duplicate Rome's more efficient and intelligent system. Advancement by merit, not birth, with the *new* aristocracy tied with ropes to the imperial dynasty."

Belisarius said nothing. He had not, in fact, "deduced" any such thing. He had not needed to. Aide, with his encyclopedic knowledge of human history, had long since acquainted the Roman general with the sweeping changes which Khusrau the Just—as future history would have called him—would make in Persian culture and society. Replacing a feudal system with an imperial one, and instituting a tax system so efficient and fairly spread that even the later Moslem conquerors would adopt it for their own.

"The Indus will be the perfect place to plant that shoot," mused Khusrau. "My army will be made up almost entirely of modest dehgans from the impoverished eastern borderlands. Not rich and haughty grandees from Mesopotamia. They'll be willing enough, in exchange for land and wealth, to accept new terms of imperial service."

He clenched his fist. "And with *them* to back me, I can deal with any fractious Mesopotamian sahrdaran as roughly as I need to." He quirked a smile. "Who knows? Perhaps, upon my eventual death, my designated successor can take the throne without having to wage the usual civil war."

Belisarius leaned over the map, planting both his

hands, and studied the terrain depicted there. "All right," he said softly. "I can see where the land campaign has a good chance for success. A *very* good chance, actually, since the one thing not even the superhuman mind of Link will be expecting is to see twenty thousand Persian heavy cavalry come charging into the Indus valley out of the Kacchi Desert."

Chuckling: "The whole idea's insane, after all. And if there's one thing that damned monster is not, it's given to illogical planning."

It will never understand the power of such myths as Rustam, came Aide's soft thought. **I would never have understood either, had I not spent so many years now living in your mind. And your heart.**

True, said Belisarius in reply. *In the end, Link and the "new gods" who sent it here will fail, as much as anything, because they tried to shape humanity's future without ever understanding its soul.*

He straightened from the table. "But that still leaves the naval problem," he said forcefully. "The fact is that none of this can possibly succeed without a total mobilization of the entire fleet for the logistical effort. That, and—of course—the actual assault on Barbaricum."

His next words sounded harsh even to himself, but they needed saying. "And that, in turn, is impossible so long as the Malwa have that great fleet of theirs in Bharakuccha. At harbor today, yes, but only because of the monsoon. By the time we can take the delta, no matter how fast we move, summer will be over and we will be into autumn. Come November, the change in winds will be upon us. At which point, the Malwa fleet will be able to ravage our own shipping. And because of the inevitable disruption in our careful planning which Antonina's scheme will create, our navy

will be ill prepared to fend them off. The only way to
get the whole army into the delta ahead of schedule
is to transport them by sea instead of having them
march. Which will completely tie up all of our shipping, military as well as civilian. Whether we like it or
not, the fact is that until the Ethiopians finish expanding their navy—which won't be for months—we haven't
got the additional maritime power to make this work.
It's as simple as that."

He gave both of them a stony look. "Without complete command of the sea—which depends on the
Ethiopian fleet—we could easily wind up in exactly the
same position we left the Malwa last year—with a huge
army stranded, and dying of starvation. We can't possibly weather through the first few months in the Indus
simply on the food which the valley's peasants might
provide us. Their own situation will have been completely disrupted also. We *need* our own stable logistics train for that first winter, no matter what else may
happen."

Neither Khusrau nor Antonina responded. They
were both bridling at the logic, but neither of them
could *quite* figure out how to gainsay it.

Still, they intended to try, clear enough. Belisarius
braced himself for renewed quarrel.

Whereupon came the second royal intervention.

The doors opened, and Agathius limped in, shouldering his way through the ornate and heavy portals
with rough abandon, even knocking one aside with a
crutch. He seemed excited—excited enough, at least,
that he began speaking in the presence of royalty
without so much as a polite cough of apology.

"You won't believe this, but a whole slew of ships
just showed up on the horizon. Biggest damn fleet I've
ever seen. Axumites, no doubt about it. And if we're

interpreting those newfangled flag signals of yours correctly, King Eon himself is leading them."

Belisarius stared at Khusrau. Then at Antonina. "You planned this," he accused.

"Nonsense!" retorted Khusrau. "How could she?"

"Indeed," concurred Antonina with demure reproof. "Just feminine intuition, that's all. As reliable as ever."

Chapter 20
THE JAMUNA
Summer, 533 A.D.

The first thing Nanda Lal saw, after Toramana ushered him into his small pavilion, was the statue resting on a small table in a corner. The statue was a representation of Virabhadra, the chief deity in the Mahaveda cult which had become the central axis of the Malwa version of Hinduism.

The Mahaveda priest who accompanied Nanda Lal wandered over and gazed upon the statue with . . . not reverence, so much as satisfaction. After a few seconds, he turned away and fixed Toramana with a stern gaze.

"And do you practice the rites?"

Toramana nodded. "Three times, every day. Have done so, since I was a child. My father was a devout man."

The priest grunted. "Good. And how is your father now?"

Toramana's face remained impassive. The big Ye-tai officer's shoulders simply shifted, in what might be interpreted as a shrug. "He's dead. Killed at Ranapur, when the rebels set off the detonation. My brother was killed there also."

Nanda Lal's jaws tightened a bit. He hadn't been given that information by his spies, before he left Kausambi. It was an oversight which several of them would regret.

But he said nothing. Nanda Lal had already made clear to the priest that he wanted him to do most of the talking. The priest had not forgotten. After a brief, quickly suppressed start of surprise, the Mahaveda cleared his throat. "I'm sorry, I didn't know. My condolences."

"It was quick. All men die. The rebels were punished."

The Ye-tai officer seemed to find those curt sentences adequate. Watching him carefully, Nanda Lal decided the man was stolid by nature. Intelligent enough, clearly—Damodara was not in the habit of promoting dullards, certainly not to general rank—but not given to excessive flights of imagination.

"My name is Vishwanathan," announced the priest. "As you perhaps already know, I was sent here specifically on the instructions of the emperor."

"So Narses informed me." Toramana extended his hand, inviting the priest to sit on the cushions before a lowset table. In some indefinable way, the hand gesture also included Nanda Lal without giving him the precedence which the chief spymaster for the entire Malwa Empire—and, like Venandakatra, a first cousin of the emperor—would normally enjoy.

Nanda Lal was impressed. He would not have expected such subtlety from a Ye-tai, not even a general officer. In a very short time, he realized, Toramana had already deduced that Nanda Lal intended to use the priest as his unofficial "envoy."

"Something to eat?" asked the Ye-tai. "Drink?"

The priest shook his head, but accepted the offer to sit. Nanda Lal remained standing, a few feet back from the table.

"I wish no servants to be present," said the priest, after settling himself comfortably on the cushions. As Toramana took a seat across from him at the table, the priest's eyes ranged through the pavilion.

The Ye-tai officer interpreted the movement of his eyes correctly. "There are no servants present, anywhere in the pavilion. If we need them, they wait outside. I assumed you wanted a private audience."

Not a dullard at all, thought Nanda Lal. *Which, in itself, is good. So long as—*

Toramana's next words surprised the spymaster. And caused him to revise upward his estimate of the Ye-tai general's intelligence.

"You wish to determine my loyalty. You are concerned over the implications of my future marriage into the Chauhar dynasty."

Vishwanathan nodded. "Exactly. There was much discussion in the Imperial Council, once the news arrived. I was present myself, at some of those discussions."

In the brief silence which followed, Nanda Lal gauged Toramana's reaction to the news that his affairs had been subjected to careful imperial scrutiny. Most Ye-tai officers—most officers of any kind in the Malwa army—would have been both surprised and apprehensive.

Toramana's reaction was—

Nothing. Might as well have told a tree it was made of wood. Or a stone that it was solid.

Before Nanda Lal's own apprehensiveness could do more than stir, Toramana surprised him again.

"I expected it would be," said the Ye-tai. "For obvious reasons, a marital alliance between Ye-tai and Rajput would be cause for imperial concern."

The priest, startled by the Ye-tai's frankness, cast a quick glance at Nanda Lal. The spymaster returned the glance with a stony gaze. The priest looked away hastily. Then, after a pause, lifted an eyebrow at the Ye-tai general, inviting further elaboration.

"Obvious," repeated Toramana. "The power of the Malwa dynasty, beyond its control of the Deva weapons, rests primarily on the pillars of the Ye-tai and the Rajputs. A tripod, as it were." Again, Toramana made that little shoulder-shifting gesture. "And the Kushans also, once—to a degree. But that leg is now cracked, and may splinter."

For the first time since he entered the pavilion, Nanda Lal spoke. "Three legs will still support a stool, even if the fourth breaks."

Toramana nodded, without looking at the spymaster. He kept his eyes on the face of the priest.

"Yes. The more so when that fourth leg was never much trusted at any time. Provided that the remaining three legs remain stationed at very different angles. Let two of them merge into one, and you no longer have a stool. You have a two-legged spill waiting to happen. Which, of course, is why the emperor is concerned about my marital plans."

The Ye-tai fell silent. After a few seconds, Nanda Lal realized that he would speak no further without another invitation. And realized, as well, that in so doing Toramana was making an invitation of his own.

The spymaster relaxed still further. He was an experienced bargainer, and could recognize a bargain in the making when he saw one.

That recognition brought another. The priest was now out of his depth, and Nanda Lal would have to abandon completely his pose of disinterested observer. The decision made, Nanda Lal stepped forward and took his own seat at the table.

"Tell me, then," he commanded, "why the emperor should permit the marriage."

Toramana's barrel chest rose in a slow, deep breath. Obviously enough, he was taking the time to marshal his arguments.

"One. The strength a stool needs depends on the weight to be placed upon it. With Belisarius threatening the Indus and Rao the Narmada, that weight has grown three- or four-fold.

"Two. A three-legged stool, more than a four-legged one, requires thick and sturdy legs. In human terms, that means loyal ones. Even devoted ones.

"Three. The weakness lies with the Rajputs. To the moment, they are bound to the Malwa by oaths alone. Not by much in the way of blood, and still less by way of confidence. Vows—even Rajput vows—are brittle things.

"Four. The surest way to bind the Rajputs tighter is to bind them with blood. Encourage high-ranking Rajputs, as you have Ye-tai, to marry into the Malwa clan."

Toramana broke off and gave Nanda Lal a long and steady gaze. "I am telling you nothing that you do not already understand. Let us suppose, for a moment, that Rana Sanga were to become a widower. Perhaps by disease, or accident—or even some unfortunate incidence of random banditry. I am certain that the dynasty would offer him a high-rank marriage into the Malwa clan. A very high-rank marriage, in fact. For the first time ever, a Rajput king—and he the greatest of them all—will be tied to the Malwa by blood, not simply by vows."

Nanda Lal could feel himself stiffening, for all his attempts to conceal his emotions. He couldn't help it. He was almost paralyzed with shock. Never—*never!*—had he imagined that this brutish-looking half-barbarian could have deduced so much, from so little. And how much else had he deduced? "By unfortunate incidence of random banditry" had been his *words*, true enough. But what thoughts—what guesses—lay beneath those words?

For a moment, Nanda Lal almost raised his voice, calling on the five assassins who waited outside the tent to come in and kill Toramana on the spot. But he managed to restrain himself. Barely.

Barely—and for two reasons. Only the second being that he was also intrigued by the possibilities which Toramana's unexpected acuity opened up.

The first reason for his restraint was even simpler. In addition to Nanda Lal's five assassins, there were dozens of soldiers within a few steps of the tent's entrance. Ye-tai, in the main, but with no small sprinkling of Rajputs among them. All of whom—so much had already become obvious to Nanda Lal—were as tightly bound to their commander Toramana as any of the soldiers of the splendid army from which they were temporarily detached were bound to Lord Damodara and Rana Sanga.

In short, this was the only army of the Malwa Empire where the work of assassins would surely be repaid, within a minute, by the work of enraged soldiers. Nanda Lal's assassins could kill Toramana, of that the spymaster had no doubt at all, even if the impressive-looking young warrior-general took two or three of them with him into the afterlife. But only if Nanda Lal was prepared to have his own hacked-apart body lying next to Toramana's a few seconds later.

And that, in a nutshell, is the entire problem. The empire cannot afford to lose this magnificent army. But can we afford to have them at all? If this razor-sharp sword ever turns in our grasp . . .

Long seconds of silence had gone by. Throughout, Toramana's eyes had never left those of Nanda Lal.

Now, still without showing a trace of anxiety—emotion of any kind—the young Ye-tai general once again made that economical shrug.

"You are worrying too much, I think. Were his beloved wife to die, for whatever reason short of Malwa involvement, Rana Sanga would have all the more reason to weld himself to the dynasty." In some subtle way, the next words came with a slight emphasis. "For all his martial prowess, you know, he is not given to subtlety."

Translation: I might have my doubts about "unfortunate circumstances," but Sanga would not.

Nanda Lal reviewed in his mind all he knew about the Rajput king, and decided the Ye-tai's assessment was accurate. That still left Damodara . . .

As if he were a mind-reader, Toramana spoke again.

"As for Lord Damodara, his gratitude at the emperor's generosity in providing his own family with a palace in the capital—safe from Roman assassins, and almost on the emperor's own doorstep—has also welded him completely to the dynasty. Not, in my opinion, that there was any reason to doubt his loyalty at all."

Nanda Lal discounted the last sentence immediately. Pure diplomacy, that was. The operative sentence was the first. *Translation: so long as Damodara's family is held hostage by the emperor, Damodara will remain obedient.*

Again, Nanda Lal reviewed the assessment; and, again, decided the Ye-tai was correct. For all his brilliance, Damodara had never once shown any inclination toward boundless ambition. Some ambition, of course—but enough to cast a death sentence on his wife and children? And parents?

No. I have seen him playing with his children myself, in days past when his family visited the capital. He is a doting father and, by all my spies' accounts, a loving husband as well as a devoted son.

"Good enough," stated the spymaster. The two words were abrupt, almost harsh. But not as harsh as the next: "That leaves you."

For the first time since he'd invited Nanda Lal and the priest into the pavilion, Toramana's face showed an expression. Humor, in the main, alloyed with a touch of irony.

"Me?" The word was almost a bark. "Do you know my clan status within the Ye-tai, Lord?"

Nanda Lal nodded; then, extended his thick hand and waggled it a bit. "Middling. Not high; not low."

"More low than high, I think," countered Toramana. The Ye-tai general cocked his head a little and gave Nanda Lal an inquisitive look. "A question, Lord. What is the chance that I would ever be offered a marriage with a lady of the Malwa clan?"

Nanda Lal hesitated. In the silence, Toramana elaborated the question. "Assume, for a moment, that I returned from the Roman war covered with glory. The victor on a hundred battlefields."

"Possible," grunted Nanda Lal. "Not likely."

Toramana's inquisitive look became almost inquisitorial. Nanda Lal sighed, and—again—revised upward his estimate of the man's intelligence.

"No real chance at all."

The Ye-tai nodded. "Purity of blood has always lain at the center of Malwa rule." He gave the priest a little nod. "As well as at the center of Mahaveda creed."

The statement did not seem to be accompanied by any anger or chagrin. In fact, the Ye-tai chuckled. "So be it. I am an ambitious man, Lord, but not a foolish one. The world has limits. So it is, so has it always been, so will it always be. I simply wish to reach my own, and nothing less."

All humor left the hard face—half-Asiatic; half-occidental, as was the usual Ye-tai visage—to be replaced by stolidity. "Now, perhaps, you understand."

Silence, once again, filled the pavilion. For quite a long period, this time. Perhaps five minutes in all. Five minutes during which a Ye-tai general and a Malwa spymaster stared at each other; and a Mahaveda priest, knowing he was well out of his depth, tried to make himself as inconspicuous as possible.

"Good," stated Nanda Lal, at the end of that silence. "Not even 'good enough.' Simply: *good.* We understand each other, I believe."

The Ye-tai general's nod was more in the way of a bow of fealty. "Yes, Lord, we do. Allow me to advance as far as I may, in this world that is, and you need have no fear at all of the consequence."

Nanda Lal spoke his last reservation. "The day might come—with Rana Sanga as your brother-in-law—when, perhaps . . ."

"If that day comes, Lord, which would surprise me greatly—rest assured that I will do what needs to be done. True, blood flows thick. Ambition flows thicker still. Like a glacier out of the mountains."

"And even a poet!" exclaimed Nanda Lal. Smiling cheerfully, he rose to his feet. For all his thickness of body, and decades of life, Nanda Lal was a vigorous and muscular man. He was on his feet before the priest had even started to rise.

"I look forward to long and mutually satisfactory relations, General. And I will make it a point to attend your wedding personally, whenever it might happen. And come what may."

Toramana, now also standing, bowed deeply at the waist. "I am honored, Lord." When his head came back up, there seemed to be a slightly mischievous twist to his lips. "But I give you fair warning—I will hold you to that promise. Come what may."

Nanda Lal waved Vishwanathan out of the pavilion ahead of him. After the priest had left, the spymaster paused at the tent flap and gave the statue in the corner a hard and scrutinizing gaze.

"Ugly damn thing," he murmured.

Toramana was standing a few feet away. The Ye-tai glanced at the statue, then made that little shrug.

"Ugly indeed. Much like me. And, like me, serves its purpose."

Nanda Lal chuckled and left, revising his estimate of Toramana's intelligence yet again. Upwards.

The thought—now—filled him with good cheer. Not so good, of course, that he didn't instruct one of his spies to keep an eye on the general at all times.

The spy, unfortunately, did not really share his master's estimate of Toramana's brains. So, late that night, the Ye-tai general had no difficulty eluding him in the darkness. Had no difficulty, even, in keeping the spy completely unaware that he had done so.

And, since Narses was equally adept at evading the spies which had been set upon him, the two men made the rendezvous which had been agreed upon earlier that evening, in the course of an exchange of a pound of tea for an equal value of incense made by two of their servants in the informal "market" which the soldiers and local villagers had set up on the banks of the Jamuna.

The exchange was also, needless to say, unobserved by Nanda Lal's spies. Both Toramana and Narses knew how to select servants.

They met in a small tent, set aside for some of the troops' more perishable goods. Narses was already there, perched on a sack. As soon as Toramana entered, he spoke.

"Tell me everything that was said. Word for word."

In the minutes which followed, Toramana may not have actually repeated the entire conversation, word for word. But he came very close. Nanda Lal, had he been present, would have revised his estimate upward once again. The Ye-tai's memory was as phenomenal as his intelligence.

When he was done, Narses issued a harsh, dry little laugh. " 'Allow me to advance as far as I may, in this world that is, and you need have no fear at all of the consequence.' That's a beautifully parsed sentence."

Toramana's shrug, as always, was a slight thing. "I know nothing about grammar. As anyone can see, I am a crude Ye-tai—not much more than a barbarian. But even as a child playing in the mud, I knew that the best way to lie is to tell the truth. Simply let he who hears the truth set his own boundaries to it. The boundaries, not the words themselves, are what make them a lie."

Narses nodded, smiling in his humorless and reptilian way. "And that, also, is a beautifully crafted sentence." The smile faded. His next words were spoken impassively.

"If the time comes—*when* the time comes—you will have to—"

Toramana cut him off with a quick, impatient wave of the hand. "Move quickly, decisively, and so forth." He rose to his feet, with even greater agility than Nanda Lal had shown in his own tent. "Have no fear, Narses. You and I understand each other perfectly well."

" 'Ambition flows thicker still,' " the old eunuch quoted softly. " 'Like a glacier out of the mountains.' "

Again, Toramana made that quick, impatient gesture.

"Poetry," he snorted. "There is no poetry in ice grinding against mountains. I know. I have seen it. I was born in the Hindu Kush, Narses. And learned, while still a boy, that ice is the way of the world."

He turned, stooped through the tent flap, and was gone. As silently as he came.

Chapter 21
CHARAX
Summer, 533 A.D.

"We thought we'd find you here," said Eon.

"Where else?" snorted Ousanas.

Startled, Antonina tore her eyes away from the mare she was staring at, and turned her head toward the stable entrance. Eon and Ousanas were standing just inside the open doors, backlit by the late morning sunshine.

Antonina began to flush. Then, dropping her eyes, she began brushing pieces of hay off her gown. When she'd entered the stable earlier that morning, after Belisarius left to rejoin his army, she'd been paying little attention to fastidiousness. Even now, the effort stemmed more from habit than any real care for her appearance.

"Am I so predictable?" she murmured.

Ousanas grinned. "Every time Belisarius goes haring off on one of his expeditions, you spend half the next day staring at a horse. Practically a thing of legend, by now."

Eon strode over to a nearby pile of hay and plumped himself down upon it. Clearly enough, the negusa nagast of Ethiopia was no more concerned with appearances than Antonina herself. He even spent a few seconds luxuriating in the sensation, for all the world like a carefree boy instead of the ruler of one of the world's most powerful kingdoms.

"Been a long time," he said cheerfully. Then, waving a hand: "Come, Ousanas! Why are you standing on dignity?"

Ousanas' grin became a bit sardonic. "Horse food! No thank you." He glared at the mare in the nearby stall. The inoffensive animal met his gaze placidly.

"Treacherous creatures," proclaimed Ousanas. "As are they all. 'Dumb beasts'—ha! I'm a hunter. Was, at least. So I know what wickedness lurks in the hearts of wild animals."

He stalked over to another nearby stall—an empty one—and leaned his shoulder against a wooden upright. "And they are all wild, don't think otherwise for a moment." He bestowed the same sardonic grin on the pile of hay Antonina was sitting on. "I'd rather feed on the horse than use its own feed for a chair. More civilized."

Antonina did not raise to the bait. She simply grinned back. For all that Ousanas often claimed to fear and loathe animals, she knew full well the man was an expert horseman as well as elephant mahout. And a superb camel driver as well, she suspected, although she had never seem him get close to one of the surly brutes.

Eon snorted his own skepticism. Then, his young face became serious. "We need to talk, Antonina. I am sorry to bother you now—I know you'd rather spend the day, ah . . ."

"Pining over a departed husband whom you've known for years, as if you were a silly lovestruck girl," concluded Ousanas unkindly.

"I *am* a silly lovestruck girl," protested Antonina. Not with any heat, however. Indeed, the ridiculous phrase brought her some comfort. Odd, perhaps. But her harsh childhood in the streets of Alexandria, followed by a long period in which she had been a courtesan—a time which had been, in some ways, even harsher—made her treasure the new life she had begun after Belisarius married her. She was catching up on things she had missed, the way she looked at it.

But—

She *was* married to Belisarius, after all. *Belisarius*, not some obscure small merchant or petty official. And, for all that she treasured the marriage, it did bring great responsibilities in its train.

She started to sigh, but suppressed it. "You want to plan the coming naval campaign. Immediately."

Eon nodded. "The change in Belisarius' tactics and timing makes it even more essential that our own expedition set forth as soon as possible. And since that expedition will now *require*"—the emphasis on that last word was perhaps a bit harsh, as if Eon expected an argument—"the involvement of the Roman fleet, we have no time to lose. Coordination between allies can be sometimes difficult. We need to, ah, establish clearly, ah—"

Eon trailed off into stumbling silence. Ousanas curled his lip, in a sneer which was as magnificent as his grin. "What the fool boy is fumbling at—supposed to be the King of Kings!—is who is going to command the thing. He or some Roman."

Antonina couldn't help bursting into laughter. "You're no longer his dawazz, you know!" she exclaimed. "And he's no longer a mere prince! Can't slap him on the head any longer!"

It was Eon's turn to grin, now. Ousanas scowled.

"Can't help it," he grumbled. "Being dawazz was easier than this silly fly whisk business. Polite! Respectful! Not my strength."

Antonina waved her hand. "It's not a problem. You will be in command, naturally. The only Roman ships which can be detached for the expedition are the half dozen new gunships which John designed. 'Carvels,' as he called them. Belisarius took the older ships with him for the assault on Barbaricum. You brought one hundred and eight war galleys. Each of them carries over two hundred men—approximately twenty thousand, all told, a far larger force than we Romans will provide. And since you refitted them all with cannons, you are even bringing a greater weight of guns to the expedition."

She broke off, distracted by a side thought. "I'm *still* amazed you managed to assemble such a fleet so quickly. How did you do it?"

Eon looked smug. "You can thank my wife Rukaiya for that. If there's anyone left in Ethiopia or Arabia who thinks a seventeen-year-old queen is still almost a child—*that* one, for sure—you could count them on your fingers."

"The fingers of *one* hand," amended Ousanas. "Huh," he grunted. "A will of iron, that girl has. As any number of quarrelsome shipbuilders discovered, not to mention supply merchants."

"And she's *smart*, too," continued Eon, not done with boasting about his wife. "It was Rukaiya's idea to refit our existing galleys for cannons, rather than trying to build gunships like you Romans have. 'Carvels,' you're calling them now?"

His expression grew somewhat apologetic. "We can build ships quickly, following the modifications which Rukaiya suggested, as long as we stick to our old methods. It would have taken us much longer to match John's design. We just don't have the same manufacturing base, especially not with metalworking."

"Couldn't have fitted carvels with the right guns,

anyway," said Ousanas. "Even your Roman armorers in Alexandria can barely produce enough of those for your own ships. But Rukaiya's design only needs small guns—four-pounders—and only four to a ship, which Alexandria could make readily enough."

Antonina nodded. And, silently, congratulated herself for having chosen Rukaiya as Eon's queen in the first place.

But the self-satisfaction was not long-lasting. She could see, from the somewhat stiff expression on the Axumites' faces, that they were still concerned over the issue of command.

"What's the problem now?" she asked bluntly, seeing no reason to be diplomatic with these two men.

Ousanas shook his head. "Antonina, I believe your assessment is based more on abstractions than concrete reality. What Irene would call 'book learning.'" He began to speak further, but Eon interrupted.

"Our ships are still basically *galleys*, Antonina." A bit of pride rallied: "Axumite galleys, of course! Which are quite capable of sailing across open sea. But . . ."

He shrugged. "But can't carry much in the way of supplies. Not with a full complement of soldiers and sailors. No more than a few days' worth. And not even Ethiopians, in a few days, can make that great voyage across the Erythrean Sea which the expedition requires for success."

"We'd run out of food and water," elaborated Ousanas. "Not to mention gunpowder and shot, after a single major engagement."

Understanding dawned on Antonina. And, with it, the source of the Axumites' concern. The Ethiopians could provide the striking force—most of it, at least—but only if the Romans provided the supply ships.

She couldn't help herself. Much as she tried to stifle the impulse, she broke into a fit of giggling.

"What's so funny?" demanded Eon, half-crossly and half-uncertainly. The king mixed with the boy.

Antonina forced down the giggles, with a hand over her mouth. Then: "Sorry. I was just thinking of a gaggle of Roman merchant ships, taking orders from Ethiopians. Like trying to herd cats."

Ousanas spread his hands. "The problem, exactly. That breed is insubordinate under the best of circumstances. There is not a chance we could maintain control over them, without threatening physical violence every leg of the voyage. Every day, most like. Which would eventually defeat its own purpose."

Antonina frowned. *Another damn problem in logistics!* But then, seeing the expectant faces of Ousanas and Eon, she realized their own solution to the quandary. One which they were apparently afraid to broach, because they feared her reaction. And probably knew, as well, that before he left Belisarius had extracted from his wife a promise to stay out of combat.

That knowledge produced, not a fit of giggling, but a gale of laughter.

"You have no idea!" she exclaimed. "I would *love* to sail across an ocean instead of staying here in this miserable city managing a pack of surly merchants and traders. And even my fussing husband agreed that I could not refrain from doing anything which was—I quote—*'necessary for the success of the campaign.'*"

Grinning: "Done!"

Ousanas grinned back. "Yes. With *you* on the expedition, I dare say no merchant will argue the fine points of command."

Antonina sniffed. "I dare say not."

Less than an hour later, Antonina gave the first order which set the new plan in motion. To Dryopus, her efficient and trustworthy secretary.

"You're promoted. I'll send a message to Photius and Theodora telling them to give you a fancy new title. Something grand. Maybe a seat in the Senate. Certainly an estate somewhere to maintain you in the style you'll need."

She swept out of the chamber where she had *formerly* made her headquarters, leaving a befuddled former secretary in her wake.

Dealing with the twenty merchant captains who would provide the expedition with its supply ships took more time.

Not much.

"Let me make this perfectly clear," Antonina said firmly, after listening to their protests for perhaps an hour while standing on the docks. She pointed her finger to the Roman carvels anchored in Charax's harbor. The red light of the setting sun gave the vessels a rather sinister appearance.

"Those warships will sink any one of you who so much as gives me a peep of protest once we set sail. Which we will do the day after tomorrow."

She allowed them some time to ponder her words.

Not much.

"And you *will* be ready to set sail the day after tomorrow." Again, the finger of doom. "Or those warships will sink whichever one of your ships hasn't cast off within an hour of the remainder of the fleet. The city's poor folk have been complaining about a lack of driftwood, anyway, so it won't be a total loss."

Dealing with Menander and Eusebius, on the other hand, took most of the evening. Their protests could not be brushed aside.

The ones which didn't involve them personally, at least. The young officers' insistence on accompanying

Antonina on the expedition, she gave short shrift.

"Don't be stupid. I'll have twenty thousand men—most of them Axumite marines—to keep me out of harm's way. I'm not *leading* this expedition, you understand—certainly not in combat! I'm simply going along to make sure that the Roman supply effort which is critical for success doesn't slack off."

Menander and Eusebius stared at her stubbornly. Antonina clapped her hands. "Enough! Belisarius will need you far more than me. Since I'm taking all the carvels and their experienced captains, he'll be relying on the two of you to fend off Malwa attacks on his supply route up the Indus. You *do* remember that he's a leading a much larger expedition, no?"

At the mention of Belisarius and his needs, Menander flushed. Eusebius, darker complected, did not. But he did look aside. No longer meeting her hard gaze, he managed a last little protest.

"You'll need the *Victrix*, Antonina. To make sure the Malwa shipping at Chowpatty and Bharakuccha is completely destroyed. And I'm really the only one who can still handle the fire cannon. Well enough under combat conditions, anyway."

Antonina hesitated. They were now moving into an area which was beyond her expertise.

Fortunately, Ezana made good the lack. The Dakuen commander had come with Eon and Ousanas to Antonina's villa, where the final arrangements for the division of Roman naval forces were being made. Before Eusebius had even stopped talking, Ezana was already shaking his head.

"Not true, Eusebius. In fact, having the *Victrix* along would be more of a problem than a help. You've been training with that odd weapon, we haven't. Trying to mix it in with Ethiopian forces and tactics—especially at the last minute—would cause nothing but grief. Like

as not, by accident, you'd wind up burning more
Axumite ships than Malwa."

Hurriedly, seeing the young Greek's gathering protest: "Not because of *your* error, but because some
eager Ethiopian captain would sail right into the spout.
Trust me. It'll happen."

Eusebius took a deep breath, then let it out slowly.
Watching, Antonina was certain that the young officer
was remembering similar veteran wisdom expounded
in times past by John of Rhodes. And, again, felt grief
at his loss. A small grief, now, softened by time. But
grief nonetheless.

"All right," said Eusebius. "But if you don't want the
Victrix along on your expedition, Antonina, I'm not
quite sure what role you *do* see for the ship." Shrugging: "The fire cannon itself would be ideal for destroying Malwa ships in the confines of the Indus. But the
Victrix is a sailing ship, not a galley. Once the monsoon ends, it'll be well-nigh impossible to move her
up the Indus—not against that current—unless we
hauled her with oxen. And what kind of a warship can
go into battle being drawn by livestock?"

Again, Antonina felt herself floundering out of her
depth. But she could tell from the expressions on the
faces of the experienced naval men around her that
they all understood and agreed with Eusebius' point.

"Difficult—at best—to convert a sailing ship to a
galley," muttered Ezana. "Have to rebuild her almost
completely."

"We could just transfer the fire cannon to an
existing galley," offered Eon. But the look on his face
didn't evidence any great enthusiasm. "True, you'd
lose the advantage of height. Be a bit dangerous, that,
in close quarters. Which"—his enthusiasm was fading fast—"is of course how the weapon can be used
best."

Ousanas started to say something, but Menander interrupted.

"Go the other way," he said forcefully. He jerked a thumb toward the southern wall of the room, pointing to an invisible harbor. "You all know the new steam-powered warship the old emperor designed arrived here three days ago. What you may not know is that the *Justinian* brought an extra steam engine with her, in case of major mechanical problems. But I can't really use the thing anyway. Can't possibly fit it in the *Justinian* as a spare engine. We could use it to refit the *Victrix* as a paddle wheeler." He paused, looking at Eusebius. "I think."

As ever, having a technical problem posed immediately engrossed Eusebius. The naval officer was still an artisan at heart. He ran fingers through his hair, staring at the tile floor through thick spectacles.

"Could be done. Easier to make her a stern-wheeler, but a side-wheeler would have a lot of advantages in a river like the Indus. Slow and muddy as it is, bound to be hidden sandbars all over the place. With a side-wheeler you can sometimes walk your way over them. That's what Aide says, anyway."

"Can't armor a side-wheeler," countered Menander immediately. Although he was not exactly an artisan himself, the young cataphract had quickly picked up the new technological methods which Aide had introduced. He was comfortable in that mechanical world in a way in which older cataphracts were not.

Eusebius lifted his head, his eyes opening wide. "Why are we messing with paddle wheels, anyway? The *Justinian* and her sister ship were designed for screws. It wouldn't be that much harder to redesign the *Victrix* for screw propulsion."

Menander got a stubborn, mulish look on his face. Seeing it, Eusebius sighed. "Forgot. You've only got one spare screw, don't you? And as many problems as the *Justinian* has already—typical prototype stuff—you don't want to find yourself stranded somewhere on the Indus without an extra propeller."

By now, Antonina and the Ethiopians were completely lost. Seeing the blank expressions on their faces, Eusebius explained.

"You can't just slap together a propeller. Tricky damn things. In the letter he sent with the *Justinian*, the emperor—I mean, the Grand Justiciar—told us he had to fiddle for months—his artisans, I mean—until they got it right. No way we could make one here, without the facilities he's got at Adulis."

Their faces were still blank. Menander sighed.

"You *do* know what a propeller is?"

Blank.

Menander and Eusebius looked at each other. Then, sighed as one man.

"Never mind, Antonina," said Menander. "Eusebius and I will take care of it. You just go and have yourself a nice ocean cruise."

Chapter 22
BARBARICUM
Autumn, 533 A.D.

The pilot in the bow of Belisarius' ship proved to be just as good as his boasts. Half an hour before dawn, just as he had promised, the heavily laden ship slid up onto the bank of the river. The bank, as could be expected from one of the many outlets of the Indus, was muddy. But even a landsman like Belisarius could tell, from the sudden, half-lurching way in which the ship came to a halt, that the ground was firm enough to bear the weight of men and horses.

For two weeks, once it had become clear that monsoon season was drawing to a close, Belisarius had been sending small parties to scout the Indus delta. Landing in small boats under cover of night, the scouts had probed the firmness of the ground along the many mouths of the river. Every year during the monsoon season, the great flow of the Indus deposited untold tons of silt in the delta. Until that new soil was dry enough, the project of landing thousands of men, horses and equipment was impossible.

"Nice to have accurate scouting," said Maurice, standing next to the general.

"It'll still be a challenge, but the ground should be firm enough. Barely, but enough."

Belisarius turned his head. In the faint light shed by a crescent moon, he could make out the shape of the next ship sliding alongside his own onto the bank. Other such ships, he knew, were coming to rest beyond that one—and many more still along two other nearby outlets of the river. Over the course of the next three days, Belisarius intended to land a large part of his entire army. Thirty thousand men, in all. Aide claimed it was the largest amphibious assault in all of human history to that day.

The general's eyes now moved to the bustling activity on his own ship. Already, the first combat engineers—a new military specialty which Belisarius had created over the past year—were clambering over the side of the ship. Those men were completely unarmored and bore no weapons of any kind beyond knives. Their task, for the moment at least, was not to fight. Their task was to make it possible for others to do so.

No sooner had the first engineers alit on the bank than others began handing them reed mats. Moving quickly, the engineers began laying the mats over the soft soil, creating a narrow pathway away from the still-soggy ground immediately by the riverbed.

"They're moving faster than I expected," grunted Maurice. "With as little training and preparation as we'd been able to give them . . ."

Belisarius chuckled. Maurice was *still* a bit disgruntled over the change of plans which had been made the past summer, after the sabotage attempt at Charax.

He's just grumbling, grumbled Aide. **That man is *never* satisfied. How much training does it take to lay down some simple reed mats, anyway?**

It's not all that simple, replied Belisarius. *Moving in the dark, in unfamiliar territory, with the fear of enemy attack in the back of their minds—and them with neither weapons nor armor? Not to mention that probably half of them are still seasick.*

He glanced at the sky. Still no sign of dawn, but the moon gave out just enough light to see that the sky was cloudless.

Pray this clear weather holds up, he continued. *The three days we spent at sea waiting for it took a toll on most of the men. They're not sailors, you know.*

Aide accepted the implied reproof without protest. For all that the crystal being had come to understand the nature of what he called his "protoplasmic brethren," Aide knew he was still prone to overlook the crude facts of protoplasmic existence. On the other hand . . . *he* couldn't have laid down those simple mats at all.

There was a new clattering noise. The Arab scouts were bringing their mounts out of the hold and beginning to walk them off the gangplank onto the reed-matted soil of the river. The horses had suffered from rough weather at sea at least as much as the men. But they were so eager to get their feet on terra firma that they made no effort to fight their handlers. The biggest problem the Arab scouts faced, in fact, was keeping the beasts from stampeding madly off the deck of the ship.

Abbu rolled over to Belisarius. The old Arab scout leader was practically swaggering.

"One day, General, no more." Abbu's pronouncement came with the certainty of a prophet. "One day from now, all opposition will be cleared to the walls of Barbaricum."

The old man's cheerful assurance transformed instantly into doom and gloom. He and Maurice exchanged a mutually satisfactory glower. Two natural-born pessimists agreeing on the sorry state of the universe.

"Thereafter, of course, disaster will follow." Abbu's thick beard jounced with satisfaction. "Disaster and ruin. The cannons will not arrive in time. The seaward assault will fail miserably, most of your newfangled gunships adrift or sunk outright. Your army will starve outside the walls of the city."

"Barbaricum doesn't have any walls," commented Belisarius mildly. "The cannons we're offloading are mostly to stop any relief ships bringing reinforcements from upriver. If there are any, that is. Khusrau should be starting his own attack out of the Kacchi desert any day now. Who knows? He may have begun already."

Abbu was not mollified. "Persians! Attacking through a desert? By now, half of them are bones bleaching in the sun. Mark my words, General of Rome. We are destined for an early grave."

Belisarius had to fight to keep from grinning. Abbu's high spirits were infectious. From years of working with the old bandit-in-all-but-name, Belisarius knew full well that Abbu's confidence stood in direct—and inverse—proportion to his grousing. A gloomy and morose Abbu was a man filled with high morale. A cheerful Abbu, dismissing all danger lightly, was a man with his back to the wall and expecting imminent demise.

"Be off, Abbu," Belisarius chuckled. "Clear any and all Malwa from my path."

"That!" The Arab scout began to turn away, heading for his horse. "That! The only thing which will go as planned!"

Within a minute or so, Abbu was over the side and organizing the Arab outriders. Within ten minutes, hundreds of lightly armed Arabs—from many ships—were disappearing into the darkness. Moving as swiftly as any light cavalry on earth, they would fall on any Malwa troops outside Barbaricum's shelter and either kill them or drive them into the port.

When the last Arab had vanished into the purple gloom of a barely breaking day, Belisarius turned to Maurice.

"So? Where are *your* predictions of catastrophe?"

Maurice grunted. "Abbu said it all. Nothing to add."

A heavier clattering began. The first of the Roman warhorses were being brought onto the deck, and the heavily armored cataphracts were clumping around to lead them off the ship.

Maurice's face seemed to lighten a bit. Or, perhaps, it was simply that daylight was beginning to spread. "Might not be so bad, though. Abbu always was a pessimist. We might be able to fight our way back through the mountains, after the disaster, with maybe a tenth of the army still alive."

By the time Belisarius caught sight of Barbaricum, the city was already burning. Burning fiercely, in fact—far more than any city made primarily from mudbrick should have been.

"No way the ships' guns caused that," said Maurice.

Belisarius shook his head. He halted his horse atop a slight rise in the landscape—more like a little mound of dry mud than a "rise"—and cocked an ear. He couldn't see the Roman fleet beyond the port, but he could hear the sound of its cannonade.

"Sounds good, though," he said quietly. "I don't think the fleet has suffered much damage."

He listened for perhaps five minutes longer. Only once, in that time, did he hear the deeper roar of one of the Malwa siege guns positioned to protect the harbor. And even that one sounded odd. Slightly muted, as if—

"They're using light powder loads," said Gregory. The commander of the artillery force which was off-loading onto the delta—miles behind them, now—had accompanied Belisarius and Maurice. "Looks like you were right, General. They're saving it for something else."

Belisarius left off listening to the cannon fire and studied Barbaricum. Much of the city was invisible, shrouded in smoke. But, here and there, he could see portions of the mudbrick buildings which made up most of the city's outlying areas.

Barbaricum was an unwalled city. But its residential areas were so tightly packed, one building abutting another, that at a superficial glance they appeared to form a defensive wall. The more so since, so far as he could see, there were no windows in any of the exterior walls of the buildings. That might be due to conscious planning, but Belisarius suspected it was simply a matter of cost. The population of Barbaricum, as the name itself implied, was polyglot and largely transient. The simplest and cheapest construction would be the norm.

He reached down into a saddlebag and pulled out his telescope. Then, looking for gaps in the smoke, he began studying the few alleyways which opened into the city's interior. Still, he could see hardly anything. The alleyways were narrow and crooked, providing only short lines of sight. Needless to say, they were filled with refuse. Only one of the alleys—the one Belisarius focused his attention upon—provided a glimpse of more than a few yards into Barbaricum.

A sudden lull in the cannon fire, perhaps combined with a slight shift in the wind, allowed him for the first time to hear sounds coming from the city itself. Sounds of screaming.

"You were right," repeated Gregory. The words were almost hissed.

Belisarius tightened his jaws. As soon as Gregory began to speak, he had caught sight through the telescope of the first signs of movement in the city. Four people, dressed in rags—two women and two children, he thought—were running down one of the alleyways. Trying to get out of the city.

As he watched, one of the women stumbled and fell. For a moment, Belisarius thought she had tripped over some of the refuse in the alley. Twisted an ankle or broken a bone, judging from the way she was writhing on the ground. Her face was distorted by a grimace. Belisarius could hear nothing, but he was quite sure she was screaming.

Then he spotted the arrow sticking out of the back of the woman's leg. An instant later, another arrow took her in the ribs. Now he *could* hear her screams.

When the woman fell, one of the children had stopped and hesitated. Began to turn back, until the other woman grabbed the child and resumed the race to get out of the city.

Too late. Three soldiers came into sight, racing down the alley. A second or two later, a Mahaveda priest became visible also. The priest was shouting something. When the soldiers reached the wounded woman lying in the alley, one of them paused just long enough to slash her neck with a sword. Arterial blood spurted against the grimy walls of the nearest building.

The other two soldiers kept up their pursuit of the surviving woman and the two children. The refugees were now almost out of the city.

Behind him, Belisarius heard one of his bodyguards snarling a curse. Priscus, that was—his eyesight was superb, and he had no need of a telescope to follow what was happening.

"We could maybe reach—" said the cataphract, uncertainly.

Before Belisarius could shake his head, Aide's voice was ringing in his mind.

No! No! That city is a death-trap!

Belisarius sighed. He lowered the telescope and turned his head.

"I'm sorry, Priscus. We can't risk it. The Malwa started those fires, not our cannons. That was deliberate. They always knew they couldn't hold Barbaricum against a serious assault. Not so long as we control the sea. So they're starting the scorched earth policy right here. And, as I feared—and expected—that will include slaughtering the populace."

He turned back, forcing himself to watch the last moments, though he saw no reason to use the telescope. The two soldiers had overtaken the fleeing woman and children just outside the city. Blades flashed in the distance. Then, moving more slowly, the two soldiers jogged back to their fellow and the priest, who were standing at the mouth of the alley. Once the small party was reunited, they began prowling back into the city's interior. They reminded Belisarius of scavengers, searching rubbage for scraps of food.

"Fucking animals," snarled Priscus. "But wait till they try to leave themselves."

The cataphract's eyes ranged the landscape behind the small command party. The sight seemed to fill his hard face with satisfaction.

Already, columns of Roman troops could be seen marching through the flat terrain. Some of those soldiers were following the path left by Belisarius and his party. Most of them, however, were ranging inland. Within a few hours, Barbaricum would be surrounded by the Roman army. The city was already surrounded by a cavalry screen.

"No prisoners," Priscus growled. He gave Belisarius a hard, almost angry stare. The Roman commander's policy of not allowing atrocities had, over the past two years, become firmly established throughout his army. With, as always, his personal household troops—*bucellarii,* as the Romans called them—ready to enforce the policy. Priscus was one of those bucellarii himself, and normally had no quarrel with the policy. Today, clearly enough, discipline was straining at the leash.

Belisarius returned the stare with one that was just as hard, if not angry. "Don't be stupid, Priscus," he said calmly. "Most of those soldiers are just following orders. And after they finish butchering the civilians, we're going to need *them* for a labor force."

His lips quirked for a moment, before he offered the consolation prize. "Mahaveda priests, on the other hand, are unaccustomed to hard labor. So I don't believe there's any need to keep *them* alive. Or any officers, for that matter."

Priscus scowled, as did Isaac and the rest of Belisarius' small squad of bodyguards. But none of them made any further argument or protest.

"Cheer up, lads," said Maurice. The words were accompanied by a burbling laugh so harsh it sounded like stones clashing in a torrent. "Nobody said anything about making their life easy."

The chiliarch—the term meant, literally, "ruler of a thousand," though Maurice commanded far more than a thousand men—turned in his saddle and grinned at Priscus and the other cataphracts. The teeth, shining in his rough-hewn, high-cheeked, gray-bearded face, gave the man more than a passing resemblance to an old wolf.

"We may not work the bastards to death," he continued cheerily. "Not *quite*. But they'll be wishing we had, be sure of it."

His words, beginning with "bastards to death," were punctuated by a ripple of sharp, cracking explosions.

"They're destroying the big guns at the harbor," pronounced Gregory.

No sooner were those words out, than a sudden roar erupted from the city. The sound of a gigantic explosion billowed across the countryside. A large part of Barbaricum—the port area, it seemed—vanished under a huge cloud of smoke and debris.

"They're blowing the whole harbor area itself, now." Gregory grimaced. "I'd have thought they'd wait a bit. Most of the men destroying the guns must have been caught . . ." His words trailed off, as he shook his head.

Belisarius was a bit surprised himself. Malwa artillery was staffed exclusively by Malwa kshatriya, the warrior caste. As a rule, the Malwa tended to coddle that elite class. He had expected the Malwa commander of Barbaricum to try to include the kshatriya in the break-out.

There won't be a break-out, said Aide suddenly. **No way to be sure, but . . .**

As with Gregory, faced with such incredible ruthlessness, Aide's thoughts trailed into silence. Belisarius could almost picture the crystalline equivalent of a headshake.

Belisarius completed the thought, speaking aloud for the benefit of the men around him.

"At a guess, I'd say the Mahaveda have usurped command in Barbaricum. Probably had the actual military commander summarily executed. For incompetence, or dereliction of duty—whatever. The priests will be running the show entirely, from now on."

Clearly enough, from the look of satisfaction which came over the faces of Maurice, Gregory, and his bodyguards, that thought caused them no great discomfort. None at all, truth be told.

"Good riddance," muttered Isaac. "Let the bastards all burn in hell."

Priscus rumbled a laugh, of sorts. "Nice. We can just sit out here and watch them fry."

Gregory's face was now creased with a frown. "Maybe not. If there are any Kushans in Barbaricum, I'd be surprised if they didn't mutiny. Once they finally understood what the priests have in store for them."

Belisarius began to speak, but fell silent once he saw Maurice shake his head. Unlike Gregory, who had been preoccupied with off-loading his troops' equipment, Maurice had been present two nights before when Belisarius heard the report of the spies returned from Barbaricum.

"There aren't any Kushans here," announced Maurice. "In fact, according to our spies, the Malwa are pulling them out of the Indus entirely." Again, he grinned like a wolf. "I'm willing to bet Kungas has been chewing his way through central Asia, and the word is spreading. Apparently, several thousand Kushans stationed in the upper valley mutinied. Last anyone saw, they were heading up the Jhelum, with the heads of Mahaveda priests and Malwa kshatriya—and not a few Ye-tai—perched on their pikes."

Geography was not Gregory's best subject. "What's the Jhelum?"

"One of the tributaries of the Indus," replied Belisarius. "It provides the easy access—relatively easy, that is—to the Hindu Kush. And Peshawar, where Kungas plans to rebuild the Kushan capital."

"Oh."

Priscus laughed. "Oh! The fucking Malwa empire is starting to come apart at the seams."

Belisarius saw no reason to correct the cataphract's overly optimistic assessment. In reality, he knew, the great Malwa empire—still the world's most powerful—could hardly be described as "coming apart at the seams."

True, the northwest Deccan was lost entirely, except

for Bharakuccha and the lowlands along the Narmada river. But the Malwa conquest of the Andhra empire was only a few years in the past, and the region had never really been incorporated by the Malwa. Even the southern and eastern portions of conquered Andhra had been sullen and restive. The northwest—Majarashtra, the heartland of the Marathas—had never stopped fighting openly, even before Shakuntala escaped captivity and provided the rebels with a rallying point.

As for the Kushans . . .

They never fit very well into the Malwa scheme of things, said Aide. **Not pampered and privileged like the Ye-tai, not locked in by custom and tradition like the Rajputs—a square peg in a round hole. Always were, at the best of times. They were bound to break away, given any chance at all.**

After a moment's silence, Aide continued his thoughts:

You can't say the Malwa empire is "coming apart at the seams" until the heartland erupts in rebellion. The Ganges valley where the tens of millions of Malwa subjects are concentrated. And not just rebels in the forests of Bihar and Bengal, either. Peasants in the plain, and townsmen in the great cities. That's what it will take. And they won't risk rebellion—not after the massacre of Ranapur—unless they see a real chance of winning. Of which there is none, so long as the Malwa dynasty stays intact and commands the allegiance of the Ye-tai and Rajputs.

Again, a moment's silence. Then, in a thought filled with satisfaction: **Still . . . I think it's fair to say that cracks are showing. Big ones.**

Belisarius said nothing in response. In the minutes that followed, as one great explosion after another announced the rolling destruction of Barbaricum, he never even bothered to watch. He was turned in the saddle, staring to the northeast. There, somewhere beyond the horizon, lay Rajputana. That harsh and arid hill country was the forge in which the Rajputs had been created.

And if they begin to crack . . .

The Malwa will still have the Ye-tai, cautioned Aide. **The Ye-tai have nowhere else to go. Especially if Kungas succeeds in reconquering the lands of the former Kushan empire, where the Ye-tai once had their stronghold. Before they accepted the Malwa offer to become the most privileged class in India after the Malwa themselves.**

Belisarius smiled crookedly. *"Nowhere else to go?" Don't be too sure of that, Aide. Enterprising men— especially ones who can see the handwriting on the wall—can find avenues of escape in many places. What was it that fellow said? The one you told me about in the future that would have been, who made so many fine quips.*

Dr. Samuel Johnson. "Depend upon it, sir, when a man knows he is to be hanged in a fortnight, it concentrates his mind wonderfully."

Chapter 23
THE DECCAN
Autumn, 533 A.D.

Rana Sanga kept his eyes firmly fixed on the ivory half-throne which supported the flaccid body of Lord Venandakatra. Not on the Goptri of the Deccan himself. Much like Venandakatra's face—with which Sanga had become all too familiar in the weeks since Damodara's army had arrived in the Deccan—the chair was carved into a multitude of complex and ornate folds and crevices.

But the Rajput king found it far easier to look at the chair than at the Malwa lord who sat in it. The piece of furniture, after all, had been shaped by the simple hand of a craftsman, not the vices and self-indulgences which had shaped Venandakatra's fat toad-lizard parody of a human face.

The Rajput king dwelled on that comparison, for a moment. He found it helped to restrain his fury. The more so since, whenever the rage threatened to overwhelm him, he could deflect it into a harmless fantasy of hacking the chair into splinters instead of . . .

Lord Venandakatra finally ceased his vituperative

attack on the Rajput troops which formed the heart of Damodara's army. Lord Damodara began speaking. The sound of his commander's calm and even-tempered voice broke through the red-tinged anger which clouded Sanga's brain.

Sanga lifted his eyes and turned them to Damodara. The commander of the Malwa forces newly arrived in the Deccan was leaning back comfortably in his own chair, apparently relaxed and at ease.

"—are more than welcome to transmit your displeasure to the emperor and Nanda Lal," Damodara was saying. His tone was mild, almost serene. "Please, Lord Venandakatra! Do me the favor! Perhaps the emperor might heed your words—unlikely though that is—and send me and my army elsewhere. To fight a war instead of attempting to indulge a spoiled child."

Venandakatra hissed at the insult. He began gobbling incoherent outrage and indignation, but Damodara's still-calm voice slid through it like a knife.

"A stupid child, as well as a spoiled one. I told you from the beginning that not even Rajputs with Pathan trackers could hope to match Rao's Maratha hillfighters on their own terrain. The Panther has hillforts scattered throughout the Great Country. If we match him in the hills and valleys, he retreats to the hilltops. If we besiege the forts—which is easier said than done, Venandakatra—he fades down the slopes. Not without, each time, bleeding us further."

Gobble, gobble, gobble.

Damodara heaved a little half-snort, half-sigh. Derision mingled with exasperation. "From the day I arrived, I told you to cease your terror campaign. Butchering and torturing Maratha villagers does nothing beyond swell the ranks of Rao's army. By now, that army is at least as large as my own. Half again the size, I estimate."

The gobbling began producing coherent half-phrases. *Have you impaled yourself . . . I am the emperor's first cousin . . . you only distantly related . . . insubordination and mutiny and treason . . . on a short stake . . .*

"Be silent!" snarled Damodara. For once, the Malwa military commander's normal placidity was frayed. "Just exactly *how* do you propose to have me impaled, you foul creature?"

Damodara's round face twisted into a sneer. He waved a hand at Venandakatra's bodyguards. The five Ye-tai were standing against the rear of the audience chamber. They seemed a bit nervous.

"With them?" demanded Damodara, his sneer turning into a savage grin. Sitting next to him, Sanga casually placed a powerful hand on the hilt of his sword. That sword had been a minor legend throughout India even before the war began. Today, the legend was no longer minor.

The five Ye-tai bodyguards were definitely nervous.

Behind Sanga and Damodara, where they squatted on cushions, Sanga could sense the slight manner in which his two Rajput and one Ye-tai officers shifted their own stances. Without having to look, Sanga knew that all three men were now ready to leap to their feet in an instant, weapons in hand.

The Ye-tai bodyguards were *very* nervous. For all the outwardly respectful manner of their unmoving stance, the five men against the wall practically exuded fear and apprehension. Their eyes were no longer on their master, Venandakatra. They were riveted on the men sitting behind Sanga, even more than on Sanga himself.

One of those men, rather. Sanga knew—and suddenly had to fight down a cheerful laugh—that it was the Ye-tai officer squatting behind him who most thoroughly intimidated the bodyguards. Not so much because Toramana was a fearsome warrior, but simply because he was Ye-tai himself.

Ye-tai, yes—just like the bodyguards. But it was already known by all the Malwa forces in the Deccan that Rana Sanga, the greatest king of Rajputana, had promised one of his own half-sisters to Toramana as a wife. And had done so, because Toramana had requested marriage into the Chauhar dynasty.

The implications of that liaison had not escaped anyone. *Certainly not Venandakatra . . .*

The Goptri of the Deccan was now glaring past Sanga's shoulder. Past his hip, rather, where the face of Toramana would be visible to him. For all his fury and his self-indulgence, Venandakatra had not missed the subtleties of the matter at hand.

"This—this absurd marriage has *not* been agreed to by the emperor! All Ye-tai are still—"

He choked off whatever might have been the last words. As the pressure of the Roman–Persian campaign led by Belisarius mounted on the Malwa empire, the Malwa were being forced to relax the long-standing principles of their rigid system of caste, status and hierarchy. Venandakatra knew full well that Nanda Lal had already given his approval to the marriage. The emperor's approval was bound to follow.

In times past, of course, they would not have done so. Would, in all likelihood, have punished any Rajput or Ye-tai who even proposed it. High-ranking and meritorious Ye-tai, and occasionally Rajputs, had been allowed to marry into the Malwa clan as a means of cementing their allegiance to the ruling dynasty. But never had the two principal pillars of Malwa rule been allowed to marry each other. The threat of such liaisons was obvious.

In times past . . .

Damodara chuckled harshly. "Times past are times

past, Venandakatra. In times past, Belisarius was not at our borders."

The Malwa army commander thrust himself abruptly to his feet. "There's no point in this," he said, again speaking calmly and evenly. "If you wish to do so, you may complain to the emperor. But, after all your complaints and failures over the past three years, I doubt he will give you an ear."

For a moment, Damodara studied his nominal superior. Then, still as calmly as ever:

"You are a military cretin as well a pustule, Venandakatra. 'Vile One' you are called, and never was a man more justly named. I will no longer subject my soldiers to casualties because of your asinine demands. Henceforth, my army will patrol the approaches to Bharakuccha and the line of the Narmada river. Let Rao have the hills and the rest of the Great Country."

He clasped his hands behind his back and stared down at Venandakatra. The Goptri of the Deccan returned the stare with a pale face, and eyes which seemed as wide as lilypads. *People did not speak to the emperor's first cousin in such a manner!*

"So long as Bharakuccha remains firmly in our grasp," continued Damodara, "we have our hands on the throat of Majarashtra. When the time comes, and we have once again the strength to do so, we shall squeeze that throat. But in the meantime—"

Again, he sneered. "*Cretin,* I named you, and named you well. Tomorrow is tomorrow, and today is today. *Today* the task at hand is beating down Belisarius. For that we need Bharakuccha intact—intact, along with the great fleet in its harbor."

Finally, Venandakatra found his voice. "I want you out of Bharakuccha!" he screeched. "Out—do you hear? Out! *Out!* You and every one of your stinking Rajputs!" For an instant, the Goptri glared at Toramana. "Every one of your soldiers! Out of the city! Live in camps along the river!"

The Goptri was shaking with rage. He began beating the armrests of his chair with his thin-boned, pudgy hands. "Out! Out! Out! This minute!"

Damodara shrugged. "So be it. Although you'd be wiser to keep at least a third of my army in the city itself. But"—another shrug—"I've long since given up any hope of teaching you wisdom."

Damodara's gaze moved to Sanga and, then, to the three officers squatting behind him. "Come," he commanded. "I want the army out of this city by tomorrow night."

"At once!" screamed Venandakatra. "Not tomorrow night! Now! *Now!*"

Damodara's ensuing laugh was one of genuine amusement. " 'Cretin,' didn't I say?" The next words were spoken as if to a child. A badly spoiled brat.

"You do not move an army of forty thousand men—*and* their horses, *and* their equipment, *and* their supplies—in the blink of an eye. Vile One."

He turned away and began walking toward the entry to the chamber. "As it is, I think we'll be working a miracle. By tomorrow night."

Shakuntala, Empress of Andhra, spent four hours searching her palace at Deogiri before she finally accepted the truth. It had been a waste of time, and she knew it. Not by accident, the search ended with her standing in her baby's room. She took the boy from his nurse's arms and cradled him in her own.

"He's gone, Namadev," she whispered, fighting back the tears. Then, slumping into a chair, she caressed the little head. "Once he knew his son was healthy . . ."

The baby smiled happily at his mother's face, and gurgled pleasure. Namadev was a cheerful boy.

Cheerful and healthy. As good an assurance that the ancient Satavahana dynasty would continue as anyone could ask for.

Which, therefore, freed the father for a long-postponed task. Once again, the Wind of the Great Country was free to roam, and wreak its havoc.

Chapter 24
THE INDUS
Autumn, 533 A.D.

As soon as Belisarius emerged at daybreak from his small cabin on the cargo vessel which was slowly moving up the Indus, he began scanning the area on both sides of the river with his telescope.

He was relieved by what he saw. The monsoon season, by all reports as well as his own experience escaping from India three years before, ended earlier in the Indus valley than it did in the subcontinent itself. The view through the telescope seemed to confirm that. Everywhere he looked, the fertile grasslands which constituted the alluvial plains of the Indus seemed dry and solid. Except for the canals and small tributaries which divided the landscape into wedges—*doabs*, as the natives called them—he could not spot any indications of the wet terrain which would be a serious obstacle to his campaign plans.

For a moment, basking in the knowledge and the bright, dry, early morning sunshine, he spent a few idle seconds following the flight of a kingfisher up the riverbank. Then, his eyes arrested by the sight of a white heron perched on the back of a water buffalo, he burst into laughter.

Maurice had arisen still earlier, and was standing at his side. The chiliarch, when he saw what Belisarius was laughing at, issued a chuckle himself. For once, it seemed, even Maurice was in a good mood.

Belisarius lowered the telescope. "Wheat and barley, everywhere you look. Some rice, too. And I saw a number of water buffaloes. Say whatever else you will about the Malwa, at least they maintained the irrigation canals. Extended and developed them, it looks like."

Maurice's inevitable scowl returned. "We still don't have a labor force. There aren't any *people* anywhere. At least, I haven't seen any except a small fishing craft at sundown yesterday. And they beached the boat and scuttled into the grasslands as soon as we came near."

"Do you blame them?" Belisarius turned his head and looked back down the river. As far as his eye could see, moving up the Indus behind his own ship, the great Roman fleet was bringing as many of his troops as could be fit into their hulls into the interior of the river valley. The bulk of his army, including most of the infantry, was marching up the river under the command of Bouzes and Coutzes. Belisarius and his waterborne troops were now almost entirely out of the coastal province called Thatta, and entering the heartland of the Sind.

After the seizure of Barbaricum—the rubble that had been Barbaricum, it might be better to say—Belisarius had immediately begun building a new port. The work would go slower than he had originally planned, because his decision to accept Antonina's change of schedule meant that the preparations for that port had lagged behind. But his combat engineers assured him they could get the harbor itself operational within days.

Fortunately, Belisarius' attack seemed to have caught the Mahaveda in the middle of their own preparations as well. The fanatic priests had succeeded in destroying the city, along with most of its population and garrison, but they had been able to do little damage to the breakwater. The biggest problem the engineers faced was erecting enough shelter for the huge army that was beginning to offload behind the initial wave which had taken Barbaricum.

There too, the change in timing had worked to Belisarius' advantage. Even along the coast, the monsoon season was ending. They were now entering India's best time of year, the cool and dry season Indians called *rabi*. That season would last about four months, until well into February, before the heat of *garam* arrived. But *garam*, for all its blistering heat and the discomfort of dust, was a dry season also. Not until next May, when the monsoon returned, would Belisarius have to deal with the inevitable epidemics which always accompanied large armies on campaign. Until then there would be some disease, of course, but not the kind of plagues which had crippled or destroyed armies so many times in history.

Movement would be easy, too. And even though Belisarius knew full well that the kind of fluid maneuver warfare which he preferred would be impossible soon enough—fighting his way through the Malwa fortifications in the gorge above Sukkur would be slogging siege warfare—he intended to take full advantage of the perfect campaign conditions while he still could.

That thought brought the telescope back to his eye. This time, however, he was not scanning the entire countryside. His attention was riveted to the north. There, if all had gone according to plan—or even close to it—the Persian army of Emperor Khusrau would be hammering into the mid-valley out of the Kacchi desert.

Between Belisarius coming from the south, and Khusrau from the northwest, the Roman general hoped to trap and crush whatever Malwa forces hadn't yet been able to seek shelter in the fortifications along the river.

He hoped to do more than that, in truth. He hoped that the Malwa army stationed in the lower valley would still be confused and disorganized by the unexpectedly early Roman assault—and the completely unexpected heavy Persian force coming out of the western desert. Disorganized enough that he might be able to shatter them completely and actually take the fortifications all along the lower Indus. According to his spies, none of those river fortifications except for the city of Sukkur had been completed yet. He might be able to drive the Malwa out of the lower valley altogether. They would have to regroup at Sukkur and the upper valley north of the Sukkur gorge.

If Belisarius could accomplish *that*—and provided his army and Khusrau's could salvage enough of a labor force from the Malwa massacre—he would have a position from which the Malwa could not hope to dislodge him. Not, at least, so long as Rome and its Axumite allies retained naval superiority. The entire lower valley of the Indus would be securely in Roman and Persian hands. An area sizeable enough and rich enough to provide them with far more than a mere "beachhead." The theater of war would have been irrevocably shifted entirely into Indian territory.

"All of the Sind . . ." he murmured.

Maurice, as was usually true except when Belisarius' crooked mind was working through some peculiar stratagem, was following his commander's thoughts. "Remind me to compliment Antonina on her feminine intuition," he said, with a little smile.

"Isn't that the truth!" laughed Belisarius. His own

smile was not little at all—nor even in the least bit crooked.

The experience of the past few days had driven home to him quite forcefully how much Antonina's insistence on moving up the invasion schedule had ultimately worked to his advantage. Impulsive and narrowly focused that insistence might have been, but in the end it had proven wiser than the sagacity of experienced soldiers. From everything Belisarius could determine, the Malwa had been caught by surprise. As much surprise, at least, as an opponent could be when faced by an inevitable invasion route.

He chuckled harshly. "I suspect Nanda Lal's excellent spy service worked against him, too. He *knew* we wouldn't attack this soon. He had hundreds of spies feeding him information on every stage of our preparations and planning. Down to every amphora full of grain, I don't doubt. Of course, once we changed plans and started scrambling, he would have heard of that as well. But—"

"Too late," finished Maurice. "That's the problem with having such a gigantic and powerful empire. It's just too big to react quickly."

Like a stegosaurus, chimed in Aide, flashing an image of a bizarre giant reptile into Belisarius' brain. **By the time the nerve impulse gets to the brain . . . True, that brain is Link's, not a stupid reptile's. But Link can't be everywhere. The monster has no magic powers. It's not clairvoyant. It relies on information provided by others.**

Aide's words reminded Belisarius of a phrase the crystal had used occasionally, when Aide lapsed into the language of a future accustomed to artificial intelligence. The expression had never *quite* made sense to Belisarius, until this moment.

Again, he smiled. *Garbage in, garbage out. GIGO.*

Belisarius' good cheer was not entirely shared by Maurice. "They'll recover from the surprise soon enough. Not quick enough, maybe, to keep us from taking the Sind up to Sukkur and the gorge. But that won't do us much good if we don't get a labor force to bring in the food. Not to mention maintaining the irrigation works. Not to mention keeping the towns and cities working."

The gray-bearded chiliarch glared at the carpet of doabs which stretched to the horizon. The multitude of canals and riverlets winkled in the sun, holding the dry patches of land in place like lead holding stained glass. "Picture soldiers doing that, will you? Even if most of them were peasants not too long ago. It'd take us half the army to keep the other half working."

The telescope was back at Belisarius' eye. "Unless I miss my guess, Maurice, those grasslands are practically crawling with peasants and their families. Laying low, out of sight. By now, the Malwa must have begun their butchery, and word travels fast.

"Besides," he added, sweeping his telescope around to the north, "they can't be too thrilled to see us coming, either."

Maurice didn't argue the point. He knew from his own experience, both as a peasant and a cataphract, how astute a rural population could be when it came to keeping out of sight of a passing army. And knew, as well, that they usually had good reason to do so.

As it happened, they had little to fear from Belisarius' army. That army, in fact, was all that would save their lives. But Maurice knew perfectly well that the Romans had as much chance of "convincing" the Indus peasantry of that as a cat would have convincing mice it was a vegetarian. Especially a peasantry which had been yoked by Malwa for half a century now. First they would have to force the peasantry out of hiding. Only then, as experience unfolded, could they hope to gain their allegiance. Or, at the least, their acquiescence in the new regime. And it would all have to be done fairly quickly, or the Roman army pouring into the Sind would begin starving.

He began to say something to that effect. But then, seeing the sudden tension in the way Belisarius pressed the telescope to his eye, Maurice fell silent. Something was happening.

"I think—" Belisarius muttered. "I think—"

An instant later he removed the telescope and nodded his satisfaction. "Sure of it. That's Abbu in the prow of that oncoming galley. And those oars are beating to double time."

He folded up the telescope with a vigorous motion. The cleverly designed eyepiece collapsed with not much more than a slight clap. The superb workmanship involved reminded Maurice of John of Rhodes, who had built the thing, and a little wave of sadness rolled over him.

Just a little wave, however, and not for long. Maurice had been a soldier for decades. Men died in war; it was the nature of the beast. Often enough, as with John, from pure and simple bad luck.

"Finally!" exclaimed Belisarius. "We'll get some real news. Abbu wouldn't be returning—not in a war galley beating double-time, for sure—unless he had something to report."

Maurice grunted his own satisfaction. Like Belisarius—like any soldier worthy of the name—he *hated* being forced to maneuver blindly. And since the capture of Barbaricum, and a few initial clashes with Malwa detachments down in the delta, the Romans had lost contact with their enemy. Someone in Malwa command had moved quickly, so much was clear enough, and ordered a withdrawal.

But where had they withdrawn? How many? To what end? Those questions and a hundred others remained unanswered.

Abbu provided some of the answers as soon as he clambered aboard Belisarius' little "flagship." The old Arab was grinning, and practically danced across the deck.

"Khusrau hit them like a sledge!" he barked. Then, slapping one hand into the other: "Broke the Malwa outside Sukkur when the fools sallied, thinking they faced only light cavalry—ha! Persian dehgans! They must have voided their bowels when they realized—and then—" The scout leader paused for dramatic effect and, again, slammed one hand into the other. "Then he took the city itself!"

Belisarius and Maurice were frozen, for an instant.

"He *took* Sukkur?" demanded Belisarius. "But—that city was supposed to be walled. I even got descriptions of the walls from two of my spies!"

"He had no siege guns," protested Maurice.

Abbu grinned. "It *is* a walled city, General. Very great walls, too—I have seen them myself." The grin widened. "Great enough to withstand even the great Malwa army which is now besieging it themselves."

Maurice was still groping with the puzzle. Belisarius' quick mind leapt immediately to the only possible solution.

"The populace rebelled. The moment word arrived that Khusrau had broken the Malwa in the field, the populace rose up against the garrison."

Abbu nodded vigorously. "Butchered plenty of the bastards, too, before Khusrau arrived. Of course, they couldn't have subdued the garrison once it rallied. They would have been massacred. But they drove them off a section of the walls long enough to open the gates.

And once the Persians were into the city, the Malwa were so much carrion."

Belisarius' thoughts were still ranging far. His eyes were fixed on the northern horizon, as if by force of will he could study everything that was transpiring there. Then, slowly, he scanned the surrounding countryside.

"I was wrong," he murmured. "I saw only their fears." His tone was half-bemused—and half-sad. "I have been a soldier too long."

Aide understood, if no one else did.

Malwa has terrorized them for two generations. And now the fabled Emperor of Persia arrives, in his splendor and his glory, thundering out of the desert and surrounded by the might of his iron dehgans. The thoughts came soft and warm. **Even peasants in the Sind will have heard tales of Rustam and his great bull-headed mace. Dim legends, and those of another people to boot. But for all their scarred memories, they will want to *believe* those legends. Especially now, with Malwa sharpening the ax.**

"Yes," said Belisarius. "Yes. It's become a war of liberation. In *name* as well as in deed. And with Khusrau here himself, there is an immediate pole around which confused and frightened—and angry—people can rally. Khusrau will bring a *legitimacy* to the thing, which a purely military invasion force could not. A foreign ruler, true enough—but so what? The Sind has been ruled by foreigners for centuries. Now, at least, they will have one who is splendid as well as mighty. *Just*, as well as fearsome."

He turned to Maurice. "Pass the word. Make sure everyone understands it. Brand it into their foreheads if you have to—or I will brand it into their corpses. Any Roman soldier who commits any crime in this valley will be summarily executed. *Any* crime, Maurice, be it so much as pilfering a goat."

The general's brown eyes were glaring hot, something which was almost as rare as a solar eclipse. Maurice turned his own head and gazed at the three couriers who accompanied him at all times.

"You heard the general," he said curtly. "Do it. Now. Use as many men as you need to pass the word."

His eyes fell on Leo. Antonina had insisted that Belisarius add Leo to his personal bodyguard, retaining only Matthew for herself. The ugliest and most savage-looking of Belisarius' small squad of bodyguards—and they were all enormous, savage-looking men—was standing well within earshot.

"You heard?" Leo nodded heavily.

"You understand?" Leo nodded heavily.

Maurice glanced at Belisarius. The general smiled crookedly. "I shouldn't imagine I'll need Leo for a bit," he murmured.

Maurice turned back to Leo. "Would you like a break from your normal duties?"

Leo nodded heavily.

For a moment, Maurice hesitated. Outside of battle, where his strength and trained reflexes were quite sufficient, Leo was so dull-witted he was often mistaken for a deafmute.

"You sure you understand what—"

Leo interrupted. "Not hard to understand. Do what the general says or I will hit you."

Leo hefted the huge mace which was his favored weapon. True, the thing was simply-made; no fancy bull-headed carving here. But perhaps not even the Rustam of Aryan legend could have hefted it so lightly.

"Hit you very hard. Two, three, maybe ten times. General burns his name into what's left. Not much."

Everyone standing on the deck of the ship who was

close enough to hear burst into laughter. Even Abbu laughed heartily, despite the fact that maintaining discipline over his own scouts during the days to come would tax him greatly. For the most part those scouts were bedouin, who considered pillaging a conquered village an act as natural as eating. Nothing outrageous, of course, unless the village had done something to aggravate them. But—*goats*?

Before Leo and the couriers had even begun lowering themselves over the rail into the galley tied up alongside, Belisarius was issuing new orders. For one of the few times in his life, Belisarius' normally relaxed and calm demeanor had vanished. He was pacing back and forth on the deck like a tiger in a cage.

"This breaks it wide open!" he exclaimed. He slapped both hands together like a gunshot. Once, twice, thrice. Then, come to a decision, he abruptly halted his pacing and spun around to face his officers.

"Separate the army, Maurice. I want the sharp-shooters and the engineers in the galleys. As many field guns as you can manage also, along with their crews, as long as you leave room for Felix's musketeers to defend the counter-siege. The galleys can get there faster than the sailing ships, with this damn erratic wind."

Belisarius now turned to Ashot, the Armenian cataphract whom Belisarius considered the best independent commander among his subordinates, save Maurice himself. "You're in charge of pinning the Malwa at Sukkur, from the south. You'll have to hold them, Ashot. It won't be easy. You'll be heavily outnumbered. But unless I miss my guess, the Malwa are still fumbling at the new situation. They'll be so preoccupied with trying to storm into Sukkur that if they're building lines of circumvallation at all they'll be doing so only fitfully. Probably haven't even started yet."

Ashot nodded, immediately grasping the implication of the general's words. "Lines of circumvallation" meant the fortifications which a besieging army built to protect itself from other armies while, using their "lines of countervallation," they tried to reduce the fortress or city. The terms came from a future history, but did not confuse him in the least. Over the past year, as they prepared for this campaign, Belisarius had spent countless hours training his top subordinates in the complex methods of siege warfare he expected to witness in the Indus. Aide had taught Belisarius those methods, from the experience of future wars. The Roman general had no doubt at all that Link had done as much for its own Malwa subordinates.

"Without good lines of circumvallation," Ashot elaborated, "the sudden appearance of Roman soldiers relieving the siege—seeming to, anyway—will pose an immediate threat. They'll *have* to attack us. No choice."

He cocked his head. "Which, I assume, is exactly what you want. We're not really a relief column. We're a decoy."

"Exactly," replied Belisarius. He paced back and forth again, just for a few steps. Stopped, jabbed a finger to the north, then swept it to the east. "If we can get you planted just south of the Malwa besieging Khusrau in Sukkur—"

He broke off and looked to Abbu. "Two questions: Are all of the Persians forted up in Sukkur? And *is* there any suitable terrain to the south where Ashot can set his lines?"

"Not all the Persians, General. After he broke the Malwa in the open field—maybe thirty miles northwest of Sukkur—and then heard the city had risen in rebellion, Khusrau sent a good part of his army back to Quetta. Almost all his infantry, except the gunners."

For a moment, Belisarius' face registered confusion.

Then: "Of course. He was thinking ahead. His dehgans could hold the walls of Sukkur, with the populace in support. The biggest danger would be starvation, so the fewer soldiers the better. And his infantry can stabilize the supply lines back to Quetta—and Quetta itself, for that matter, which controls the pass into Persia."

For the first time since he got the news of Khusrau's seizure of Sukkur, Belisarius seemed to relax. He scratched his chin, chuckling softly. "Bold move, though. And he's counting on me a lot. Because if we don't relieve that siege . . ."

"And relieve it pretty soon!" barked Maurice. "Fewer soldiers be damned. He's still got thousands of dehgans in that city, and dehgans mean warhorses. Each one of those great brutes will eat six to seven times as much as a man."

Belisarius nodded, and cocked an eye at Abbu. "And the other question?"

The old Arab glowered. "Am I a be-damned gunman?" The last term was almost spit out. Abbu was a ferocious traditionalist. He transferred the glare to Gregory. "Who knows what those newfangled devices need in the way of terrain?"

Gregory laughed. "Nothing special, Abbu. Something flat, with soft soil my gun crews and the engineers can mound up into berms." He glanced at Felix Chalcenterus. The Syrian officer was the youngest member of the staff of superb officers which Belisarius had forged around him since the war began. Although Felix was primarily a commander of musketeers, both Belisarius and Gregory thought his knowledge of artillery tactics was good enough for this purpose. Which Felix immediately proved by chiming in confidently:

"Trees would be useful, for bracing. Beyond that, anything which allows the guns to control the approaches, at least a bit. And lets me station musketeers and pikemen to protect the guns from Malwa sallies. Rivers would be ideal, or canals. Marshes will do."

"Bad for horses," muttered Abbu, who was reputed to sleep with his own.

"That's more or less the idea," retorted Gregory. "The *Malwa* will have the cavalry, not Ashot. The more they have to slog to get at him—in the face of Felix's guns—the better."

Abbu ran fingers through his thick beard. "Yes. I will leave you the men who went with me to Sukkur, and many of my other scouts. They can find you such ground. There is a great bend in the Indus, just below Sukkur. Little creeks and rivers and loops—like Mesopotamia. Somewhere in there will be a place where your be-damned *guns* can strike at Malwa. While they—"

Good cheer returned. "While they feed themselves against your gunfire. Nowhere wide enough to extend their lines. No way to flank you without boats. Many boats."

The fingers stroking the beard turned into a fist, tugging it. "Malwa don't have so many boats." Now he was practically bearding himself. "My Arabs—true bedouin!—will burn those boats they have. You watch."

He turned to Belisarius and gave the general a little bow. "Your plan will work, General. So long as you get there in time." Abbu's eyes ranged the northeast like a hawk's. Beyond those grasslands lay the edge of the great Thar desert. "It will be a difficult march. But if you can circle to the east—especially if you keep the Malwa from seeing you—"

Belisarius shrugged. "We'll get spotted, sooner or later. But by then—if all goes well—it will be too late for the Malwa to extricate themselves from their entanglement with Ashot and Felix. Thousands of their soldiers will be mired in flood river terrain. They simply can't maneuver them quickly. And they also can't release too many of their troops from the lines around Sukkur. Not with Khusrau and his dehgans inside, ready to sally. They'll be trapped between Ashot to the south and Khusrau to the north—and me hitting them from the east. With every cataphract Sittas can bring along. And once Bouzes and Coutzes get the mass of our infantry up to Sukkur, the Malwa there will be finished. They'll have to retreat back to the Punjab, with all the losses that kind of forced march always brings."

As always, Abbu was unmoved by the subtlety of a Belisarius maneuver. "Fancy, fancy. Maybe. But it will work. Provided you get there in time."

Chapter 25

Belisarius began his march to outflank the Malwa besieging Emperor Khusrau once the flotilla of small cargo vessels and river barges carrying his cavalry and field artillery was well past the great bend of the Indus. In straight line distance he was less than a hundred miles from the besieged city.

But Belisarius had no intention of approaching Sukkur either from the river or even directly from the south. He intended, once his troops off-loaded, to move almost due east. He would cross the Khairpur canal, skirt the hills directly south of Sukkur where the ancient fortress city of Kot Diji was perched, and find the channel of the Nara. Then, following the Nara just east of the Kot Diji hills, he would eventually reach the Indus again at Rohri.

Rohri, of course, was on the wrong side of the river for any army which proposed to relieve a siege of Sukkur—and Maurice had poured sarcasm and derision all over Belisarius' plan the moment the general started explaining it.

Sittas, on the other hand, was enthusiastic.

"Oh, be quiet, you old grouch," he said, half-scowling.

(Half-laughing, too, for Maurice's witticisms had been genuinely amusing. If grossly uncouth and disrespectful of an acknowledged military genius.)

"He's an acknowledged military genius, you know," continued Sittas, with a sly glance at Belisarius. The Roman commander returned the glance with a glare. "I'll bet all the history books will say so in the future."

Then, more seriously, tracing the route of the Indus on the map with a thick finger: "You should know his methods by now. Our young genius likes to force his enemies to attack *him*, not the other way around. 'Strategic offensive, tactical defensive,' he likes to call it, when he's in a philosophical mood."

Sittas' finger slid past Sukkur and Rohri and moved up the line of the Indus until it reached the juncture of the Chenab, the first major fork in the Punjab. "Right here. That's where we'll really hit them. If we can bypass Sukkur and that damned gorge north of it, we'll have a powerful force of cataphracts and field artillery in the Punjab, where the flood plain opens up again."

" 'Punjab' means 'land of five rivers,' " chimed in Belisarius. "That gives you an idea of how much maneuvering room we'll have when we resume the offensive next year. We'll be in a vastly better position than trying to fight our way out of the lower valley. *If* we can keep pushing Malwa off balance and prevent them from stabilizing the front further south at Sukkur."

Maurice did not seem mollified. "You've already divided your forces into three separate detachments, as risky as that is." He began counting off on his fingers. "You left Bouzes and Coutzes behind to bring up the infantry, who are still far to the south marching up the Indus. You're peeling off Ashot to continue straight up the river and take up positions against the

Malwa with your big guns and Felix's musketeers. And now, you're proposing a forced march of heavy cavalry and field artillery across hundreds of miles—"

"Three hundred, by my estimate."

Maurice plowed on. "—through unknown terrain—poorly known, at best—with a fragile supply route and a pitched battle at the end where you'll have cavalry trying to fight on the defensive." Stubbornly: "It's too big a gamble. You should stick to the original plan."

Belisarius gazed at his most trusted subordinate. His expression was attentive and solemn, not sarcastic. No one but a fool would dismiss Maurice's advice when it came to war.

But, when he spoke, his tone was as firm as ever. "What 'original' plan, Maurice? The original plan to attack Barbaricum weeks after we did? We've already scrapped that plan, and—you know it as well as I do—I'm improvising as I go along. I was planning to concentrate on Sukkur, but now . . . the more I think about it, I've come to the same conclusion Sittas obviously has. We'll hit them at Sukkur, leave enough of a force to make them *think* we're stopping there, but keep going up the Indus. By now, Malwa communications have *got* to be tattered. They have *got* to be confused. Their command structure has *got* to be rattled, maybe even cracking. And don't forget that Link is still in Kausambi, not in the Punjab where it might rally them quickly."

Belisarius leaned over the map and began making fierce little jabs with his finger. "If I didn't have an army and officers I trusted, I wouldn't dream of trying this. But . . ." Jab, jab, jab. "While Bouzes and Coutzes bring up the main forces, I want to move as fast as possible, hitting the Malwa again and again. Pin them in one place, force them to attack the forces I leave behind in good defensive positions, while I keep outflanking them by moving east by north."

The jabbing turned into a more thoughtful drumming of the fingers. Belisarius' eyes seemed slightly out of focus, as if he were trying to visualize enemy armies like a clairvoyant. "They'll be doing the same thing I am, right now, except I'm willing to bet they're less organized and not moving as quickly. And don't have commanders as good as Bouzes and Coutzes. They'll be bringing big forces down the river from the Punjab, just as I'm bringing them up from the lower valley. A race to see who gets to Sukkur first."

The drumming ended in an sharp, emphatic slap of his hand on the map. "But I'm not going to play their game. I'll let them get drawn into Sukkur while I move around them to the northeast. Then, if we can reach the fork of the Chenab and set up our own field fortifications, we'll have broken into the Punjab."

Maurice tugged at his beard fiercely, reluctance and eagerness obviously contesting within him. The grizzled veteran understood exactly what Belisarius was counting on. *The chaos and fog of war.* If the Romans could ride that chaos while the Malwa floundered in it . . .

"If we can end this campaign with a foothold in the Punjab," said Belisarius, "we can avoid entirely the problem of fighting our way out of the Sind through that damn bottleneck at Sukkur. And you know what a bloodbath that would be! We'll need some time to refit and recuperate after that, of course, but once we're ready to resume the offensive we'll be in a far better position to do it. We'll be attacking the Malwa in the Punjab, which spreads out before us with five rivers to serve as supply lines and invasion routes. As good a terrain as you could ask for, even given that the Malwa will have the Punjab covered with fortresses and lines of fortification. And—*and*—by then Kungas might be threatening them from the northwest, which will force them to fight on two fronts.

"I know it's a gamble, Maurice," concluded Belisarius quietly. "But I think it's not as risky as you do, and the payoff would be gigantic."

A crooked little smile replaced the solemn expression. "I can also remember a veteran telling me, years ago when I was a sprat of an officer, that the stupidest thing you can do in war is let the enemy regain his balance once you've staggered him. 'Knock 'em off their feet entirely, and kick 'em when they're down,' as I recall his words. And I recall them perfectly, because he repeated them, oh, maybe a thousand times."

Maurice scowled. Belisarius continued.

"Moving up the assault on Barbaricum surprised the Malwa. Khusrau's strike out of the Kacchi caught them completely off guard. Now they're staggering, off balance, trying to restabilize the front lines. That's why they'll be so completely preoccupied with crushing Khusrau at Sukkur. If we can hammer them hard enough at Sukkur to keep them pinned, then make a lightning strike into the upper valley and establish a stronghold at the fork of the Chenab, we'll force the Malwa—*force them*, Maurice, they won't have any choice—to lift the siege at Sukkur and try to bring their entire southern army back into the Punjab. An army which will be caught between us and Khusrau, and forced to march along the Indus where *we* can control the river with our river fleet." Shrugging: "They might be able to escape the pocket, but they'll suffer big losses in the doing."

Belisarius' eyes ranged over the map. "Of course, we'll probably encounter other Malwa armies on the way. But I'm willing to bet the Malwa forces converging from everywhere their commanders can scrape them up on short notice will be coming in ragged and disorganized. We've got a powerful and concentrated field army here, with a cohesive leadership. We can probably defeat them in detail and complete the march to the fork of the Chenab with enough of our army intact to hold it."

"And then what? You're sliding over the fact that we will *also* be caught between two armies," countered Maurice. He set his feet like a wrestler beginning a match. "You can be certain that the Malwa will bring every soldier they've got in the upper valley to hit us at the Chenab—keep *us* pinned down—while they bring that army up from Sukkur to crush us. And they've got a huge army in the Punjab, all the spies say so. Leaving aside the fact that by the time we get to the Chenab our logistics train won't be 'fragile.' It'll be in complete tatters. They don't even have to crush us. They can starve us out."

As if they were one man, the eyes of Maurice, Belisarius and Sittas came to rest on the figure of Menander. Menander had left Eusebius behind in newly conquered Barbaricum and followed Belisarius' flotilla up the Indus on the steam-powered warship named after its designer. He and the *Justinian* had caught up with Belisarius' army in time for Menander to participate in this staff meeting. The young officer had been standing a few paces back from the table in Belisarius' command tent where the argument between the general and his top staff had been occurring.

Belisarius was a bit amused—and very pleased—to see that the young Thracian managed to speak without any of the flushed embarrassment which had often characterized Menander in times past when he was called upon to give his opinion. The inexperienced cataphract who had accompanied Belisarius on his scouting expedition into the Malwa heartland had been transformed, during the four years which followed, into a self-confident officer. A commander in his own right. Uncertainty-covered-by-braggadocio had been replaced by relaxed assurance.

"I can do it, Maurice," he said firmly. "*Provided* we move at once. We're still catching the tail end of the monsoon winds. For a few more days—although it'll be hit-or-miss any given day—we can use the wind to move the ships upriver and the current to bring us back down. But once rabi settles in—"

Without a second thought, Menander used the Indian term for the cool, dry season where the winds came out of the Himalayas. India was no longer an exotic and foreign place to him.

"—it'll be a different story," he continued. "After that, moving supplies upriver will be a matter of pure sweat. The sailing ships will be almost useless, unless we can tow them with oxen. Eusebius is already starting up the river with the *Victrix*, but that hurried reconversion he did to turn her into a steam-powered paddle wheeler isn't . . . all you could ask for. So I doubt he'll be able to tow more than one barge behind him. That means we'll have to use galleys, for the most part, which aren't anywhere near as good for supply ships because so much space has to be taken up by the rowers."

"There's always your ship," said Belisarius. His smile was now more crooked than ever. "The *Justinian*."

Menander was startled. Then, running fingers through his straw-colored hair: "Yes, I suppose. Wouldn't even really require much in the way of refitting to enable it to tow several barges. And a courier vessel just brought word from Queen Rukaiya that the *Justinian*'s sister ship has left the shipyards at Adulis. So the *Photius* ought to be available to us also, before too long. Between the two of them—"

The young officer winced. "Jesus, when Justinian finds out . . ."

A little burst of laughter erupted in the tent. The new steam-powered warships were Justinian's pride and joy. The former emperor had spent years overseeing a large team of artisans to build those engines and design the ships which they would drive.

Drive into *combat,* not—not—

"Glorified tug boats!" barked Maurice, grinning. "Justinian will have apoplexy, if he finds out. Probably demand that Theodora have Menander flayed alive."

Menander did not seem to find that last particularly amusing. Neither Justinian nor Theodora was famous for their sweet temper.

"Have to keep it a secret . . ." he muttered, grimacing with anxiety.

"Don't worry about it!" boomed Sittas, taking two steps and buffeting Menander with a hearty backslap. The young officer staggered a bit under the blow. Sittas was built like a boar; his idea of a "hearty backslap" was on the excessive side. "You won't even have to lie about it. If those supply ships being towed upstream by your fancy new boats aren't forced to fight their way through every time, it'll be a miracle. Guns blazing the whole way. According to our spies, there's even a big new Malwa fortress in the Sukkur gorge they'll have to run if they try to get into the Punjab."

The fact that Menander so obviously found the prospect of desperate river battles a great relief brought another round of laughter to the tent.

Maurice, still smiling faintly, went back on the offensive. "All right, but that still leaves the critical moment up in the air." His stubby finger jabbed at the map. "You know as well as I do, General, that this 'lightning strike' of yours is most likely to come apart at the seams right at the start. In order for it to work, we've got to get the expedition through open terrain. Six thousand Arab and Syrian light cavalry can probably do it easily enough. But fifteen thousand cataphracts and two thousand artillerymen and combat engineers? And don't forget we'll be *crossing* rivers and canals, not using them for supply routes."

Scowling again, all trace of humor gone: "That's a recipe for disaster, young man. They always said Julian was a military genius too, when he was hacking his way into Persia. Until the damn fool burnt his ships and tried to march overland through Mesopotamia."

Belisarius shrugged. "Julian had four or five times as many soldiers as I'm taking. And—if I say so myself—my logistical methods are better than his were."

He paused for an instant, giving Maurice a level gaze. The chiliarch tightened his lips and looked away. Years earlier, when Maurice had been training a brilliant but inexperienced Thracian officer, he had convinced the youth to adopt the logistical methods of the great Philip of Macedon. Use mules as much as possible for his supply train, instead of the cumbersome wagons preferred by other Roman armies. The methods had proved themselves in action since, over the course of many campaigns.

"Still . . ." he grumbled, staring at that portion of the map which showed the terrain in question. "We don't know how good the foraging will be. Mules can only carry so much, and you *have* to use some wagons for the artillery supplies. And if that territory is all that fertile, you can be sure the Malwa will have plenty of troops stationed there."

Belisarius scratched his chin. "I doubt it, Maurice. Not now. The Malwa commanders have probably pulled most of their soldiers back to the river. They'll be expecting us to use the Indus as our marching route, not the Nara. The more so since—"

He fell silent, groping for a way to explain. Over the years, fighting Link, Belisarius had come to have a certain sense for how the monster's mind worked. The same superhuman intelligence imparted to Link by those "new gods" of the future was also, often enough, a gap in its armor.

Aide understood. **It always knows so much, but the knowing comes from recorded history. Not experience. And it doesn't *listen*, really. It hears, but it does not pay attention. Because it "knows" already. History—the records Link will have, which are the same as I do—will tell it that the Indus valley is largely arid. But that's because of the environmental degradation caused by the later centuries of human habitation. Its subordinates may have told it otherwise, but . . .**

The thought trailed off for a moment, then came back as firm as ever. **It will not really think about it. I have been surprised myself, many times, by how much more life there is in lands which my "knowledge" told me was half-barren. But I am not Link. I do not think the way it does. So I have learned to listen, not just hear.**

Belisarius nodded. To his subordinates, the gesture carried that certain solid air about it which they had come to recognize and respect deeply even if they were not privy to its origin. *Aide agrees with me.*

"I doubt they stationed a large force there to begin with," he stated firmly. His officers, recognizing the weight of Aide's opinion which nestled inside that confident statement, nodded their acceptance. Even Maurice.

The chiliarch sighed. "All right, then. But we should take all the mitrailleuse with us. And all the sharpshooters." He gave Mark of Edessa, standing well back in the tent, a glance of approval. "They've been trained as dragoons, so they'll be able to keep up."

Belisarius eyed him skeptically. Maurice snorted. "*All* of them, dammit. Ashot will be counter-besieging the Malwa at Sukkur, with a supply route as wide as the Indus—literally—and a fortified position guarded by our entire infantry once Bouzes and Coutzes arrive."

Another look of approval came to Maurice's face, as he thought of the twin brothers who, in the course of the Mesopotamian and Zagros campaigns, had hammered Belisarius' infantry into shape. If there was one thing in the world that Maurice treasured, it was *veteran* troops. True, most of the soldiers in the gigantic Roman army which was now taking the war to the Malwa were recent recruits, pouring into military service in hopes of sharing the spoils which smaller armies of the famous Belisarius had gleaned from earlier campaigns. But every branch of that army had been built around a core of veterans, experienced against the Malwa.

Bouzes and Coutzes' Syrian infantry and cavalry, Gregory's artillerymen, Felix's musketeers and pikemen, Mark of Edessa's new force of sharpshooters, Belisarius' own Thracian bucellarii directly commanded by Maurice himself—and, not least, the magnificent Greek cataphracts who had broken the Malwa at Anatha and the Dam, and held off Rana Sanga's ferocious cavalry charges at the Battle of the Pass.

For a moment, Maurice exchanged glances with Cyril, the man who had succeeded to command of the Greek cataphracts after Agathius was crippled at the Battle of the Dam. The glance was full of mutual approval.

Sittas suddenly laughed. "And will you look at those two? As if I don't know what they're thinking!"

He bestowed another "hearty backslap," this time on the shoulder of Cyril. The Greek cataphract, more sturdily built than Menander, did no more than flinch.

"Don't worry, my lowborn comrade. I'll see to it that my haughty noble cataphracts follow your lead." Sittas frowned. "Even if I can't say I'm too thrilled myself at the idea of fighting dismounted behind fortifications."

His face lightened. "But—who knows? There's bound to be the need for an occasional sally, now and then. History may still record that the last great charge of heavy lancers was led by Sittas the Stupendous."

Again, laughter filled the tent. This time, not so much with humor as simple satisfaction. Whether Belisarius' daring maneuver would lead to victory or defeat, no one could say. But all hesitation and doubt would now be set aside. If the plan *could* work, these men would see to it.

Chapter 26
INDIA
Autumn, 533 A.D.

Kungas studied Irene carefully. The sly humor which was normally to be found lurking somewhere in his eyes was totally absent.

"You are certain?" he demanded.

She nodded. Quite serenely, she thought. Such, at least, was her hope. "What is there to fear, Kungas? The fact that the Malwa put up only a token fight to hold Begram tells us that Belisarius must be hammering them in the south. They are apparently withdrawing all their troops into the Punjab."

Kungas said nothing in response. Instead, he stepped over to the edge of the roof garden and planted his hands on the wide ledge which served it for a railing. From there, atop the palace that his men had seized to serve as the residence for the reborn Kushan monarchy, he gazed onto the streets of Begram. He swiveled his head slightly, studying the scene below. Listening to it, for the most part.

The city was awash in sound and moving color, almost rioting with celebration. After the Ye-tai had destroyed Peshawar long years before, Begram had become the major city of the Kushans. Four fifths of the population, approximately, was either Kushan or part-Kushan by descent. And the Pathans who formed most of the remaining population had no great allegiance to Malwa. None at all, truth be told. So if the Pathans were not exactly joining the Kushan festivities, they were not huddling in fear from it either. And there was certainly no indication that they were planning any sort of countermoves.

No expression at all could be read on his face. It was a pure mask. But Irene, now long experienced in what she jokingly called "Kungas interpretation," could tell that her husband was not happy with the situation.

On a purely personal level, she found that knowledge warming. More than warming, really—she felt a little spike of passion race through her body. But she suppressed that spike even more firmly than the warmth. Not so much from the old habits of a spymaster but from the new habits of a woman who had come to think like a queen. Thoughts which were, in truth, even more cold-blooded.

Although she did feel a moment's regret that there would be no time to satisfy her passion. Time was of the essence, now.

"Stop this, Kungas," she said firmly. "You know as well as I do—more than I do, for you are a general and I am not—that you *must* march on the Khyber pass immediately. *Now.* Today!"

Kungas did not look at her. The only sign that he had heard her words was that his fingers began tapping the ledge on which his hands were planted.

"Move fast," he mused. "Yes, I should. All signs point to a Malwa empire in panic. Their troops are racing out of the Hindu Kush, not making an orderly withdrawal." He snorted wryly. "They certainly aren't doing so in fear of my small army. They are not being *forced* out of the mountains—they are being *sucked* out. As if, somewhere in the Indus valley, a great whirlpool has erupted into existence. A greater monster than Charybdis has arrived. Belisarius, at his work."

Sensing the shift in Kungas' mood, Irene pressed home the advantage. "If you move now—instantly—you can catch them at the Khyber before they have time to stabilize a defensive position. It will still be hard fighting, though—which is why you need to take the *entire* army—but if you move fast we can end this campaign with *us* in control of the Khyber. Which would mean that the gateway to our new kingdom is in *our* hands, not Malwa's."

He said nothing. The fact that his finger-tapping had become a little drumbeat was, again, the only sign that he was paying attention to her.

"You are only hesitating because of me!" Irene protested. Then, chuckling: "If I weren't a bedraggled bag of bones—almost dead from exhaustion—you'd probably insist on hauling me along."

Finally, the mask cracked. Kungas' trace of a smile emerged. "Hardly that," he said cheerfully. "At least, you didn't seem to be dying from exhaustion last night. Nor do I recall that you felt like a bag of bones. Quite the opposite, in fact."

He turned his eyes and gave Irene's figure a quick and warm appraisal. "The trek has been good for you, I'd say, for all the aches and pains."

Irene grinned. As it happened, she agreed with Kungas' assessment. Her figure was still as slim as ever, but the somewhat flaccid flesh of a Greek noblewoman was now long gone. The change, of course, would not have met with approval from high society in Constantinople. Pale skin and soft flesh was the female ideal in that aristocratic society. But her bronzed skin and firm muscle tone fit her new kingdom far better.

"Exhausted," she insisted. "On the edge of the grave."

Then, more seriously: "Kungas, I couldn't possibly keep up with the march you must now undertake, and we both know it. I may not be a whimpering Greek noblewoman any longer, but I'm hardly in the same condition as your soldiers. In truth, I doubt if even the camp followers will be able to keep up."

He stopped the little finger-drumming and slapped the ledge firmly. "Won't even try! I'm leaving them all behind."

The decision finally made, Kungas, as was his way, cast all hesitation aside. "This will be a march out of legend. My whole army will put the memory of that pitiful Athenian runner from Marathon into the shade. Twenty-six miles, pah. A trifle. And then—drop dead at the end? Not likely. Not Kushans."

He began pacing slowly along the ledge, running his hand across the smooth surface as if he were caressing the stone. Remembering the feel of that hand on her body the night before, Irene felt a moment's regret that Kungas was accepting her advice. But if she rued the coming absence of fleshly pleasure, she took a greater pleasure in Kungas' words. Not because of his decision, but because of the classical allusions. It had been she who told Kungas of Charybdis, and Marathon. And, as always, her husband had forgotten nothing of what she said to him.

"I will be safe," she said softly.

Kungas stopped his pacing and turned to face her. The little crack of a smile vanished without a trace.

"You will be in deadly peril, and we both know it. With the entire army gone from Begram—except for the handful of soldiers I will leave you for a bodyguard—you will be at the mercy of any sizeable force in the area. Doesn't even have to be Malwa. Any Pathan tribe in the region could swoop down and take the city."

Irene began to brush back her hair, from old habit, but halted the gesture midway. The long, flowing chestnut tresses she had once possessed had vanished along with the rest of the Greek noblewoman she had once been. The hair was still there—still chestnut and still long, in fact—but it was bound up tightly in the female equivalent of the Kushan topknot. What the Kushan women called a "horse tail."

"You let me worry about the Pathans. There won't be any danger from them immediately, no matter what. Begram is not a village, after all. It is a sizeable city, with walls, and a large population to guard it. An *enthusiastic* population, to boot."

She inclined her head, indicating the riotous celebration going on in the streets below. "Any Pathan chief will know full well that, while he might take Begram, he will pay a hard price for it. And if the price is too hard—which it is likely to be; the populace is Kushan, after all—his tribe will be at the mercy of your army when you return."

"*If* we return."

" 'If' you return," Irene allowed. "But the Pathans will wait to see what happens at the Khyber, Kungas. Not even the most hot-headed tribesman will make any attempt on Begram until they are certain your army is not something to be feared. And besides—"

Old habit triumphed. She reached back, drew the horse-tail over her shoulder, and began stroking it. "And besides," she said softly, almost crooning with anticipation, "I will not be spending those weeks idly. Diplomacy, after all, can often accomplish greater wonders than feats of arms."

❖   ❖   ❖

"You must be joking," hissed Valentinian. He stared at the implements in Ajatasutra's hands as if they were so many cobras. In the moonlight, his narrow face and close-set features made him look not so much like a weasel as a demon.

And a greatly offended demon, at that.

Ajatasutra shrugged. "There is another alternative, if you prefer."

Lifting his left hand, still holding one of the digging tools, he indicated Ajmer at the bottom of the slope which served the city for a cemetery. "I can purchase a suitable woman and three children in the slave market. A quick bit of blade work—much less effort than all this digging—and we'll have what we need."

He lowered the digging tool and gave Valentinian a hard-eyed stare. "Of course, *you* will have to do the work. Not me."

Valentinian stared down at the city below, his face even sharper than usual. Clearly enough, he was considering the alternative . . .

Anastasius heaved up a sound which was as much of a sigh as a humorless chuckle. "Not even you, Valentinian. And you know it. So there's no point postponing the inevitable."

The giant cataphract stepped forward and took one of the tools from Ajatasutra. "You *do* know which graves we want, I hope. Or are we digging at random?"

Ajatasutra's chuckle was quite full of humor. "Please! I am no fonder of labor than either of you. I did not spend my weeks here idly, I assure you." Handing one of the tools he still had in his hands to Valentinian, he began working at the soil with the other. "One grave will do. This one. A big family, it was, although we will need only four of the bodies. One woman and three children. Two boys and a girl, of approximately the right age."

Although he began sharing in the work, Valentinian was still sour. "Died of the plague? Wonderful. We're digging up disease too."

"No disease. Just an impoverished family—one of many, now—huddling in a shack on the outskirts of the city. Easy pickings for a street gang. So the bodies will even show suitable injuries."

Some time later, after the four bodies had been extracted, Valentinian's sourness was still as strong as ever.

" 'Suitable injuries,' " he mimicked. "Who could possibly tell?" He scowled down at what was left of four corpses, still wrapped in what was left of rags. Which was not much, in either case.

Ajatasutra shrugged. "There will be enough signs to satisfy anyone who investigates. We will burn the caravan after the attack, so there wouldn't be much left anyway."

Anastasius, unlike Valentinian, was devoted to the study of philosophy. So he had already walked through the steps of the logic. And, having done so, heaved another great sigh.

"It gets worse," he rumbled. "The corpses will be suitable. But those rags have got to go."

Valentinian's eyes began widening with new indignation. Indignation which became outrage, when he saw what Ajatasutra was hauling out of a sack he had brought with them.

"Indeed," said the assassin cheerfully, as he began tossing items of clothing to the two Romans. "These cost me a small fortune, too. Narses, at least. The garments of Rajput royalty are enough to bankrupt a man."

That same night, in Kausambi, Lady Damodara entered the chamber where her new maids slept. It was the first time she had ever done so.

The two sisters drew back a little, on the bed where they were both sitting. For all the subtlety of the movement, it exuded fear and apprehension.

"I'm sorry, great lady," said the older hastily. She bounced the little boy in her arms, trying to quiet the squalling infant. "He isn't usually so bad."

Lady Damodara swept forward to the bed and leaned over, studying the child. She was a short woman. But, though she was as plump as her husband had been in times past, there was a certain solidity to her form which made her stature seem much greater than it was. The fact that she was wearing the expensive garments of a member of the Malwa royal clan, of course, added a great deal to the impression.

"He's sick," she pronounced. "You should have told me, Como."

She straightened and swept out of the chamber. Confused and fearful, the two sisters followed her.

In the course of the next few hours, their fear abated. Almost vanished, in fact. But their confusion grew. It was unheard of, after all, for a great Malwa lady to serve as a physician for a slave servant's infant. Using her own chamber for the purpose! Feeding him potions with her own hands!

As they began to leave, the infant having finally fallen asleep, Lady Damodara's voice stopped them in the doorway.

"You remember, I trust, what Ajatasutra told you?"

The sisters, more confused than ever, turned around and stared at her.

Lady Damodara sighed. "Spymasters, assassins," she muttered. "He did not even tell you his name?"

After a moment or two, the meaning of her words finally registered on them. Both sisters' eyes widened.

"What did he tell you?" demanded Lady Damodara. "The most *important* thing?"

"Ask no questions," the younger sister whispered. "Do as you are told. Say nothing to anyone."

Lady Damodara stared at them. Short she might have been, and plump besides, but in that moment she resembled a great hawk. Or an owl, which is also a predator.

The moment lasted not more than seconds, however. "Oh, pah!" she suddenly exclaimed. "Spymasters are too smart for their own good. If any part of the thing is discovered, we are all dead anyway. Better you should know, so that when the time comes you are not overwhelmed with confusion."

She moved over to her own great regal bed and sat down on the edge. "Come here, girls," she commanded, patting the bedding. "Sit, and I will tell you who you are."

The sisters—now completely confused, and again fearful—moved toward the bed. On the way, the youngest clutched to the only certainty which their universe had possessed for years. "We are the daughters of Dadaji Holkar."

Lady Damodara laughed. Softly, with gentle humor. "Indeed so!"

And then, in the minutes which followed, she told them who their father was. Told them that the humble small town scribe from whom they had been torn had since become the peshwa of mighty Andhra. An Andhra growing mightier by the day.

By the time she finished, both girls were weeping. From joy, because they knew their father—and mother, too—were still alive. From grief, hearing of the death of their brother.

But, mostly, from fear and heartbreak.

"You are holding us hostage, then," whispered the youngest.

"Our father will never want us back, anyway," sobbed

the older, clutching her child to her breast. "Not now.
Not so great a man, with such polluted daughters."

Lady Damodara studied them for a moment. Then,
rose and went to the window of her bedchamber. Once
at the window, she stared out over great Kausambi.

"Hostages?" The question seemed posed as much
to herself as anyone. "Yes. It is true. On the other
hand . . ."

She studied the sleeping city. It reminded her of a
giant beast, washing on the waves of a deep and black
ocean.

"Let us rather think of it as a pledge. Malwa has
much to answer for. Many fathers struck childless, and
children orphaned." She turned her head away from
the window and gazed on the sisters. "So perhaps the
day may come when a family reunited will serve as an
offering. And so a father grown powerful might be
moved to hold his hand from vengeance, and counsel
others to do the same. Because the sight of his living
children might remind him of the cost of more dead
ones."

The sisters stared at her, their eyes still wet with
tears. "We will mean nothing to him now," repeated
the oldest. "No longer. Not after everything which has
passed."

Lady Damodara issued another soft, gentle laugh.
"Oh, I think not." She turned her face back to the
window, this time studying not the city so much as the
land it sat upon. As if she were pondering the nature
of the great, dark ocean through which the beast swam.

"Whatever happens," she said quietly, "India will
never be the same. So I would not be so sure, children, that your father will think as he might have once.
A man does not go from such obscurity to such power,
you know, if he is incapable of handling new truths.
And besides—"

Again, the laugh. "He is said to be a philosopher. Let us all hope it is true!"

When she turned back from the window this time, the movement had an air of finality. She came to stand before the two sisters on her bed, and planted her hands on her hips.

"And now, I think, it is time for us to start anew as well. You will continue in your duties, of course, for that is necessary. Ask no questions. Say nothing to anyone. But, for the rest . . . what are your *names*?"

That simple question seemed to steady the girls, and bring them back from the precipice of fear and sorrow.

"I am called Lata," said the youngest, smiling a bit timidly. "My sister is named Dhruva."

"And my little boy is Baji," concluded her sister. "Who is as dear to me as the sunrise, regardless of whence he came."

Lady Damodara nodded. "A good start. Especially that last. We will all need your wisdom, child, before this is through."

No one took any notice of the beggar squatting outside Venandakatra's palace. He was simply one among many beggars. The old man had been plying his trade there for several weeks, and had long since become a familiar part of the landscape. Few people paid any attention to him at all, in truth—and certainly not the arrogant Ye-tai who guarded the Goptri.

Some of the other denizens of the city's slums noticed him, of course. For all the old man's apparent poverty, his garments were a bit unusual. Not in their finery—they were rags, and filthy at that—but simply in their extent. Most beggars wore nothing more than a loincloth. This old man's entire body was shrouded, as if by a winding sheet.

There was a reason for that, which was discovered

by a small band of street toughs when they assaulted the old beggar. The attack occurred a few days after he first began plying his trade, in the crooked alley where the old beggar slept at night. The toughs had noticed that the beggar's bowl had been particularly well-endowed that day, and saw no reason such a miserable creature should enjoy that largesse.

The first thug who seized the old beggar by the arm was almost paralyzed with shock. Beneath the filthy garment, that arm was not the withered limb he had been expecting to feel. It was thick, and muscled so powerfully that the thug thought for a moment that he had seized a bar of iron.

The impression was reinforced an instant later—very briefly—when the elbow attached to the arm swept back and crushed the thug's throat. And that first attacker's new wisdom was shared, within a matter of a few seconds, by his three comrades. A very brief enlightenment, it was.

A few days later, another gang of toughs made the same discovery. Thereafter, the old beggar was left alone. The word spread, as it always did in such crowded and fetid slums, that the new beggar who lived in that alley was guarded by a demon. How else explain the mangled and battered corpses which had appeared of a morning—twice, now—in the mouth of that alley? While the beggar himself emerged unharmed, at the break of day, to resume plying his pathetic trade.

No word of this, of course, ever came to the ears of the authorities. Nor, if it had, would they have paid any attention. The slums of any city—especially a great metropolis like Bharakuccha—are full of superstition and rumor.

And so, day after day, the old beggar plied his trade against the wall of the palace. And so, day after day, the Ye-tai who guarded the entrance gave him no more than a casual glance.

Venandakatra himself did not give the beggar so much as a glance, in his own comings and goings. Such creatures were simply beneath the Goptri's notice. So he was completely oblivious to the way in which, without seeming to, the beggar's eyes followed his every movement while the beggar's head remained slumped in abject misery. Showing, in their hidden depths, a gleam which would have seemed odd in such a man. Almost yellow eyes, they were, like those of a watchful predator.

Chapter 27
THE SIND
Autumn, 533 A.D.

Belisarius and his army encountered the first Malwa force shortly after rounding the southern slopes of the Kot Diji hills and crossing the Nara. Fortunately, the Romans had received forewarning that enemy troops were in the vicinity—not from any spies or scouts, but from the stream of refugees coming south from the Indus.

Abbu and his scouts captured a small group of the refugees, what appeared to be an entire extended family. Not knowing their language, he brought the group to the general. Belisarius' fluency in foreign tongues was a byword among his troops. The Talisman of God allowed him to understand any language—even, some said, the speech of animals.

The truth, of course, fell far short of that legend. Aide did provide Belisarius with a great facility for *learning* foreign languages. But it was not magic, and did not allow Belisarius to understand and speak a language in an instant.

So the group of peasants huddling on the ground before him, with their few belongings strapped to their backs and their one precious cow "guarded" in the center, were unable to communicate with him. In truth, the people were so terrified that Belisarius doubted they would have been able to speak in any event. The eyes of the men and women were downcast. They stared at the soil before them as if, by ignoring the armed and armored men who surrounded them, they could change reality itself.

The children were less bashful. Or, at least, less ready to believe that reality was susceptible to such easy manipulation. They ogled the Roman soldiers around them, wide-eyed and fearful. One young girl—perhaps six or seven—was sobbing wildly, ignoring the way her mother was trying to shake her into silence. Because of the mother's own terror, the shaking was a subdued sort of thing, not the kind of ferocious effort which could hope to subdue such sheer hysteria.

Belisarius winced and looked away. His eyes met those of a boy about the same age. Perhaps the girl's brother; perhaps a cousin. Between the dirt and grime which covered the peasants, and the distortion which fear produced in their faces, it was hard to detect family resemblance. More accurately, family resemblance was buried under the generic similarity which makes all desperate people look well-nigh identical.

The boy was not sobbing. He was simply staring at the general with eyes so open they seemed to protrude entirely from his face. Belisarius gave him a smile. The boy's only reaction was to—somehow—widen his eyes further.

There was nothing of childlike curiosity in those wide eyes. Just a terror so deep that the lad was like a paralyzed rodent, facing a cobra.

"Oh, Christ," muttered Maurice.

Belisarius sighed. He dismissed any thought of trying to interrogate the peasants. They would tell him nothing, in any event. *Could* tell him nothing, even if he spoke their language. The war had smote the peasants as war always does—like a thunderstorm cast down by distant and uncaring deities, sweeping them aside like debris in a river raging in flood. They would understand nothing of it, beyond chaos and confusion. Troop movements, maneuvers, terrain as a military feature rather than just a path of panic-stricken flight—these were beyond their ken and reckoning.

"Let them go," he ordered. "Make sure you have our own Thracians escort them to the rear. I don't expect there'd be any trouble with other soldiers, but . . ."

"There's no reason to risk the temptation," finished Maurice, scowling a bit. "Not that these have anything worth stealing, but some of the Greeks—the new ones, not Cyril's men—are starting to complain about the lack of booty."

He eyed one of the peasant girls. Older, she was— perhaps sixteen or seventeen. "They might take out their frustration with other pleasures. And then—" He grated a harsh little laugh. "You'd give the army another demonstration of Belisarius discipline, and we'd look a bit silly charging into battle dragging executed cataphracts behind us."

Belisarius nodded. "The fact these people are here at all tells me what I need to know. The Malwa have started their massacre."

He gathered up the reins of his horse. His brown eyes, usually as warm as old wood, glinted like hard shells in a receding tide. "Which means they'll be spread out and disorganized. So it's time for another demonstration." The next words were almost hissed. *"I will put the fear of God in those men. Old Testament fear."*

❖   ❖   ❖

He fell on the Malwa less than two hours later. Early afternoon it was, by then. The Arab scouts had begun bringing in further reports, this time based on direct observation of the enemy. As Belisarius had expected, the Malwa soldiers were spread out across miles of terrain.

"Some burning, not much," summarized Abbu. The old desert chief's face was tight with anger. "Probably they plan to do the burning later. Now it is just the killing."

That too, Belisarius had also deduced. As they marched forward, the Roman army had encountered other refugees since the first group. The trickle had become a stream, until the entire countryside seemed to have little rivulets of frantic people pouring through it. The Malwa were butchering everyone in the area they could catch. A scorched earth campaign Tamerlane would have been proud to call his own. Tear out the ultimate roots of the land by destroying the work force itself, not simply the products of its labor.

"Is there a depression in the land we can drive them toward?" he asked.

Abbu pointed east by north. "Yes, General. That way, not far—maybe five miles. A little riverbed, almost dry. Runs northwest by southeast."

The scout leader's face tightened still further. The anger was still there, but it was now overlaid with anticipation. He understood immediately Belisarius' purpose.

"Good killing ground," he snarled. "The opposite bank will channel them downriver. Not high, but sharp and steep."

He pointed again, this time more east than north. "There. A small rise slopes down toward our bank of the river, which is shallow."

Belisarius nodded. Then:

"Sittas, take all your cataphracts and flank them on the west. Take Cyril's, too. Roll the bastards up. Don't try to smash them, just herd them toward Abbu's river. As disorganized as they are, they'll run, not fight."

He gave the big Greek general a hard stare. "Run, not fight. As long as you don't corner them."

Sittas returned the stare with a grin. "Stop fussing at me. I do know how to do something other than charge, you know." He began turning his horse. "Besides, I like this plan. We'll show these swine how to run a *real* slaughter."

Before Sittas had finished, Belisarius was issuing new orders. "Gregory, set up the artillery on that rise. But *don't* use the mitrailleuse or the mortars unless I give the command. In fact, keep them covered with tarpaulins. I want to keep those weapons a secret as long as possible, and they require special ammunition anyway. Which we need to use sparingly, this early in the campaign. Abbu, guide them there—or have one of your men do it."

As Gregory and Abbu peeled off to set their troops into new motion, Belisarius continued to issue orders. They were obeyed instantly, with one exception.

"No, Mark," said Belisarius forcefully. "I know you want to give your sharpshooters their first real taste of battle, but this is not the time and place. We can't replenish your ammunition from the general stock, and we'll need it later."

He eased any sting out of the rebuke with a slight smile. "You'll have plenty of combat, soon enough. At Sukkur and elsewhere. For today, I just need you to guard the guns. They'll do the killing."

Mark, as always, was stubborn. It was a trait Belisarius had managed to wear down some, over the years. But not much, because in truth he had never really made much of an effort to do so. If there was any single word which captured the spirit of Mark of Edessa, it was *pugnacious*—a characteristic which Belisarius prized in his officers.

At the Battle of the Pass, that pugnacity had broken a Ye-tai charge like so much kindling. That it would do so again, and again—or die in the trying—was one of the lynchpins of Belisarius' entire campaign.

"The damn artillery doesn't have much ammunition either," grumbled Mark. "And they chew it up like a wolf chews meat."

"They can also chew up enemy troops like a wolf," pointed out Belisarius. "Especially at close range, with canister. And I can keep them restocked from any kind of gunpowder. Even that cruddy Malwa stuff, if I have to. I can't replace your special cartridges easily."

Mark of Edessa knew he had pushed the general as far as he could. Stubborn he was, yes, but not insubordinate. So, still scowling, he trotted off on his horse, venting his resentment by barking his commands to the sharpshooters. He sounded like a wolf himself.

"God help the Malwa if they try to overrun the batteries," said Maurice, smiling grimly. "Mark's been wanting to test the bayonets, too. And don't think he won't, if he gets half a chance."

Maurice too, it seemed, had caught the general bloodlust. "Not that I wouldn't enjoy watching it, mind you. But, you're right—this is not the time and place." He sighed with happy satisfaction. "This is just a time and place for butcher's work."

By the time the real butchery began, the Malwa were already badly blooded. Sittas, if he had not violated the letter of his orders, had obviously stretched the spirit of them as far as he could. Watching the Malwa soldiers pouring down the river bed in complete disorder, Belisarius knew that Sittas and his Greek cataphracts had "rolled them up" the way a blacksmith rolls a gun barrel—with hammer and flame.

Belisarius had chosen to take his own position with the artillery and the sharpshooters. These were his least experienced troops—in the use of these weapons, at any rate—and he wanted to observe them in action.

The slant of the terrain gave him a view of at least half a mile of the riverbed. The first Malwa units had almost reached the slight bend where he intended to hold them. Behind, moving more like fluid water than solid men, came enough enemy soldiers to fill the riverbed from bank to bank.

"How many, do you think?"

Maurice shook his head. "Hard to say, exactly, with a mob like that. At a guess, we'll wind up facing maybe twelve thousand."

That was a little higher than Belisarius' own estimate, but not by much. He nodded, continuing to study the oncoming enemy. Some of the Malwa soldiers, perhaps instinctively sensing a trap, were trying to clamber out of the riverbed over the shallow southwestern bank. But Sittas—who, for all the fury with which he could drive home a charge, was as shrewd as any cataphract commander in the Roman army—had foreseen that likelihood. So he had peeled off Cyril's men to flank the enemy yet again. The Greek cataphracts were already on the southwestern bank, ready and eager to drive the Malwa back with lance and saber.

A few Malwa tried to clamber over the opposite bank. But, as Abbu had said, that far bank was steep if not especially high. Close to vertical, in many places; and, nowhere that Belisarius could see, shallow enough to allow a man to scamper rather than climb.

The opposite bank ranged in height from eight to twelve feet. Not much of a climb, perhaps—except for a man laden with armor and weapons, being driven in a packed crowd of confused and frightened soldiers. Not many of the Malwa even attempted to make that climb, and most of them were swept off the bank by their fellows pouring past in a rout. And for the few who made it, the ground beyond proved no refuge in any event. Abbu and his Arabs had crossed the river-bed and taken up positions on the opposite bank half an hour earlier. Their lances and sabers were just as eager as those of the cataphracts.

"It's working," said Maurice. "Damned if it's not."

Belisarius nodded. His tactics for this battle were proving themselves in action. Sittas and the main body of cataphracts had caught the Malwa infantry spread out, in the open. And the forces were evenly matched—twelve thousand against twelve thousand. The heavily armed and armored cavalry might be "obsolete" in this new age of gunpowder weapons, but obsolescence does not happen overnight.

A cataphract charge struck like a mailed fist. Well-organized and prepared troops could withstand such a charge, even bloody and break it, with pikemen shielding musketeers and volleys coming like clockwork thunder. But an army caught off-guard, driven off balance and never allowed to regain it, was like grain in a thresher.

Routed soldiers, like water, will follow the path of least resistance. Especially with Sittas and his cataphracts pouring into the riverbed themselves and driving the Malwa before them. With Cyril and his men guarding the shallow bank and Abbu guarding the other, almost the entire Malwa army was being herded toward the guns. Penned into a perfect killing ground.

The rise where Gregory had stationed the field guns had a clear line of fire into the river bed, and at enough

of an angle to enfilade the coming troops. There
remained only to place the "stopper" in the bottle.

"Now, I think," said Maurice.

Belisarius nodded. The chiliarch made a motion and
the cornicenes began blowing. The Thracian bucellarii,
awaiting the signal, trotted across the riverbed some
two hundred yards down and took up positions. As
the lead elements of the Malwa spotted them, they
began slowing their pell-mell race. Several of them
stopped entirely. Behind them, the Malwa soldiers
started piling up in a muddle. They formed a perfect
target for cannon fire, not more than four hundred
yards away—almost too close, for round shot.

Belisarius leaned toward Gregory, who was sitting
a horse to his left. "You're loaded with round shot, or
canister?"

"Round shot," came the immediate and confident
reply. "On that ground—most of the near bank is shale
and loose rock—the ricochets will work as well as
canister. And I've got more round shot than anything
else."

Belisarius wasn't quite sure Gregory was right, but
he wasn't about to second-guess him and order the
guns reloaded. In truth, the artillery commander was
more experienced at this than he was, at least in training and theory. This would be the first time ever in
the Malwa war that either side used field guns as the
major element in a battle. And since the range was at
the outer limits of canister effectiveness, anyway . . .

"Go ahead, then. Fire whenever you're—"

"*Fire!*" bellowed Gregory, waving his arm. The
cornicenes, waiting for the cue, began blowing the call.
But the sound of the horns was almost instantly
drowned under the roar of the guns. Gregory's entire
battery—thirty-six three-pounders—had fired at once.

That volley . . . did much less than Belisarius

expected. True, a number of Malwa soldiers went down—ripped in half, often enough. But instead of cutting entire swaths, the volley had simply punched narrow holes in the packed mass of soldiers.

He rose up in his stirrups, now tense. His whole battle plan *depended* on those field guns. And he didn't want to be forced to use the mitrailleuse and the mortars this early in the campaign. He turned to Gregory, about to order a switch to canister.

But Gregory was no longer there. The artillery commander had sent his horse trotting behind the guns. Gregory was up in his own stirrups, bellowing like a bull.

"Down, you sorry bastards! Lower the elevation! I want grazing shots, damn you!"

The artillerymen were working feverishly. In each gun crew, two men were levering up the barrels while the gun captain sighted by eye. On his command, a fourth man slid the quoin further up between the barrel and the transom, lowering the elevation of the gun and shortening the trajectory of the fire. That done, they raced to reload the weapons. Again, with the cast iron balls of simple round shot.

Belisarius hesitated, then lowered himself down to his saddle. He still wasn't sure Gregory was right, but . . .

Good officers need the confidence of their superiors. Best way for a general to ruin an army is to meddle.

While the guns were reloading, the Greek cataphracts who were now massing on the southwestern slope began firing their own volleys of arrows into the packed mass of Malwa troops in the riverbed. As Belisarius had insisted—he wanted to keep his own casualties to a minimum—Sittas and Cyril were keeping the armored horse archers at a distance. But, even across two hundred yards, cataphract arrows struck with

enough force to punch through the light armor worn
by Malwa infantrymen.

Belisarius could see a knot of Malwa begin to form
up and dress their ranks. Somewhere in that shrieking and struggling pile of soldiers, apparently, some
officers were still functioning and maintaining order.
Good ones, too, from the evidence—within the few
minutes it took for the Roman guns to reload, they
managed to put together a semblance of a mass of
pikemen, flanked by musketeers. Within a minute or
so, Belisarius estimated, they would begin a charge.

He glanced at his own artillerymen. They were
getting ready to fire again, waiting for Gregory to give
the order. Belisarius moved his eyes back to the enemy.
He wanted to study the effect of this next volley.
"Grazing shots," Gregory had demanded. Belisarius
understood what he meant, but he was uncertain how
effective they'd be.

"*Fire!*" The cannons belched smoke and fury.
Then—

"*Sweet Mary,*" whispered Belisarius.

Gregory got his wish. Almost all of the cannonballs
struck the ground anywhere from twenty to fifty yards
in front of the Malwa soldiery. Three-pound cast-iron
balls came screaming in at a low trajectory, hit the
ground, and caromed back up into the enemy at knee
to shoulder level. Where the first volley had plunged
into the middle and rear of the Malwa soldiery, killing and maiming a relative few, this volley cut into
them from front to back.

Far worse than the balls themselves, however, was
the effect of the ricochets. The ground which those
cannonballs struck was loose rock and shale. The impact
sent stones and pieces of stone flying everywhere. For
all practical purposes, solid shot had struck with the
impact and effect of explosive shells. For each Malwa

torn by the balls, four or five others were shredded by stones.

Most of those ricochet wounds, of course, were not as severe as those caused by the cannonballs themselves. But they were severe enough to kill many soldiers outright, cripple as many more, and wound almost anyone not sheltered from the blow.

That single volley also put paid to the charge the Malwa were trying to organize. Whether by accident or design, the worst effects of the cannon fire were felt by the semi-organized men in the middle.

The riverbed was a shrieking, blood-soaked little valley now. The cataphracts continued their own missile fire while the guns reloaded again.

"Fire!"

Another round of perfect grazing shots. Belisarius was beginning to sicken a little. Through his telescope, he could see Malwa soldiers trying to stand up, slip and slide on bloody intestines and every other form of shredded human tissue, fall, stagger to their feet again . . .

He lowered the telescope and waved at Sittas. But then, seeing that the big Greek general was preoccupied with keeping his men from moving too close and therefore hadn't seen his wave, Belisarius turned in his saddle and shouted at the cornicenes. For a moment, the buglers just stared at him.

Cease fire was the last order they had been expecting to blow. But, seeing Belisarius' glare, they obeyed with alacrity.

Startled, Gregory and his artillerymen lifted their heads. Belisarius swore under his breath.

"Not you, Gregory! You keep firing! I want the *cataphracts* to hold their fire!"

Gregory nodded and went back to his work. Sittas, meanwhile, started trotting—then cantering—his horse toward Belisarius. Seeing him come, Belisarius didn't know whether to scowl or smile. He had no doubt at all that Sittas was going to protest the order.

But, to his surprise, when Sittas pulled up his horse the big man was smiling broadly.

"I was going to chew your head off—respectfully, of course—until I figured it out." He hefted himself up in the stirrups and studied the Malwa. Another volley of cannon fire ripped them again.

"You've got no intention of finishing them off, do you?" The question was obviously rhetorical. "Which means we wouldn't be able to recover our arrows. No small problem, with our light supply train, if we use up too many this early in the campaign."

It had been a long time since Belisarius had actually been on campaign with his barrel-chested friend. Sittas looked so much like a boar—and acted the part, often enough—that Belisarius had half-forgotten how intelligent the man was underneath that brawler's appearance.

"No, I'm not. At close quarters, we'll suffer casualties, no matter how badly they're battered. There's no purpose to that, not with almost the whole campaign still ahead of us." For a moment, he studied the enemy. "That army's finished, Sittas. By the end of the day, what's left of that mass of men will be of no military value to the Malwa for weeks. Or months. That's good enough."

Sittas nodded. "Pity not to finish 'em off. But, you're right. Cripple 'em and be done with it. We've got other fish to fry and"—he glanced up at the sun—"at this rate we can still manage to make another few miles before making camp."

He gave the bleeding Malwa his own scrutiny. Then, with a grimace: "No way we want to camp anywhere near this place. Be like sleeping next to an abattoir."

❖   ❖   ❖

For the next half an hour, Belisarius forced himself to watch the butchery. Eight more volleys were fired in that time. That rate of fire could not be maintained indefinitely, since firing such cannons more than ten shots per hour over an extended period ran the risk of having them become deformed or even burst from overheating. But against such a compact and massed target, eight volleys was enough. More than enough.

For Belisarius, too, this was the first time he had been able to see with his own eyes the incredible effectiveness of field artillery under the right conditions. He had planned for it—he wouldn't have made the gamble this whole campaign represented without that presumption—but, still . . .

Gustavus Adolphus' guns broke the imperialists at Breitenfeld, said Aide softly. **And those men in that riverbed are neither as tough nor as well led as Tilly's were.**

Belisarius nodded. Then sighed. But said nothing.

I know. There are times you wish you could have been a blacksmith.

Belisarius nodded; sighed; said nothing.

By the end of that half-hour, Belisarius decided to break off the battle. There was no point in further butchery, and the Malwa soldiers were finally beginning to escape from the trap in any event. By now, corpses had piled so high in the riverbed that men were able to clamber over them and find refuge on the steep, opposite bank. Abbu and his Arabs were no longer there to drive them back. Belisarius had pulled them back, fearing that some of the light cavalry might be accidentally hit by misaimed Roman cannons—as he and Agathius' cataphracts had been at the battle of Anatha, by Maurice's rocket fire.

Most of the killing was done by the big guns, but not all of it. Twice, early on, bold and energetic Malwa officers succeeded in organizing sallies. One sally charged down the riverbed toward the Thracian bucellarii, the other upstream against Sittas' Greeks. Both were driven back easily, with relatively few casualties for the armored horsemen.

Thereafter, Belisarius gave the Malwa no further opportunities for such sallies. To his delight, Mark of Edessa was finally able to give his sharpshooters their first test in battle. Whenever it seemed another group of officers was beginning to bring cohesion back to some portion of the Malwa army bleeding to death in the riverbed, Belisarius would give the order and concentrated fire from the sharpshooters would cut them down. Mark's men, shooting weapons which were modeled after the Sharps rifle, were still indifferent marksmen by the standards of the nineteenth-century America which would produce those guns. But they were good enough, for this purpose.

By the time Belisarius broke off the engagement, the enemy forces had suffered casualties in excess of fifty percent. Far more than was needed to break almost any army in history. The more so because the casualty rate was even higher among officers, and higher still among those who were brave and capable. For all practical purposes, a Malwa army had been erased from the face of the earth.

Even Maurice pronounced himself satisfied with the result. Of course, Maurice being Maurice, he immediately moved on to another problem. Maurice fondled worries the way another man might fondle a wife.

"None of this'll mean shit, you understand, if the Ethiopians can't give us supremacy at sea." The comfort with which he settled back into morose pessimism was almost palpable. "Something will go wrong, mark my words."

❖   ❖   ❖

"I can't see a damned thing," complained Antonina, peering through the relatively narrow gap between the foredeck's roof and the bulwarks which shield the cannons in the bow.

"You're not supposed to," retorted Ousanas, standing just behind her. "The sun is down. Only an idiot would make an attack like this in broad daylight on a clear day."

Scowling, Antonina kept peering. She wasn't sure what annoyed her the most—the total darkness, or the endless hammering of rain on the roof.

"What if we go aground?" she muttered. Then, hearing Ousanas' heavy sigh, she restrained herself.

"Sorry, sorry," she grumbled sarcastically. "I forget that Ethiopian seamen all sprang full-blown from the brow of Neptune. Can see in the dark, smell a lee shore—"

"They *can*, as a matter of fact," said Ousanas. "Smell the shore, at least."

"Easiest thing in the world," chimed in Eon. The negusa nagast of Axum was standing right next to Ousanas, leaning on one of the four cannons in the bow. In the covered foredeck of the large Ethiopian flagship, there was far more room than there had been in the relatively tiny bow shield of the *Victrix*.

"People call it the 'smell of the sea,'" he added. "But it's actually the smell of the seacoast. Rotting vegetation, all that. The open sea barely smells at all." He gestured toward the lookout, perched on the very bow of the ship. "That's what he's doing, you know, along with using the lead. Sniffing."

"How can anyone smell *anything* in this wretched downpour?" Antonina studied the lookout. The man's position was well forward of the roof which sheltered the foredeck. She thought he looked like a drowned rat.

At that very moment, the lookout turned his head and whistled. Then whistled again, and twice again.

Antonina knew enough of the Axumite signals to interpret the whistles. *Land is near. Still no bottom.*

For a moment, she was flooded with relief. But only for a moment.

"We're probably somewhere on the Malabar coast," she said gloomily. "Six hundred miles—or more!—from Chowpatty."

Suddenly she squealed and began dancing around. Eon was tickling her!

"Stop that!" she gasped, desperately spinning around to bring her sensitive ribs away from his fingers.

Eon was laughing outright. Ousanas, along with the half dozen Axumite officers positioned in the foredeck, was grinning widely.

"Only if you stop making like Cassandra!" boomed Eon. Who, at the moment, looked more like a very large boy than the Ethiopian King of Kings. A scamp and a rascal—royal regalia and vestments be damned. The phakhiolin, as Ethiopians called their version of an imperial tiara, was half-askew on Eon's head.

With a last laugh, Eon stopped the tickling. "*Will* you relax, woman? Ethiopian sailors have been running the Malwa blockade of Suppara for almost two years now. Every ship in this fleet has half a dozen of those sailors aboard as pilots. They know the entire Maratha coastline like the back of their hand—good weather or bad, rain or shine, day or night."

He went back to lounging against the cannon, and patted the heavy flank of the great engine of war with a thick and powerful hand. "Soon enough—soon enough—we will finally break that blockade. Break it into pieces."

Antonina sighed. Abstractly, she knew that Eon was right. Right, at least, about the dangers of the voyage itself.

A long voyage that had been, and in the teeth of

the monsoon's last days. The entire Axumite warfleet had sailed directly across the Erythrean Sea, depending entirely on their own seamanship—and the new Roman compasses which Belisarius had provided them—to make landfall. A voyage which would, in itself, become a thing of Ethiopian legend. Had the negusa nagast not led the expedition personally, many of the Ethiopian sailors might well have balked at the idea.

But, just as Eon and his top officers had confidently predicted weeks before, the voyage had been made successfully and safely. That still left . . .

A voyage, no matter how epic, is one thing. Fighting a successful battle at the end of it, quite another.

Antonina went back to fretting. Again, her eyes were affixed to the view through the foredeck.

"Silly woman!" exclaimed Eon. "We are still hours away. That Malwa fleet at Chowpatty is so much driftwood. Be sure of it!"

Again, for a moment, her fears lightened. Eon's self-confidence was infectious.

To break the Malwa blockade . . . Break it into pieces!

Such a feat, regardless of what happened with Belisarius' assault on the Sind, would lame the Malwa beast. The Maratha rebellion had already entangled the enemy's best army. With Suppara no longer blockaded, the Romans would be able to pour supplies into Majarashtra. Not only would Damodara and Rana Sanga be tied down completely—unable to provide any help to the larger Malwa army in the Indus—but they might very well require reinforcements themselves. Especially if, after destroying the Malwa fleet at Chowpatty which maintained the blockade of Suppara, the Ethiopian fleet could continue on and . . .

That "and" brought a new flood of worries. "It'll never work," Antonina hissed. "I was an idiot to agree to it!"

"It was your idea in the first place," snorted Ousanas.

"Silly woman!" she barked. "What possessed sane and sensible men to be swayed by such a twaddling creature?"

The Roman army made camp that night eight miles further north of the "battle" ground. North and, thankfully, upwind.

Just before they did so, they came upon the ruins of a peasant village. Bodies were scattered here and there among the half-wrecked huts and hovels.

There was a survivor in the ruins. An old man, seated on the ground, leaning against a mudbrick wall, staring at nothing and holding the body of an old woman in his arms. The woman's garments were stiff with dried blood.

When Belisarius rode up and brought his horse to a halt, the old man looked up at him. Something about the Roman's appearance must have registered because, to Belisarius' surprise, he spoke in Greek. Rather fluent Greek, in fact, if heavily accented. The general guessed that the man had been a trader once, many years back.

"I was in the fields when it happened," the old man said softly. "Far off, and my legs are stiff now. By the time I returned, it was all over."

His hand, moving almost idly, stroked the gray hair of the woman in his arms. His eyes moved back to her still face.

Belisarius tried to think of something to say, but could not. At his side, Maurice cleared his throat.

"What is the name of this village?" he asked.

The old peasant shrugged. "What village? There is no village here." But, after a moment: "It was once called Kulachi."

Maurice pointed over his shoulder with a thumb. "Today, we destroyed the army which did this. And now, as is Roman custom, we seek a name for the victory."

Belisarius nodded. "Quite right," he announced loudly. "The Battle of Kulachi, it was."

Around him, the Roman soldiers who heard growled their satisfaction. The peasant studied them, for a moment, as if he were puzzled.

Then, he shrugged again. "The name is yours, Roman. It means nothing to me anymore." He stroked the woman's hair, again, again. "I remember the day I married her. And I remember each of the days she bore me a child. The children who now lie dead in this place."

He stared to the south, where a guilty army was bleeding its punishment. "But this day? It means nothing to me. So, yes, you may have the name. I no longer need it."

On the way out of the village, several soldiers left some food with the old man. He seemed to pay no attention. He just remained there, stroking a memory's hair.

Aide did not speak for some time thereafter. Then, almost like an apology:

If you had been a blacksmith, this would have happened also. Ten times over, and ten times worse.

Belisarius shrugged. *I know that, Aide. And tomorrow the knowledge will mean something to me. But today? Today it means nothing. I just wish I could have been a blacksmith.*

Chapter 28
CHOWPATTY
Autumn, 533 A.D.

Just after daybreak, the first Malwa ship at Chowpatty was sunk by ramming. Unfortunately, the maneuver was completely unplanned and badly damaged an Ethiopian warship in the process. Coming through the pouring rain into the bay where the Malwa kept their fleet during the monsoon season, the lead Ethiopian warship simply ran over the small Malwa craft stationed on picket duty.

The Malwa themselves never saw it coming. The crew—exhausted by the ordeal of keeping a small ship at sea during bad weather—had been preoccupied with that task. They had no lookouts stationed. The thought that enemy warships might be in the area didn't even occur to them.

As it was, they considered their own commander a lunatic, and had cursed him since they left the docks. Nobody, in those days, tried to actually "maintain a blockade" during the stormy season. The era when English warships would maintain year-round standing blockades of French ports was in the far distant future.

In times past, once the monsoon came, the Malwa

fleet blockading Suppara had simply retired to the fishing town of Chowpatty further south along the coast, which the Malwa had seized and turned into their naval base. There, for months, the sailors would enjoy the relative peace and pleasures of the grimy town which had emerged on the ruins of the fishing village. The fishermen were long gone, fled or impressed into labor. Those of their women who had not managed to escape had been forced into the military brothels, if young enough, or served as cooks and laundresses.

But this monsoon season had been different. The Malwa ruler of southern India—Lord Venandakatra, Goptri of the Deccan—had always been a foultempered man. As the strength of the Maratha rebellion had grown, he had become downright savage. Not all of that savagery was rained down upon the rebels. His own subordinates came in for a fair portion of it.

So . . . the Malwa commander of the Suppara blockade had taken no chances. As preposterous and pointless as it might be, he would keep one ship stationed at sea at all times. Lest some spy of Venandakatra report to the Goptri that the blockade was being managed in a lackadaisical manner—and the commander find himself impaled as several other highranked officers had been in the past. Their flayed skins hung from the ceiling of the audience chamber of the Goptri's palace in Bharakuccha.

The Ethiopian ship did have a lookout posted in the bow. But he, too, had not been expecting to encounter enemy ships at sea. He had been concentrating his attention—with his ears more than his eyes—on spotting the first signs of approaching landfall. So he didn't see the Malwa vessel until it was too late to do anything but shout a last-minute warning.

Seconds later, the Ethiopian seaman died. When the prow of the Axumite craft struck the Malwa vessel amidships, he was flung from his roost into the enemy ship and broke his neck against the mast. His body then flopped onto two Malwa sailors huddling next to the mast, seeking shelter from the rain. Panic-stricken, the sailors heaved his corpse aside.

They had good reason to panic. The Ethiopian ship was not only heavier and larger, its bow was designed to serve as a platform for cannons. The hull structure was braced to support weight and withstand recoil. The small Malwa craft, on the other hand, was nothing more than a small fishing boat refitted as a warship. Even that "refitting" amounted to nothing more than mounting a few rocket troughs along the side.

The Ethiopian ship, running with the wind, caved in the hull of the Malwa vessel and almost ran over it completely before falling away. Within half a minute of the collision, half the Malwa sailors were in the water and the other half would be within another minute.

Cursing, the captain of the Ethiopian ship raced below deck to check the extent of the damage. His lieutenant, in the meantime, hastily ordered the signal rockets fired which would alert the rest of the Axumite fleet that they had reached their target.

Those signal rockets, of course, would also alert the Malwa defenders of the port. But Eon and his top advisers had already decided that it was too risky to attempt a complete surprise attack in bad weather. The Axumite ships might very well destroy or strand themselves by running ashore. Besides, Eon and his officers were confident that prepared and ready Axumite marines could overwhelm any Malwa garrison caught off guard during monsoon season. Half of those garrison sailors and soldiers—at least half—would be carousing or sleeping or foraging. And the ones on duty would be concentrated primarily on the inward walls of the town, guarding against attacks from Rao's guerrillas.

The negusa nagast even took the time, as his ship loomed out of the rain-drenched sea, to pull alongside the crippled Ethiopian warship. By then, the captain had returned from below, scowling more fiercely than ever.

"What's the damage?" hailed Eon.

The captain shook his head. "Taking water badly!" he shouted back. "She'll sink soon enough if we don't beach her for repairs!"

On his flagship, Eon didn't hesitate for more than a few seconds. Nor did he bother to consult with Ousanas or Ezana or Antonina, all of whom had gathered by the rail next to him.

"Forget repairs!" the Ethiopian king shouted. "Beach her in the middle of the Malwa fleet and do what damage you can! We'll salvage what we can after we take the port!"

Before he had even finished, the captain was shouting new orders. The fact that he had just been sent on what seemed to be a suicide mission did not faze him in the least.

Nor did it faze Ousanas and Eon, although Antonina's face registered a bit of shock.

"Good plan," grunted Ezana. Seeing the distress on the Roman woman's face, he chuckled harshly and shook his head. "Have no fear, Antonina. Those men will hold off the Malwa until we get there. Axumite marines!"

And so it was that the Ethiopian assault on the Malwa fleet at Chowpatty was led by a crippled ship limping into the harbor. The few sailing ships possessed by the Malwa—again, refitted sailing craft—were sheltered behind a small breakwater. The war galleys which constituted the heart of the fleet had simply been drawn up on the beach itself. That great beach had been the main reason the Malwa had chosen Chowpatty for their monsoon naval base.

The Ethiopian captain ignored the sailing ships in their little marina. His target was the galleys. So, when his ship grounded, it grounded on the beach right in the middle of the Malwa warships.

Near them, rather. By now the Ethiopian ship had taken so much water that it grounded while still twenty yards offshore. The captain issued a string of bitter curses, until he saw that his gunnery officer was practically dancing with joy as he ordered the two guns in the stern of the ship levered around to face forward as much as possible. The crews of the two guns in the bow were already getting ready to fire.

The curses trailed off. The captain of the ship had been thinking in terms of the Axumite traditions he grew up with. War at sea, to him, was a matter of boarding. His gunnery officer, trained by Antonina's Theodoran cohort, understood the realities of gunpowder combat better than he did. A ship grounded offshore provided a reasonably level firing platform. Had they actually reached the beach, the ship would almost certainly have canted so far over that none of the cannons could be brought to bear.

In effect, the crippled Ethiopian ship was now a small fortress planted in the midst of the enemy. Once he realized that, the scowl which had been fixed on the captain's face since the collision vanished instantly.

"Sarwen to the side!" he bellowed. "Prepare to repel boarders!"

The Ethiopian marines who had been pulling on the oars left the benches and began taking positions in the bow and alongside the rails. Any Malwa who tried to silence those guns would be met by spears and the heavy cutting swords favored by Ethiopian soldiers.

That still left—

The captain squinted into the rain, trying to spot the Malwa fortress which guarded the harbor. The fortress, perched on a hill overlooking the bay, held at least eight large siege guns, any one of which could destroy his vessel with a single well-placed shot. Especially if they had time to use the heated shot which all fortresses—allied or enemy alike—had adopted over the past year of the war. Fortunately, five of the eight field guns in the fortress were positioned to protect Chowpatty on its landward side from Maratha rebels.

The Ethiopians knew of that fortress. They had been in regular contact with the Marathas for two years, and Shakuntala's spies had given them a good description of Chowpatty's defenses. But they did not possess any of the detailed battle maps which would be taken almost for granted by armies of the future. Warfare was still, for the most part, a matter of words and muscle.

The rain seemed to be lightening, and the captain estimated that they were already into the afternoon. But visibility was still too poor to see more than perhaps fifty or sixty yards. He couldn't spot the fortress at all.

"Good," grunted his lieutenant, standing next to him. "If we can't see them, they can't see us."

The words echoed the captain's own thoughts. He now turned his gaze to the breakwater, barely visible through the rain. Already, two Ethiopian warships had come alongside the pier and were offloading marines, and two more were not far behind.

There was—had been, rather—a wooden structure perched on the very end of the breakwater where the

Malwa kept a small squad of soldiers on guard at all times. The thing had been a glorified shack, really. Now it was half-collapsed—not by gunfire but simply by the spears and swords of the first marine contingent. The captain could see no corpses anywhere, although some enemies might have been buried beneath the shattered planking. But he suspected the handful of Malwa soldiers stationed there had run away before the marines landed.

"They're coming now," said his lieutenant. "Finally! What a sorry lot of bastards."

The captain followed the pointing finger. Sure enough, Malwa soldiers were beginning to appear at the land end of the breakwater and, here and there, streaming onto the beach where the galleys rested.

Small streams. More like hesitant and uncertain trickles. Most of the Malwa soldiers were still buckling or strapping on their gear. The way they held their weapons did not, even at the distance, seem to indicate any great confidence and enthusiasm to the captain.

"Garritroopers," he muttered. "What do you expect?"

The Malwa getting organized at the end of the breakwater must have had a fairly efficient officer, however. By the time the first Ethiopian marines reached them, the Malwa had managed to set up an actual shield wall of sorts, bristling with spears. A handful of musketeers, positioned in the rear, sent a ragged little volley at the Axumites.

It did them about as much good as a picket fence against charging bulls. Ethiopian boarding tactics leaned very heavily on shock. The Axumites marines were trained and conditioned to expect an initial round of severe casualties. Over the decades, obtaining a "boarding scar" was a matter of pride and honor.

These marines didn't bother with an initial volley

of javelins, or even use their stabbing spears. They just raced forward and hammered into the line; deflecting spears as best as possible with their small light shields and getting into the enemy's midst with those horrid, heavy swords which were basically big meat cleavers. Strength and fury did the rest. Wolverine tactics, developed by an African nation which had never heard of the beasts.

The lieutenant had better eyesight than the captain. Suddenly he emitted a sharp, wordless cry full of distress.

"What's wrong?" demanded the captain, squinting at the distant melee. So far as he could tell, the Ethiopian marines were shredding the Malwa line.

"The negusa nagast is leading the charge!" came the hissing response. "Damned idiot!"

The captain's jaws tightened. So did his squint, as he tried to force slightly nearsighted vision to his will.

"Idiot," he echoed. Then, with a small sigh: "Always the danger, with a young king. Especially one who never fought enough battles while still a prince."

Yet, for all the condemnation in the words, the tone in which they were spoken—as had been true of the lieutenant's—echoed a dim but profound contentment. A mighty empire, Axum had become over the centuries. Its King of Kings might rule over half of Arabia and have a navy whose power could stretch across an ocean. But at the heart of that power still lay the fierce highland warriors whose sarwen, as Axumites called their regiments, were the spine and sinew of Ethiopian might.

Today's negusa nagast might carry, as had all those before him, a long list of grandiose and splendid titles. "He who brings the dawn" being not the least of them. But he had begun his life simply as Eon bisi Dakuen—*Eon, man of the Dakuen regiment*.

That was his most important name, the one that captured his true soul. Today, did any man doubt it, he would prove it true. Even without good eyesight, the captain knew full well that the first Axumite marine who had hurled his lightly armored body onto that shield wall had been the king who commanded his loyalty.

And so, despite the disapproval of his brain, the man's heart erupted. And, like every Ethiopian soldier in that fleet now pouring its strength against the Malwa bastion at Chowpatty, he spent the remaining time in that battle—even while he oversaw the cannonade which began shredding Malwa galleys on the beach and turning them into kindling for the torching squads—shouting the name of his emperor.

The *name*, not the titles. *Eon bisi Dakuen!*

From beginning to end, the battle lasted slightly longer than three hours. Throughout, the captain kept shouting that name.

The battle was ferocious enough, once the Malwa commander was able to organize the resistance. "Garritroopers," the Ethiopian captain had called his men, but the term was quite unfair. Most of the Malwa stationed at the port had been seamen, accustomed to the hardships of naval life and no stranger to savage boarding actions. Nor were they strangers to Axumite tactics, for they had clashed many times over the past year with Ethiopian ships running the blockade. And the soldiers, because Chowpatty was an isolated bastion surrounded by the Maratha rebellion, were no strangers to bitter fighting.

Still, the contest was uneven. The Ethiopians had been prepared, ready, on edge. The Malwa caught off guard, even if their commander rallied them before they were completely routed. Most of all, the difference in leadership was simply too great to withstand.

Not military leadership, as such. The Malwa commander was a capable and courageous officer, experienced in both land and naval combat. As an infantry officer, one of the Malwa kshatriya who fought with grenades in the front lines, not cannons in the rear, he had been one of the first to pour through the breach of Amaravati's walls which brought down the Andhran empire ruled by Shakuntala's father. Later, transferred into the navy, he had shown the same aptitude with maritime warfare. Promotions had come quickly enough, and not one of those promotions had come from bribes or favoritism.

If truth be told, he was not only more experienced than the king who led his enemies, but a more capable commander as well. In that battle, the negusa nagast could hardly have been said to "command" at all. He simply *led*, cutting his way through the Malwa defenders like any one of the marines at his side. Like Alexander the Great before him—though with little if any of Alexander's strategic and tactical genius—Eon bisi Dakuen would lead a battle in the front ranks, wielding a sword himself.

Indeed, in the course of that battle, Eon even managed to restage one of Alexander's most famous exploits. The negusa nagast was among the first marines who reached the walls of the fortress and began erecting their siege ladders. And then—despite the vehement protests of the soldiers surrounding him—insisted on being the first to scale the wall.

Stupid, really—even idiotic. Eon's great strength carried him to the parapet and cleared it quickly enough of the handful of Malwa soldiers who guarded his section. Just as Alexander's strength had carried him to the parapet at one of the cities he conquered from the Mallians. And then, just as happened to Alexander, he was isolated atop the parapet when the defenders pushed aside the scaling ladders.

Finding himself now the target of every Malwa bowman within range, and with nowhere to take shelter from the arrows on the *inside* of the parapet, Eon was forced to emulate Alexander again. He leapt into the interior of the fortress itself—alone, but at least no longer as vulnerable to missiles. There he took his stand next to a small tree, just as the Macedonian had done—although this was not a fig tree as in the Alexandrian legend—and began fiercely defending himself against a small mob of Malwa attackers.

The Malwa commander died not long afterward. By the time the sarwen poured over the walls of the fortress, taking no prisoners in their fury, the commander had managed to organize a rear guard action which enabled him to lead a small column of soldiers down to the beach. There, in a brief but savage melee, he tried to stop the Axumite marines who were putting the Malwa ships to the torch.

Tried, and failed, and died himself in the doing. In his case, died in the actual combat, not in the slaughter which followed as the sarwen pursued the routed Malwa soldiers for miles inland until the fall of night gave the few Malwa survivors blessed sanctuary.

There would be no mercy for Malwa that day. Although, the next day, the sarwen retrieved the body of the Malwa commander from the piled corpses on the beach and gave him a solemn burial. That was done at the command of Ezana, the leader of the Dakuen sarwe, who also commanded the erection of a small, simple gravestone over the commander's grave.

Another nation's warriors might have mutilated that

body. But the Dakuen soldiers, like their commander, came from a different tradition. One whose origins in tribal custom was not so far removed. Beneath the civilized names of regiments, lurked the not-so-dim faces of old totems. And it was that tradition which gave honor to the commander.

A hunting people will kill a tiger, but they will not dishonor it. Not even—especially not even—when the tiger, in its death throes, manages to slay the leader of the hunting party.

Eon bisi Dakuen had gained his treasured boarding scar. The wound, rather. The scar itself would never form, because the negusa nagast of Ethiopia would die from it before it could.

His soldiers had known, from the moment, still fighting their way over the rampart, they saw the spear thrust which took Eon in the belly as he fought alone inside the fortress. The knowing fueled the rage which destroyed the Malwa fleet and slaughtered Malwa's men.

Eon himself had known, and the knowing had fueled his own fury as he beat down his last assailants before collapsing unconscious to the packed-earth floor.

Ousanas had known, from the moment he reached the body and examined the wound. The young king he had reared in the way of kingship since he was a boy would be gone from this earth within a time measured by, at most, a few days. And for the first time in years, the man named Ousanas had no philosophical insights and no quip to make and no sarcasm to utter and no grin to present to the universe. He fell to his knees and simply wept, and wept, and wept.

And Antonina had known, from the moment she saw the first Ethiopian warship pull away from the break-water and begin rowing toward the flagship on which she had remained throughout the battle. Slow, solemn oarstrokes, accompanied by a rhythmic drum beat which was not so much a time-keeper as a lament.

In truth, deep inside, she had known from the moment she saw the blazing fury with which Axum's marines cut down the Malwa sailors attempting to protect the ships along the strand. Ethiopian sarwen were always ferocious in battle, to be sure, but this went beyond ferocity. This was pure slaughter, animal rage tearing at flesh, the bloodlust of maddened wolverines.

When Eon's body was brought aboard the flagship and carried into the negusa nagast's cabin, Antonina had accompanied it. Had done what she could, with the aid of an Axumite healer, to minimize the damage of the horrible wound. But, long before Ousanas came into the cabin, his face drawn and haggard, Antonina had faced the truth. The negusa nagast would live, for a time. Might even, if she and the healer used every method at their disposal, regain consciousness and speak. But he would not live to see another month go by. Probably not more than two weeks. Not with that wound. The spear had cut great slices of his intestines; damage that would inevitably bring fatal disease in its train.

In her heartbreak and despair, Antonina thought of summoning Belisarius and Aide—somehow, someway— but gave up that thought soon enough. Aide would know of some method of the future which could save Eon—*did* know, for her husband had ordered experiments begun to create the medications of the future. But there had been no time—*no time*—for that, along with everything else. And now, time had run out. Even if—somehow, someway—she could summon Aide, the crystal being from the future would be able to do no more than Antonina herself.

Weep, and weep, and weep. And, as she wept, nestled in Ousanas' arm while he joined her in the weeping, Antonina wondered, now and then, how a crystal might weep as well.

Not whether. Simply how.

Chapter 29
SUKKUR
Autumn, 533 A.D.

When Belisarius first heard the guns roaring at Sukkur, he felt a great sense of relief. Granted, Abbu's scouts had already reported that the Roman and Persian forces at Sukkur were holding back the Malwa besieging the city. Still, there was nothing quite as comforting as hearing the sound of those Roman cannons himself.

Even at a distance—Sukkur and the Indus were still a mile away—he could tell the difference in the sound between the Roman and the Malwa guns. The difference, ironically, was not in the guns themselves. Most of the siege guns which Belisarius had brought with him to the Indus—and all of the forty-eight-pounders—were Malwa in origin. Belisarius and the Persians had captured them in Mesopotamia the year before. But the Roman powder was uniformly "corned" powder, whereas the Malwa often used the older "serpentine" powder.

Here, as in many areas, the Malwa were handicapped by their sluggish economy—a handicap which was inevitable, given their insistence on maintaining rigid caste distinctions. The enemy *had* corned powder, but not enough of it to keep all their units supplied through a long battle or siege. Just as they were perfectly capable of making horseshoes and the new harnesses for draft animals—but, making them without replacing caste handicraft methods by the "industrial" system the Romans had adopted, they weren't able to supply enough for their entire army. Where every single one of Belisarius' cavalryman rode a shod horse, and all of his supply train animals used the new harnesses instead of the old collars, at least half of the Malwa army was not so equipped.

With large, small-number items like cannons or even muskets, the Malwa could compensate for their more primitive methods by substituting a mass of production. Even workers using older methods, remaining within caste boundaries, could produce a lot of such items—given that enough of them were put to work on the projects. Where the Malwa's reactionary fanaticism tended to really show up was in their inability to mass produce small and cheap items like horseshoes and large quantities of corned powder.

What pleased Belisarius the most, listening, was the comparative rate of fire. The Malwa were firing volleys, where Ashot's guns were firing individually. Under some circumstances, that would have concerned Belisarius. A volley was more effective in breaking a charge than uncoordinated fire. But Ashot knew that as well as anyone, and the fact that he was allowing his gun crews to set their own pace meant that he was not repelling any assaults. He was simply engaged in an artillery duel.

"Good," grunted Maurice, who had reached the same conclusion. The chiliarch leaned back in his saddle. "We're still in time, then."

He scanned the surrounding area, his gray beard

bristling. "Which is a good thing, since *this* little part of your plan came all to pieces. Greedy damn Greeks!"

Belisarius' jaws tightened a little. He shared Maurice's anger at the indiscipline of the Greek cataphracts, and had every intention of chewing on Sittas' ear about it. But . . .

He sighed heavily. "I suppose it couldn't have been avoided." His eyes moved to the right, where what was left of Rohri was being plundered by Sittas' Constantinople cataphracts. Then, with considerably greater satisfaction, moved on to examine the ordered ranks of his Thracian bucellarii and the Greeks who were under the command of Cyril.

The "old Greeks," as they were called by the rest of Belisarius' troops, were the cataphracts who had served with Belisarius in Mesopotamia. Along with the Thracians and the field artillery, they were almost back in formation after the assault which took Rohri. Belisarius would be able to resume his advance with *them* within the hour.

The others . . .

"Leave them to it," he growled. "I'll have words with Sittas later. Not fair to him, really, since he's been doing his best to rein them in. But he'll take out his anger at getting reprimanded on his own troops. All the better. Sittas will gore them worse than I would, with his temper up."

Maurice nodded, stroking his beard. "Then, after Sittas rages at them, you can give them a calm little speech about the need for discipline—*if* we're to win this campaign and get ten times more in the way of booty than this piddly little river town provides."

"Bound to happen, I suppose," repeated Belisarius. "They've been complaining for weeks about the lack of booty. As if our men last year just walked into a treasure room without fighting for months!"

"Well, look on the bright side. The Greeks paid for it, well enough."

Maurice's words didn't bring Belisarius much in the way of satisfaction. True, the enthusiastic assault of Sittas' cataphracts had overwhelmed the Malwa garrison in Rohri, far quicker than Belisarius could have done with the siegecraft he had been planning to use. And, true also, had thereby gained him more precious days in which to continue outmaneuvering the enemy.

But the cost had been steep. At a rough estimate, he had lost a thousand cataphracts in that pell-mell—and completely impromptu—charge. And he knew he would lose as many afterward to wounds suffered in the course of taking the city. As always, war had been an unpredictable mistress. Gain something, lose something, then shift plans accordingly.

There was no point dwelling on it. And there was this much to be said: at least the "Greek fury" was not producing the atrocities against native civilians which usually accompanied the uncontrolled sacking of a city. Not because the Greeks were restraining themselves—they had already put the entire Malwa garrison to the sword, refusing any and all attempts at surrender—but simply because there were no civilians left in Rohri. The Malwa garrison had already massacred them.

"It's insane," snarled Belisarius. "The Malwa are still carrying out their orders long after the situation which called for those orders has changed. No point in a scorched earth policy in the Sind *now*. We're already at the gates of the Punjab. They ought to be corralling the populace in order to use them for a labor force themselves."

Half-gloomily, half with philosophical satisfaction, he studied the ruins of Rohri's outer fortifications. The only reason the first charge of the Greek cataphracts had broken through, for all its headlong vigor, was that

the fortifications had not been completed before the
Roman army arrived unexpectedly from the south. The
civilians who could have finished the work were dead
before it got well underway.

"Insane," he repeated. Then, shaking his head,
looked away and studied the terrain ahead. What was
done was done.

"Send a courier to Sittas and tell him to follow us
whenever he can get those maniacs back under control. If we wait here for them, we'll lose the initiative.
I think, judging from Abbu's report and the sound of
those guns, that if we move now we can take the good
ground on the south bank."

Maurice nodded, summoned a courier, and gave him
the necessary commands. By the time that was done,
Belisarius had already set his army into motion.

What was left of it, at least, with the Greek
cataphracts now out of action for a time. So, the army
which finally reached the bank of the Indus across from
Sukkur was the smallest Belisarius had led in years.
Three thousand of his own bucellarii, two thousand of
Cyril's men, several thousand Arab and Syrian light
cavalry, two thousand artillerymen—and, fortunately,
Felix's five hundred sharpshooter dragoons.

Which rump of a rump army was what made the
difference, in the end. Because by the time Belisarius
and his army reached the south bank, the Malwa
commander of the great army besieging Sukkur across
the river had already sent thousands of his men across
the Indus to relieve the garrison under attack in Rohri.

But . . . that flotilla of barges and river boats hadn't
quite reached the bank, when Belisarius arrived.
Quickly, Gregory began bringing up the field guns to
repel the looming amphibious assault. In the meantime, moving much more quickly, Felix had his
sharpshooters—firing under discipline, at coordinated

targets—begin taking out the helmsmen and sailors controlling those ships.

It was a close thing. But Felix managed to throw the oncoming flotilla into enough confusion to give Gregory the time he needed to position the field guns. Thereafter, volleys of cannon-fire added their much heavier weight to the battle between land and water. By then it was already sunset. And if three-pounders were far too small to make much of a dent in good fortifications, they were more than enough to hammer river boats into pieces. Enough of them, at least, for the Malwa to call off the assault and retreat back to the opposite bank.

Not for long, of course. Early the next morning, just after dawn, the Malwa boats came again. This time, spreading out to minimize the damage of the cannon and sharpshooter fire. The Malwa suffered considerable casualties in that crossing, but they did manage to land a total of ten thousand men in three separate places along the south bank by midmorning. In numbers, at least, they now had almost as many men as Belisarius on his side of the Indus.

It did them no good at all. By then, Sittas had restored order among his cataphracts and pulled them out of Rohri. The Malwa had barely gotten their feet on dry land when yet another furious cataphract charge, sallying from the Roman lines, crushed them like an avalanche. Eight thousand armored horsemen, using bows and lances and sabers, throwing their weight atop the forces Belisarius already had hammering the Malwa in their three enclaves, were more than enough to destroy yet another Malwa army.

Although, this time, Belisarius was able to save the Malwa soldiery trying to surrender. The Greeks had sated their bloodlust in Rohri the day before. Even they, belatedly, had come to understand that a captured soldier was someone *else* to do the scut work of erecting fieldworks. And even they, belatedly, were beginning to realize that real war was a lot more complicated than simply a series of charges.

Three battles and three victories, thus, were added to the luster of Belisarius' name by the time he finally reestablished contact with Ashot and Emperor Khusrau. *Kulachi. Rohri. The Battle of the Crossing.*

None of those battles was exactly a "major" battle, of course, measured in any objective sense. Two small armies destroyed, and a town taken. But it mattered little, if at all. The importance of the names lay in the names themselves, not the truth beneath them. Belisarius had a blooded army, now, whose new troops—which was most of them—had the satisfaction of adding themselves into that long roll call of triumph against Malwa which began at Anatha.

Eight times, now, since the war began, Belisarius and his army had met the Malwa on the battlefield or in savage siege. Anatha, and the Dam; The Battle of the Pass and Charax and Barbaricum—and now these new victories. Except for the Battle of the Pass against Damodara and Sanga, each clash had ended in a Roman victory. Even the defeat at the Pass had been a close thing, tactically—and had set up, strategically, the annihilation of the giant Malwa army at Charax.

Such a string of victories gives confidence to an army. A kind of confidence which doubles and triples their strength in war. Real war, which, unlike the maneuvers drawn by pen on paper, is as much a thing of the spirit as the flesh.

Confidence alone, of course, is not enough. As important is an army's sense of cohesion and solidarity. Achieving *that* was a bit more difficult. The indiscipline and selfish greed of the Greeks at Rohri had infuriated the rest of the army—the more so when they found themselves forced to fend off a Malwa assault immediately afterward, unaided by their supposed "comrades" for a full day.

For their part, the Greeks were outraged to discover that the rest of the army expected them to *share* the loot they had obtained by their own furious energy (and loss of blood) in the assault which took Rohri. Abstractly, they knew of that traditional policy of Belisarius' army. But . . . but . . . applied to *them? Here and now?*

Belisarius let the troops sort the matter out in their own manner. He was busy enough, as it was, preparing for his coming council of war with Ashot and Khusrau. Even if he hadn't been, he probably would have stayed out of it. Some things are best handled informally, when all is said and done.

He *did* grow a little concerned when Gregory's artillerymen began training their field guns on the Greek encampment, true. And he kept an eye cocked on the maneuvers of the Thracian cataphracts to the south and Cyril's men to the east, blocking the Greek line of retreat. Not to mention the enthusiasm with which Felix's sharpshooters began making wagers on how big a hole their magnificent rifles could punch through a Greek nobleman's finest armor.

But . . . it all sorted itself out after a single tense day. Soon enough, the Greeks decided that largesse and generosity on the morrow of victory and triumph was a fine and splendid thing. And, for their part, the Thracians and others allowed that the Greek charges at Rohri and the south bank had been conducted with panache and flair well worthy of any man who ever marched with Belisarius.

In the end, the worst problem left to Belisarius was trying to make himself heard in the command tent while discussing stratagems and tactics with Ashot and Khusrau. The din of the great victory celebration was well nigh overwhelming: Greek cataphract shouting his praise of Thracian, artilleryman lifting his voice in chorus with sharpshooter—*a capella* which sent every frog nearby into shock—and Arab ululation adding its own special flavor to the acoustic stew.

"What *is* that incredible racket?" demanded Khusrau, as soon as he entered the command tent.

"Music to my ears," replied Belisarius.

"We can withstand them," said Khusrau confidently. "It was a tight thing, for a time. Once, they even breached a small section of the walls before we drove them back. But since Ashot arrived and took positions to the south, the Malwa have become more cautious."

The Persian emperor gave the Armenian cataphract a look full of approval. "Most clever, he's been!" he stated cheerfully. "His positions are so well designed and camouflaged that the Malwa have no real idea how few soldiers he has."

"They made two major assaults early on," chimed in Ashot. "The second one came close to over-running our positions. But—"

He bestowed his own look of approval on Abbu. "The Arabs found us splendid ground for a defensive stance. Both times the Malwa charged, the terrain bunched them in front of our guns. Their casualties were horrendous, and I don't think their commanders even realize how close they came to success in the second assault. I don't believe they'll try that again."

Belisarius scratched his chin. "So now, in effect, everything has bogged down into a long siege and continual counter-battery fire. We're tying up a very large Malwa army with much smaller forces of our own."

Both Khusrau and Ashot nodded.

"What is your stock of powder?" Belisarius asked the Armenian.

"Good enough for a bit," replied Ashot, shrugging. "Although if Menander doesn't get us some supplies within a few days, that will change."

The Armenian officer frowned. "It's those big guns that really keep them at bay, General. The truth is that with as few troops as I have, the Malwa *could* over-run our position. Not without taking great losses, of course. But Malwa is always willing to shed the blood of its soldiers. And if their commanders ever realize how much our defenses rely on the big guns, they'll pay the price."

"Which means you can't afford to slack off your fire," interjected Maurice, "in order to conserve ammunition. That would give away your weakness."

All the men in the tent turned their heads, look-ing to the south, as if they could see the river through leather walls.

"I hope this Menander of yours is a capable officer," mused Khusrau. "He seems very young."

"He'll do the job, if it can be done," said Belisarius firmly. "The problem isn't him, in any case. It's whether those steam engines of Justinian's work properly. Which, unfortunately, we'll have no way of knowing until Menander gets here. Or Bouzes and Coutzes arrive with the main army."

Maurice heaved a sigh. "Even that last won't do it, by itself. With the twins' infantry added into the mix, of course, the Malwa will not have a chance of breaking Ashot's position. In fact, they'll have to retreat back to the Punjab. But those soldiers will need food and supplies themselves, especially if we hope to pursue. Unless Menander can get the logistics train working—which means using the river; no way to haul that much by land—we're hanging on here by our fingernails."

For the first time since the conference began, Gregory spoke. "True. But at least once Bouzes and Coutzes arrive, we'll be back in touch with all of our forces strung out along the river—all the way back to Barbaricum. They're laying telegraph wire as they come."

He gave a sly little glance at Abbu. As always whenever "newfangled ways" were brought up, the old Arab traditionalist was glowering fiercely.

"My scouts can maintain communications down the river!" he snapped. Then, reluctantly: "If need be."

Belisarius shook his head. "I've got a lot better use for your men than being couriers." He decided to toss Abbu a bone—and a rather large one at that. "This newfangled system is fine for staying in touch with the rear. Only *men* can scout the front."

Abbu's chest swelled. The more so, after Belisarius' next words: "Which is precisely where I propose to go. Back to the front. I want to keep pushing Malwa off balance."

Leaning over the map, Belisarius gave the Persian emperor a concise summary of his plans. To his relief, Khusrau immediately nodded agreement. Belisarius was not under the command of Khusrau, of course, but maintaining good and close relations with the Persians was essential for everything.

"Yes," stated the emperor forcefully. "That is the way to go. The Aryan way!"

The last, boastfully barked statement was perhaps unfortunate. The last time the Roman officers in that tent had seen an Aryan army attacking in "the Aryan way" was when they charged Belisarius at Mindouos.

And lost an army in the doing, in one of the worst defeats in Persia's long history.

Obviously sensing the little awkwardness in the room, Khusrau smiled. "Not, of course, as stupidly as has sometimes been done in the past."

Maurice—of all people—played the diplomat. "You broke Malwa yourself, Emperor, not so long ago. When you led the charge in the Aryan way which cleared the road to Sukkur."

Khusrau's smile turned into a grin. "I? Nonsense, Maurice." The emperor slapped the shoulder of the young Persian officer standing at his side. "*Kurush* led that magnificent display of Aryan martial prowess. I assure you I stayed quite some distance behind. Arrayed in my finest armor, of course, and waving my sword about like the great Cyrus of ancient memory."

A little laugh swept the room. For all the historic animosity between Rome and Persia, every Roman officer in Belisarius' army had long since fallen under the sway of Khusrau's magnetic personality. That little witty remark of his being a good part of the reason. Of Khusrau Anushirvan's personal courage, no man in the tent had any doubt. But it was refreshing, for once, to see a Persian monarch—any ruler, for that matter—who did not fear to speak the truth as well.

"God save us from reckless leaders," murmured Maurice. "Especially those who try to assume the mantle of Alexander the Maniac. Nothing but grief and ruin down that road."

Belisarius straightened. "Mention of your sagacity outside Sukkur, Emperor of the Aryans, leads me to the next point I wanted to raise." He hesitated. Then, seeing no way to blunt the thing:

"Now that you have smuggled your way out of Sukkur, you should not return. If Sukkur falls, that is just a setback. If you fall with it, a disaster."

Sagacious or not, Khusrau's back was stiffening. Before he could utter words which might irrevocably commit him to any course of action, Belisarius hurried on.

"But that is only one reason you should not return. The other—the more important—is that your people need you in the Sind."

As Belisarius had expected, and counted on, the last words broke through Khusrau's gathering storm of outrage. The Persian emperor's eyes widened.

"*My* people?" he asked, confused. "In the *Sind*?"

Belisarius nodded sagely. "Exactly so, Emperor. The Sind—as we agreed—is now Persian territory. And it is filled with terrified and desperate people, fleeing from the Malwa savagery. *Your* subjects, now, Khusrau of the Immortal Soul. Who have nowhere to turn for aid and succor but to you. Which they cannot do if you are locked away behind a Malwa siege at Sukkur."

Sittas—would wonders never cease?—took his turn as diplomat. "The Malwa were not able to do that much damage to the Sind itself, Emperor, before they were driven out. Burn some crops, destroy some orchards, ravage some towns and break open a part of the irrigation network. It is not irreparable damage, and much of the land remains intact. The problem is that the people who work that land are scattered to the winds. Still alive, most of them, but too confused and terrified to be of any use."

Belisarius picked up the thread smoothly. "That is where you are truly needed now, Emperor. Kurush can hold Sukkur, if any man can. You are needed in the south. Touring the countryside, visible to all, reassuring them that their new ruler has their interests at heart and will protect them from further Malwa outrages. And, as you go, organizing them to return to their villages and fields."

Khusrau swiveled his head and looked at Kurush. The young Persian officer straightened and squared his shoulders. "I agree, Emperor. No one can replace you in *that* work. I can—and will—hold Sukkur for you, while you forge a new province for our empire."

Khusrau took a deep breath, then another. Then, as was his way, came to quick decision.

"So be it." He paused for a moment, thinking, before turning back to Belisarius. "I do not wish to drain any significant number of the men in Sukkur. Kurush will need them more than I."

The emperor jerked his head, pointing toward the entrance of the tent. "Twenty Immortals accompanied me here. I will keep those, as an immediate bodyguard. But I will need some of your Roman troops. Cavalrymen. Perhaps a thousand, in all."

Belisarius did not hesitate for an instant. He turned toward the small group of officers standing toward the rear of the tent. His eyes found the one he was seeking.

Jovius. He's steady and capable, but slow on maneuvers. An asset to Khusrau, and a bit of a headache to me.

"Take five hundred men, Jovius. All from the Thracian bucellarii. The emperor will want to start by going down the Indus"—he gave Khusrau a glance; the emperor nodded—"so you should encounter the Syrian cavalry coming north soon enough. When you do, tell Bouzes and Coutzes to provide you with another five hundred men. Or whatever number the emperor feels he might need. I'll write the orders to that effect later tonight."

Jovius nodded. Belisarius now gave Maurice a glance, to see if the commander of the bucellarii had any objection.

Maurice shrugged stolidly. "Five hundred Thracians won't make a difference, to us. Not where we're going.

Your fancy plans will either work or they won't. And if they don't, five *thousand* Thracians couldn't save us from disaster."

Another little laugh arose in the tent. "Besides," continued Maurice, listening for a moment to the revelry still going on outside, "from the sound of things we won't be having too many discipline problems in the future. And those Greeks—I'll say it, just this once—are probably as good as Thracians on an actual battlefield."

"Done, then," said Khusrau. He cocked his head quizzically at Belisarius. "And is there anything else? Any other subtle Roman stratagem, which needs to be finagled past a dimwitted Aryan emperor?"

The laugh which swept the tent this time was neither small nor brief. And, by its end, had given the alliance between Rome and Persia yet another link of steel.

Odd, really, came Aide's soft thoughts in Belisarius' mind. **That humor can be the strongest chain of all, binding human destiny.**

Belisarius began some philosophical response, but Aide drove over it blithely. **It's because you protoplasmic types are such dimwits, is what it is. Logic being beyond your capability, you substitute this silly fractured stuff you call "jokes."**

Whether or not Belisarius' face got a pained expression at those words was impossible for him to determine. Because it certainly did as Aide continued.

Speaking of which, did I tell you the one about the crystal and the farmer's daughter? One evening, it seems, the daughter was in the field—

Chapter 30

Trying not to wince, Belisarius studied the young—the *very* young—officer standing in front of him. As always, Calopodius' smooth face showed no expression at all. Although Belisarius thought—perhaps—to detect a slight trace of humor lurking somewhere in the back of his eyes.

I hope so, he thought, rather grimly. *He'll need a sense of humor for this assignment.*

Aide tried to reassure him. **It worked for Magruder on the peninsula.**

Belisarius managed his own version of a mental snort. *Magruder was facing McClellan, Aide. McClellan! You think that vaudeville trickery would have worked against Grant or Sherman? Or Sheridan?*

He swiveled his head, looking through the open flap of his command tent toward the Malwa across the river. He couldn't see much in the way of detail, of course. Between the width of the Indus and the inevitable confusion of a large army erecting fieldworks, it was impossible to gauge the precise size and positions of the Malwa forces besieging Sukkur.

But Belisarius wasn't trying to assess the physical characteristics of his enemy. He was trying, as best he could, to gauge the mentality of the unknown Malwa officer or officers who commanded that great force of men. And, so far at least, was not finding any comfort in the doing.

True, the enemy commander—whoever he was—seemed to be somewhat sluggish and clumsy in the way he handled his troops. Although, as Belisarius well knew, handling large forces in siege warfare was a sluggish and clumsy task by its very nature. "Swift and supple maneuvers" and "trench warfare" fit together about as well as an elephant fits into a small boat.

But the enemy commander didn't *have* to be particularly talented to make Belisarius' scheme come apart at the seams. He simply had to be . . . determined, stubborn, and willing to wrack up a butcher's bill. If anything, in fact, lack of imagination would work in his favor. If McClellan hadn't been such an intelligent man, he wouldn't have been spooked by shadows and mirages.

It's not the same thing, said Aide, still trying to reassure. **If Magruder hadn't kept McClellan pinned in the peninsula with his theatrics, Richmond might have fallen. The worst that happens if Calopodius can't manage the same—**

For a moment, the crystal's faceted mind shivered, as if Aide were trying to find a term suitably majestic. Or, at least, not outright . . . But he failed.

All right, I admit it's a stunt. But if it doesn't work, all that happens is that Calopodius and his men retreat to the south. There's no disaster involved, since you're not depending on him to protect your supply lines.

Another pause, like a shivering kaleidoscope, as Aide tried to find another circumlocution. Belisarius almost laughed.

Because I won't have any supply lines, he finished. *Because I'm going to be trying a stunt of my own.*

Marching through two hundred miles of enemy territory, living off the land as I go.

Aide seemed determined to reassure, no matter what. **It worked for—**

I know it worked for Grant in the Vicksburg campaign, interrupted Belisarius, a bit impatiently. *I should, after all, since this whole campaign of mine is patterned after that one—except that I propose to take Atlanta in the bargain. Well . . . Chattanooga, at least.*

This time he did laugh aloud, albeit softly. *Even Grant and Sherman would have called me a lunatic. Even Sheridan!*

Apparently realizing the futility of reassurance, Aide got into the mood of the moment. Brightly, cheerily: **Custer would have approved.**

Belisarius' soft laugh threatened to turn into a guffaw, but he managed to suppress it. The face of young Calopodius was now definitely showing an expression. A quizzical one, in the main, leavened by—

I'd better explain, lest he conclude his commander has lost his mind.

Quickly, pushing his doubts and fears aside, Belisarius sketched for Calopodius the basic outlines of his plan—and the role assigned for the young Greek nobleman. Before he was halfway into it, as Belisarius had hoped—and feared—Calopodius' eyes were alight with enthusiasm and eagerness.

"It'll work, General!" exclaimed the lad, almost before Belisarius completed his last sentence. "Except—"

Calopodius hesitated, obviously a bit abashed at the thought of contradicting his august commander. But the hesitation—as Belisarius had hoped, and feared—didn't last for more than a second.

Almost pulling Belisarius by the arm, Calopodius led the way out of the tent onto the sandy soil beyond. There, still as eager and enthusiastic as ever, he began pointing out his proposed positions and elaborating on his subterfuges

"—so that's how I'd do it," he concluded. "With logs disguised to look like cannons, and the few you're leaving me to give some teeth to the illusion, I can make this island look like a real bastion. That'll put us right in the face of the Malwa, intimidate the bastards. They'll never imagine we'd do it unless we had big forces in reserve at Rohri. And I'll keep the walking wounded on the mainland marching around to seem like a host."

Belisarius sighed inwardly. *Smart lad. Exactly how I'd do it.*

He directed his thoughts toward Aide: *Which is what I was really worried about. If Calopodius loses the gamble, it won't be a disaster for me. True enough. But he and well over a thousand men will be doomed. No way they could retreat off this island in the middle of the Indus if the Malwa launch a major assault on them, and press it home.*

Aide said nothing. Belisarius scowled. *It's a damned "forlorn hope," is what it is. Something of which I do not generally approve.*

Seeing his commander's scowl, and misinterpreting it, Calopodius began expanding on his proposal. And if his tone was somewhat apologetic, the words themselves were full of confidence.

Belisarius let him finish without interruption. Partly to gauge Calopodius' tactical acumen—which was surprisingly good for such a young officer, especially a noble cataphract asked to fight defensively, on foot—but mostly to allow his own nerves to settle. Throughout his career, Belisarius had tried to avoid inflicting heavy casualties on his own troops. But, there were times . . .

And this was one of them. "Forlorn hope" or not, if Calopodius could succeed in this tactical military gamble, the odds in favor of Belisarius' own great gamble would be much improved.

Belisarius scanned the island, following the eager finger of Calopodius as the teenage officer pointed out his proposed field emplacements. As he did so, Belisarius continued his own ruminations on the larger strategy of which this was a part.

In order for his campaign to break out of the Sind to work, Belisarius needed to effectively disappear from his enemy's sight. For at least two weeks, more likely three, as he took his army away from the Indus—and thus out of sight of the Malwa troops who would be marching and sailing down the river to reinforce the siege of Sukkur. He would lure them into a trap at Sukkur, while he marched around them to lock the door shut in their rear.

Belisarius would take his main army directly east and then, skirting the edges of the Cholistan desert, sweep to the northeast. He would be marching parallel to the Indus, but keeping a distance of some thirty miles between his forces and the river. Enough, with a screen of Arab scouts, to keep his movements mysterious to the Malwa.

Even if Abbu's men encountered some Malwa detachments, the enemy would most likely assume they were simply a scouting or foraging party. Never imagining that, behind the screen of light cavalry, a powerful striking force of Roman heavy cavalry and artillery was approaching the Chenab fork—two hundred miles away from the pitched siege warfare raging around Sukkur.

The plan relied on its own boldness to succeed. That—and the willingness of Calopodius and fewer than two thousand cataphracts left behind to die, if necessary, on a island across from the huge Malwa army besieging Sukkur. Again, the very boldness of the gambit was the only thing that gave it a chance to succeed. Belisarius estimated—and Calopodius obviously agreed—that the Malwa commander would assume that the forces on the island were simply a detachment of Belisarius' main force. Which, he would assume—insanity to think otherwise!—were still positioned in Rohri.

Positioned, refitted—and ready to take advantage of a failed Malwa assault on the outlying detachment on the island to push across the Indus and link up with the Persians forted up in Sukkur and Ashot's Roman forces south of the city.

Aide chimed in, back to his mode of reassurance: **By now, after Anatha and the Dam and Charax, the Malwa will be terrified of another "Belisarius trap." Their commander at Sukkur will stare at that island and wonder. And wonder. What trap lies hidden there? He will study that island, and conclude that Calopodius is simply bait. And—wise man!—he will conclude that bait is best left unswallowed.**

Belisarius nodded, responding simultaneously to Aide and the young and eager officer standing in front of him.

"It'll work," he said firmly, his tone exuding a confidence he did not really possess. But . . .

Belisarius had made up his mind, now. As much as anything, because listening to Calopodius' enthusiastic words had convinced him of the key thing. If this scheme had any chance of success, it would be because of the boldness and courage of the officer who led it. And while some part of Belisarius' soul was dark and grim—almost bitter—at the thought of asking a seventeen-year-old boy to stand and die, the cold-blooded general's mind knew the truth. For some odd reason buried deep within the human spirit, such "boys," throughout history, had proven their willingness to do so.

Time and time again they had, in places beyond counting. It was a characteristic which recognized neither border, breed, nor birth. Such "boys" had done so in the Warsaw Ghetto, and at Isandhlwana, and in the sunken road at Shiloh. As if, on the threshold of manhood, they felt compelled to prove themselves worthy of a status that no one, really, had ever challenged—except themselves, in the shadowy and fearful crevices of their own souls.

He sighed. *So be it. I was once seventeen years old myself.* Coldly, his eyes moved over the landscape of the island, remembering. *And would have—eagerly—done the same.*

There remained, only, to sharpen the sacrificial blade. Belisarius steeled himself, and spoke.

"Remember, Calopodius. *Bleed them.* If they come, spill their guts before you die." His tone was as hard as the words. "I'm hoping they don't, of course. I'm hoping the fake guns and the constant movement of a few troops will convince the Malwa my main force is still here. The few guns and troops I'm leaving you will be enough to repel any probes. And once Menander gets here with the *Justinian*, any Malwa attack across the river will get savaged. But—"

"If they come across in force before Menander gets here, they'll mangle us," concluded Calopodius. "But it won't be all that easy for them, if we stand our ground. Don't forget that we captured or destroyed most of their river boats in the Battle of the Crossing. So they can't just swamp me with a single mass attack. They'll have to work at it."

He shrugged. "It's a war, General. And you can't live forever, anyway. But if they come, I'll bleed them. Me and the Constantinople cataphracts you're leaving behind." His young voice rang with conviction. "We maybe can't break them—not a large enough assault— but we will gore them badly. Badly enough to give you that extra few days you need. That much I can promise."

Belisarius hesitated, trying to think of something to add. Before he could shape the words, a small sound caused him to turn his head.

Maurice had arrived. The chiliarch looked at him, then at Calopodius. His eyes were as gray as his beard.

"You agreed, boy?" he demanded. Seeing the young officer's eager nod, Maurice snorted.

"Damn fool." But the words glowed with inner fire. Maurice, too, had once been seventeen years old. He stepped over and placed a hand on Calopodius' shoulder. Then, squeezing it:

"It's a 'forlorn hope,' you know. But every man should do it at least once in a lifetime, I imagine. And—if by some odd chance, you survive—you'll have the bragging rights for the rest of your life."

Calopodius grinned. "Who knows? Maybe even my aunt will stop calling me 'that worthless brat.' "

Belisarius chuckled. Maurice leered. "That might not be the blessing you imagine. She might start pestering you instead of the stable boys."

Calopodius winced, but rallied quickly. "Not a problem!" he proclaimed. "I received excellent marks in both rhetoric and grammar. I'm sure I could fend off the ploys of an incestuous seductress."

But a certain look of alarm remained on his face; and it was that, in the end, which reconciled Belisarius to the grim reality of his scheme. There was something strangely satisfying in the sight of a seventeen-year-old boy being more worried about the prospect of a distant social awkwardness than the far more immediate prospect of his own death.

You're a peculiar form of life, observed Aide.

I sometimes wonder if the term "intelligence" isn't the ultimate oxymoron.

Belisarius added his own firm shoulder-squeeze to Maurice's, and strode away to begin the preparations for the march. As he began issuing new orders, part of his mind examined Aide's quip. And concluded that, as was so often true, humor was but the shell of reason.

True enough. An intelligent animal understands the certainty of his own eventual death. So it stands to reason his thought processes will be a bit—what's the word?

Weird, came the prompt reply.

Two days later, Belisarius and his army moved out of their fieldworks on the banks of the Indus near Rohri. They left behind, stationed on the island in the new fieldworks which had been hastily erected, three field guns and their crews and a thousand of Sittas' cataphracts. Also left behind, in Rohri itself, were all of the wounded. Many of those men would die from their injuries in the next few days and weeks. But most of them—perhaps six or seven hundred men—were healthy enough to provide Calopodius with the troops he needed to maintain the pretense that Rohri was still occupied by Belisarius' entire army.

They pulled out shortly after midnight, using the moonlight to find their way. Belisarius knew that his soldiers would have to move slowly in order not to make enough noise to alert the Malwa positioned across the river that a large troop movement was underway. And he wanted—needed—to be completely out of sight by the break of dawn.

Under the best of circumstances, of course, heavy cavalry and field artillery make noise when they move. And doing so at night hardly constituted "the best of circumstances." Still, Belisarius thought he could manage it. The cavalry moved out first, with Gregory's field artillery stationed on the banks of the Indus near Rohri adding their own fire to that of Calopodius' guns on the island. At Belisarius' command, the guns were firing staggered shots rather than volleys. The continuous sound of the cannons, he thought, should serve to disguise the noise made by the cavalry as they left the river.

Then, as the night wore on, Gregory would start pulling his guns away from the river. Taking them out one at a time, following the now-departed cavalry, leaving the rest to continue firing until those leaving were all gone. As if Belisarius was slowly realizing that an artillery barrage at night was really a poor way to bombard an unseen and distant enemy entrenched within fieldworks. By the end, only Calopodius' three guns would remain, firing until a courier crossing to the island on one of the few small boats left behind would tell Calopodius that his commander had succeeded in the first step of his great maneuver.

That barrage, of course, would cost Belisarius still more of his precious gunpowder. But he had managed to save all of the special ammunition used by the mitrailleuse and the mortars, and most of the sharpshooters' cartridges. And he was sure he would have enough gunpowder to keep the field guns in operation against whatever enemy he encountered on the march to the Chenab. Whether there would be enough ammunition left thereafter, to fend off the inevitable Malwa counterattack once he set up his fortifications at the fork of the Chenab . . .

Worry about that when the time comes, he thought to himself. Yet, despite that firm self-admonition, he could not help but turn around in his saddle and stare back into the darkness over the Indus.

He was staring to the southwest now, not toward

the guns firing on the river. Trying, as futile as the effort might be, to find Menander somewhere in that black distance. In the end, the success of Belisarius' campaign would depend on yet another of the young officers whom he had elevated to command in the course of this war. Just as he was relying on the courage and ingenuity of Calopodius to cover his break from enemy contact, he was depending on the energy and competence of Menander to bring him the supplies he would need to make this bold maneuver something more than a reckless gamble.

Perhaps oddly, he found some comfort in that knowledge. If Belisarius was willing to condemn one young man to possible destruction, he could balance that cold-blooded deed with his willingness to place his own fate in the hands of yet another. Throughout his military career, Belisarius had been firmly convinced that the success of a general ultimately rested on his ability to forge a leadership team around him. Now that he was taking what was perhaps the boldest gamble in that career, he took no little satisfaction in the fact that he was willing, himself, to stake his life on his own methods of leadership.

In for a penny, in for a pound. You stick with the ones who got you here. Put your money where your mouth is.

On and on, as he guided his horse through a moonlight-dim landscape, Belisarius recited proverb after proverb to himself. Some of which he had long known, others of which Aide had taught him from future saws and sayings.

Aide remained silent, throughout. But Belisarius thought to detect a faint trace of satisfaction coming from the crystal being. As if Aide, also, found a philosophical comfort in matching actions to words.

❖   ❖   ❖

Far to the southwest, at one of the many bends in the Indus, Menander was in the hold of the *Justinian*, cursing fate and fortune and—especially!—the never-to-be-sufficiently-damned gadgetry of a far-distant one-time emperor.

"Justinian and his damn contraptions!" he snarled, glaring at the steam engine and the Greek artisans feverishly working on it. His own arms were covered with grease up to the elbows, however, and the curse was more in the way of a ritual formality than anything truly heartfelt. This was not the first time the *damned gadget* had broken down, after all. And, judging from past experience . . .

"That's it," said one of the artisans, straightening up. "She should be all right again. Just that same miserable stupid fucking—"

Menander didn't hear the rest of the ritual denunciation. Before the artisan was well into the practiced litany, he had clambered onto the deck and was beginning to issue orders to resume the voyage upriver.

Ten minutes later, studying the river barges being towed behind the *Justinian* and the *Victrix*, Menander's mood was much improved. Even in the moonlight, he could see that the flotilla was making good headway. Far better—far, far better—than any galleys could have done, sweeping oars against the current of the great river. And the four cargo vessels, needing only skeleton crews, were carrying far more in the way of supplies—far, far more—than five times their number of galleys could have done.

His eyes lifted, looking into the darkness to the south. Somewhere back there, many miles behind, a much larger flotilla of sailing ships was moving up the river also, carrying men and supplies to reinforce Ashot at Sukkur. But the monsoon winds were but a fickle remnant now. The sailing craft were not making much faster headway than were Bouzes and Coutzes, who were marching the main forces of the Roman army along the riverbanks.

Still, they were not dawdling. They were moving as fast as any huge army made up primarily of infantry could hope to do. Fifteen miles a day, Menander estimated. And Bouzes and Coutzes, when he left them, had been confident they could maintain that pace throughout the march.

"Three weeks," Menander muttered to himself. "In three weeks they'll be at Sukkur." He growled satisfaction, almost like a tiger. "And once they get to Sukkur, the Malwa there are done for. If Khusrau and Ashot can hold out that long, Bouzes and Coutzes will be the hammer to the anvil. The Malwa will have no choice but to retreat back to the Punjab."

He pictured that retreat in his mind. Practically purring, now.

Two hundred miles they'll have to retreat. With our main forces coming after them, Belisarius blocking their way—the possibility that Belisarius might fail in his attempt to reach the Chenab never crossed Menander's mind—*and me and Eusebius to hammer them from the river with the* Justinian *and* Victrix. *And the* Photius, *coming later.*

Fondly, Menander patted the thick wooden hull of the newfangled steam-powered warship. According to the last message received by Bouzes and Coutzes over the telegraph line they had been laying behind them, the *Justinian*'s sister ship had reached Barbaricum and was starting up the Indus herself. Towing yet another flotilla of precious supplies to the front.

"Fine ships!" he exclaimed, to a distant and uncaring moon.

❖   ❖   ❖

Not long after daybreak, the next morning, Menander was snarling at the rising sun. But, this time, simply at the vagaries of fate rather than the madness of a far-distant one-time emperor besotted with gadgetry.

For the fifth time since the voyage began, the *Justinian* had run aground on an unseen sandbar in the muddy river. While the ship's navigator dutifully recorded the existence of that sandbar on the charts which the expedition was creating for those who would come after them, Eusebius towed the *Justinian* off the sandbar with the *Victrix*, its paddle wheels churning at full throttle. Once the *Victrix* succeeded in breaking Menander's ship loose, the *Justinian*'s own engine did the rest.

A few minutes later, having cleared the obstruction and carefully towing the cargo vessels away from it, Menander's mood became sunny once again.

So was that of his chief pilot. "Good thing the old emperor"—such was the affectionate term which had become the custom in Menander's river navy, to describe a blind emperor-become-craftsman—"designed this thing to go in reverse. Odd, really, since he never planned it for river work."

Menander curled his lip. "Who says he never planned it for river work?" he demanded. Then, shaking his head firmly: "Don't underestimate the old emperor. A wise man, he is—ask anyone who's ever been up for judgement in his court."

The pilot nodded sagely. "True, true. No bribing the old emperor to make a favorable ruling for some rich crony. Worth your head to even try."

Affectionately, the pilot patted the flank of the ship and cast an approving glance at one of the heavy guns nearby. "She'll put the fear of God in the Malwa. You watch."

Menander began to add his own placid words of wisdom to that sage opinion, but a shrieking whistle cut him short.

"Again!" he bellowed, racing for the hatch leading to the engine room below. "Justinian and his damned contraptions!"

The same rising sun cast its light on Belisarius' army, now well into its march away from the Indus.

"We've broken contact, clear enough," said Maurice with satisfaction. "The men will be getting tired, though, after marching half the night. Do you want to make camp early today?"

Belisarius shook his head. "No rest, Maurice. Not until nightfall. I know they'll be exhausted by then, but they'll get over it soon enough."

He did not even bother to look behind him, where he had left two young men to bear a load far heavier than their years warranted.

"Drive them, Maurice," he growled. "By the time we reach the Chenab, I want every man in this army to be cursing me day and night."

Maurice smiled. "Think they'll take it out on the Malwa, do you?" The smile became a grin. "I imagine you're right, at that."

Chapter 31
THE GULF OF KHAMBAT
Autumn, 533 A.D.

"Tomorrow you will strike the Malwa at Bharakuccha," whispered Eon. The voice of the dying king, for all its weakness, did not tremble or waver in the least. Nor did any of the people assembled in the royal cabin of the flagship, which consisted of all the top commanders of the Axumite navy, have any difficulty making out the words. If they leaned forward on their stools, bracing hands against knees, it was not because they strained to hear. It was simply from deep respect.

Antonina, watching from her own position standing toward the rear of the cabin, found herself fighting back tears. Now, at the end of his short life, all traces of Eon the rambunctious young prince were gone. What remained was the *dignitas* of the negusa nagast of Axum.

Eon reminded her of his father, in that moment, the Kaleb who had gone before him—and had also been slain by Malwa. And not simply because his face, drawn by pain and exhaustion, made him look much older than he was. Kaleb had possessed little of his younger son's intellect, but the man had exuded the aura of royal authority. So too did Eon, now that he was on the eve of losing authority and life together.

"You will destroy their fleet completely. The merchant vessels as well as the warships." The words issued by Eon's dry and husky voice blurred together a bit. The blurring did not detract from their weight. They simply made the words come like molten iron, pouring into molds. Not to be denied, but only received. The sarwen commanders nodded solemnly.

"You will destroy the docks. Destroy the shipyards. Burn and ravage the entire harbor." Again, came the solemn nods.

Eon shifted slightly, where he lay reclined against his cushions. No sign of pain came to his face with the movement, however. For all intents and purposes, it seemed like a face carved in monumental stone.

And would be, Antonina knew, soon enough. As they had done with Wahsi the year before, the Axumite sarwen were transforming a stupid battle death into a thing of legend and myth. Before a year had passed, she had no doubt at all, Eon's face would be carved into monuments throughout the Ethiopian highlands. And woven into the tapestries of Yemen and the Hijaz.

"This I command," said Eon. "Let the navy of Axum be destroyed in the doing, if need be—*this I command.*"

He took a long and shuddering breath before continuing. "Our people can build new ships, raise new sarwen. But only if Belisarius is given the time to break Malwa. Time only we can give him, by penning Malwa to the land." Slowly, laboriously: "Let them, even once, get loose on the sea, and the great Roman's back will be exposed."

The heads of the sarwen did not so much nod as bow in obedience. Eon watched them for a moment, as if to assure himself of their fealty, before he concluded.

"Bharakuccha is the key. It is the only great port left to Malwa on its western coast. Destroy that great fleet, destroy that harbor"—finally, a little hiss came—"and by the time they can recover their naval strength, Belisarius will have his sword to Malwa's neck. Ethiopia's future will be assured, even if no man in this fleet lives to see it."

Ezana cleared his throat. The other sarwen commanders turned their heads to gaze upon him. Formally, Ezana was simply one of many sarawit commanders, no greater than they. But, over the past two years, he had become the "first among equals." He and the great hero Wahsi had been Eon's personal bodyguards, had they not? Eon's son had been named after Wahsi, and Ezana was the commander of the royal regiment to which Eon himself belonged. As would young Wahsi himself, once his father was dead.

"It will be done, negusa nagast. Though this navy die in the doing."

The words were echoed by all the regimental commanders. *Though this navy die in the doing.*

"Indeed so," added Ousanas. The aqabe tsentsen, as always, had been sitting in lotus position on the floor rather than on a stool. Now he unfolded and rose with his inimitable grace. Then, stooping a little, he placed a hand on Eon's brow.

"It will be done, negusa nagast. Have no doubt of it. And now you must rest."

"Not yet, old friend," whispered Eon. "There is still another task to be done." His dark eyes moved to the only woman in the cabin. "Step forward, Antonina."

Antonina felt herself grow tense. Dread piled upon heartbreak. Eon had said little to her, since he regained consciousness after the battle of Chowpatty. But she was certain of the subject he would now broach.

Not this, Eon! You cannot ask me—your mother in all but name—to do this! Anything else, but not this!

Eon's eyes had never left her. Slowly, trying not to let her reluctance show, Antonina moved toward the bed where Ethiopia's king lay dying.

Once she was standing alongside Ousanas, however, Eon's thoughts seemed to go elsewhere. Antonina felt a moment's relief. The negusa nagast's eyes moved to Ezana.

"At the end, I am a man of the Dakuen. So I will be in that battle myself, Ezana. As my commander as well as my subject, I demand that right."

Ezana's eyes widened a bit. A veteran of many battles, the sarwen knew full well that Eon would probably be dead before the coming battle even started. He certainly would be incapable of even standing, much less wielding a weapon.

But then, as if some mysterious signal had passed between them, Ezana nodded his head gravely. "Be certain of it, negusa negast. Eon bisi Dakuen will lead us to victory at Bharakuccha, as surely as he led us at Chowpatty."

Antonina remained confused by that exchange, but she had no time to puzzle over it. Eon's eyes were now resting on her. The moment she dreaded was here.

"With my death," husked Eon, "the dynasty will be in danger."

Antonina forced herself not to hiss. Behind her, she could sense the commanders of the sarawit stiffening. Eon had now, for the first time, exposed to the light the great shadow which had hung over everyone since his mortal injury.

To her astonishment, Eon managed a chuckle. The effort seemed to wrack his body with pain, though the amusement did not leave his face.

"Look at them," he half-gasped. "Like saints accused of sin."

He broke off, coughing a bit. Then, very firmly: "It is true, and all here know it. My son is but a babe, his mother an Arab. A queen from Mecca, to rule over Ethiopians? With every Axumite suspicious of her family's ambitions? And every sarwe eyeing the rest with equal suspicion?"

For a moment, he bestowed a stony haze on the regimental commanders. None of them but Ezana could meet that gaze for long. Within seconds, they were staring at the deck of the cabin.

"True!" stated Eon. "I know it. You know it. All know it."

He paused, drawing in a slow and painful breath. "I will not have it. First, because Rukaiya is my wife and Wahsi is my son, and they are dear to me. I will not have my wife and child suffer the fate of Alexander's. Second, because Axum is poised on the threshold of grandeur, and I will not see my empire brought down by my own rash folly."

Again, he coughed; and, again, fought for breath.

"Let the dynasty survive—survive and prosper—and my folly will become transformed into a glorious legend." He managed a faint smile. "As, I suspect, has usually been true with legends. Let it fall . . ."

He could no longer prevent the pain from distorting his features. "It will all have been for nothing," he whispered. "The Diadochi reborn in Axum, and Ethiopia's empire—like Alexander's—torn into shreds."

The king's strength was fading visibly, now. Ezana cleared his throat. "Tell us your wish, negusa nagast." For an instant, his hard eyes ranged right and left. "We—I, for one—will see it done."

For a moment, Antonina felt a rush of hope. She

held her breath. But then, seeing Eon's little shake of the head, she felt herself almost trembling.

No! Not this!

"I am too weak," whispered Eon. "Too—not confused, no. But not able to think well enough. The thing is too difficult, too complex. And—"

Again, he broke off coughing. "And, to be truthful, cannot think beyond my own love for Rukaiya and Wahsi. Only the sharpest mind can find the way forward in this fog. And only one whose impartiality and wisdom is accepted by all."

Understanding, finally, the eyes of the all the regimental commanders moved to Antonina. An instant later, seeing their nods—nods of agreement; even relief—Antonina knew that protest was impossible.

She stared at Eon. There was nothing of majesty left in those dark eyes. Simply the pleading of a small boy, looking to his mother—once again, and for the last time—for salvation and hope.

She cleared her own throat. Then, to her surprise, managed to speak with a voice filled with nothing but serenity.

"I will do it, Eon. I will see to the safety of your wife and child, and the dynasty. I will ensure that your death was not in vain. There will be no Diadochi seizing power in Axum and Adulis. Your heritage will not be destroyed by ambitious generals and scheming advisers."

Her eyes moved from the dying king to the regimental commanders. Serenity, cool serenity, hardened into diamond. "You may be sure of it."

"*Sure of it,*" echoed Ousanas. His great powerful arms were crossed over a chest no less powerful. He made no effort to shroud his own glare at the sarawit commanders with anything which even vaguely resembled serenity. Unless it be the serenity of a lion studying his prey.

"Sure of it," repeated Ezana, his voice ringing as harshly as that of the aqabe tsentsen. Ezana did not even look at his fellow commanders. He kept his eyes fixed on those of his king. Eon, clearly enough, was about to lapse back into unconsciousness. Ezana almost rushed to speak the next words.

"The negusa nagast has appointed the Roman woman Antonina to oversee the transition of authority in Axum. I bear witness. Does any man challenge me?"

Silence. Ezana allowed the silence to stretch unbroken, second after second.

"*Any man? Any commander of any sarwe?*"

Silence. Stretching unbroken.

"So be it. It will be done."

The negusa nagast seemed to nod, perhaps. Then his eyes closed and his labored breathing seemed to ease.

"The king needs rest," pronounced Ousanas. "The audience is over."

When all had gone except Antonina and Ousanas, she leaned weakly against the wall of the cabin. Slow tears leaked down her cheeks.

Through blurred vision, she met the sorrowing eyes of Ousanas.

"I married him, Ousanas. Found him his wife and gave him his son. How can I—?"

Almost angrily, Ousanas pinched away his own tears with thumb and forefinger.

"I would not have wished it on you, Antonina," he said softly. "But Eon is right. The dynasty could shatter into pieces—*will* shatter, if there is not a strong mind and hand to lead us through. And no one but you can provide that mind and hand. All the rest of us—Ethiopian and Arab alike—are too close to the thing. The Ethiopians, fearful that Rukaiya's relatives will grow too mighty, will seek to humble the Arabs. And then, in the humbling, squabble among themselves over which regiment and which clan will be paramount. The Arabs, newly hopeful of a better place, will fear reduction to vassalage and begin to plot rebellion."

"You are neither Arab nor Ethiopian," retorted Antonina. "You could—"

Ousanas' old grin almost seemed to make an appearance. "Me? A savage from the lakes?"

"Stop it!" snapped Antonina. "No one thinks that— has not for years—not even you! And you know it!"

Ousanas shook his head. "No, not really. But it hardly matters, Antonina. If anything, my sophistication will make everyone all the more suspicious. What does that odd man really want? He reads philosophy, even!"

Now, the grin did appear, even if for only an instant. "Would *you* trust someone who could parse sophisms with Alcibiades?"

Antonina shrugged wearily. "You are not Alcibiades. Nor does anyone believe so." She managed a semblance of a grin herself. "Assuming that hardheaded and practical sarwen knew who Alcibiades was in the first place. But if the name is unfamiliar, the breed is not. I do not believe there is one man or woman in all of Axum or Arabia who believes that Ousanas is a scheming, duplicitous adventurer seeking only his own gain."

Ousanas shrugged. "That, no. I believe I am well enough trusted. But trust is not really the issue, Antonina. The problem is not one of treachery, to begin with. It is simply—confusion, uncertainty. In which fog every man begins to wonder about his own fate, and worry, and then—" He took a breath. "And then begin scheming, and lying, and seeking their own gain.

Pressing to their own advantage. Not from treason, simply from fear."

Antonina tried to protest, but could not. Ousanas was right, and she knew it.

"Only you, Antonina, are far enough away from the thing. Have no ties at all to any part of Axum, except the ties of loyalty and wisdom. They might trust me, but they would never trust my *judgement*. Not in this. Whereas they will trust the judgement—the ruling— made by you. Just as they did before."

She slumped. Ousanas came over and embraced her. Antonina's tears now trickled down his chest.

"I know," he whispered. "I understand. You will feel like a spider, weaving a web out of your own son's burial shroud."

And now, all of it said, she began sobbing. Ousanas stroked her hair. "Ah, woman, you were never a hunter. Many hours I spent, waiting in the thickets for my prey, whiling away the time in a study of spiderwebs. There is, in truth, nothing so beautiful in all the world. Gossamer delicate yet strong; and does it really matter how it came to be? All of creation, in the end, came from the humblest of substance. Yet is there, now, and it is glorious."

The battle of Bharakuccha began early the next morning, when the Axumite galleys came into the harbor, followed by the handful of Roman warships. The Malwa defenders were waiting, alert. There was no surprise here. Except, perhaps, the lack of surprise itself. The Ethiopian fleet came forward, not like a lioness springing from ambush, but with an elephant's almost stately rush of fury.

Certain in its might, imponderable in its wrath, unheeding of all resistance. On the deck of each galley, the drummers pounded a rhythm of destruction.

The sarwen at the oars kept time with their own chants of vengeance. The commanders in the bow, standing atop the brace of four-pounders, held their spears aloft and clashed the great blades with promise.

And, on the great flagship at the center of the fleet, the Malwa commanders peering through their telescopes could see the leader of the fleet. An emperor himself, of that they were instantly certain. Who else would come to a battle ensconced on a throne and garbed in royal finery? The sun gleaming off the iron blade of his pearl-encrusted, gold-sheathed spear was almost blinding.

The commanders, uncertainly, looked to their own leader. Venandakatra the Vile, Goptri of the Deccan, was on the ramparts of the harbor himself, glaring at the oncoming enemy fleet through his reptilian eyes. His thin-boned, flabby hand patted the great siege gun next to which he was standing.

"Fire on them as soon as they are in range," he commanded. "Soon enough, that fleet will be so much flotsam. The fools!"

The commanders glanced at each other. Then the most senior, almost wincing, cleared his throat and said: "Goptri, I believe you should summon Lord Damodara. We will be needing his Rajputs, soon enough, and it will take them hours to return to the city. Even if you summon them immediately."

Venandakatra almost spit. "Rajputs? *Rajputs*?" He pointing a finger, quivering with outrage and indignation. "That's just a fleet, you idiot! Of what use would Rajput cavalry be?" Again, he patted the cannon; almost slapped it. "Sink them—that is enough!"

The senior commander hesitated. Incurring the Vile One's wrath was dangerous. But—

His eyes returned to the enemy warship. But the commander had fought Axumites, before, and . . . he could *sense* the fury under those drums, and he could *sense* what the strange sight of that royal figure on the flagship held in store.

"They will not stop, Goptri. That is not a raiding fleet. That is an army bent on destruction. They will accept the casualties to get into the harbor. And then—"

Venandakatra spluttered fury, but the commander pressed on. He was a kshatriya, after all, bred to courage even in Malwa lands. The commander squared his shoulders. "I have fought Axumite marines. We will need the Rajputs."

When the first Malwa gun was fired, it did not signal the start of a volley. It was a single shot, and the missile fell far short of the Ethiopians. Pieces of flesh have poor aerodynamic properties, after all, and Venandakatra the Vile had chosen to start the battle of Bharakuccha by blowing his top commander out of the barrel of a siege gun.

The sound of a cannon shot startled Antonina. She lifted her head from the book in her lap and stared at the still-distant ramparts which protected the fleet sheltered in Bharakuccha's harbor.

"Why have they—"

Standing on the other side of Eon's throne, Ousanas shrugged. "Nerves, I suppose. No way that shot could reach us." He chuckled savagely. "God help the commander of that battery. Venandakatra will punish him, be sure of it."

The sound also seemed to stir Eon. His drooping head lifted, bringing the tiara and phakhiolin which was the symbol of Axumite royalty against the headrest of the great throne which his sailors had erected on the deck of his flagship. For a moment, his eyes opened again.

The wasted, pain-wracked body which was all that a mortal wound had left of his once-Herculean physique, was invisible now. The full robes and imperial regalia which Eon had not worn since the weddings at Ctesiphon shrouded him completely. He was strapped to the throne, lest he slip aside; and the spear held proudly in his hand, the same. Even his fist was bound to the spear with cloths. Come what may, Eon would sail through this battle.

"What—?" he murmured.

"Nothing, negusa nagast," pronounced Ousanas. "The Malwa squall in fear. Nothing more."

Eon nodded heavily. Then, his eyes closing, he whispered: "Keep reading, Antonina."

Antonina's eyes went back to the book. A moment later, finding the place, she continued her recitation of the feats of ancient warriors beneath the walls of Troy. Eon had always loved the *Iliad*.

He did not hear the end of it. Perhaps an hour later, when the battle was in full fury, Eon stirred to wakefulness and spoke again.

"No more, Antonina," he whispered. "There is no time. I am done with battles forever. Read from the other."

Clenching her jaws to keep from sobbing openly, Antonina lowered the *Iliad* to the deck. Then, picked up the book which lay next to it. She spent a few seconds brushing aside the splinters of wood which covered it. A Malwa cannonball, minutes before, had struck the rail of the flagship. Eight Axumite marines had been killed or badly injured. Many others, including Antonina herself, had suffered minor wounds from the splinters sent flying everywhere.

It had been a lucky shot. Eon would have risked himself, but not Antonina or Ousanas. So he had ordered the flagship to stay out of the battle once it began, just beyond cannon range. But Venandakatra, either because he recognized what a blow sinking the flagship would have struck at Ethiopian morale or simply because he was beside himself with rage, had ordered a volley with overloaded powder charges. One of the cannonballs had struck the flagship. Four had missed widely. The last shot had barely cleared the rampart—the gun had exploded, killing most of its crew.

The effort of lifting the heavy tome opened the gash in her hand. Blood seeped anew through the cloth bandage, staining the pages of the book as she opened it. That was a shame, really. It was a beautiful book. But Antonina thought it was perhaps appropriate.

She began reading from the New Testament. The Gospel According to Mark was Eon's favorite, and so that was the one she selected. She read slowly, carefully, enunciating every word. Throughout, until she came to the end, she never lifted her eyes from the book, never so much as glanced at the king beside her.

Eon bisi Dakuen died somewhere in those pages, as Antonina had known he would. But she never knew when or where, exactly. And, to the day of her own death, would thank the gentle shepherd for allowing her that blessed ignorance.

Chapter 32

Venandakatra squalled, scrambling from the masonry collapsing not more than three yards away. He tripped and fell, knocking the wind out of himself. As he gasped for breath, he stared spellbound at the cannonball that had shattered that portion of Bharakuccha's defenses. The ugly iron thing, almost all its energy lost in the impact with the wall, rolled slowly toward him. Then, following some unseen little imperfection in the stone platform, veered away until it dropped out of sight over the edge. A second or two later, dimly, Venandakatra heard the thing come to its final rest. From the sound, the horrid missile had taken yet another life in the doing, falling on one of the Malwa soldiers cowering in the supposed shelter below.

Silently, still fighting for breath, Venandakatra cursed that soldier and savored his destruction. Just as he cursed all the soldiers who cowered beside him, and all the others who had failed to drive back the Axumite assaults and the Roman cannonade.

Almost glazed, his eyes now stared at the hole that the cannonball had made in the ramparts. Venandakatra was astonished by the power of the gun that had fired it. He had not expected that.

He should have—and would have, had he paid any

attention to his military advisers or Damodara. But Venandakatra, whose last personal experience with naval warfare had been years before, had not really grasped the rapid advances that both the Malwa and their enemies had made in gunpowder weaponry since the war began. His memory had been of war galleys armed with rockets, not cannons. And his logic had told him that galleys, by their nature, could never carry many guns in any event.

On that, of course, he was correct. Like all war galleys armed with cannon, the Axumite vessels carried only as many guns as could be fit in the bow and stern. Firing a "broadside" was impossible because of the rowers' benches. And the Ethiopian ships, for all that they were designed to cross the open sea under sail, were still essentially oared galleys in time of battle.

So, yes, they had few guns on each ship—four only, on most of them, two in the bow and two in the stern. Nor were the guns particularly powerful. But the Ethiopians had many ships—and still had, even after running through Venandakatra's volleys. And the Roman ships coming behind them *were* designed to fire broadsides, and *did* carry powerful guns. Venandakatra was not certain, but he thought every Roman vessel was firing what his own gunners called "elephant feet." The Romans, if he remembered correctly, called them thirty-two-pounder carronades. For the most part, the Romans were firing grapeshot, designed to kill the men manning the huge Malwa guns. But they fired solid shot at regular intervals also, and those heavy balls had proven more than powerful enough to begin shattering the ramparts which protected Malwa's batteries. The ramparts were old stonework, erected long ago in an era of medieval warfare, not the newer style of fortifications designed to withstand cannon fire. The Malwa had simply never expected to be defending

Bharakuccha against such an attack—at least, Venandakatra hadn't—so the Goptri had not ordered new construction to replace the ancient walls.

The battle had now been raging for hours. The Ethiopians had lost many ships to gunfire, true. But even those losses had been turned to their purpose, as often as not, by the sheer fury of the Ethiopian assault. Unless a ship was destroyed completely, sunk in the harbor, the Axumite sailors had driven their crippled ships into the midst of the anchored Malwa fleet. Then, after pouring over the side in that now all-too-familiar and terrifying way of boarding, had turned their own ships into floating firebombs. Between the gunfire of their galleys and the torchwork of their marines, the Ethiopians completed the destruction of the Malwa navy and began doing the same to the merchant fleet.

With any chance of being intercepted by Malwa galleys now eliminated, the Romans had sailed their warships directly before the Malwa fortifications guarding the harbor and begun firing broadsides at a range which was no more than two hundred yards. So close, ironically, that the Malwa could no longer depress the huge siege guns enough to strike back.

At which point, to Venandakatra's shock, *all* of the surviving Axumite galleys had offloaded their marines onto the piers of Bharakuccha itself.

Insane! Are they maddened bulls? This was a raid! They cannot hope to take one of Malwa's greatest cities!

Then, as their marines rampaged through the harbor area of the city, putting everything to the torch—the shipyards, the warehouses, everything—the galleys had pulled away from the docks. Again, Venandakatra had been shocked. Manned by skeleton crews, the Ethiopian warships had turned their guns on the fortifications. With the Ethiopians now firing the grapeshot which kept the ramparts clear of troops, the Romans had been freed

to hammer the fortification themselves with those terrifying great iron balls.

*Why? Why? Not even those guns are great enough
to collapse these walls!*

Which, indeed, they weren't. But, again, Venandakatra had misgauged the fury of Axum. Collapse the
walls, no—but splinter them, and break them in pieces
here and there, yes. As he had just discovered himself. And, as he was discovering himself, do enough
damage to suppress Venandakatra's own guns and send
his artillerymen rushing to shelter.

*While the marines in the harbor below, finished with
their work of destruction, began storming . . .*

Venandakatra finally realized the truth. The Ethiopians could not take Bharakuccha, true enough. But,
driven by that near-suicidal fury which still bewildered
the Goptri, they could ruin the city completely as a
working port and naval base. They would not stop until
they had stormed the fortifications guarding the harbor, spiked all the siege guns and blown up the maga-
zines. Even if half their marines died in the assault.

Frantic with fear, now, Venandakatra levered himself painfully erect. Still gasping for breath, he staggered toward the steps which led to the city below.
The Axumite marines would be coming soon, he
knew—and knew as well that his pitiful artillerymen
had no more chance of repelling those insensate
madmen than children could repel rogue elephants.

Damodara! And his Rajputs! Only they—!

Venandakatra was flooded with relief to see that his
squad of chaise-bearers had remained faithful to their
post. Despite the fear so obvious in their faces, they
had not left the conveyance and run away, seeking
shelter from the fury deep in the city's bowels.

He repaid them with curses, lashing the leader with
a quirt as he clambered aboard.

"To the palace!" he shrieked. *"Any slave who stumbles will be impaled!"*

One of them *did* stumble, as it happens. Inevitably, some of the Roman guns had badly over-ranged their targets, sending iron cannonballs hurtling into the streets and tenements of Bharakuccha beyond the harbor. One such ball, striking a tenement wall—by accident, but at a perfect angle—had collapsed the front of the mudbrick edifice into the street. The chaise-carriers were forced to clamber over the rubble bearing their awkward burden, and one of them lost his feet entirely.

Fortunately, although Venandakatra was tumbled about in the chaise, he barely noticed. Partly because his own terror made him oblivious to the sudden terror of his slave. Mostly, however, because he was preoccupied with cursing all the modern technology and devices which Malwa had adopted so eagerly over the years.

There had been a time, once, when he would have had mounted couriers with him at all times. Ready to carry the Goptri's messages everywhere, to all his subordinates—and Damodara *was* still his subordinate in name, even if Venandakatra's authority was threadbare in reality.

But Damodara would have come, in answer to a courier-borne summons. Of that, Venandakatra had no doubt at all. For all that the Vile One hated the little military commander, he did not doubt either his courage or his competence.

Damodara *would* come, in fact, once Venandakatra *did* summon him. The only way Venandakatra now had available to do so, unfortunately, was with the telegraph which connected his palace with Damodara's field camp miles upstream on the Narmada. The marvelous, almost magical, device which Link had brought to Malwa from the future.

As his chaise-bearers lumbered toward the palace, panting with exhaustion and effort, Venandakatra kept up his silent cursing of all *technology*. Belatedly, he was realizing that the very splendor of the gadgetry disguised its inner weakness. Men were cheap and plentiful; technology was not. In the old days, he would have had many couriers. Today, he had only a few telegraph lines.

Only two, really—the line which connected Bharakuccha and Damodara's army camp, and the line which went over the Vindhyas to the imperial capital city of Kausambi. Early on, Rao's bandits had realized the importance of those new wires stretching across Majarashtra. So, wherever they roamed—and they roamed everywhere in the badlands which they called "the Great Country"—they cut the wires.

No, did more than cut them! Copper was valuable, and the polluted Marathas were born thieves. So, until Venandakatra stopped even trying to maintain the telegraph lines anywhere except where Damodara's tough Rajputs could patrol them, the filthy Maratha rebels simply stole the lines and filled the coffers of the bandit Rao—he and his whore Shakuntala—with Malwa's precious magic.

For a few satisfying moments, Venandakatra broke off his cursing of technology to bestow various curses on Rao and Shakuntala. But that entertainment paled, soon enough, and he went back to damning the never-to-be-sufficiently-damned *telegraph*.

Because the problem, at bottom, was that humanity itself was a foul and despicable creature. Except for those favored few who were beginning—just beginning—to forge a new and purer breed, all men were cast in that despised Maratha mold. *All* men were thieves, if the truth be spoken plainly.

Venandakatra, understanding that truth, had naturally taken steps to protect the valuable telegraph. The precious device was guarded at all times, and only one such device had he permitted being installed in the city—the one adjoining his own personal chambers in the palace. Lest the grandeur of his dynasty be polluted by still more thievery.

They were almost at the palace, now. The roar and fury and the flames and the smoke of the battle in the harbor was a faded thing, two miles behind him. Venandakatra leaned forward in his chaise and began lashing the bearers with his quirt.

Faster! Faster! I'll impale the slave who stumbles!

At the end, just as they drew up before the palace entrance, the slaves did stumble—and not just one alone, but three of the four. Venandakatra had driven them at an impossible pace, and they were utterly exhausted. The sudden end of their exertions simply overcame them.

It would have been better, in truth, if the fourth man had collapsed as well. Then, falling all at once, the slaves might have lowered Venandakatra more or less gently to the ground. Instead, one man standing erect with the pole on his shoulder—too dazed and weary to realize what was happening—the sudden tipping of the chaise dumped Venandakatra onto the flagstones like a flabby fruit from an upended basket.

Shrieking with rage, he lashed the sole standing slave with the quirt. But the lash was feeble. Barely landed at all, in fact, because the Vile One had bruised his shoulder when he fell. The pain of lashing caused him to hiss and clutch the shoulder.

Then, turning away, he half-stumbled and half-lunged through the palace doors. Fortunately, the doors were already open, as they always were during daylight to allow the edifice to ventilate. As soon as he passed into the shadows of the vestibule, Venandakatra pointed with his quirt to the slaves and snarled at the guards.

"Impale them! All of them!"

Then . . .

Snarled again. There *were* no guards. The three men who were stationed at all times inside the palace entrance were absent. Gone.

Gone. Not there.

For a moment, Venandakatra simply gaped. Then, a new fury piling onto existing fury—he felt like he might burst from sheer rage—he hurried toward the staircase which led to his chambers above.

"I will have them impaled also!"

Some remote part of his mind tried to caution himself that, in the middle of a raging battle, soldiers might have gotten involved in the fighting. But Venandakatra ignored it. Duty was duty, and there's an end to it—especially the duty of servants to their master. Those guards were *supposed* to be there. At all times!

At the top of the stairs, he snarled again. Then, so great was his rage, uttered a wordless shriek.

And where were these guards? Two of them—at all times!

The almost-animal shriek seemed to steady his nerves. He managed to control himself enough to march, not stagger or stumble, to the doors which led to his own chambers.

He was not surprised to discover that the soldier who was supposed to remain on guard just inside his personal quarters—at all times!—was also gone.

Not there. No one.

Venandakatra realized, then, what had happened. He had been too lenient with his men. Had allowed them to soften with garrison duty, while the Rajputs and Ye-tai of Damodara and Rana Sanga campaigned in the hills against the Maratha bandits. The sudden and furious battle had panicked them all. They had fled—abandoned their lord!

He stalked toward the door which led to the telegraph chamber. On the way, he made himself a vow.

Two vows. First, every member of his personal bodyguard—whether stationed on duty that day or not—would be impaled on the morrow. Second, despite his hatred for Damodara, he would accept the military commander's proposal to rotate the garrison soldiers into the field along with the Rajputs.

Venandakatra did not stride through the door to the telegraph chamber so much as burst through it. He noticed, but ignored—*why should he be different?*—the absence of the guard who was normally to be found inside the chamber. At all times.

He *was* surprised, however, to see that the telegraph operator had remained faithful to his duty. The man was there, as he was supposed to be, sitting on a chair in front of the telegraph apparatus.

"Someone!" he barked. Then, striding forward, he grabbed the man's shoulder.

"Send an immediate tele—"

He stopped in mid-word. The telegraph operator's head lolled back. Too stunned to think—though that remote part of his mind was shrilling and shrilling and shrilling—Venandakatra simply stared at the man's neck.

It took him a few seconds to understand what he was seeing. The device which had strangled the operator was almost invisible. So mighty had been the hands which had driven that silk cord that it was almost buried in the flesh.

A soft voice spoke from behind him.

❖   ❖   ❖

"I have bad news, Venandakatra."

Slowly, the Vile One turned his head, looking to the corner of the room behind him and to his left. He could barely discern a figure in the shadows.

"My son, as you may well know, was born recently. And now the priests who attend him say he is healthy. Has every chance of reaching his manhood."

The shrilling voice in Venandakatra's mind began to shape a name. But he was too paralyzed to really hear.

The shadows moved. The figure stepped forward into the light.

Prowled forward, it might be better to say. He moved more like a predator than a man. Then, as he began slipping an iron-clawed gauntlet over his right hand, assumed the form of a predator completely.

"So now it is time for our unfinished business. Let us dance, Vile One. The dance of death you would have once given my beloved, I now give to you."

Finally, Venandakatra broke through the paralysis. He opened his mouth to scream.

But it never came. It was not so much the powerful left hand clamped on his throat which stifled that scream, as the pure shock of the iron claws on the right hand which drove into his groin and emasculated him.

The agony went beyond agony. The paralysis was total, complete. Venandakatra could not think at all, really. Simply listen to, and observe, the monster who had ruined him.

So strange, really, that a panther could talk.

"I trained her, you know, in the assassin's creed when slaying the foul. To leave the victim paralyzed, but conscious, so that despair of the mind might multiply agony of the body."

The iron-clawed gauntlet flashed again, here and there.

When Venandakatra's mind returned, breaking over

the pain like surf over a reef, he saw that he was still standing. But only because that incredible left hand still held him by the throat. Under his own power, Venandakatra would have collapsed.

Collapsed and never walked again. Nor fed himself again. His knees and elbows were . . . no longer really there.

"Enough, I think. I find, as I age, that I become more philosophical."

The monster, still using only the one hand, hefted Venandakatra's body like a man hefts a sack full of manure and drew him toward the corner where it had waited in ambush. On the way, that remote part of Venandakatra's mind was puzzled to see the gray hair in the monster's beard. He had never imagined a panther with a beard of any kind. Certainly not a grizzled one.

Now in the corner, the monster swept aside the heavy curtain over the window. Tore it aside, rather, sweeping the iron claws like an animal. Sudden light poured into the chamber.

When Venandakatra saw the chair now exposed, he suddenly realized how the monster had whiled away the time he spent lurking in ambush. The chair had been redesigned. Augmented, it might be better to say. The remote part of his brain even appreciated the cunning of the design and the sturdiness of the workmanship.

The rest of his mind screamed in despair, and his ruined body tried to obey. But the monster's left hand shifted a bit, the iron claws worked again, and the scream died with the shredded throat which carried it.

"You may bleed to death from that wound, but I doubt it. It certainly won't kill you before the other."

The claws worked again, again, again.

"Not that it probably matters. There are no guards left in this palace to hear you. It seems a great wind has scoured it clean."

Venandakatra now stood naked, his expensive clothing lying tattered about the chamber. The iron claws raked his ribs, the iron left hand turned him. He was now facing away from the chair. His throat and joints leaked blood and ruin.

Despair of the mind, to multiply agony of the body. That was Venandakatra's last, fully conscious thought, except for the final words of his executioner.

"I thought you would appreciate it, Vile One. You always did favor a short stake."

Chapter 33
THE INDUS
Autumn, 533 A.D.

Abbu leaned over the map and studied it. His face was tense, tight; half-apprehensive and half-angry. The lighting shed by the lamps hanging in Belisarius' command tent brought out all the shadows in the old man's hawk face. Brow and nose were highlighted; thick beard framed a mouth and cheeks in shadows; the eyes were pools of darkness. He looked, for all the world, like a sorcerer on the verge of summoning a demon. Or, perhaps, about to sup with the devil—and wishing he had a longer spoon.

Belisarius glanced quickly around the table. Judging from their stiff expressions, he thought Maurice and Sittas and Gregory were fighting the same battle he was—to keep from laughing outright at the scout chief's reluctance to have anything to do with the *cursed new-fangled device*. The detested, despised—*map*.

Maps were toys for children! *At best*. Real men— father teaching son, generation after generation!—relied on their own eyes to see; their memory to recall; the verbal acuity of a poetic race to describe and explain!

Too bad he doesn't mutter, except in his own

mind, mused Aide. **I'm sure he could give even Valentinian an education in the art.**

Belisarius' lips tightened still further. If so much as a single chuckle emerged . . .

"Here," rasped Abbu, pointing with a finger at a bend in the Chenab. The mark on the map was recent. So recent the ink had barely dried. Which was not surprising, since Belisarius had just drawn that stretch of the Chenab himself, following Abbu's stiff directions.

"A bit far to the north," rumbled Sittas. Now that real business was being conducted, the big general was no longer having any trouble containing his amusement. His heavy brows were lowered over half-closed eyes, and his lips were pursed as if he'd just eaten a lemon.

Abbu flashed him a dark glance. "Here!" he repeated. "The ships at Uch are big. Both of them. The whole army could be transferred across the river in a single day. And there are good landings at three places on the opposite bank."

He leaned over the map again, his earlier reluctance now lost in the eagerness of a prospective triumph.

"Here. Here. Here." Each word was accompanied by a jab of the finger at a different place on the map, indicating a spot on the opposite bank of the Chenab. "I would use the second landing. Almost no risk there of grounding the ships."

For a moment, Abbu hesitated, reluctant again. But the reluctance, this time, stemmed from simple tradition rather than outrage at newfangled ways. Like any master scout, Abbu hated to allow any imprecision into his description of terrain.

But . . . Abbu was the best scout Belisarius had ever had because the man was scrupulously honest as well as infernally capable. "I can't be certain. We did not cross the river ourselves, because there is no ford. But the river looks to run deep at that second landing, with no hidden sandbars. Not even a beach. So the fishing village built a small pier over the water. Too small for these ships, of course, but the simple fact it is there at all means that we could unload the big ships without running aground."

Sittas was still scowling. "Too far to the north," he grumbled again. "Both the town and the landing across the river. A good twenty or thirty miles past the fork of the Chenab and the Indus. Hell of a gamble." He straightened up and looked at Belisarius. "Maybe we should stick to the original plan. Seize *this* side of the Indus and set up our lines right at the fork itself."

Belisarius did not reply immediately. He understood Sittas' reluctance, but . . .

What a coup if we could pull it off!

You'd have no line of retreat at all, said Aide.

"No line of retreat," echoed Maurice. The chiliarch had no way of hearing Aide's voice, of course, but the situation was so obvious that Belisarius was not surprised their thoughts had run in tandem. "If it goes sour, we'll be trapped in the triangle, bottled up by the Malwa. The Chenab to our right and the Indus to our left."

Sittas shook his head. "I can't say I'm much concerned about *that*. Once we make the thrust into the Punjab—wherever we strike, and wherever we set up our fieldworks—'lines of retreat' are pretty much a delusion anyway."

He gestured toward the army camped just outside the tent, unseen behind its leather walls. "You know as well as I do, Maurice, that we'll have no way to retreat across the country we just passed through. Even if we *could* break contact with the Malwa after the fighting starts. Which isn't too likely, given how badly we'll be outnumbered."

"We've already foraged the area clean," said

Belisarius, agreeing with Sittas. "As it was, the thing was tight. If the peasants hadn't been panicked by reports of Malwa massacres in the Sind and fled, we might not have had enough to get this far."

Maurice winced a little, but didn't argue the point. The stretch of territory which Belisarius' army had marched through, with the Indus to one side and the Cholistan desert to the other, had been—just as Aide suspected—far less barren than future history would record. But it had still not been anything which could be called "fertile." If the fleeing peasantry hadn't left a good deal of already collected food behind them, the Roman army would have been forced to move very slowly due to the need for constant foraging.

As it was, they had been able to make the trek in sixteen days—better than Belisarius or his top subordinates had expected. But, in doing so, they had stripped the land clean of all easily collectable food. Trying to retreat through that territory, with much larger forces in pursuit, would be a nightmare. Most of the Roman soldiers would never make it back alive. And it was quite possible that the entire army would be forced to surrender.

"Surrender," into Malwa hands, meant a rather short stint in labor battalions. The Malwa had the charming practice of working their prisoners to death.

"Do or die," said Sittas calmly. "That's just the way it is, regardless of where we hit the enemy in the Punjab."

He leaned over the map, placing both large hands on the table it rested upon. "But I still think it's too much of a risk to go for the inside of the big fork. The problem's not retreat—it's getting supplies from downriver."

Belisarius understood full well the point Sittas was making. In order to reach a Roman army forted up in the fork itself, Roman supply vessels would have to run a gauntlet of enemy fire from the west bank of the Indus. Whereas if the Romans set up their fortifications on the opposite bank of the Indus just below the Chenab fork, the supply ships would be able to hug the eastern shore.

Still—

He scratched his chin. "The ships will *still* have to run the supplies in under fire, Sittas. Not as heavy, I grant you, but heavy enough. The Malwa have already built a major fortress on the west bank of the Indus, still further south, and you can be certain they've positioned big siege guns in it. The river's a lot wider south of the Chenab fork, true enough, but not so wide that those big guns won't be able to carry entirely across. So, no matter where we set up, the supply ships will be under fire trying to reach us."

Maurice started to say something, but his commander cut him off. Belisarius had relied on boldness throughout this campaign. His instincts told him to stay the course.

"I've made up my mind. We'll follow Abbu's proposal. Take Uch in a lightning strike, smash that small Malwa army there, and then use the ships to ferry our army into the triangle. We'll set up our lines across the triangle, as far down into the tip as we need to be to have enough of a troop concentration. Then—"

He straightened. "Thereafter, we'll be relying on the courage of our cataphracts to hold off the Malwa counterattack. And the courage of Menander to bring the supplies we need to hold out. Simple as that."

He scanned the faces of the men at the table, almost challenging them to say anything.

Maurice chuckled. "I'm not worried about their *courage*, general. Just . . . These damn newfangled contraptions of Justinian's better work. That's all I've got to say."

Sittas, like Maurice, was not given to challenging

Belisarius once a decision had been made. So, like the excellent officer he was, he moved directly to implementation.

"Leaving the logistics out of it, the position in the fork is the best possible from a defensive point of view. We can design our fieldworks to provide us with continual lines of retreat. The more they press us, the more narrow the front will become as we retreat south into the tip of the triangle. As long as we can provide the men with enough to eat . . ."

Suddenly, he burst into laughter. "And they'll demand plenty, don't think they won't! Ha! Greek cataphracts—half of them aristocrats, to boot—aren't accustomed to digging trenches. They'll whine and grouse, all through the day and half the night. But as long as we keep them fed, they'll do the job."

"They won't have much choice," snorted Abbu. "Even Greek noblemen aren't that stupid. *Dig or die.* Once we cross the Chenab, those are the alternatives."

"I just hope they don't argue with me about the details," grumbled Gregory. "Those hide-bound bastards of Sittas'—on the rare occasions when they think about fieldworks at all—still have their brains soaked in legends about Caesar. The first time I use the words 'bastion' and 'retired flank' and 'ravelin' they're going to look at me like I was a lunatic."

Sittas grinned. "No they won't." He gestured with a thick thumb at Belisarius' chest. "Just tell them the Talisman of God gave you the words. That's as good as saints' bones, far as they're concerned."

Gregory still looked skeptical, but Belisarius was inclined to agree with Sittas. Even the notorious conservatism of Greek noble cataphracts could be dented, on occasion. And all of them, by now, were steeped in the Roman army's tradition of awe and respect for the mysterious mind of Aide.

"If I need to," he chuckled, "I'll give them a look. Aide can put on a dazzling show, when he wants to."

Great, muttered Aide. **I travel across the vastness of time in order to become a circus sideshow freak.**

Belisarius was back to scratching his chin. And his crooked smile was making an appearance.

"I like it," he said firmly. "Let's not get *too* preoccupied with logistics. There's also the actual fighting to consider. And I can't imagine better defensive terrain than the triangle."

"Neither can I," chimed in Gregory.

All the men in the tent turned their attention toward him. Other than Agathius—who was far to the south in Barbaricum, organizing the logistics for the entire Roman army marching north into the Sind—no one understood the modern methods of siege warfare better than Gregory.

The young artillery officer began ticking off on his fingers.

"First—although I won't be sure until we get there—I'm willing to bet the water table is high. Flat terrain with a high water table—those are exactly the conditions which shaped the Dutch fortifications against the Spanish. Whom they held off—the most powerful army in the world—for almost a century."

The names of future nations were only vaguely familiar to the other men in the tent, except Belisarius himself, but those veteran officers could immediately understand the point Gregory was making.

"Earthen ramparts and wet ditches," he continued. "The hardest things for artillery to break or assaulting infantry to cross. Especially when there's no high ground anywhere in the area on which the Malwa could set up counterbatteries."

He stroked his beard, frowning. "We can crisscross

that whole area with ditches and fill them with water. Biggest problem we'll have is keeping our own trenches dry. Raised ramparts—using the same dirt from the ditches—will do for that. The Dutch used 'storm poles'—horizontal palisades, basically—to protect the ramparts from escalade. I doubt we'll have enough good wood for that, but we can probably use shrubbery to make old-style Roman hedges."

The mention of old methods seemed to bring a certain cheer to Sittas. He even went so far as to praise modern gadgetry. "The field guns and the sharpshooters will love it. A slow-moving, massed enemy, stumbling across ditches . . . What about cavalry?"

"Forget about cavalry altogether," said Gregory, almost snapping the response. He gave Sittas a cold eye. "The truth is—like it or not—we'll probably wind up eating our horses rather than riding them."

Both Sittas and Abbu—especially the latter—looked pained. Maurice barked a laugh.

"And will you look at them?" he snorted. "A horse is a horse. More where they came from—*if* we survive."

"A good warhorse—" began Sittas.

"Is worth its weight in silver," completed Belisarius. "And how much is your life worth?"

He stared at Sittas, then Abbu. After a moment, they avoided his gaze.

"Right. If we have to, we'll eat them. And there's this much to be said for good warhorses—they're big animals. Lots of meat on them."

Sittas sighed. "Well. As you say, it's better than dying." He cast a glance to the south. "But I sure hope Menander gets here before we have to make *that* decision."

The *Justinian* and the *Victrix* encountered the first Malwa opposition barely ten miles from Sukkur.

Menander could hear, even if dimly, the guns firing in the north.

It was nothing more than a small cavalry force, however. A reconnaissance unit, clearly enough. The Malwa, perched on their horses by the riverbank, stared at the bizarre sight of steam-powered warships chugging upriver, towing four barges behind them. Menander, perched in the armored shell atop the bridge which held one of the *Justinian's* anti-boarding Puckle guns, stared back.

For a moment, he was tempted to order a volley of cannon fire, loaded with canister. The Malwa were close enough that he could inflict some casualties on them. But—

He discarded the thought. The cavalry patrol was no danger to his flotilla, except insofar as they brought word of his approach back to the Malwa forces besieging Sukkur. And since there was no possibility of killing all of them, there was no point in wasting ammunition.

Quickly, Menander did some rough calculations in his head. The result cheered him up. By the time the cavalry patrol could return and make their report, Menander's flotilla would already have reached Ashot's positions. Thereafter, freed from towing all but one or two of the barges, Menander could make better time up the Indus. The Malwa would have a telegraph line connecting their army around Sukkur with their forces in the Punjab, of course. But—assuming that Belisarius had succeeded in his drive to reach the fork of the Chenab—the Malwa were probably too confused and disorganized, too preoccupied with crushing this unexpected thrust into their most vital region, to organize a really effective counter against Menander's oncoming two-ship flotilla.

So, he simply watched as his ships steamed past the foe. A rare moment, in the midst of bitter war, when enemies met and did nothing about it. He even found himself, moved by some strange impulse, waving a cheerful hand at the Malwa cavalrymen. And three of them, moved by the same impulse, waved back.

Odd business, war.

The Malwa did make a feeble attempt to intercept his flotilla when he was less than a mile from Ashot's fortifications. Two river boats, crammed with soldiers, came down the Indus toward him. Their movement was slow, however, because the wind was fitful at best. The Malwa boats were sailing ships, not galleys, so they were forced to rely mainly on the sluggish current.

Menander gave the order to prepare for battle. He and Eusebius had planned to leave such work to the *Victrix*, but the *Victrix*'s engine—every bit as balky as the one in Menander's ship—had broken down a few miles back. By the time Eusebius could repair the problem and arrive, the battle would be over. Menander was not overly concerned.

One boat, soon enough. Ashot, ever alert to the possibility of an amphibious attack on his flank, had two field guns stationed on the river. A few well placed shots were enough to sink one of the boats.

Menander, stationed next to one of the long twenty-four-pounder bowchasers was fascinated by what happened next. So fascinated, in fact, that he paid little attention for a time to the enemy ship still approaching him.

The Malwa commander was quite clearly doing his best to steer the vessel to the bank before it foundered completely. Right into the waiting arms of the Roman forces. He almost made it before his men were forced into the water. But the swim was short—many of them were actually able to wade ashore. And, sure enough, Roman troops were there to accept their surrender.

There was no fighting, no resistance of any kind. The wet and bedraggled Malwa troops seemed quite resigned to their new condition.

Menander looked away. The surviving enemy warship was almost within range of his forward guns, and soon he would give the order to fire. But he took the time, before concentrating all his attention on the coming little battle, to ponder over his great commander's methods of war. Methods which were sometimes derided—but never by those who had witnessed them.

Mercy can have its own sharp point. Keener than any lance or blade; and even deadlier to the foe.

"Will you look at the sorry bastards scramble!" laughed one of the gunners. "Like ducklings wading to mama!"

Menander met the gunner's jeering face. Then, softly: "And who do you think has been doing all of Ashot's digging for him? You can be damned sure that *Ashot's* men haven't been worn out by it. Fresh for the fighting, they've been. Day after day, while Malwa prisoners work under conditions not much worse than they faced in their own ranks. Which makes them always ready enough to surrender."

The amusement faded from the gunner's face, as he grappled with a new concept. Seeing his confusion, Menander was hard-pressed not to laugh himself.

Mind you, I think Ashot will be ecstatic when we arrive. I'll bet his supply problems have been even worse than he expected, with all those extra mouths to feed.

A few minutes later, the battle began. A few minutes after that, it was over. The two big guns in the bow of the *Justinian* simply shredded the Malwa river boat. The two shots the Malwa managed to fire from their own little bowchaser missed the *Justinian* by a wide margin.

Again, Malwa soldiers and sailors spilled into the water. But, this time, they were too far from shore for many of them to have a chance of reaching it.

Menander hesitated, for an instant. Then, remembering a friendly wave and his revered commander's subtleties, he made his decision.

"Steer right through them!" he barked. "And slow down. Any Malwa who can grab a line we'll tow ashore with us."

He turned and moved toward the rear of the ship, issuing orders to his soldiers as he went. By the time the desperate Malwa in the river had managed to seize one of the tow lines tossed by the Romans, Menander had soldiers ready to repel any possible boarding attempt. And he had both Puckle guns manned, loaded and ready to fire.

Long before they reached the docks that Ashot's men had erected in anticipation of their arrival, however, Menander was no longer worried about boarders. It was clear as day that the Malwa being towed to safety had no more intention of turning on their rescuers than ducklings would attack their mama. On those faces which were close enough for Menander to read any expression, he could see nothing beyond relief.

For those men, obviously, the war was over. And glad enough they were, to see the end of it come. Most of them were peasants, after all. Hard labor on too little food was no stranger to them. Nothing to enjoy, of course. But also—nothing to fear.

Ashot himself met Menander at the dock, shouting his praise and glee, and clapping the young officer on the shoulder.

"Knew you'd make it! Good thing, too—we're running low on everything."

Ashot's merry eyes moved to the Malwa surrendering as they came ashore. "And another fine catch, I see. I tell you, Menander, there have been times over the past weeks when I've felt more like a fisherman than a soldier."

Chapter 34
THE HINDU KUSH
Autumn, 533 A.D.

"How many Pathans, do you figure?" asked Kungas.

As Vasudeva pondered the question, Kungas kept studying the Malwa positions through the telescope which Belisarius had given him when he left Charax. His position, standing atop the ruins of a centuries-old Buddhist stupa destroyed by the Ye-tai when they conquered the Kushans, gave him a good view of the fortress which blocked the Khyber Pass at its narrowest point.

"Hard to say," muttered his army commander. "They're scouts and skirmishers, only, so they move around too much to get a good count."

"Not more than a few hundred?"

"If that many. With Sanga and the Rajputs a thousand miles away, the Pathan 'allegiance' to the Malwa is threadbare at best. At a guess, the only Pathans the Malwa have under their command down there are maybe two hundred tribal outcasts. The tribes themselves seem to be pulling back to their fortified villages and assuming a neutral stance."

"Let's hope Irene can keep them there," murmured Kungas. He lowered the telescope. "Which will depend, more than anything, on whether we can take that fortress and drive the Malwa out of the Khyber Pass entirely."

He began clambering down from the ruins. "With that few Pathans on the other side, we can seize the high ground. Use grenades to clear the outlying fortifications and then set up mortars and the field guns to start bombarding the big fortress across the narrows. Stupid bastards! They haven't fought in mountain country for too many years."

Now that they were on level ground, Vasudeva was able to concentrate on Kungas' plan. The way he was tugging the tip of his goatee and the furrows in his face indicated some doubts.

"Mortars, yes. Easy enough to haul up those rocks. But field artillery too? We could get them up there, sure enough. Not easily, mind you, but it can be done. But what's the point? All we have in the way of field guns are three-pounders. They're too light to break down the walls and—firing round shot, which is all we have—they won't produce many casualties."

Kungas shook his head. "I got a better look at that fortress than you did, Vasudeva, using the telescope. The outer walls are thick enough, to be sure, but everything—including all the interior walls and pits—is typical sangar construction. Nothing more than piled up fieldstone. They weren't expecting to be defending the Khyber Pass—of all places!—so that fortress was built in a hurry. Probably didn't even finish it until a few weeks ago, judging from what I could see of the outlying forts. Half of those forts are unfinished still."

Vasudeva was still frowning. Although he actually had more experience than Kungas using gunpowder weaponry, his mind was slower to adjust to the new reality than was that of his king.

Kungas helped him along. "Think what will happen when a solid ball of iron hits that loose fieldstone."

Vasudeva's face cleared, and he left off tugging the goatee. "Of course! As good as shrapnel!"

The army commander looked down at the soil between his feet and gave it a little stamp. "Solid rock, for all it matters. No way to dig rifle pits *here*." His eyes lifted, and he studied the distant fortress. "There neither. All their men will be above ground, using elevated sangar instead of holes in the ground. May as well have surrounded themselves with shells."

All hesitation gone, Vasudeva became as energetic and decisive as ever. "It will be done, King! We will take the high ground—clear the Malwa from every outlying hillfort with grenade and sword—bring up the mortars and artillery . . . and then! Place half the army further down the pass to stymie any Malwa relief column. It'll be a siege, with us holding them in a grip of iron."

Kungas smiled, in a manner of speaking. "I give them two weeks. Maybe three. And they can't even try to retreat back to the Vale of Peshawar, once we've blocked their route. We outnumber them three to one. We'd cut them to pieces on open ground, and they know it. They'll have no choice but to surrender."

He planted his hands on his hips and surveyed the mountains surrounding the Khyber Pass with approval. "After which—using them to do the scut work—we can fortify this pass the way it *should* be done. And we'll have plenty of time to do it, with the Malwa preoccupied with Belisarius in the plains. Before Malwa can counterattack, the Hindu Kush will be secure. The Pathans will bow to our rule—and why not, since it will be lighter than Malwa's—and next year . . ."

But he was speaking to himself, now. Vasudeva, being no more prone than his king to worry about formality, was already hurrying away to send the Kushan army back into motion.

Kungas remained in the ruins of the stupa for the rest of that day, and all the days which followed. He thought it was fitting that the founder of the new Kushan kingdom should make his headquarters in a holy place desecrated by those who had destroyed the old one. By the morning of the third day, Kushan shock troops had taken the outlying hillforts in two solid days of savage hand-to-hand combat, using both their traditional swords and spears as well as the Roman grenades for which all Kushan soldiers had developed a great affection. The Malwa troops were good—much better than usual—but they were not Rajputs. Nor did they have more than a few hundred Ye-tai to stiffen them.

So began, on the morning of the fourth day, the bombardment of the Malwa fortress which was the key to control of the Khyber pass. The Kushan troops were able to place many mortars within a thousand yards of the fortress. The devices were crude, true. They had been patterned after what Belisarius called a "coehorn mortar," nothing more complicated than a brass tube mounted at a fixed forty-five-degree angle on a base. The only way to adjust the weapon's range was by adjusting the powder charge. But the four-inch shells they fired, with a fuse ignited by the powder, could still wreak havoc within the fortress even if they could not shatter the walls.

And, two days later, once the Kushans had wrestled the field guns into the hillforts they had taken, the mortar fire was augmented by solid shot. Which, in the days which followed, began slowly pulverizing the inner fortifications and—more slowly still—crumbling the outer. Fieldstone being returned to fieldstone, with blood and flesh lubricating the way.

And each morning, as he arose, Kungas completed the thought. Speaking aloud, to the mountains which would shelter a kingdom being reborn.

"Next year—*Peshawar!*"

The oldest and most prestigious of the Pathan chiefs stroked his beard, frowning fiercely. Part of the frown was due to his ruminations. Most of it was because, being the grand patriarch of a patriarchal folk, he did not approve of the woman sitting on the chair across from him. Outrageous, really, for this self-proclaimed new king to have left his *wife* in charge of his capital!

Still—

Different folk, different customs. So long as the Kushans did not meddle with his own—which the scandalous woman had assured him they would not—the chief did not much care, in the end, what silly and effeminate customs the dwellers of the towns maintained.

Too, there was this: effeminate they might be, in some ways, but there was no doubt at all that the Kushans were not to be taken lightly on the battlefield. And the fact that—judging from reports which Pathan scouts had brought from the siege in the Khyber Pass—they seemed as much at home fighting in the mountains as in the plains, was added reason for caution.

As a rule, the Pathans did not much fear the armies of civilization. *Plains armies.* Dangerous enough on flat ground, but ill-prepared to challenge the Pathans in their own mountains. But the chief had not lived to such an age, nor risen to such prominence, by being an arrogant fool. Civilized kingdoms, with their wealth and rich soils, could field much larger armies than the Pathans. And whenever those armies proved capable of adapting to mountain warfare . . .

It had happened once before, after all. The old chief barely managed to repress a shudder, remembering the savage punitive expeditions of the Rajputs.

"Done," he said firmly, bowing his head—slightly, and a bit reluctantly—to the woman seated before him. Then, rising from his own chair, he cast an imperious gaze over the eight other Pathan chiefs seated alongside him. As he expected, none of them seemed prepared to challenge his decision.

"Done," he repeated. "So long as you do not meddle with us—nor interfere with our caravans—we will respect the peace. Send annual tribute to the King of the Kushans."

Three of the other chiefs seemed to stir a bit. The oldest, snorting, added the final condition for Pathan allegiance to the new realm:

"This all presumes, you understand, that the King of the Kushans can take the Khyber. And *hold* it, once Malwa strikes the counterblow. We will not face Rana Sanga again!"

The Kushan queen nodded her head. The old chief could not tell, but he suspected that the *damned woman* was smiling at him. Impossible to tell, for sure, because of the heavy veil she was wearing. But he did *not* like the hint of humor and wit which seemed to lurk in her eyes.

Damned Kushans! He had been told that the Kushan queen had only donned the veil when the Pathans arrived. He could well believe it. She was reputed to be a sly creature, tricky and devious.

Still—

Customs were customs. And they depended, in the end, on survival. So, controlling his bile in the way such a wise old patriarch had learned how to do over the decades, he kept his face from showing his distaste.

"I am not concerned about Rana Sanga," said the woman, speaking as softly and demurely as she had since the Pathan chiefs first entered her audience chamber. "I have been led to believe, for reasons I cannot divulge, that he will remain preoccupied elsewhere. For years, probably his lifetime."

The old Pathan chief stared down at her. The idle chatter of a silly woman? Perhaps.

Still—

Perhaps not, also. The woman was reputed to be *very* cunning, and so well-informed that some were already whispering about witchcraft. That possibility, oddly enough, brought the fierce old patriarch a certain relief. Customs were customs, survival was survival. And so he allowed that it was perhaps just as well—since the effeminate Kushans seemed determined to be ruled by a woman—that they had at least had the good sense to choose a sorceress.

Chapter 35
CHOWPATTY
Autumn, 533 A.D.

Antonina stared down at the crowd gathered in the harbor of Chowpatty. The gathering, it might be better to say, crowding onto the narrow stone causeways and spilling dangerously onto the rickety wooden piers. Some of those piers were far worse than "rickety," in truth. In the time since the Ethiopians had departed Chowpatty and then returned, bearing triumph and grief in their ships, the Marathas who had poured into Chowpatty after the destruction of the Malwa garrison had begun rebuilding the city. But the work was only beginning, and had not yet extended to the harbor. Partly, because the harbor was the most ravaged portion of the town; but, for the most part, because the fishermen who would have used it had not returned.

For them, who had once been its center, Chowpatty was and would remain a name of horror. A place of ruin and rapine. They wished no part of it, now or forever more. They would use other ports, other towns, to ply their ancient trade. Not Chowpatty. Never Chowpatty.

But to the hill people who came, Chowpatty was a name of victory and hope. The place where Malwa had been broken yet again—and by the same folk who were now seen as Majarashtra's closest ally. Closer, even, than great Belisarius and the Romans.

Belisarius was a legend among them, true enough. But, except for that handful who had met him during his time in India, years before, it was a vague and distant legend. The Marathas had heard of Anatha and the Dam; and Charax. And now, Barbaricum added to that list of triumphs. (Soon, too, they would hear of Kulachi.) But none of them knew those places. Few could even say exactly in what direction they were to be found, other than somewhere to the west or, possibly, the north.

Chowpatty, they knew. Bharakuccha, they knew. So the black folk who had taken Chowpatty and shattered Bharakuccha—had done more, had dragged the Vile One himself to his impalement post—were as real as the sunrise. Not a legend, but heroes walking among them.

Oh, yes—dragged him to it they had, even if no African hand had ever touched the monster. For all Marathas knew, from the mouth of their champion himself, that without Axum's assault on Bharakuccha he could not have finally dealt the Great Country's vengeance. In the short time since his return, Rao had said so time and again. And those who heard his words directly passed them on to others, and they to others, and they to others still. For it was now the great tale of Majarashtra, and would be for generations to come.

No wind could have swept that palace clean, except that a greater wind had smote its city. Not even the Panther could have cut his way to the Vile One through the mass of soldiery who normally protected the beast. But the soldiery had been drawn aside, all save a handful, in order to fend off the wrath of Ethiopia. Into that sudden emptiness, the Wind had slipped its way. Softly, quietly, stealthily, before it struck the mighty blow.

The deed was done by the hand of the Great Country, yes—and all Marathas swelled in the knowledge. But only because a black folk had broken Bharakuccha, half breaking themselves in the doing, and lost their king besides.

So the crowd gathered—or the gathering crowded—onto those treacherous piers. Because that was where they could see the people of Africa, and touch them, and speak to them, and bring what little gifts their village or town might have scraped together.

Antonina had been standing on the battlements of the fortress above Chowpatty since the break of day. She had come there, at first, out of some obscure need to see for herself the place where Eon had received his death wound. She had watched the sun rise over that place, gazing hollow-eyed into the fortress for perhaps an hour or so.

But then, finally, the sounds growing behind her had registered. So she had turned away from the fortress, to look down at the harbor it guarded. And, in the hours which followed, had begun to find some warmth returning to her soul. Perhaps . . .

Perhaps . . .

Ousanas' harsh voice broke into her thoughts. "Do not presume, woman."

Startled, Antonina jerked her head around. She had never heard Ousanas' steps, coming up to the battlements. Not surprising, really, given his skill as a hunter.

"What?" Her mind groped for the meaning of the words. "Presume what?"

Ousanas crossed his powerful arms over his chest. Then:

"You think you are Ethiopia's curse? The foreign woman—the Medea—who wreaked havoc upon it? Slew two kings—the father, and then the son? Spilled half a nation's blood, and broke half its ships in the bargain?"

Antonina looked away. She tried to find words, but could not.

Ousanas snorted. "Do not presume, woman."

"How many of them will return, Ousanas?" she whispered, almost choking. "How many?" She brought tear-filled eyes back to face him.

"This year? None," he replied forcefully. "Except the Dakuen sarwe, which will escort Eon's regalia home. That half of it, at least, which is still alive and not so badly injured that they can make the trip across the sea."

Her eyes widened. Ousanas snorted again.

"For the sake of God, Antonina—*think*. Think, for once, instead of wallowing in this stupid misery." He waved an arm toward the harbor. "That is a warrior nation, woman. Traders too, yes, but a nation built on the training ground of the highland regiments."

The next snort was more in the way of a laugh. "I will grant you the beauty of Helen. But it was not because of you that Axum bled. So will you *please* desist from this idiot imitation of that puerile woman, standing on the walls of Troy."

The image caused Antonina to giggle, and then laugh outright. Ousanas smiled, stepped forward, and placed an arm around her shoulders. Once Antonina had managed to stifle her laughter, he turned her to face the harbor.

"Look at them, Antonina. There is no grief in those faces. Sorrow for a young king they loved and treasured, yes. Sadness for those of their brave comrades who have died or been maimed, yes. But grief? Not a trace."

Watching Axum's sarwen below, as they moved easily among the crowd—jesting, laughing, strutting, preening, basking in the admiration of old men and young girls alike (especially the latter)—Antonina knew he spoke the truth. And that small *perhaps* in her heart seemed to grow like a shoot in spring.

"They know, Antonina. They *know*. Now, at last—they truly *know*. That which Eon promised them, if they would follow him, has truly come to pass. Ethiopia is great, now. Axum has its empire. And that empire spans the seas themselves. No obscure land tucked away in a corner of Africa, but a nation which could reach its strength across the ocean and buckle great Malwa itself."

He drew in a deep breath, gazing across the very ocean of which he spoke. "Who will doubt now? Who will question Axum's rule of the Erythrean Sea *now*? Not Malwa! Nor, in the future, Rome or Persia, or anyone else. Axum's coinage will be as good as Roman here. And don't think"—he pointed to the crowd below—"that every one of those sarwen isn't thinking about it, in at least one part of his mind."

Another snort. "That part, at least, which is not preoccupied with seduction, and wallowing in the knowledge that no great skill will be needed for that *here*. Not this night, for a certainty."

Antonina chuckled. Ousanas continued:

"No, they are already starting to think about the future. About the time *after* the war, when they will return. War heroes one and all, with the holds of their trading ships full to bursting. Bringing wealth back to their towns and villages, to add golden luster to their already glorious names."

He gave her shoulder a little shake. "So it is time—past time—for you to do the same. We do not need your guilt and misery, Antonina. Nor want it. We *do* need your shrewdness and wisdom. Athena we could use. Helen is nothing but a damned nuisance."

❖   ❖   ❖

On the way down from the battlements, Antonina paused. "But why aren't the other regiments returning with the Dakuen?"

Ousanas gave her a stony stare.

"Oh." She giggled. "Of course. Silly of me not to have seen that."

"Praise God," he sighed. "I think the woman's wits may be returning."

After they reached the foot of the battlements, picking their way carefully through the rubble which still lay strewn about, Antonina started giggling again. "That's *such* a devious tactic, Ousanas."

The aqabe tsentsen shrugged. "Not really. Every regimental commander understands the logic perfectly. And why not? Ezana explained it to them plainly enough."

"You stay here," chuckled Antonina, "too far away to even think of meddling. Win more fame and fortune both for Axum and yourselves. While I, commander of the royal regiment to which Wahsi is sworn, will return and give the newborn negusa nagast the large fist the baby needs. Should it be needed."

She looked at Ousanas through the corner of her eyes. "And they did not balk? Not even a bit?"

"Not a bit. In truth, I think they were all secretly relieved. None of them *wants* a disruption in the dynasty, Antonina. With your hand to guide the thing, and Ezana to provide the fist, their distance relieves them of any burden at all. They are simply left with a warrior's simple task, far away in a foreign land. Win more fame, more glory, more fortune."

His famous grin made its appearance. "You noticed, I'm sure, that every sarwen in that harbor—wounded or whole—is practically staggering under his load of treasure. So careless of the Malwa, to leave their gold and silver and gems in the fabled vaults of Bharakuccha's harbor."

The grin began to fade. "So. How *do* you plan to guide the thing?"

Antonina scrutinized him, almost as if he were a sphinx posing a riddle.

"I don't know yet," she said abruptly. "I'm thinking about it."

He scrutinized her in return. Almost as if he were a man studying a riddle. Then grimaced, as a man might do when he cannot find the riddle's answer—and remembers that sphinxes have an unfortunate diet.

"Maybe you should go back up," he muttered.

"Not a chance," she replied, taking him by the arm and leading him away. "For one thing, I would be late for Shakuntala's audience. She's an empress, you know. And for another—" She broke off, studying Ousanas out of the corner of her eyes. "I'm thinking."

"I have wakened a monster." Ousanas rolled his eyes. "I can sense a demon rising."

"Nonsense. I'm just a woman, thinking."

"Same thing," he whined.

The empress shook her head. "I will not presume to override my commanders, but I think you are misreading the man completely. Rao most of all."

Shakuntala's officers stared at her in confusion. Her husband most of all. They were seated on cushions in a semicircle, facing the empress. She too sat on cushions, and those no higher than their own. Yet, despite her short stature, Shakuntala seemed to loom over them. As always, her posture was so erect that the small young woman seemed much larger than she really was.

Rao stroked his beard. "I will not deny the possibility. Still, Empress, I know something about Rajputs. And that army is entirely Rajput now, in all that matters. The name 'Malwa' applied to Lord Damodara has become a bare fiction. A tattered cloak, covering very different armor. Even the Ye-tai in his army are adopting Rajput ways and customs. The top Ye-tai commander, Toramana, is said to be marrying into the Chauhar clan itself. A half-sister of Rana Sanga's, no less."

"Others are doing the same," added Shakuntala's cavalry commander Shahji, "and not only Ye-tai. Nothing happens in Bharakuccha now that we do not learn almost within the day. We have gotten innumerable reports from Maratha merchants and vendors. Day after day, they tell us, Rajput soldiers are conducting marital negotiations with their Ye-tai and other comrades—even Malwa kshatriya— who seek to weld themselves to Rajputana."

Somehow, Shakuntala seemed to sit even more erect. "Yes, I know. And you think that means Damodara and Sanga will now wage war against us in the Rajput manner? Sally forth, finally, to meet us on a great open field of battle?"

"They will *try*," murmured Rao. "Whether we accommodate them is another manner." Perhaps sensing the sudden stiffness in the posture of the Maratha officers who sat to either side, he smiled slightly.

"Oh, do be still. It is no dishonor to say that our army is not yet a match in the open field against Damodara and his men. And will not be, for some time to come. Do not forget that army fought Belisarius—and won."

The officer Kondev stirred. "Belisarius was outnumbered at the Pass, by all accounts. Our forces are as great as Damodara's. Greater, if we bring in all the outlying units."

"And so what?" shrugged Rao. "Damodara's army has fought great battles, against Roman and Persian alike. They are experienced, sure, confident. Our forces have fought no such thing as that. A thousand skirmishes and ambushes, yes. A hundred small battles in narrow terrain, yes. Defended and taken a dozen hillforts, yes. It is not the same. In the open field, Damodara would break us like a stick."

An uncomfortable silence fell. From the sour look on their faces, it was plain to see the officers *wanted* to deny Rao's words. But . . .

Couldn't. And the fact that Majarashtra's greatest champion had been so willing to say them, calmly and openly, made denial quite impossible. Who were they to tell the Wind of the Great Country that he was mistaken in a matter of war?

Shakuntala, as it happened.

"You are wrong, Rao." She made a small, abbreviated gesture with her left hand. "Not about the correct tactics *if* Damodara comes out for battle. On that, I can say nothing." Her tone of voice, for just a moment, became demure. As demure, at least, as the empress was capable of. "I would not dream of disagreeing with my husband on such matters."

Rao grinned. But his wife the empress ignored him aloofly. "Where you are wrong is in the *politics* of the thing. Damodara, I am quite sure, knows that he could break us in battle. But not without suffering great losses himself. And *that*, I think, lies at the heart of things. He is waiting, and will continue to wait."

Rao frowned. "For what?" His eyes opened a bit. Then, for just one moment, the old Rao returned. The hill chieftain who had once trained an emperor's daughter. Long before he married her, in a time when such a marriage was unthinkable.

"Nonsense, girl! *Rajput*, I tell you. Even if Damodara himself were willing to seize the Malwa throne—and with his family hostage in Kausambi, what is the chance of that?—his soldiers would not follow him. Were he to press the matter, Rana Sanga himself would cut him down. The Rajputs swore an oath of fealty to the emperor of Malwa. And a Rajput oath—you know this well as I do—is as hard to break as iron."

Shakuntala shook her head. If the empress was displeased by her consort's sudden reversion to old and uncouth ways of addressing her, she gave no sign of it. Indeed, from the hint of a smile on her lips, one might almost think she enjoyed it.

Still, the headshake was vigorous.

"That was not my meaning—although, Rao, I think you are forgetting the lessons in philosophy you once gave an impatient and headstrong girl." Yes, she *was* smiling. "The business about truth becoming illusion, and illusion truth. The veil of Maya is not so easily penetrated as you might think."

A little chuckle swept the room. The officers seemed to relax a bit. Badinage between the empress and her consort was a familiar thing. Familiar, and immensely relaxing.

Shakuntala continued:

"It is Damodara's nature to *wait*. People miss that in him, because he is so capable in action when he moves—and moves so often, and so fast when he does. But, mostly, he is a waiting man. That is the core of his soul. He does not *know* the difference between truth and illusion, and—most important—knows that he doesn't. So . . . he waits. Allows the thing to unfold itself, until truth begins to emerge."

"What 'truth'?" asked Rao, a bit crossly.

She shrugged. "The same 'truth' we are all pondering. The 'truth' which is unfolding in the Indus, not here. We have no knowledge of what has happened with Belisarius, since he left Barbaricum and led his expedition into the interior of the Sind."

She glanced at Antonina, who, along with Ousanas and Ezana, was sitting on a stool not far to Shakuntala's left. Antonina shook her head slightly. *I don't know anything more than you do.*

Rao and the officers caught that little exchange, as Shakuntala had so obviously intended them to do. She pressed on.

"What will happen in the Indus? When Belisarius and Malwa clash head on? Who will win, who will lose—and how great will be the winning or the losing?"

She paused, defying anyone to answer. When it was obvious no answer was coming, she made that little hand wave again.

"So Damodara will wait. Wait and wait. Until the truth begins to emerge. And, in the meantime, will do nothing beyond rebuild Bharakuccha's harbor and fortifications. He will send nothing beyond patrols, up the Narmada—large enough to defeat any ambush, but not so large as to risk any great losses to himself."

Kondev stroked his beard. "It is true that all the punitive expeditions have ceased, since Damodara took command after the Vile One's death. But it was known that he had already opposed them, even while the beast was alive. So I am not sure that tells us much of anything regarding his future plans."

Antonina decided it was time for her to speak up. She cleared her throat, to gain everyone's attention. Then, as soon as Shakuntala nodded her permission, began to speak.

"I agree with the empress. Not so much with regard to Damodara's intentions"—she shrugged, waving her hand more broadly than Shakuntala had done—"although I suspect she is right there also. But who can read that man's soul? The key thing, however, is what she *proposes.* And in that, I am in full agreement with her."

Rao seemed a bit frustrated. "That means we would do nothing."

Antonina shook her head. "That is not what the empress said. She did not propose doing *nothing*, Rao. She proposes, instead, that we *prepare*."

She turned her head, looking toward the wide window which looked out over the city. Half-ruined Chowpatty was invisible, for the window was too high. But Antonina could see the ocean beyond, calm now that the monsoon season had ended.

"The Axumites will need to spend much time, in any event, recuperating from their wounds and repairing damaged ships. As soon as the eastern monsoon begins, Ousanas and I and the Dakuen sarwe will return to Ethiopia. But the rest of the Axumite army could use a long period in which to rest and rebuild their strength."

There was a little stir in the room. The officers had heard that most of Ethiopia's forces would stay in India, but this was the first time that rumor had been confirmed by an authoritative voice. They glanced at Ousanas and Ezana, and saw by their stern and solemn faces that Antonina had spoken truly. The stir grew a bit, before it settled. The news, clearly enough, filled all the Marathas with satisfaction.

Majarashtra and Axum combined. Now there might be a force which could even challenge Damodara and the Rajputs in open battle.

"Not yet," said Antonina firmly, as if gainsaying her earlier skepticism about the possibility of mind reading. "Axum needs time." More forcefully: "And so do *you*. If you intend to face Damodara and Rana Sanga in anything other than ambush, you will need to train your army. Marathas are not accustomed to such methods of warfare. You are not ready yet."

Although there was no expression on Shakuntala's face beyond respectful attentiveness, it was plain as day that Antonina's words encapsulated her own opinion.

And Antonina, though she herself was not Belisarius, carried the penumbra of his reputation for strategic sagacity.

"Wait," repeated Antonina. "Train, prepare. Let the Axumites rest, and then begin training with them. Prepare."

She sat up as straight as Shakuntala. "The time will come, do not doubt it. But when it comes—when the truth has begun emerging from the mists—you will be ready for it."

Whether or not Rao agreed with her was impossible to tell. The Panther of Majarashtra, when he so desired, could be as impenetrable as any man. But, clearly enough, he was ready to bring the thing to a close. He was facing Shakuntala now, not Antonina.

"This is your desire, Empress?"

"Yes."

"So be it, then." Rao bowed his head. There was nothing of the husband in that gesture, simply the servant. "It shall be as you command."

Later, as Rao and Shakuntala and Antonina relaxed in the empress' private chambers, Rao suddenly chuckled and said: "That went quite well, I think. Even my hot-blooded Marathas are satisfied enough to settle for the rigors of training camp."

Shakuntala gave her husband a skeptical lifted eyebrow.

"Preposterous!" he exclaimed. "I was merely playing a part. Surely you don't think I—Raghunath Rao himself!—would have been so foolish as to advocate challenging Damodara on the morrow?"

"Tomorrow, no." Shakuntala sniffed. "The day after tomorrow . . ." The eyebrow lifted and lifted.

"I am wounded to the heart," groaned Rao, a hand clutching his chest. "My own wife!"

The air of injured innocence went rather poorly with the sly smile. Not to mention Rao's own cocked eyebrow, aimed at Antonina.

"And you, woman of Rome? Are you still immersed in this role of yours? What did Ousanas call it—someone named Helen?"

Antonina's sniff matched Shakuntala's own in imperial dignity. "Nonsense. I'm thinking, that's all."

Before Rao could utter a word, she scowled at him and snapped: "Don't say it! One Ousanas is bad enough."

Chapter 36
RAJPUTANA
Autumn, 533 A.D.

The Ye-tai guarding Rana Sanga's family reacted to the attack as well as Malwa imperial troops could be expected to. No sooner had Kujulo and the Kushans charged out of ambush than the Ye-tai had their weapons cleared and were moving their horses out to intercept them. But, as Ajatasutra had foreseen, the anvaya-prapta sachivya commander of the escort had placed himself and all of his men at the front of the little caravan. So, since the Kushans were attacking from the front, within seconds the ornately carved and heavily decorated wagon which carried Rana Sanga's wife and children was left isolated.

"Now!" cried Ajatasutra. A moment later, pounding out from their own hiding place in a small grove of trees which was now to the caravan's right rear, the assassin and the two cataphracts raced their horses toward the wagon and the three carts following it.

Seeing them come, five of the six men guiding the supply carts—already on the verge of bolting after seeing the Kushans spring from ambush—sprang off the carts and began running toward a nearby ravine.

The sixth man, a Rajput from his clothing, snatched up a bow and began frantically groping for one of the arrows in a quiver attached to the side of the cart.

He never got as far as notching an arrow to the bowstring. Before he could do so, Valentinian's first arrow took him in the chest. The arrow, driven at less than forty yards range from a powerful cataphract bow, punched right through the man's light armor and drove him off the cart entirely. He was dead before he hit the ground.

Anastasius' first arrow and Valentinian's second did the same for the two Rajput guards riding on Lady Sanga's wagon, except that Anastasius' man was not killed outright. Anastasius had neither Valentinian's accuracy with a bow nor his speed. His arrow took the man in the shoulder. On the other hand, Anastasius used such a powerful bow that the wound was terrible. For all practical purposes, the Rajput's shoulder was destroyed. The man slumped off the wagon, unconscious from shock.

By now, the battle between the seventeen Kushans and twelve Ye-tai was in full melee. Three of the Ye-tai—the commander not being one of them—spotted the three enemy bandits attacking the wagon and tried to come to the rescue. But the Kushans, taking advantage of their sudden distraction, killed two of them within seconds. Only the third Ye-tai was able to break free from the small battle and return to the wagon. He came on, galloping his horse and waving his sword and bellowing curses.

"I'll deal with it," rumbled Anastasius. "You see to the wagon." The giant trotted his horse forward a few paces, drew the mount to a halt, and notched another arrow. When the Ye-tai was less than ten yards away, he drew and fired. At that range, not even Anastasius could miss. The arrow drove right through the Ye-tai's chest armor, his sternum, his heart, and severed the spine before it emerged. The bloody blade and eighteen inches of the shaft protruded from the man's back armor. When he fell off the horse, the arrow dug into the ground, holding the corpse up as if it were on display.

Ajatasutra and Valentinian, meanwhile, had left their horses and clambered into the small balcony at the rear of the great wagon which provided Lady Sanga and her children with a place where fresh air could be obtained, partially sheltered from the dust thrown up by their escort. The door leading to the interior was shut. Locked, too, as Ajatasutra immediately discovered when he tried the latch.

"Stand back!" he ordered. Valentinian drew off to the side, holding his spatha in one hand and a knife in the other. He had left his shield behind on the horse. Ajatasutra had not even bothered to bring his sword. He was armed only with a dagger.

The assassin stepped back the one pace the balcony allowed, lifted his knee to his chest, and kicked in the door. No sooner had the door flown open than a man charged out of the wagon's interior. His head was lowered, allowing no glimpse of his face beneath the turban. He was unarmored, wearing nothing but regular clothing, and carrying a short sword.

Valentinian's blade began the swing which would have decapitated the man, but Ajatasutra's sudden cry—*stop!*—stayed his hand. Ajatasutra avoided the awkward sword thrust easily, seized the man by his clothing, slammed him back against the wall of the wagon, and rendered him unconscious with two short, swift, merciless strikes with the dagger's pommel. As he dropped the man's body, the face was finally visible.

Valentinian bit off the curse with which he had been about to condemn Ajatasutra's recklessness. That was the face of an old man. A relative, perhaps. More likely, from the plainness of the clothing, an old and faithful retainer. Ajatasutra's quick action in sparing the man's life—maybe; those head blows had been ferocious—might save them trouble later.

A woman's voice was screaming inside the wagon. Valentinian stooped and entered, both his weapons ready for combat. Ajatasutra delayed a moment, leaning his head over the side to assess the progress of the battle between the Kushans and the Ye-tai. Then, grunting soft satisfaction, he followed Valentinian within.

"The Kushans should have it wrapped up soon," he said cheerfully. "I think we only lost four of them, too. Better than I expected."

Then, seeing Valentinian's rigid stance, Ajatasutra tensed. He couldn't really see most of the wagon's interior, because the cataphract was in the way. All Ajatasutra could spot was a young servant huddled in one far corner, shrieking with terror. The moment his eyes met hers, the servant's screaming stopped abruptly. Clearly enough, her terror had now gone beyond shrieks.

Crouched in the other corner, wearing very fine clothing, was a little girl. Sanga's daughter, he supposed. The girl's face was pale, and she was wide-eyed as only a six-year-old girl can be. But she seemed otherwise composed. At least she hadn't been screaming like the servant.

But what was in *front* of Valentinian? Ajatasutra had never seen the deadly cataphract so utterly prepared for mortal combat. As taut and alert as a mongoose facing a cobra. Apparently—Ajatasutra had not foreseen this possibility—Lady Sanga had brought one of her husband's most capable Rajput warriors along as a personal bodyguard.

"You draw him off to one side," Ajatasutra hissed, speaking in Greek "I'll take him from the other."

Valentinian began to mutter something. Then, as he obeyed Ajatasutra's instructions, the mutter became something more in the way of a laughing exclamation.

"Good! *You* figure out how to handle this, you genius!"

With Valentinian out of the way, Ajatasutra could finally see the whole interior of the wagon. Lady Sanga, a plump, plain-faced and gray-haired woman, was sitting on the large settee at the front of the wagon. On her lap, clutched tightly, she was holding a four-year-old boy.

In front of her, standing between his mother and Valentinian, was the last of Sanga's children. A twelve-year-old boy, this one was. Ajatasutra knew that his name was Rajiv, and that the gap in age between himself and his two siblings was due to the death in infancy of two other children.

What he *hadn't* known . . .

—although he *should* have assumed it—

"Great," muttered Valentinian. "Just great. 'You draw him off and I'll take him from the other side.' "

Suddenly, the cataphract straightened and, with an abrupt—almost angry—gesture, slammed his spatha back in its scabbard. A moment later, the knife vanished somewhere in his armor.

Now empty-handed, Valentinian crossed his arms over his chest and leaned casually against the wagon's wall. Then he spoke, in clear and precise Hindi.

"I fought the kid's father once already, Ajatasutra. And once is enough to last me a lifetime. So *you* can kill the kid, if you want to. *You* can spend the rest of your life worrying that Sanga will come looking for you. *I* am not an idiot."

Ajatasutra stared at the boy. Rajiv held a sword in his hand and was poised in battle stance. Quite adeptly, in fact, given his age.

Of course, the boy's assurance was not all *that* surprising, now that Ajatasutra thought about it. He *was* the son of Rana Sanga, after all.

Ajatasutra was still trying to figure out how to disarm the boy without hurting him, when Rajiv himself solved his quandary. As soon as Valentinian finished speaking, the boy curled his lip. Quite an adult sneer it was, too.

"Had you truly fought my father, bandit, you would not be alive today." The twelve-year-old spit on the floor of the wagon. Quite a hefty glob of spittle it was, too. Ajatasutra was impressed.

"Only two men have ever faced my father in battle and lived to speak of it afterward. The first was the great Raghunath Rao, Panther of Majarashtra. The other was—"

He broke off, his eyes widening. Then, for the first time since Ajatasutra got sight of him, the boy's eyes lost that slightly vague focus of the trained swordsman who is watching everything at once, and fled to Valentinian's face.

His eyes widened further. Behind him, his mother uttered a sharp little cry. Ajatasutra couldn't tell if the wordless sound signified fear or hope. Possibly both.

"*You* are the Mongoose?" Rajiv's question was barely more than a whisper.

Valentinian grinned his narrow-faced weasel grin. Which was a bit unfortunate, thought Ajatasutra. That was *not* a very reassuring expression.

But then, moving quickly but easily, Valentinian removed the helmet from his head and dropped to one knee in front of the boy. Seeming completely oblivious to the naked blade not more than inches from his neck, he reached up a hand and parted the coarse black hair on his head.

"You can still see the scar," he said quietly. "Feel it, too, if you want to."

Rajiv lowered the sword, a bit. Then, slowly and hesitantly, reached out his other hand and ran fingers over Valentinian's scalp.

"It's a big scar," he said wonderingly. And now, in a tone of voice more appropriate to his age.

His mother finally spoke, after clearing her throat. "My husband always said the Mongoose was an honorable man. And certainly not a bandit or cutthroat."

Ajatasutra sighed with relief and sheathed his own dagger. "Nor is he, Lady Sanga. Nor am I or the men who came with us. I apologize for killing and injuring your Rajput companions. But we had no choice."

Mention of those men brought home to Ajatasutra that all noise coming from without the wagon had ceased. Clearly enough, the battle was over.

Proof came immediately. Making very little noise, Kujulo landed on the balcony and stuck his head into the interior.

"The Ye-tai are all dead. We're driving off those gutless cart-drivers now. Killed three so far. We thought to leave two, maybe three alive."

Ajatasutra nodded. "Just so long as they're driven far away. Near enough to see the caravan burn, but too far to see any details."

"What about the one guard? He'll never use that shoulder again—not for much, anyway—but he'll live if we take care of the wound. So will the old man."

Ajatasutra hesitated. There had been no room in his plans for bringing badly injured men with them. But, seeing the new stiffening in Rajiv's stance, he decided the alternative was worse. Clearly enough, Sanga's son—probably the mother, too—would put up a struggle to save their close retainers.

"Bind them up," he ordered curtly. "We can probably

disguise them as diseased men. Or simply the victims of a bandit attack. Who knows? That might even help keep prying eyes away."

That done, he turned back to Lady Sanga. "We did not come to kill you, but to save you from harm. It is all very complicated. I do not have time now to explain it to you. You will just have to trust us, for the time being. We *must* move immediately or—"

"*Malwa*," hissed Lady Sanga. "Men and their stupid oaths! I told my husband they would play him for a fool." Seeing her son stiffening in front of her, she reached out a hand and swatted his head. Half-playfully, half . . . not.

"Stupid!" she repeated. "Even you, at twelve! Malwa will ruin us all."

When her eyes came back to Ajatasutra's, the assassin was almost stunned by the warmth and humor gleaming in them. For the first time, he began to understand why the great Rana Sanga had such a reputation for fidelity, despite the lack of comeliness of his wife.

An hour later, as they rode away from the scene of an apparent massacre, a pillar of smoke rising behind them, Valentinian claimed to have *almost* fallen in love with her.

"Would have, actually, except not even *that* woman is worth fighting Sanga again."

"You'd do anything to get out of doing a stint of honest work," jibed Anastasius.

Valentinian sneered. "Pah! The way she arranged the bodies from the cemetery? Perfect! Didn't even flinch once. Didn't even grimace."

The cataphract turned in his saddle and bestowed a look of mighty approval on the woman who was following them not far behind on a mule, wearing the clothing of a bandit's woman and clutching a rag-wrapped bandit's child before her. Two other bandit children—wrapped in even filthier rags—rode tandem on a mule alongside hers.

"I'll bet you my retirement bonus against yours that woman can cook anything. She probably laughs while she's chopping onions."

By evening, Valentinian was feeling positively cheerful. As it turned out, Lady Sanga apparently *could* cook almost anything.

"I was getting *so* sick of that damned Kushan food," he mumbled, around a mouthful of some savory item which Lady Sanga had prepared. Out of what, exactly, no one knew. The one item Lady Sanga had insisted on salvaging from her wagon, before the thing was put to the torch with the corpses from the cemetery in it, was a small chest full of her cooking supplies.

"No one will notice its absence," she'd claimed. Ajatasutra, despite some misgivings, had not pressed the point. He'd simply insisted that she transfer the supplies—which consisted mostly of onions, packets of herbs and spices and other savories, and a small knife—into various sacks, leaving the empty chest behind to burn in the flames. He agreed with her that no one would notice the absent supplies. But the chest, though not an expensive item likely to be stolen, had solid fittings which would survive the flames. Someone—someone like Nanda Lal and his best spies, at any rate—*might* notice the absence of those fittings, and start to wonder.

"Got onions in't," Valentinian continued happily. "I love onions."

Anastasius sighed heavily. "I don't miss their cooking, but I do miss the Kushans. I felt better with Kujulo and his maniacs around."

Ajatasutra began to say something, but Anastasius waved him down. "Don't bother! I understand the logic, you damned schemer. Five men—two of them injured, and one of them elderly—a woman, and three children can make their way across the Ganges plain without being noticed much. No way a large party of armed men could. Especially not Kushans. Not when we got to Kausambi, for sure."

Valentinian had finished devouring the savory by then, and Anastasius' last words brought back his normal gloom.

"I still say this plan is insane. We could get Lady Sanga and the children out *now*." He pointed to the southwest. "Easy enough—well, after a hard trek through the Thar—to reach the general's forces. Then—"

Ajatasutra began to speak again, but, again, Anastasius waved him down. "I'll deal with the little weasel." Glowering: "Valentinian, that'd be even more insane. This whole little rescue operation was a side trip added on at the last moment. We *still* have the main thing to accomplish. If we brought out Lady Sanga now that would expose the whole scheme—no way it wouldn't come out, in the middle of a whole army—and make the rest of it impossible. The only way to keep the secret is to hide it in the belly of the beast. In Kausambi, the last place Nanda Lal would think to look."

"*Narses!*" hissed Valentinian. "Too clever by half!" But he left off arguing the point.

The supremacy of logic having been restored, Anastasius went back to his own worries. "I just miss having the Kushans around. I don't begrudge it to them, mind you, getting back to their own folk. And since they'll pass through the Sind on their way, they can probably give the general word of how we're doing.

But—" He sighed, even more heavily than before. "It's going to be tricky, with just the three of us, if we get attacked by *real* bandits."

Lady Sanga and the children had eaten earlier, and she had given the two wounded Rajputs what care she could. So now she and her children were sitting around the campfire listening to the exchange. No sooner had Anastasius finished than Rajiv sprang to his feet, drawing his sword and waving it about.

"Bandits—*pah*! Against the Mongoose? And there are *four* of us!"

The twelve-year-old boy's enthusiasm did not seem to mollify Anastasius. Ajatasutra shared the giant cataphract's skepticism. Having an overconfident and rambunctious lad as an "additional warrior" struck him as more trouble than help.

And, judging from the fierce scowl on his face, Valentinian felt even more strongly about it. But Valentinian's displeasure, it became immediately apparent, had a more immediate focus.

"You hold a sword that way in a fight, boy, you're a dead man."

Rajiv lowered the blade, his face a study in contradiction. On the one hand, chagrin. On the other, injured—even outraged—pride.

"My father taught me to hold a sword!" he protested. "Rana Sanga himself!"

Valentinian shook his head, rose with his usual quick and fluid speed, and drew his own sword. "He didn't teach you *that* grip," he growled. "If he had, I wouldn't have this scar on my head and he'd be buried on a mountainside in Persia."

The cataphract stalked off a few paces onto an empty patch of ground. The sun had set over the horizon, but there was still enough light to see. He turned, and made a come-hither gesture with his sword.

"May as well start tonight, boy. If you're going to be any help against bandits, your swordwork has got to get better."

Eagerly, Rajiv trotted forward to begin his new course of instruction. Behind him, Lady Sanga shook her head, not so much ruefully as with a certain sense of detached irony.

"There's something peculiar about all this," she chuckled. "The son being trained by the father's great enemy. To fight whom in the end, I wonder?"

"God is prone to whimsy," pronounced Ajatasutra.

"Nonsense," countered Anastasius. "The logic seems impeccable to me. Especially when we consider what Aristotle had to say about—"

Chapter 37
THE PUNJAB
Autumn, 533 A.D.

Belisarius went across on the first ship, leaving Maurice to stabilize the Roman defensive lines at Uch. He had no intention of trying to hold Uch, beyond the two or three days necessary to transfer the entire army across the Chenab. But keeping an army steady while it is making a fighting withdrawal requires a very firm hand in control, a characterization which fit Maurice perfectly.

Belisarius wanted to get a sense of the land he would be holding as soon as possible, which was why he decided to take the risk of being part of the initial landing. His subordinates had protested that decision, rather vehemently, but Belisarius fit the description of "very firm" quite well himself.

Besides, he thought the risk was minimal. The small triangle of land formed by the confluence of the Chenab and the Indus was not well situated to defend *against* an invasion of the Punjab. For that purpose, it made far more sense to fortify the Indus south of the fork—which was exactly what the Malwa had done. So Belisarius expected to encounter no enemy troops beyond cavalry patrols. And against those, the cataphracts and Arab scouts crammed into the ship should suffice.

"Crammed" was the operative term, however, and Belisarius was thankful that the river crossing took not much more than an hour. By the time his own ship began offloading its soldiers, the second ship the Romans had captured when they took Uch was half-way across the river bearing its own load of troops.

Belisarius landed on the bank of the Chenab just north of Panjnad Head, which marked the confluence of the Chenab and the Sutlej. That position was much too far north for him to hold for long. The Indus was fifteen miles away, and the confluence of the Indus and the Chenab was twenty-five miles to the south-west, forming a triangle well over sixty miles in circumference—more likely eighty or ninety miles, considering all the loops and bends in the two rivers. With the twenty thousand men he still had left, he could not possibly hope to defend such a large territory for more than a few days.

But unless the Romans encountered a sizeable Malwa force in the triangle—which he didn't expect to happen—Belisarius *could* hold that position for those few days. Just enough time to begin throwing up his fortifications further south, in a much smaller triangle, while his men foraged as much food and fodder as possible. Their supplies were now running very low. They had captured a fair amount of gunpowder in Uch, but not much in the way of provisions.

Even more important, perhaps, than rounding up food would be rounding up the civilian population. The Punjab was the most fertile region of the Indus, and the population density was high. Here, the Malwa had not conducted the savage massacres of civilians which they had in the Sind—although word of those massacres had undoubtedly begun spreading. Which, from Belisarius' point of view, was all to the good. The peasants in the triangle would not have fled yet, but they would be on edge. And more likely to fear their Malwa overlords than the Roman invaders.

Once again, Belisarius intended to use mercy—defining that term very loosely—as a weapon against his enemy. His cavalry would cut across to the Indus and then, much like barbarian horsemen in a great hunt on the steppes, drive the game before them to the south, penning them into a narrower and narrower triangle. Except the "game" would be peasants, not animals. And the purpose of it would not be to eat the game, but to use them as a labor force. The kind of fortifications Belisarius intended to construct would require a *lot* of labor—far more than he had at his disposal from his own soldiers, even including the thousands of Malwa prisoners that they had captured.

How many, Aide, do you think?

Aide gave that shivering image which was his equivalent of a shrug. **Impossible to say. There are no records of such things, at this point in history. In later times, the Punjab would hold a population numbering in the millions, with a density of five hundred people to a square mile. It won't be that high today, of course, but I wouldn't be surprised if it was half that. So you may well wind up with tens of thousands of people for a work force. Many of them will be oldsters and children, of course.**

Belisarius paused to exchange a few last words with Abbu. The Arab scouts were offloading first. As always, Abbu and his men would provide Belisarius with reconnaissance. That done, he returned to his mental conversation with Aide.

So many? Better than I had hoped. With twenty

*thousand, I am confident I can erect the fortifications
I need before the Malwa can organize a serious siege.*

**I cannot be positive. But—yes, I think so. With
no more civilians than that, Gustavus Adolphus
was able to erect the fortifications at Nürnberg
in two weeks time. On the other hand . . .** *those*
**civilians were enthusiastic partisans of the Prot-
estant cause. These Punjabi peasants you will be
rounding up could hardly be described as
"partisans" of Rome.**

Belisarius chuckled. *True, true. But that quip of Dr.
Johnson's will apply here as well, if I'm not mistaken.
I think the Malwa savagery in the Sind will come back
to haunt them. If you were a Punjabi peasant con-
scripted to build fortifications for Roman troops fending
off a Malwa siege, would you be a reluctant laborer?*

"The prospect of being hanged . . ." mused Aide.
**No, I think not, especially if you maintain dis-
cipline among your own soldiers and do not allow
the civilians to be abused. Beyond being forced
into hard labor, at least. They will know full well
that if the Malwa overrun you, they will be
butchered along with the Roman troops. The
Malwa will consider them "rebels," and they
showed at Ranapur the penalty for rebellion.**

Three days later, Maurice came across with the last
of the Roman forces. By then, Belisarius had an
approximate count.

"Better than twenty thousand civilians, for sure,"
were the first words he spoke when Maurice entered
the command tent Belisarius had erected near the
village of Sitpur. "Probably at least twenty-five. Maybe
even thirty thousand."

Maurice grunted satisfaction. He removed his helmet and hung it on a peg attached to a nearby pole

supporting the small pavilion. The helmets of Gregory and Felix and Mark of Edessa were already hanging there.

That grunt of satisfaction was the last sign of approval issued by the chiliarch. Before he had even reached the table where a new map had been spread, showing the first sketched outlines of the terrain, he was already accentuating the negative.

"You're too far north, still. If you think you can hold this much land with so few troops, you're out of your mind. What is it to the Indus from here? It must be a good ten miles!"

Gregory and Felix and Mark of Edessa burst into outright laughter. Belisarius satisfied himself with a crooked smile.

"Oh, *do* be quiet. I have no intention of building my principal lines up here, Maurice. I intended to erect them—have started to already, in fact—ten miles southwest of here." He pointed to a place on the map where lines indicating heavy fortifications had been drawn. "That far down into the tip of the triangle, the distance from the Chenab to the Indus is no more than six miles. And I'm building the outer line of fortifications here, a few miles north of that."

"We're just setting up field camps here," added Gregory. "Nothing fancy. Enough for large cataphract units to sally out and keep the first Malwa contingents held off for another few days. We have *got* to keep Sitpur in our hands as long as possible."

"Why?" demanded Maurice.

Belisarius' three other top commanders grinned. "Would you believe—talk about luck!—that Sitpur is the bakery center for the whole area?"

Maurice exhaled so forcefully it was almost as if he were spitting air. His hard gray eyes fell on Belisarius, and grew harder still.

"You don't deserve it, you really don't. This is almost as bad as the silly *Iliad,* where every time that reckless Achilles gets himself into a jam Athena swoops in and saves him."

Belisarius winced, acknowledging the hit. Then, shrugged. "I'll admit I assumed the local bread would be made by village women. Like trying to collect pebbles on a beach, that would have been. But I was prepared to do it."

"Instead," interrupted Mark, "we've had the villagers rounding up everything else—mostly lentils, and lots of them—while we keep the bakers in Sitpur working night and day. The biggest problem we're having right now is finding enough carts to haul the bread off to the south."

By this time, even Maurice was beginning to share in the excitement. Although he did make a last rally, attempting to salvage some portion of sane pessimism. But the effort was . . . feeble.

"I suppose the so-called 'bread' is that flat round stuff. Tastes awful."

"It's called *chowpatti,*" chuckled Felix, "and I think it tastes pretty good, myself."

Maurice did not argue the point. Culinary preference, after all, was a small issue in the scope of things. Food was food, especially in a siege. Before it was all over—assuming things went *well*—Maurice fully expected that at least half of the Roman horses would have been eaten.

"Lentils too, eh?" he murmured, stroking his beard and staring down at the map. "And we'll be able to get fish from the rivers."

That last thought seemed to relieve him. Not because it suggested that the Roman army would be able to stave off starvation, even in a long siege, but because it brought a new problem to the fore.

"We'll have enough fishing boats for that," he growled, "but don't think the Malwa don't have plenty of boats of their own. And no little fishing vessels, either. They have enough large river craft in the Punjab, from what I can see, to start ferrying their own troops across to the triangle before we'll have the fortifications finished."

He turned and pointed back in the direction of Uch. "The whole area is starting to crawl with Malwa troops. With a lot heavier artillery than anything we have. As we were pulling out of Uch, the Malwa were starting to set up twenty-four pounders around the town. Real siege guns, those, not like these little popguns we've got."

The chiliarch was comfortably back in his favorite groove. He began stroking his beard with great vigor and satisfaction. "They must have thirty thousand men within a week's march. Three times that, within a month. And once they start transferring troops from the Ganges valley, we'll be looking at two hundred thousand." A bit lamely: "Soon enough."

"Maurice," said Belisarius patiently, "nobody can move that many troops that far very quickly. It took us months to get our army from Mesopotamia to the Indus, and we could use the sea. The Malwa cannot possibly move any large number of soldiers through Rajputana. The area is too arid. That means they'll have to march any reinforcements from the Ganges to the headwaters of the Jamuna, and then cross over to the headwaters of the Sutlej. It'll take them until well into next year, and you know it as well as I do."

He jerked his head backward, pointing to the north. "Until then, the Malwa will have to rely on whatever forces they already have in the Punjab. Which is a massive army in its own right, of course, but I'll willing to bet—I *am* betting—that by now they're scattered all over the place. Half of them are probably in or around Sukkur, hammering themselves into a pulp against Khusrau and Ashot."

Maurice did not argue the point, but he was not mollified either. "Fine. But they can still bring three or four times as many men to bear as we've got. Sure, with good fortifications across the neck of the triangle, we can mangle them before they break through. But there are enough boats in these rivers to enable them to land troops downstream."

With his finger, he traced on the map the Indus and Chenab rivers as they converged south of their own location. "Almost anywhere along here. So we have to leave enough of a striking force, centrally positioned, to stop any landing before it gets established." Gloomily: "We can manage it for a while, sure. We've still got twelve thousand cataphracts, and we can use half of them for a quick reaction force against any amphibious attack. But . . ."

Gregory finished the thought for him. "But sooner or later, they'll establish a beachhead. And when they do, the whole thing will start unraveling."

"So let's make sure it happens later than sooner," said Belisarius firmly. "Because sooner or later, Menander and Eusebius are going to get here also. There's been no indication at all that the Malwa have any real warships on these rivers. Once the *Justinian* and the *Victrix* arrive, we should be able to control the banks of the triangle well enough."

At the moment, neither Menander nor Eusebius quite shared the general's confidence. First, because they still had to run the fortress which the Malwa had built on the Indus below the Chenab fork. Secondly, because they had found themselves laden with a far greater cargo than they had expected. Instead of towing one barge behind the *Justinian*, the gunship was towing three and the fireship yet another. One of the three extra barges was loaded with all six of the twenty-four pounders which Ashot had possessed; the second with the artillerymen and engineers needed to set them up and keep them in operation; and the third with the powder and shot to get them in operation through pitched battles.

Ashot had insisted. Rigorously.

"I don't need them anymore," he'd told them. "After Calopodius broke that Malwa assault on the island—the one they must have been *sure* would succeed—the Malwa stopped all their attacks on the Roman positions. They must be getting a little desperate now. Their food is running low, and now that you've arrived—don't think they didn't spot you—they'll know that they're most likely going to be losing their water supplies. They don't have any boats on the river which can stand up to either the *Justinian* or the *Victrix*, much less both combined."

"You'd think they would!" protested Eusebius.

Ashot shook his head. "You're thinking like an engineer instead of a military man, Eusebius. A year ago, the Malwa still thought they were conquering Mesopotamia. The last thing in their minds was building armed and armored gunships to defend the heartland of the Indus valley. And that's not the kind of thing you can do overnight, as you well know."

"You think they're going to lift the siege of Sukkur?" asked Menander.

"Who knows?" shrugged Ashot. "If they had any sense, they would. Unless they can break into Sukkur, which there's no sign they can after weeks of trying, they'll start starving before too long. But I'm pretty sure the general was right: Link is still way off in Kausambi, not close enough to the scene to make informed decisions. So the Malwa commanders are probably operating based on the kind of 'stand at all cost' orders which seem reasonable to a commander a thousand miles away. And the Malwa high command has made crystal clear what the penalty is for disobeying orders.

"So take the twenty-four pounders," he'd concluded. "That'll still leave me the really big guns, in case of another Malwa assault. And Belisarius can use them up north. Those monsters *can* break down walls, if the Malwa start building lines of countervallation, which they will if he's managed to take the triangle. His little three-pounder field artillery can't."

On their way up the Indus, Menander and Eusebius had picked up another load as well. A small one, however—just one man. When they came ashore on a boat to the island where Calopodius had made his stand, in order to pay him their regards, Calopodius pleaded with them to take him along.

Menander and Eusebius stared down at him. The young Greek officer was lying on a pallet in his tent. Nothing of his face above the mouth could be seen. The entire upper half of his head was swathed in bandages. Calopodius' trickery had delayed a Malwa assault, but it had not prevented it. He had still managed, by his heroism and that of his men, to beat off that attack. But not without suffering a great price. His force had suffered terrible casualties, and Calopodius himself had been blinded by the shrapnel from a mortar shell.

"Please," he whispered. "I'm useless here, now. Anthony of Thessalonica has taken charge of the forces since I was injured—doing a good job of it, too—and I've got nothing to do but lie here." He managed a weak chuckle. "Practicing my rhetoric and grammar. A pastime which pales very quickly, I assure you."

The two naval officers hesitated. Neither one of

them wanted to come right out and make the obvious rejoinder: *there'll be nothing for you to do up north, either, except die if Belisarius can't hold.*

The rejoinder was so obvious that Calopodius already had an answer prepared. Clearly enough, his request was not a spur-of-the-moment impulse. The young nobleman—not much more than a boy, really—must have been lying there for days hoping for an opportunity to leave the place where he had lost his eyesight. And, in the fierce manner of youth, try to return to the fray despite the loss.

"The general will be able to use me in some fashion or other," he insisted. "He'll be fighting what amounts to a siege, on the defensive. Lots of quartermaster work, and a lot of that can be done without eyes. Most of it's arguing with soldiers over what they can and can't get, after all." Again, the weak chuckle. "And I really *am* quite good in rhetoric and grammar."

Menander looked at Eusebius, then shrugged. "Why not? If he really wants it."

Eusebius had his doubts. But, within a day after leaving the island, the doubts began to recede. Much to his surprise—astonishment, rather—the noble Greek youth proved to have an aptitude for machinery. Or, at least, didn't look upon it as utterly unfathomable.

Working down in the hold with the steam engine, of course, was far too dangerous for a blind man. But, after a bit of experimentation, Eusebius discovered that a blind man who was willing to learn could manage the work of pumping the chamber of the fire cannon readily enough.

"It's kind of dangerous," he said hesitantly.

"All the better," replied Calopodius. Then, after thinking about it: "Unless I'd be putting you and the crew at risk."

Eusebius began to shake his head, until he realized the gesture would be meaningless to Calopodius. "I didn't mean it that way. I meant it'll be risky being stationed up here when we run the fortress. There'll be picket boats, sure as anything. I'll have to torch them as we go past, or they might board the cargo ships. That will give the big Malwa guns on the fortress as good a target as anyone could ask for at night. You'd really be safer on the *Justinian*."

But he didn't press the issue. Safety, clearly enough, was not what Calopodius was seeking. There was something almost suicidal about the young officer's eagerness to return to combat. As if, by sneering at death itself, he could somehow restore his sight. That part of it, at least, with which a young man measures his own worth.

Chapter 38

Belisarius hunched, covering his head with his hands. The motion was more instinctive than reasoned, since his helmet would provide far more protection than his hands. From the sound of it, the mortar shell had landed too far away to be any danger anyway.

"Those are the worst," said Gregory. "The round shot, even from their big twenty-four pounders, can't really make a dent in these soft-earth berms. But those damned big mortars of theirs . . ."

"Just one of them killed eight men earlier this morning," muttered Felix. He gave Belisarius a keen scrutiny. "Are you sure . . ."

Belisarius shook his head, as he rose up from his crouch. "Not yet, Felix. Don't think Sittas hasn't been hounding me about it, either." The general placed the periscope back over the rampart. The optical device was one of twenty which Belisarius had brought with him from Charax. Aide had recommended the things, and, sure enough, they had proved invaluable once the Malwa siege began biting in.

"He's champing at the bit to lead a sally, because he's positive he can get to those trenches and butcher the Malwa mortar crews without losing too many cataphracts."

Belisarius slowly scanned the enemy forces in the trenches not more than a few hundred yards away. "He's probably right, too. Unless I miss my guess, the Malwa commanders are still preoccupied with getting their forces into position. Those fieldworks are pretty badly designed. Sloppy. The kind of thing soldiers throw up in a hurry, each unit working on its own, without any real overall planning or coordination."

He heard the soft *whump* of a Roman mortar being fired, and followed the trajectory of the shell with his naked eyes. A few seconds later, the missile struck almost dead on in a Malwa trench. By now, two days since the fighting at the forward fortifications had begun, the Roman crews manning the coehorn mortars had become very accurate with the crude devices. They were using Malwa powder instead of Roman, since Belisarius had wanted to reserve the better grade for his field guns. But, with a little experimentation, the Roman mortar crews had adapted handily. This many years into the war, even Malwa gunpowder was far more uniform and standard in grade than had been the case earlier.

"I don't think those men out there are convinced yet that they've got a *real* siege on their hands," he mused. "Which, if I'm right, means that they'll be mounting a mass assault pretty soon. That's why I've kept the mitrailleuse out of sight, and have been using your sharpshooters so sparingly. I want to mangle them as badly as possible when they come in. *Then*—when they're retreating—Sittas can lead out his beloved sally. That'll turn the whole thing into a complete bloodbath."

The savage nature of the words went poorly with the soft, almost serene voice. But Belisarius had long since learned to put his personal feelings aside in the middle of a battle. A man who was warm by nature was also capable of utter ruthlessness when he needed to be. He no longer even wondered much at the dichotomy.

Neither did Aide. The crystal's thoughts were even more cold-blooded than the general's. **They won't have any real experience with modern fortifications, either. Even if they've been instructed, the instructions won't mean much. They'll come straight at the curtain wall, instead of the bastions like they should. The mitrailleuse will catch them enfilade, piled up against the wall with scaling ladders.**

Belisarius was standing in one of those bastions himself. The bastion was shaped liked an arrowhead, with the rear sides of the "blade" facing the curtain wall at a ninety-degree angle. Those sides were what was called a "retired flank," invisible to an attacking enemy because of the protecting lobes of the "arrowhead"—what were called, technically, "orillons"—and sheltered from cannon fire. The gun ports in the retired flanks were empty now. But mitrailleuse crews waiting in a bunker below would bring the weapons up once the attack began. From those gun ports, the crews would have a protected and perfect line of fire down the entire length of the curtain wall which separated this bastion from the next one, some two hundred and fifty yards away.

The fortifications, which were thick earthen ramparts rather than stone construction, were fronted by a wide ditch. There was perhaps two feet of water in the ditch, due to natural seepage from the high water table. In the more elaborate fortifications which Belisarius was having built several miles to the rear, where he planned to make his real stand, his engineers were designing the ditches to be suddenly flooded by ruptured dikes. But these simpler outer fortifications had no such elaborate designs.

They didn't need to. The purpose of the outer fortifications was twofold:

First, give Belisarius the time he needed to finish scouring the area north of his "inner line" of any and all foodstuffs. That work was now almost finished.

Second—hopefully—draw the Malwa into an ill-conceived mass assault which would enable Belisarius to bleed them badly. That remained to be done. But, from what he could detect through the periscope—and even more from his well-honed "battle sense"—it should be happening very soon.

"Tomorrow," he pronounced. "No later than the day after." His gaze, looking through the gun ports in the retired flank, ranged down the length of the curtain. He could envision already the mass of Malwa soldiers piled up against that wall, and the pitiless enfilade fire of the mitrailleuse and canister-loaded field guns which would turn a muddy ditch bright with color.

It was a cool thought, for all that the color red figured so prominently in it. Containing no more in the way of mercy than a blacksmith shows mercy to a rod of iron. As he examines the metal's own red glow, gauging the strength of his hammerstrike.

That night, Menander and Eusebius ran the fortress on the Indus. Ideally, they would have preferred to wait for another week, when they could take advantage of a new moon. But time was critical. They still had no way of knowing if Belisarius had succeeded in his plan to seize the lowest fork in the Punjab. But, if he had—and neither of them was prone to doubt on that score—the general would soon enough be in desperate need of the men and supplies they were bringing. And, perhaps even more, the control of the river which the *Justinian* and the *Victrix* would provide.

Ideally, also, they would have hugged the eastern bank of the Indus, keeping as far away as possible from the huge guns in the Malwa fortress. But the river was uncharted this far north—at least, for Romans if not Malwa—and Menander was far more concerned about the danger of running aground at night on a hidden sandbar. So he would stick to the middle of the river, where that risk was lowest.

The *Victrix* would have to take the risk, of course. In order to intercept the Malwa picket boats which were certain to be stationed on the river near the fortress, Eusebius would have to steam close to the western shore. Although it was theoretically possible to "walk" a side-wheeler across a submerged sandbar, neither Menander nor Eusebius had any desire to test the theory under enemy fire. So the *Victrix* would have to rely on speed alone. For which reason, the barge which the fireship had been towing was now attached to the *Justinian*.

"Talk about sitting ducks," muttered Menander to himself, as he watched the outlines of the fortress looming up to his left. "I'm moving as slow as a snail, and Eusebius is practically walking into the lion's den."

The faint light shed by a crescent moon didn't provide enough illumination to make it possible to discern the details of the fortress' construction. It just looked very dark, very big—and very grim. Already Menander could spot the glowing lights which indicated that the fortress had long since fired up the hearths where the shot was being heated.

There would be no surprises here. Belisarius' drive to the Punjab had shredded the enemy forces stationed to the east of the Indus, but the Malwa retained complete control of the west bank north of Sukkur. Malwa cavalrymen had been keeping pace with the small Roman flotilla since it steamed out of Rohri, reporting its whereabouts to the fortress by using the telegraph line which the Malwa had stretched from their

camp besieging Sukkur all the way to their headquarters in the Punjab. And from there, Menander had
no doubt at all, to the capital at Kausambi.

Still, he and Eusebius had one "secret weapon" up
their sleeve. Menander turned his eyes away from the
fortress and studied the fireship which was starting to
pull out ahead of him. Any moment now . . .

A sudden flash of light came from a dinghy being
towed behind the *Victrix,* as the small explosive charge
was ignited. Within seconds, the infernal chemical
concoction which Eusebius had prepared was burning
fiercely and emitting a huge cloud of smoke. Less than
a minute a later, the *Justinian* and its four barges began
disappearing into that smoke. Until the powder burned
itself out, or the boat sank from the heat of the burning, Menander would have a certain amount of protection. The Malwa would be firing blind.

The thought did not comfort him overmuch. The
big Malwa siege cannons were so inaccurate that they
could just as well hit from a miss, as it were. He had
only to remember the fate of John of Rhodes to be
reminded that perhaps the real mistress of battle was
the Goddess of Luck.

The damned stuff was acrid, too. Within seconds,
Menander was trying to hold his breath as much as
possible. And he was already regretting the fact that
just as the Malwa could no longer see him, he could
no longer watch the progress of the *Victrix* as it went
against the picket boats.

"Good luck, Eusebius."

Eusebius, a proper artisan, did not really believe in
luck. Even his new career as a naval officer had not
much shaken his faith in logic and order. So, as he
positioned the barrel of the fire cannon to rake the
oncoming picket boats, he did not give much thought

to the possibility of being sunk by cannon fire coming from the guns on the fortress. If for no other reason, he would be sailing so close to the picket boats that they would not fire at him for fear of sinking their own craft.

A great roar announced the first volley being fired by the fortress. Not too many seconds later, Eusebius was muttering fierce curses and frantically repositioning the barrel of the fire cannon.

His intended target had disappeared. The Malwa *had* fired at the *Victrix*. They had undershot, however, and managed to sink the lead picket boat coming toward him.

Whether from chagrin or simply because the Malwa commander of the fortress decided that Menander's ships made a more suitable target, the second volley was fired at the *Justinian* and the four barges it was towing. As was the third.

And Menander, cursing even more bitterly than Eusebius, was confirmed in his belief that the Goddess of Luck reigned supreme in battle. None of the ships were hit by the fortress' fire. Indeed, none of the great cannon balls landed closer than thirty yards to any of the Roman vessels. But one ball, guided by incredible good fortune, did manage to neatly sever the cable towing the last barge.

That barge, containing most of the powder and shot for the twenty-four pounders, fell away and began drifting aimlessly in the sluggish current. The handful of soldiers stationed on the barge were completely helpless. None of them were really sailors; even if they had known how to raise the sails, there was no wind to fill them; and they were far too few—nor was the barge properly designed for the task anyway—to drive it against the current using oars. All they could do was drift, awaiting their certain doom.

Menander was not even aware of the problem immediately. The change in the flotilla's speed due to the sudden lightening of the load was too minor to register. It was not until the *Justinian* and the three barges still attached to it had steamed completely out of the smoke bank that he realized what had happened.

For a moment, he was torn by indecision. He was still within range of the fortress' guns, and would remain so for several minutes. If he cast loose the three barges he was towing in order to steam back to rescue the fourth, he might lose them all. On the other hand, if he waited until he had towed them far enough upstream to be safe from cannon fire, it would take him quite some time to rescue the stray and return— assuming he wasn't hit himself. During which time, the three barges cast off might very well ground ashore or drift back into range. The Indus' current was not swift, but it was irresistible for a barge not under any form of powered control.

His eyes fell on the *Victrix*, now almost a mile away. He could see another gout of flame spurting from its bow and engulfing a Malwa picket ship. In the fireship's wake, he could see that two others were burning fiercely. As expected, river craft could not hope to match the *Victrix* in close quarter combat. A single burst of that hideous weapon was enough to turn any small vessel into an inferno.

There was only one Malwa picket boat left. The commander of that boat, no coward, was still rowing toward the *Victrix*. Menander could see a small flash in the bow of the boat, as it fired the puny little bowchaser it carried. That would be a three pounder, at best. Even at short range, the heavy timber which shielded the *Victrix*'s bow would shrug it off.

To Menander's surprise, however, the *Victrix* began

to turn away. Within seconds, he realized that Eusebius had spotted the orphaned barge—which was now not more than three hundred yards away from him—and was intending to go to its rescue.

"You fucking idiot!" shouted Menander. He was so infuriated that he repeated the curse three time over, despite the utter impossibility that Eusebius could hear him.

He started pounding the rail of his ship with frustration. Already he could see the Malwa picket boat picking up the tempo of its oars. The *Victrix*'s advantage in combat lay entirely in a head-on attack, using its irresistible weapon protected within that heavy bow shield. From astern—and the clumsy jury-rigged paddle wheeler was no faster than an oared ship—the advantage would lie entirely with a vessel designed for boarding. Between the steam engine which drove it and the fire cannon in the bow, the *Victrix* was far too cramped to carry a large crew. And half of them were mechanics, not soldiers. Before the *Victrix* could reach the drifting barge and secure another cable, the Malwa picket boat would have overhauled it and overwhelmed the fireship's crew.

The only thing the *Victrix* had to fend off such an attack was the Puckle gun mounted in an armored shell atop the engine house. It was basically a large, long-barreled cap-and-ball revolver on a stand, which was operated by a two-man crew. All nine of its chambers could be fired in quick succession by a gunner turning a crank, whereupon the cylinder could be removed by the loader and replaced by another. It gave them the closest thing possible to a true machine gun, short of the heavy and unwieldy mitrailleuse assigned to the field artillery.

The Puckle gun was a handy little weapon, admittedly. But Menander had no illusions that it would be enough to drive off as many men as the Malwa had crammed into that picket boat.

The pilot of the *Justinian* came to Menander's side. Clearly enough, the man had reached the same conclusion. "What you get for trying to make a damned artisan a naval officer," he snarled. "He's just going to lose his own ship in the bargain."

Menander sighed. He took the time, before bowing to the inevitable, to regret once again that the mad rush in which Belisarius' change of strategy had thrown everything had left many projects unfinished in its wake. Among them had been the plans which he and Eusebius had begun to develop in Charax for designing an effective signaling system by which a fleet could be controlled by a single officer. Which would be *him*, not—not—*that damned artisan*!

As it happened, he and Eusebius had developed part of the system. The easy part. Signal flags hoisted in daylight. But those flags—all of them neatly arrayed in a nearby chest—would be useless in the middle of this dark night. They had never gotten as far as designing a system of lamp signals.

"Nothing for it," he growled. "If we turn back, we'll just be compounding the damage. Maintain course."

"Aye," said the pilot, nodding his approval. "Spoken like a navy man."

"Let's hope this works," muttered Eusebius. They had almost reached the stranded barge. He was standing just outside the bow shield, leaning over the rail in order to gauge the distance between the *Victrix* and the pursuing picket boat. Then, deciding the range was about right, he looked up at the fortress.

So far, the Malwa had maintained volley fire. Eusebius wasn't quite sure why they were doing so, since the undoubted advantage of volley fire on a battlefield was a moot point in this situation. He suspected that the Malwa commander was afraid that, working in the dark, crews left to their own pace might hurry the work and cause a disastrous accident.

Whatever the reason, he was glad of it. The maneuver he was about to try would leave the *Victrix* more or less stationary for a time. He was still far too close to the fortress to want to take that risk, until a volley had been fired. Thereafter, it would take the Malwa gunners long minutes to reload the huge guns. Long enough, Eusebius thought, to carry out his hastily conceived plan.

The dark outlines of the fortress were suddenly backlit by the enormous flash of the guns. The instant Eusebius saw the guns erupting, he leaned into the bow shield and shrilled at Calopodius: *"Now! Now!"* The words barely carried over the roar of the cannons.

As soon as he saw Calopodius begin pumping the lever which would fill the fire chamber, Eusebius leaned back over the rail to get a final look at the distance between the *Victrix* and her pursuer.

Started to, rather. He was almost knocked off his feet by a wave of water hammering over the rail. And then, almost pitched overboard as the *Victrix* began rolling wildly.

The Malwa volley had missed again. Just barely.

Sputtering and coughing, Eusebius began shrilling new orders. The helmsman, awaiting those orders, disengaged the gears to the left paddle wheel and then reengaged them in reverse. With the two paddle wheels now working in opposite directions, the *Victrix* shuddered to a halt and began—slowly, painfully—swinging back to face the oncoming picket boat.

The worst of it was the first half minute or so. Thereafter, the bow of the *Victrix* began turning more rapidly. As it swung around, Eusebius could see the picket boat begin frantically trying to turn itself.

"Too late, you bastards," he hissed. Then he plunged into the gloom of the bow shield and worked his way to the barrel of the fire cannon. The two-man crew in the shield had already positioned the barrel in the first slot which would come to bear on the picket ship. As Menander squeezed past Calopodius, the blind young Greek handed him the striker and said cheerfully: "Ready to go—but don't miss."

"Not likely," replied Eusebius, just as cheerfully. Looking through the slot, he could see that the picket boat had drifted inexorably within range. "Roast Malwa, coming up."

A moment later he turned the valve and lit the striker, and matched the deed to the word.

Looking back, watching the *Victrix* begin steaming upstream again with the lost barge once again secured, Menander heaved a sigh of relief.

The pilot had returned to his side. "God bless the old emperor!" he exclaimed. "If he hadn't designed these gears to work both ways . . ."

Menander nodded sagely. "There's something to be said for artisans, you know."

Shortly thereafter, Menander's superstition was confirmed. A cannon ball from the fortress' final volley, fired at extreme range, smashed into the barge's stern. Fortunately, the powder was not ignited—or the *Victrix* towing the barge would probably have been destroyed along with the barge itself. But within a minute, it became obvious that there was no hope of saving the vessel. Eusebius was just barely able to put the engines in reverse and reach the barge in time to save the crew before it sank. The cargo he had maneuvered so cleverly to salvage was a complete loss.

Chapter 39
INDIA
Autumn, 533 A.D.

As the great vessel which Eon had used for his flagship
sailed out of Chowpatty's harbor, Antonina and Ousanas
remained on the stern of the ship. That position gave them
the best possible view of the long, steep-sided promontory which overlooked the harbor. The fortress where Eon
had met his end was atop that promontory. Malabar Hill,
as the natives called it. And so was his tomb.

Antonina had thought the Ethiopians would want to
return Eon's body to Axum. But, leaving aside the
practical difficulties of transporting a corpse across an
ocean, the sarawit commanders—with Ousanas and
Ezana agreeing—had decided it would be more fitting
to bury him on Malabar Hill. So, like Alexander, Eon
would be laid to rest in the land he had conquered
rather than the land of his origins.

Conquered, yes, not simply occupied. At a great
ceremony three days earlier, Empress Shakuntala had
formally bestowed ownership of Chowpatty and the
immediate region surrounding it onto the kingdom of
Axum. That area would become a piece of Ethiopia

on Indian soil, an enclave where Axumite traders and merchants and factors could establish an anchor for the Erythrean trade which everyone expected to blossom after the war.

"It is only just and fitting," Shakuntala had told the crowd of Andhran and Maratha notables who had assembled in her palace for the ceremony. "Our debt to Axum is obvious. And I have a debt of my own to pay."

Then, for the first time to any Maratha except her husband, Shakuntala told the tale of how she first met the prince of Ethiopia, in the days when she was still a princess, and of the manner in which Eon had rescued her from Malwa captivity.

It was lively tale. The more so because the empress made no attempt, as she normally did in imperial audience, to restrain her own lively sense of humor. And if the tale bordered on salaciousness—Shakuntala depicted in lavish detail the episode where Eon kept her out of sight from Malwa soldiers searching his quarters by tossing the princess into his bed and pretending to mount her—himself, if not she, stark naked—none of the assembled notables reacted with anything but laughter. For all their obsession with ritual purity, Indians were not prudes. Anyone had but to walk a short distance from the palace to see a temple whose exterior carvings depicted—in even greater detail than the empress' story—copulations which were real and not simulated.

"I thought, once," she concluded, "that a day might come when I would marry Eon. For the sake of advancing Andhra's cause, of course. But the thought itself was not unpleasing to me."

Her little hand reached out and squeezed the large hand of her husband. Unusually, for such an affair,

Shakuntala had insisted that Rao stand by her side throughout the audience.

"Destiny decreed otherwise, and I am glad of it. But there will always remain a part of me which is still that young princess, sheltered from harm by the noblest prince in the world. And so, I think, it is fitting that Andhra should give Axum the dowry which would have come in a different turn of the wheel. I would not be here—none of us would be here—except for Eon bisi Dakuen."

She rose and stepped down from the throne, then presented it to Saizana, the commander of the Hadefan regiment, whom Ousanas had appointed the Axumite viceroy of the new territory.

Watching the feverish work of the Axumites and the Marathas they had hired atop Malabar Hill, Antonina began to laugh softly. Not satisfied with simply rebuilding those portions of the Malwa fortress which they had destroyed in the assault, the Ethiopians were dismantling it still further. Antonina had heard, from Ousanas himself, the plans which the Ethiopians had developed for the new great fortress they would build. A fortress within whose fastnesses the body of Eon was buried, and which they intended to serve as his monument.

"I was just remembering," she said, in response to Ousanas' quizzical expression, "the time Eon took me on a tour of the royal ruins at Axum. So sarcastic, you were, on the subject of royal aggrandizement congealed in stone."

She pointed to the fortress under construction. "And now—look! By the time you're finished, that thing will make any monument in Axum seem like a child's pile of pebbles."

Ousanas grinned. "Not the same thing at all, Antonina!" He clucked his tongue. "Women. Never

practical. That *thing* is not a monument of any kind.
True, it will be gigantic and grandiose and—between
us, in private—rather grotesque. But it is really a
fortress, Antonina. Living proof of Axum's real power,
not"—here, he waved his hand in a regal gesture of
dismissal—"some silly curio recalling a long-dead and
half-forgotten petty monarch."

Antonina stared at him, her eyebrows arched in a
skeptical curve.

"It is true! We Ethiopians are a practical folk, as all
men know. Very economical. We saw no reason to
waste all that space, and so why not use a small corner of it to serve double duty as a modest grave?
Rather than require some poor grave digger to do
unneeded and additional work?"

A very arched curve, those eyebrows made. "I have
seen a sketch of that 'modest grave,' Ousanas. Saizana
showed it to me, bragging fiercely all the while. He
told me, furthermore, that the design originally came
from none other than *you.* Some dawazz you turned
out to be!"

Ousanas' grin never wavered, never flinched. "True,
true. Actually, I got it from Belisarius. Long ago, during one of those evenings when he was passing along
Aide's secrets of the future to me. I've forgotten how
we got onto the subject. But we starting talking about
great conquerors of the future that would have been
and Aide wound up describing a monument which
rather caught my fancy. Mainly because it was perhaps
the most garish and tasteless one imaginable. And what
better, I ask you, for a nation to remind all skeptics that
what it did once it might still do again, if it is crossed?"

His grin was now positively serene. "Indeed, it
seemed fitting." He pointed to the gigantic fortress
under construction, within which a "modest grave" was
being placed. As if it were the heart of the thing.

"Napoleon's Tomb, that is. A replica of it. Except"—he spread his hands wide—"I decreed that it should be much bigger."

The expression on Antonina's face was still quizzical, but all traces of sarcasm had vanished. "That's the first time I've ever heard you say that," she murmured. " 'We Ethiopians.' "

Ousanas shrugged, a bit uncomfortably. "A man cannot be a hunter and a rover forever, it seems. Not even me."

Antonina nodded, very serenely. "I had come to the same conclusion."

"You're _thinking_ again," accused Ousanas, frowning worriedly. Then, when she made no attempt to deny the charge, the worry deepened.

"A demon," he muttered. "Same thing."

"Make way! Make way!" bellowed the Ye-tai officer trotting down the road which paralleled the Jamuna river. Here, in the Malwa heartland of the Ganges valley not far from the capital at Kausambi, the road was very wide and well-made. The small party of petty merchants hastily moved aside, barely managing to get the cart which held two sick men off the paved road and into the weeds before the Ye-tai soldiers who followed the officer stormed past.

The red and gold colors they were wearing, which matched those of the great banners streaming from their lances, indicated that these soldiers were part of the imperial troops which served the Malwa dynasty for an equivalent to the old Roman Praetorian Guard. And, as more and more soldiers thundered past the party of merchants—hundreds and hundreds of them—it became apparent that a very large portion of the elite unit was traveling down that road.

Mixed in with the soldiers were many Malwa officials,

of one sort or another. From the pained look on most of their faces, it was obvious that those splendidly garbed men were unaccustomed to riding a horse instead of traveling in a palanquin or howdah.

There were some exceptions, however. One of them was a very large and barrel-chested man, who apparently served as some kind of herald. He had a herald's ease in the saddle, and certainly had the voice for the job.

"Make way! Make way!" he boomed. *"Prostrate yourselves before the Great Lady Sati!"*

Seeing the enormous wagon which was lurching behind the soldiers, almost careening in the train of twenty horses drawing it, the merchants hastily prostrated themselves. No grudging formality, either. It was noticeable—had any bothered to notice, which none did—that all of the men, as well as the woman and even the children, kept their faces firmly planted to the soil. Not even daring so much as a peek, lest a haughty imperial dynast be offended in her passage by the sight of polluted faces.

The wagon flashed past, its gems and gold inlay and silk accouterments gleaming in the sunlight. It was followed by still more Malwa elite bodyguards. Hundreds and hundreds of them.

When the imperial expedition had finally gone, the merchants rose to their feet and began slapping off the dust of their passage. Despite the dust and the prospect of hard labor to haul the hand-drawn cart back onto the road, one of the merchants was grinning from ear to ear. On the man's narrow visage, the expression was far more predatory than one would have expected to see on the face of such a man.

"I'd say all hell has broken loose," he announced cheerfully. "Imagine that! The Great Lady Sati herself, racing toward the Punjab. As if some disaster were taking place. Dear me, I wonder what it could be?"

"Shut up," growled his enormous companion. "And will you *please* wipe that grin off your face. You look like a weasel in a henhouse. *Merchants*, we're supposed to be, and piss-poor ones at that."

The faces of the unarmed Malwa soldiers who marched out of the fortress in the Khyber Pass were not grinning. Although a few of them, obeying ancient instinct, did attempt to smile at the Kushan troops who were accepting their surrender, in that sickly manner in which men try to appease their masters.

"Look at 'em," snorted Vima. "Like a bunch of puppies, flat on their backs and waving their little paws in the air. *Please don't hurt me.*"

"Enough of that," commanded Kungas. His mask of a face was just that—an iron mask. Even the men who surrounded him, who had come to know the man well in the months of their great march of conquest, could not detect a trace of humor lurking beneath.

He turned his head and gazed upon them, his eyes like two pieces of amber. "There will be no cruelties inflicted on those men. No disrespect, even. Such was my word, given to their commander. And that word—the word of King Kungas—must become as certain in these mountains as the stones themselves. Or the avalanche which buries the unwary. Do you understand?"

All of his commanders bowed their heads. The obedience was instant, total. Nor was it brought by any idle humor concerning a queen in Begram, weaving her cunning webs. The king himself was enough to command that allegiance. More than enough, after the months which had passed.

King Kungas he was, and did no man doubt it. Not

Malwa, not Persian, not Pathan—not Kushan. The mask, which a man had once made of his face to conceal the man himself, was no longer a mask at all. Not of the king, at least, whatever warmth might remain in the man's heart.

"See to their well-being," the king of the Kushans commanded. "Set them to work building the new fortifications, but do not allow the labor to cripple or exhaust them. See that they are fed well enough. Some wine, on days they have done well."

He did not have to add the words: *obey me*. Such an addendum would have been quite pointless.

Toramana first caught sight of his bride-to-be when the girl and her entourage came into the palace where Lord Damodara made his headquarters. It was a different palace than the one which Venandakatra had inhabited. That palace had been designated as the residence of the Goptri, not the military commander of the Malwa forces in the Deccan. Lord Damodara, as all men knew, was not given to self-aggrandizement. He would not presume to inhabit the Goptri's palace without the emperor's permission.

On the morrow, as it happened, he would be moving into the palace. Nanda Lal had arrived three days before the Rajputs bringing Toramana's bride, as an official envoy from the emperor. Skandagupta had decided to bestow the title of Goptri upon Damodara, in recognition of his great services to the dynasty.

Toramana was pleased by the sight of the girl's face, as any groom would be seeing such a face on his bride. Nanda Lal, standing next to him, leaned over and whispered in his ear.

"I had heard Indira was comely. My congratulations."

Solemnly, Toramana nodded. His face, composed as faces should be at formal ceremonies, indicated nothing of his amusement at Nanda Lal's words. The spymaster had quite mistaken the source of his pleasure.

For the most part, at least. True, some portion of Toramana was delighted with the girl's face. But the real source of his pleasure lay in the simple fact that the face was exposed at all. Most Rajput women, at such an event, would have been wearing a veil. The fact that his bride-to-be did not told him two things. First, she was spirited, just as Rana Sanga had depicted his half-sister. Second, she saw no need to hide herself behind a disguise.

Which, since Toramana himself thought a disguise generally defeated its own purpose, boded well for the future. He had high hopes for the girl moving slowly through the palace, exchanging greetings with her Rajput kinsmen as she made her way toward Rana Sanga. Even more as a wife than a bride.

Indira had now reached her half-brother. From the distance where he was standing, Toramana could not hear the words which passed between them. But he had little doubt, from the anguish so evident on both faces, of the subject they were discussing.

"Such a tragedy," murmured Nanda Lal. "His entire family, you know."

Toramana cocked his head slightly. "Was it truly just a band of brigands? You conducted the investigation yourself, I understand."

Nanda Lal's thick lips tightened. "Yes, I did. A horrible scene. Fortunately, the bodies were so badly burned that I could, in good conscience, tell Rana Sanga that there had been no signs of torture or abuse. That much relief, at least, I was able to give him."

The Malwa empire's chief spymaster sighed heavily. "Just bandits, Toramana. A particularly bold and daring group, to be sure. Kushans, according to the few surviving eyewitnesses. By now, I'm sorry to say, the monsters have undoubtedly found refuge with the other Kushan brigands in the Hindu Kush."

Nanda Lal's lips were very thin, now. "Brigands, no more. Remember that, Toramana. All who oppose Malwa are but brigands. Which we will deal with soon enough, have no doubt of it."

Both men fell silent, watching the Rajput king leading his half-sister out of the audience chamber toward his own quarters in the palace. When all the Rajputs in the chamber were gone, Nanda Lal leaned over and whispered again.

"My best wishes on your marriage, Toramana. The emperor asked me to pass along his own, as well. We are quite sure, should it ever prove necessary, that you will do whatever is needed to protect Malwa from its enemies. *All* of its enemies, whomever they might be."

Again, Toramana nodded solemnly. "You may be sure of it, Lord. I am not given to subterfuge and disguise."

Late that night, Narses was summoned to the private chambers of Rana Sanga. The eunuch obeyed the summons, of course, though not with any pleasure. It was not that he objected to the lateness of the hour. Narses was usually awake through half the night. It was simply that the old intriguer hated to be surprised by anything, and he could think of no logical reason why the Rajput king would wish to see him.

Narses moved furtively through the dark corridors of the palace. That was simply old habit, more than anything else. Narses was not in the least bit worried of being overseen by Nanda Lal's spies. Here, in his own territory, Narses' webs of intrigue and espionage were far superior to those of the Malwa spymaster.

Very rarely, in times past, had Rana Sanga spoken to Narses at all, except in the presence of Lord Damodara. And those occasions had been in daytime, in military headquarters, while on campaign. To summon him for a private audience in his own chambers . . .

After Narses entered the Rajput king's quarters, a servant led him to the private audience room and then departed. Courteously, his face showing nothing of the grief and rage which must have lain beneath, Rana Sanga invited him to sit. The Rajput was even courteous enough to offer the Roman a chair, knowing that the old eunuch's bones did not adjust well to the Indian custom of sitting cross-legged on cushions.

After taking his own seat on some cushions nearby, Rana Sanga leaned over and spoke softly. "The news of my family's murder has caused me to ponder great questions of philosophy, Narses. Especially the relationship of truth to illusion. That is why I requested your presence. I thought you might be of assistance to me, in my hour of sorrow. My hour of great need."

Narses frowned. "I'm not even conversant with Greek philosophy, Rana Sanga, much less Hindu. Something to do with what you call *Maya*, the 'veil of illusion,' as I understand it. Don't see what help I could be."

The Rajput nodded. "So I understand. But I was not intending to ask your help with such profound questions, Narses. I had something much simpler in mind. The nature of onions, to be precise."

"Onions?" Narses' wrinkled face was deeply creased with puzzlement. The expression made him look even more reptilian than usual. "*Onions?*"

"Onions." Sanga leaned over and picked up a thick sheaf of documents lying next to him. He held them up before Narses and waggled them a bit. "This is the official report of the ambush and killing of my family. Nanda Lal, as you may know, oversaw the investigation himself."

The Rajput king laid the mass of documents on the carpet before him. "It is a very thorough and complete report, as you would expect from Nanda Lal and his top investigators. Exhaustive, actually. No detail was left unmentioned, except the precise nature of the wounds, insofar as they could be determined."

For a moment, his face grew pinched. "I imagine those details exist in a separate addendum, which Nanda Lal thought it would be more merciful not to include in this copy of the report. As if"—almost snarling, here—"I would not understand the inevitable fate of my wife and children in the hands of such creatures."

The Rajput straightened his back. For all that he was sitting on cushions, and Narses on a chair, he seemed to tower over the old eunuch. "But there is one small detail which puzzles me. And I have now studied this report carefully, reading it from beginning to end over and over again. It involves onions."

Seeing Narses' face—*onions?*—Rana Sanga managed a smile. "You see, included in Nanda Lal's report is a detailed—exhaustive—list of every thing which was found. Among those items was the remains of a small chest which my wife always used to carry her cooking materials. Nothing fancy, that chest. No reason for bandits to steal the thing, so they didn't."

Narses was completely lost. A state of affairs which infuriated him. But he continued to listen to Sanga with no hint of protest, allowing no sign of his anger to show. He was no fool, was Narses. And he realized—though he had no idea from whence it was coming—that a terrible peril was looming over him. Like a tidal wave about to break over a blind man.

"Nor would bandits bother to steal anything *in* that chest, Narses. Except, perhaps, the small packets of herbs and spices. Those might be of some value to them, I suppose. But, for the most part, that chest contained onions. My wife was very fond of using onions in her cooking."

Sanga glanced at the documents. "Apparently, judging from the charred remains, the bandits looted the onions also. Nanda Lal's report was so exhaustive that they measured the ashes and charred pieces which remained. There is no mention of onions. Which would not have burned up completely, after all. And something else is missing which should not have been missing at all, for it couldn't have burned—the knife which my wife always used to cut onions."

"Bandits," husked Narses. "They'll steal anything."

Rana Sanga shook his head. "I think I know more about the bandits of mountain and desert than you do, Narses. They're not likely to steal onions, much less a simple knife. The one thing such men—and their women—do *not* lack are blades. If they did, they couldn't be bandits in the first place."

The Rajput king placed his large and powerful hand atop the documents. "It is not there, Narses. Nanda Lal and his men could not have possibly overlooked it, in the course of such a thorough report. The knife was a small and simple one, to be sure, but not that small—and very sturdy. The blade would have survived the fire, at the very least. The thing was made by a Rajput peasant as a gift to my wife on her wedding. She adored it, despite its simplicity. Refused, time after time, to allow me to replace it with a finer one." He took a deep breath, as if controlling grief. "She always said that knife—that knife alone—enabled her to laugh at onions."

Seeing the stiffness of Narses' posture—the old eunuch looked, for all the water, as if he were carved from stone—Sanga emitted a dry chuckle. "Oh, to be sure, Nanda Lal himself would never have noticed the absence of onions or the knife. How could he or his spies know anything of that? The thing was just a private joke between my wife and me. To everyone else, even our own servants, it was just one of many knives in the kitchen."

"Undoubtedly, he failed to notice its absence." Narses' words were not so much husked, as croaked. "Undoubtedly." As a frog might pray for deliverance.

"Undoubtedly," said Sanga firmly. "Nor did I see any reason to raise the matter with him, of course. What would such a great spymaster and dynast as Nanda Lal know about onions, and the knives used to cut them?"

"Nothing," croaked Narses.

"Indeed." And now, for the first time, the severe control left Rana Sanga's face. His eyes, staring at Narses, were like dark pools of sheer agony, begging for relief.

Narses rubbed his face with a hand. "I am sworn to tell nothing but the truth, king of Rajputana. Even to such as Great Lady Sati. *As you know.*"

Sanga nodded deeply. The gesture reminded Narses of a man placing his neck on a headsman's block. "Give me illusion, then," he whispered, "if you cannot give me the truth."

Abruptly, Narses rose. "I can do neither, Rana Sanga. I know nothing of philosophy. Nothing of onions or the knives needed to cut them. Send for your servant, please, to show me the way out of these chambers."

Sanga's head was still bent. "Please," he whispered. "I feel as if I am dying."

"Nothing," insisted Narses. "Nothing which cannot bear the scrutiny of the world's greatest ferret for the truth. *Great Lady Sati*, Rana Sanga."

"Please." The whisper could barely be heard.

Narses turned his head to the door, scowling. "Where *is* that servant? I can assure you, king of

Rajputana, that I would not tolerate such slackness in my own. My problem, as a matter of fact, is the exact opposite. I am plagued with servants who are given to excess. Especially sentimentality. One of them, in particular. I shall have very harsh words to say to him, I can assure you, when next I see the fellow."

And with those words, Narses left the chamber. He found his way through Sanga's quarters easily enough. Indeed, it might be said he passed through them like an old antelope, fleeing a tiger.

Behind, in the chamber, Sanga slowly raised his head. Had there been anyone to see, they would have said the dark eyes were glowing. With growing relief—and fury—more than ebbing fear. As if a tiger, thinking himself caught in a cage, had discovered the trapper had been so careless as to leave it unlocked.

A state of affairs which, as all men know, does not bode well for the trapper.

Chapter 40
THE PUNJAB
Autumn, 533 A.D.

Despite the protests of his officers and bodyguards, Belisarius insisted on remaining in one of the bastions when the Malwa launched their mass assault on his fortifications. His plans for the coming siege were based very heavily on his assessment of the effectiveness of the mitrailleuse, and this would be the first time the weapons had ever been tested under combat conditions. He wanted to see them in action himself.

Blocking out of his mind the noise of mortar and artillery fire, as well as the sharper sounds of Felix's sharpshooters picking off Malwa grenadiers, Belisarius concentrated all his attention on watching the mitrailleuse crew working the weapon in the retired flank he was crouched within.

The mitrailleuse—the "Montigny mitrailleuse," to give the device its proper name—was the simplest possible form of machine gun except for the "organ gun" originally designed by Leonardo da Vinci. Like the organ gun, the mitrailleuse used fixed instead of rotating barrels. But, unlike its more primitive ancestor, the breech-loading mitrailleuse could be fired in sequence instead of in a single volley, and fire many more rounds in any given period of time.

Belisarius watched as the gun crew inserted another plate into the breech and slammed it into place with a locking lever. The plate held thirty-seven papier-mâché cartridges, which slid into the corresponding thirty-seven barrels of the weapon. A moment later, turning a crank, one of the men began triggering off the rounds while another—using the crude device of a wooden block to protect his hands from the hot jacket—tapped the barrel to traverse the Malwa soldiery piled up in the ditch below the curtain wall.

Belisarius had wanted a more advanced type of machine gun, preferably something based on the Gatling gun design which Aide had shown him and which he had detailed for John of Rhodes. But all the experiments of John's artificers with rotating barrels—much less belt-designed weapons like the Maxim gun—had foundered on a single problem.

Roman technology was good enough to make the weapons. Not many, perhaps, but enough. The problem was the ammunition. Rotating barrel and belt-fed designs all depended on uniform and sturdy brass cartridges. John's artificers could make such cartridges, but not in sufficient quantity. As had proven so often the case, designs which could be transformed into material reality in small numbers simply couldn't be done on a mass production scale.

The sixth-century Roman technical base was just too narrow. They lacked the tools to make the tools to make the tools, just as they lacked the artisans who could have used them properly even if they existed. That was a reality which could not be overcome in a few years, regardless of Aide's encyclopedic knowledge.

Since there was no point in having a "machine gun"

which ran out of ammunition within minutes on a battlefield, Belisarius had opted for the Montigny design. The small number of brass cartridges which could be produced would be reserved for the special use of the Puckle guns mounted on river boats. The mitrailleuse, because it used a plate where all thirty-seven cartridges were fixed in position, did not require drawn brass for the cartridges. Rome *did* have plenty of cheap labor, especially in teeming Alexandria. The simple plate-and-papier-mâché units could be mass produced easily enough, providing the mitrailleuse with the large quantities of ammunition which were necessary for major field battles.

It was a somewhat cumbersome weapon, but, as he watched it in operation, Belisarius was satisfied that it would serve the purpose. The two mitrailleuse which were raking the Malwa along the curtain wall—one firing from each opposed retired flank of two adjacent bastions—were wreaking havoc in the closely packed and unprotected troops. Combined with the grenades being lobbed by soldiers on the curtain wall, and the grapeshot being fired by field guns positioned in the sharply raked angle of the bastions themselves, the water in the ditch where hundreds of Malwa soldiers were already lying dead or wounded had become a moat of blood.

Satisfied by that aspect of the battle, Belisarius began studying the sharpshooters at work. There were a dozen such men positioned in each bastion, whose principal responsibility was to target those Malwa soldiers carrying grenades or satchel charges. Or, possibly—although Belisarius had so far seen no indication of such a weapon in use—attempting to use a Malwa version of the flamethrower which John of Rhodes had designed for the *Victrix*.

He didn't envy the sharpshooters their task. The crude design of the breech-loading rifles—again, a result of the severe shortage of brass cartridges, which required a rifle which could fire a linen cartridge—produced a certain amount of leakage blowing upward around the breech block. Every sharpshooter soon acquired a blackened face and a few powderburns on his forehead.

The other drawback to being a sharpshooter, naturally, was that the man was singled out by the enemy for special attention. As Belisarius watched, one of the sharpshooters on the bastion wall was suddenly slammed backward, sprawling dead on the bastion's fighting surface. His face was a pulped mass of flesh and blood, with brains leaking from a shattered skull. The horrible wounds looked to have been inflicted by several musket balls striking at once.

Felix cursed bitterly. "Those damned organ guns! I hadn't counted on those. Not so many of them, at any rate."

Ignoring the murmured protests of his bodyguards Isaac and Priscus, Belisarius crawled over to the inner side of the bastion and propped his periscope over the wall. Within seconds, he was able to spot what he was looking for.

The Malwa, sensibly enough given their numerical advantage over the Romans, had opted for organ guns rather than mitrailleuse. The organ guns were even cruder in design—about the most primitive conceivable quick-firing gunpowder weapon—but they had the great advantage of being easy to produce in quantity, using the skills and material available. The Malwa had an even narrower technical base than the Romans.

An organ gun looked like a wheelbarrow more than anything else, with a dozen barrels laid side by side in a row across the equivalent of the bucket. Except that it used two wheels instead of one, like a rickshaw Aide had shown him. They were muzzle-loaders, and so required some time to reload. But they could be easily moved into position manually, with only a two-man crew, and were surprisingly easy to aim. The recoil was small enough that an experienced organ gun handler could aim simply by using the two wooden handles—even adjust the elevation of the weapon by the simple expedient of rolling it up or down on the big wheels which held up the barrels.

And the Malwa had a *lot* of them. Just in the area Belisarius could sweep easily with his periscope, he counted no fewer than seventeen. The organ guns were positioned about a hundred yards away from the bastions, providing covering fire for the troops trying to storm the walls.

He glanced again through the gun ports in the retired flanks of the bastion. Then, satisfied that the mitrailleuse and grenades were enough to hold off the Malwa soldiers trying to scale the curtain walls, he turned to Gregory and ordered:

"Tell all the three-pounder crews to start firing on the organ guns instead of providing extra coverage for the curtain wall. With grape shot, at this close range, they ought to pulverize them soon enough. The one big disadvantage of those weapons is that they pretty much *have* to be aimed and fired by men standing in the open."

Gregory nodded. A moment later, he was clambering down the ladder which provided access to the bastion's fighting platform. Below, in a shielded bunker, a telegraph operator was waiting to transmit orders to every part of the outlying fortifications. And to the inner fortifications, for that matter, since one of the first things Belisarius had had his combat engineers do was lay telegraph wire to every key location in the triangle.

One of those locations was not more than half a mile away: the nearest of the fortified camps where Sittas and his thousands of cataphracts lay waiting for the order to sally. Belisarius had seen enough of the battle from the vantage point of the bastion. It was time he returned to his communication center. The sun was beginning to set in any event.

As he made his way to the ladder, he ignored the sighs of relief loudly—even histrionically—issued by his bodyguards. He also ignored the crystalline equivalent which Aide was rattling around in his brain. He even managed to ignore Maurice's first few words when he entered the telegraph bunker.

"Finally decided to stop playing junior scout, did we?" To Isaac and Priscus, shouldering their way behind him through the narrow entrance to the bunker: "You *did* manage to keep the damn fool from actually dancing on the wall, didn't you?"

The essentials having been taken care of, Maurice moved immediately to the necessities. "It's just about time to order Sittas out," he growled. "At daybreak, tomorrow. Every fortress is now reporting the same thing: the Malwa have been beaten off the walls, and are starting to trickle through the gaps. You could call it a 'flanking maneuver,' if you wanted. Except that I doubt any high-ranked officer ordered it."

Belisarius shook his head. "I saw the butcher's bill they've been paying at the walls, Maurice. Those soldiers have had enough. They're just trying to get out of the line of fire without actually retreating."

He stared down at the map spread across a table. The map showed the location of every one of the outlying forts, as well as the camps where Sittas and his armored cavalry were lying in wait. Like tigers, ready to spring from ambush. The outer lines had been designed for that purpose. In effect, they channeled the Malwa troops away from the fortresses into four areas which were tailor-made for cataphract tactics. The most solid ground in the area, cleared of obstructions, with nowhere to take cover.

"Give the order," he said. "Tomorrow morning, let's finish this."

The biggest problem Menander faced as they neared the fork of the Chenab was restraining himself from engaging enemy forces on shore in a series of pointless gun duels. During the daytime, Malwa dragoons were constantly peppering the Roman flotilla as it made its way upriver. Menander was keeping the *Justinian* and its barges as far from the west bank as possible, while still avoiding the danger of hidden sandbars. But even at that range, a number of the Malwa shots struck his ship. The Roman vessel, with its heavy load of barges, was moving very slowly. It was for all practical purposes a stationary target.

Granted, the shots were more in the way of a nuisance than an actual danger. Especially since, so far as Menander could determine, the Malwa were firing simple muskets instead of the equivalent of the Sharps breech-loading rifle with which Belisarius had equipped his own dragoons.

Justinian had designed his namesake to fight pitched battles at sea, with little concern for speed. Something which John of Rhodes, in times past, had criticized sourly—though not within earshot of the former emperor. Like most naval men, John had prized speed and maneuverability over all else. But, as things had turned out, Justinian's decision was working to Roman advantage. Speed and maneuverability were not as important as sheer strength of armor and firepower in the close and cramped quarters of river battles. And while the only iron armor on Menander's warship was the plating which protected the pilot house and the Puckle guns, the *Justinian* was what later ages would call a "wood-clad"—a ship whose hull was so thick that most round shot could not penetrate, much less musket fire. Moreover, it was heavy and sturdy enough to carry heavy guns which could overpower any kind of easily maneuvered land-based field artillery. So the Malwa dragoons posed no real threat at all.

Still . . . it was *annoying*!

But, he restrained himself. The dragoons made poor targets anyway, and gunpowder was too precious to waste on volleys fired out of temper rather than necessity, the more so now that the barge which carried most of the powder had been sunk.

Still . . . it was *so* annoying!

Only once did he fire a broadside. That was on an occasion where the *Justinian's* engine had to be shut down for repairs. Eusebius and the *Victrix*—whose own engine, for whatever reason, was proving a lot more reliable than the *Justinian's*—attached themselves to Menander's warship with a cable. The paddle wheeler was not powerful enough to tow the entire flotilla on its own, but it could keep the Roman ships from drifting downstream out of control.

The delay gave the Malwa enough time to bring up a small battery of three-pounders, five in all, which they began positioning on a small promontory within range of the Roman flotilla. Alas, the promontory was *also* within range of the *Justinian's* much heavier guns. Eusebius had to tow the bow of Menander's warship around in order to bring the guns to bear. But, thereafter, two broadsides with Menander's thirty-two-pounder carronades were enough to destroy the little field guns and send the surviving Malwa artillerymen scampering for cover.

There had been one night engagement, when a Malwa river boat packed with marines approached from behind and tried to seize the last barge in the train. But the Romans had been alert for such a maneuver, and the men on the barge sent up a signal flare. Eusebius turned the paddle wheeler around—the *Victrix* was steaming at the head of the flotilla, as usual—and charged back downriver.

Fortunately, the Malwa boat was a sailing craft hastily refitted with oars, not an actual war galley. So its own progress upriver was slow. Not as slow as the heavy barges being towed by the *Justinian*, of course, but slow enough that Eusebius had time to come to the rescue before the enemy ship had gotten so close to the barge that the fire cannon couldn't be used.

One gout of flame from that fearsome weapon was all it took to end the engagement. Those Malwa who survived the initial holocaust dove overboard and swam for shore. The others died the peculiarly horrible death which that weapon produced.

By now, Eusebius was a hardened veteran. So he blithely ignored the screams rippling across the dark water and steamed back to his assigned position at the head of the flotilla. As he passed the *Justinian*, he spotted Menander standing on the deck and gave him a jaunty wave.

And why not? Eusebius, the former artisan, had learned enough of military strategy and tactics by now to understand a simple truth. "Simple," at least, to him—though he would have been amazed to discover how many prestigious military leaders understood it very poorly. But perhaps that was because, as an artisan, Eusebius had an instinctive grasp of the reality of *momentum* and its effects.

Mass, multiplied by *speed*. The second factor, if large enough, could offset a small mass. A bullet, after all, is not very heavy. But it can create even more damage to soft tissue than a ponderous sword.

Belisarius, by taking a relatively small force of men

and striking so swiftly into the Punjab, had shattered
the Malwa plans for grinding the Roman advance to
a bloody stalemate in the Sind. Like a bullet piercing
the soft vitals, tumbling through flesh leaving a trail
of wreck and ruin, Belisarius had effectively disembow-
eled the enemy.

The Malwa who faced him had larger forces—and
would, even after Bouzes and Coutzes arrived at
Sukkur—but those forces were like so many vital organs
spilled on the ground. One army here, another there,
yet another stranded over there . . . none of them able
to coordinate properly, and none of them with what
they needed to put up an effective resistance.

As he gazed serenely over the landscape—which was
perhaps a useless exercise, since on a moonless night
he could see almost nothing—Eusebius basked in his
invincibility. One of the many Malwa vital organs which
Belisarius had spilled on the floor of the arena was their
control of the Indus.

The Malwa had not expected to be contesting the
Indus at all, until Belisarius destroyed their army at
Charax. Then, realizing that they were now on the
defensive, they had begun a belated program of shipbuilding.

But—too late, after Belisarius struck at the Punjab.
Too late, in any event, to provide them this year with
armored and steam-powered warships which could
contest the Indus with such craft as the *Justinian* and
the *Victrix*.

Next year might be different. Eusebius knew that
the Malwa were creating a major shipbuilding complex
near Multan, the city which the enemy had turned into
their military headquarters for the Punjab. According
to spies, the Malwa were starting to build their own
steam-powered riverboats—and these would apparently
be ironclads. Once those warships came into action,

Menander's two screw-driven warships and the *Victrix* would be hard-pressed.

But—that was still many months away. And by then, Eusebius was certain, Belisarius would have figured out a way to stymie the Malwa again.

How? He had no idea. But he was serene in his confidence in his great commander. And so, as the *Victrix* paddled its slow way up the Indus, still more was added to its *momentum*. For that, too, the former artisan Eusebius had come to understand about warfare. The tide of victory was flowing with the Romans, as much because of their own confidence as the weight of men and material they brought with them.

The next morning, just after daybreak, Eusebius spotted a Malwa warship under construction tied up to a small pier along the river bank. The effort had all the earmarks of a last-minute, jury-rigged project. From what he could see of the half-completed ship, the Malwa had taken a small oar-powered river barge and were attempting to armor it with iron plate and place a handful of field guns aboard.

A pitiful thing, really, even had it been completed.

But, pitiful or not, no lion allows a jackal to contest its domain. So, after a quick exchange of signals with Menander—the flags were working quite well—Eusebius paddled over to put paid to *that* upstart nonsense.

Before he got there, the Malwa managed to wrestle around one of the field guns and fire two shots at the *Victrix*. One shot missed entirely. The second struck the heavy bow shield a glancing blow which did no worse than loosen a few bolts and scatter some chips of wood into the river.

Thereafter, the enemy gunners ceased their efforts and scampered hurriedly off the half-finished little warship. Which, within a few minutes, made a splendid bonfire to warm Roman souls as they continued chugging up the river toward Belisarius.

They were not far away now, if Menander was reading the skimpy charts correctly. (Charts which had become very far from skimpy as they made their way upriver. Future expeditions would not have to guess and grope their way through hidden sandbars.) And Eusebius had no doubt at all that the great uncertainty in the equation—had Belisarius reached the fork of the Chenab and seized it?—was no longer uncertain at all. Everything about the Malwa behavior that he could see practically shrieked panic and confusion.

Which, of course, is what you expect from a pack of jackals after a lion enters their lair.

Chapter 41

Whatever else could be said of Sittas, he was the most aggressive cavalry commander Belisarius had ever known. As soon as the order was given, not long after daybreak, the Greek nobleman led all eight thousand of his cataphracts in a charge out of the four camps in which they had been waiting. In four columns, the heavily armored horsemen smashed into twice that number of Malwa soldiers who had piled up in the areas between the fortresses during the preceding day and night.

Despite the disparity in numbers, the battle was really no contest. The Malwa were confused and disorganized. More often than not, their soldiers were no longer part of coherent and organized units. Nothing but individuals, in many cases, who had sought shelter from the bloodbath beneath the fortress walls.

Their shelter lasted no longer than the darkness of night. With dawn, the cataphracts turned it into yet another holocaust. Well-led, properly organized and coordinated volley fire—with the musketeers braced by pikemen—could stave off any cavalry assault. But a huge mass of infantrymen out of formation, even when many of them were armed with guns and grenades, could not possibly stand up to the weight of a heavy cavalry charge.

The more so when that charge was made by *cataphracts*. The Roman armored horsemen bore no resemblance at all to the sloppy hordes which a later medieval world would call "cavalry." They were highly disciplined, fought in formation, and obeyed orders. Orders which were transmitted to them by officers—Sittas most of all—who, for all their occasional vainglory, were as cold-blooded and ruthless as any commanders in history.

Although the cataphracts emerged from the camps at a gallop, in order to cross the distance to the enemy as soon as possible, the charge never once threatened to careen out of control. As soon as the cornicenes blew the order, the cataphracts reined their mounts to a halt and drew their bows. Then, firing volley after volley from serried ranks, they shredded whatever initial formations the Malwa officers had hastily improvised.

At close range—a hundred yards or less—cataphract arrows struck with as much force, and far greater accuracy, than musket balls. And even Roman cataphracts, though not such quick archers as their Persian dehgan counterparts, could easily maintain a rate of fire which was better than any musketeers of the time.

A better rate of fire, in truth, than even Roman sharpshooters could have managed, using single-shot breech-loading rifles. The drawback to the bow as a weapon of war had never been its inferiority to the gun, after all—not, at least, until firearms developed a far greater sophistication than anything available until the nineteenth century. In the hands of a skilled archer, a bow could be fired faster and more accurately than a musket, much less an arquebus. Nor, in the case of the hundred-pound-pull bows favored by cataphracts, with anything less in the way of penetrating power.

The real advantage to the gun was simply its ease

of use. A competent musketeer could be trained in weeks; a skilled archer required years—a lifetime, in truth, raised in an archer's culture. Moreover, powerful bows required far more in the way of muscle power than guns. Only men conditioned to the use of the weapons for years could manage to keep firing a bow for the hours needed to win a battle. The wear which a musket placed on its user was nothing in comparison.

And so, the bow was doomed. But in the conditions which prevailed on *that* battlefield, on *that* day, the bow enjoyed one of its last great triumphs. Within minutes, whatever might have existed of a Malwa "front line" resembled nothing so much as a tattered and shredded piece of cloth.

That done, the cornicenes blew again. The cataphracts put away their bows and took up their lances. Then, cantering forward in tight formation, they simply rolled over the thousands of Malwa soldiers who were now trying to scramble out of the way.

Within a few more minutes, the scramble turned into a precipitous rout. The cornicenes blew again, and the cataphracts took up their long Persian-style sabers. And then, in the hour which followed, turned the rout into a massacre. As always, infantry fleeing in panic from cavalry were like antelopes pursued by lions—except *these* lions, seeking victory rather than food, were not satisfied with a single prey. They did not give up the pursuit until the open terrain between the fortresses was almost as red with blood as the moats which surrounded them. In their wake, thousands of enemy bodies lay strewn across the landscape.

When the cornicenes blew again, sounding the recall, the cataphracts trotted back to their camps. Full of fierce satisfaction, and arguing among themselves over what proper name to use to label yet another battlefield triumph.

In the end, although the town itself was no longer within Belisarius' line of outer fortifications, they settled on the name of *Sitpur*. Perhaps because the name was short, and had a nice little ring to it. More likely, because the cataphracts had become rather fond of the chowpatti which had been baked there, and which gave them their strength. Even Maurice was now claiming to have developed a taste for the foreign bread.

"The Battle of Sitpur!" roared Sittas triumphantly, as he strode into Belisarius' new command post many miles to the south. "You can add that one to your list, O mighty Belisarius!"

Belisarius smiled. Then, so infectious was Sittas' enthusiasm, grinned outright. "Has a nice sound, doesn't it?"

"Yes, it does," proclaimed Sittas. The words came out in a bit of a mumble, because the cataphract general was already stuffing himself from the pile of chowpatti on a small table just inside the bunker entrance. "Great stuff," he mumbled.

"Any problems?" asked Maurice. Like Belisarius himself, Maurice had retreated to the inner line of fortifications as soon as the charge began. Neither one of them had expected Sittas to fail, and they had the next stage of the siege to plan.

"Not much," mumbled Sittas, waving what was left of the chowpatti. An instant later, that fragment joined its fellows in his maw. Once he finished swallowing, Sittas was able to speak more coherently.

"Only real problem was the organ guns. A few places, here and there, they managed to put together a little line of them. Firing at once, that makes for a pretty ferocious volley. Killed and injured probably more of my men than everything else put together."

Despite the grim words, Sittas was still exuding good cheer. Which became still cheerier with the next words, which were downright savage:

"Of course, that ended soon enough. Once my cataphracts made clear that there'd be no quarter given to organ gun crews, the rest of them left the damned gadgets lying where they were and scampered off with all the others. Tried to, at least."

Belisarius started to speak, but Sittas waved him silent. "Oh, do be still! Yes, we took as many prisoners as possible. We're already starting to shepherd the sorry bastards to the south. Tame as sheep, they are. You'll have plenty more men to add to your labor gangs. At least five thousand, I'd say."

Belisarius nodded. Then, resuming his study of the map which depicted the complex details of his inner line of fortifications, he said: "We'll need them. The civilians need a rest, as hard as they've been working. So do the prisoners we took earlier."

Sittas laughed. "From what I've been told, those civilians of yours will need as many guards to keep them *from* working as you need to keep the prisoners at it."

Maurice echoed the laugh. "Not far from the truth, that. Once they sized up the new situation, the Malwa civilians—"

"*Punjabis*," interrupted Belisarius forcefully. "It's a war of liberation now, Maurice. Those people are *Punjabi*—not Malwa."

Maurice nodded cheerfully, accepting the correction without quarrel. "Punjabis, right. Anyway, once they saw what was happening, they became the fiercest Belisarius loyalists you could ask for. Their necks are on the chopping block along with ours, and they know it perfectly well—and know the Malwa ax better than we do."

"What about the prisoners?" asked Sittas. The casual way in which he reached for another chowpatti suggested he was not too concerned with the answer. "Any trouble there?"

Gregory shrugged. "Since Abbu and his scouts aren't much use in the siege warfare we're starting, the general put them to work guarding the Malwa prisoners."

Sittas choked humor, spitting pieces of chowpatti across the table. "Ha! Not much chance of any prisoner rebellion, then. Not with bedouin watching them!"

For all the cruel truth which lurked beneath those words, Belisarius couldn't help but smile. Abbu and his Arabs had made as clear as possible to the Malwa under their guard that the penalty for rebellion—even insubordination—would be swift and sure. As much as anything, Abbu had explained to their officers, because bedouin hated to do any work beyond fighting and trading.

Far easier to behead a man than to do his work for him, after all. A point which the old man had demonstrated by beheading, on the spot, the one Malwa officer who had raised a protest.

Thereafter, the Malwa prisoners had set to work with a will—and none more so than the officers who commanded them. Abbu had also explained that he was a firm believer in the chain of command. Far easier to behead a single officer, after all, than twenty men in his charge. A point which the old man had demonstrated by beheading, the next day, the Malwa officer whose unit had done a pitiful day's work.

Under other circumstances, Belisarius might have restrained Abbu's ferocious methods. But siege warfare was the grimmest and cruelest sort of war, and now that he had put the arch stone of his entire daring campaign into place, he would take no chances of seeing it slip. So long as Belisarius could hold the area within the fork of the Indus and the Chenab—the "Iron Triangle," as his men were beginning to call it—the Malwa would have no choice but to retreat from the Sind entirely. Belisarius would be in the best possible position to launch another war of maneuver once his forces recuperated and were refitted. He would have bypassed the Sukkur bottleneck entirely and opened the Punjab for the next campaign. The Punjab, the "land of five rivers," where all the advantages of terrain would lie with him and not his enemy. And he would have saved untold Roman lives in the process—even Malwa lives, when all was said and done.

If he could hold the Iron Triangle long enough to relieve the pressure on Khusrau and Ashot at Sukkur and allow a reliable supply route to become established on the Indus, using Menander's little fleet of steam-powered warships to clear the way.

One challenge to him having been beaten off, another immediately came to fore. One of the telegraphs in a corner of the large bunker began chattering. Seconds later, as he leaned over the telegraph operator's shoulder and read the message the man was jotting down, Belisarius began issuing new orders.

"The Malwa are trying to land troops in that little neck of land at the very tip of the Triangle," he announced. "Eight boats, carrying thousands of men."

Then, straightening and turning around: "We'll use the Thracians for this, Maurice. Give the Greeks a rest. See to it."

Maurice snatched his helmet from a peg and hustled toward the bunker's entrance, shouting over his shoulder at Sittas: "You Greeks won't get all the glory this day! Ha! Watch how Thracians do it, you sorry excuses

for cataphracts! You'll be crying in your wine before
nightfall, watch and see if . . ." The rest trailed off as
the chiliarch passed through the entrance into the
covered trench beyond.

Sittas smirked. "Poor bastard. I guess he doesn't
know yet that the wine's all gone. My Greeks finished
the last of it yesterday. Come nightfall, when they're
wanting to celebrate, his precious Thracians will be
drinking that homemade beer the Malwa civilians—I
mean, *Punjabi* civilians—are starting to brew up." He
stuck out his tongue. "I tried some. Horrible stuff."

Belisarius gave no more than one ear to Sittas'
cheerful rambling. Most of his attention was concentrated on the map, gauging the other forces he could
bring to bear if Maurice ran into difficulty. His principal reserve, with the Thracians thrown into action,
were the two thousand cataphracts which Cyril had
under his command. Those "old Greeks" hadn't par-
ticipated in Sittas' charge. Belisarius trusted their discipline far more than he did those of Sittas' men, and
so he had put them in charge of the small city which
was being erected in the very center of the Iron
Triangle. A city, not so much in the sense of
construction—its "edifices" were the most primitive
huts and tents imaginable—but in population. Over
twenty-five thousand Punjabi civilians were huddled
there, along with Cyril's men and half of Abbu's Arabs.
Already, Belisarius' combat engineers were working
frantically to design and oversee the construction of
a crude sanitation system to forestall—hopefully—the
danger of epidemic which siege warfare always entailed.

That worry led to another. *Supplies.* They were starting to get low again. Not so much in terms of food
as gunpowder. Even with the Malwa gunpowder which
Sittas' men would have captured in their sally this
day . . .

Belisarius' train of thought was cut short by another burst of chatter from the telegraph. This time, he charged out of the bunker himself as soon as he read enough of the message to understand the drift. After Sittas read it, the big Greek nobleman came fast on his heels.

"No glory for you today!" Sittas cheerfully informed Maurice, as soon as he trotted his horse alongside the Thracian's. "Just as well, really. You would have been *so* disappointed by the libation cup."

Maurice, perhaps oddly, didn't seem discomfited in the least. "I don't think the local beer is really all *that* bad," he said. "I've tried it already. No worse than the stuff a Thracian villager grows up with, after all." The chiliarch stroked his gray beard complacently. "We Thracians are a lot tougher than you pampered Constantinople Greeks, you know. What's more to the point, we're also a lot smarter."

He pointed to the three Malwa ships drifting down the Indus, wreathed in flame and smoke. Five others could be seen frantically trying to reach the opposite bank. "Let Eusebius and his artisans do all the work, what we say. Charging into battle on a horse—all that damned armor and equipment—is too much like farm labor. Hot, sweaty, nasty business, when you get right down to it."

"That last one's not going to make it," opined Gregory. The artillery commander was perched on his own horse on Maurice's left, opposite Sittas. "Anyone want to make it a wager?"

Sittas was known to be an inveterate gambler. But, after a moment's pause while he gauged the situation, the Greek nobleman shook his head firmly. "I don't know enough about these newfangled gadgets to figure out the odds. But since Eusebius is a *Greek*

artisan—best in the world!—I don't think I'll take the
bet. He'll catch it, you watch."

Five minutes later, Eusebius did catch the trailing
ship. Another spout of hellfire gushed from the *Victrix*,
and yet another Malwa would-be landing craft became
a scene of hysterical fear and frenzy, as hundreds of
Malwa soldiers stripped off their armor and plunged
into the river.

Those who could swim started making their way
toward the west bank of the Indus. The others—perhaps
half of them—floundered helplessly in the water. Most
of them would drown. Those who survived did so only
because they were close enough to the lines which the
Victrix's sailors tossed from the stern to be towed ashore
into Roman captivity.

"Reminds me of fishing," mused Maurice. "A good
catch, that. Maybe we'll be able to get enough latrines
dug to stave off an epidemic after all."

Belisarius took no part in that exchange. He had
ridden his horse directly to the pier which his combat engineers had started erecting from the first day
the Iron Triangle was seized. Even the pier itself was
still unfinished, much less the massive armored "sheds"
which Belisarius had ordered built to provide shelter
from enemy fire for the Roman warships once they
arrived. But enough of it was in place to allow
Menander and his barges to start offloading.

"We lost most of the gunpowder and shot,"
Menander confessed, as soon as he came ashore. "Their
damned fortress in the gorge did for that. We'll need
to take that, as soon as possible, or we'll probably lose
supplies on every trip. Might even lose the *Justinian*."

The news about the gunpowder was of some concern to Belisarius, but not much. "We'll have enough

gunpowder to get by, through at least two more major assaults. Maybe three. By that time, hopefully, the *Photius* will have brought more supplies. But there's no chance at all of the *Justinian* being sunk—not by that fortress, at least. You're staying here, Menander. You and Eusebius both. With the *Justinian* and the *Victrix* here, the Malwa have no chance at all of bypassing the fortified lines across the neck of the Triangle with an amphibious attack."

That cheerful thought drove all worries about gunpowder aside. "And wait till you see what those fortifications look like! Even now, before they're completely finished, those earthworks are the strongest the world's ever—"

He broke off, seeing a figure being helped onto the pier by one of Menander's sailors. Even with the bandage covering half the man's head, Belisarius immediately recognized him. All trace of gaiety vanished.

"Oh, Christ in Heaven," he murmured. "Forgive me my sins. That boy wasn't more than eighteen years old."

Chapter 42

Calopodius' first words, almost stammered, were an apology if his presence proved to be nothing but a burden for the general. But he was sure there was *something* he could do—quartermaster work, maybe, or—

"I've got plenty of clerks to do that!" snapped Belisarius. "What I *really* need is an excellent officer who can take command of this mare's nest we've got of telegraph communications." A bit hurriedly: "Blindness is no handicap for that work, lad. You have to listen to the messages anyway, and we've got plenty of clerks to transcribe them and transmit orders."

Calopodius' shoulders seemed to straighten a bit. Belisarius continued. "What I *really* need is an officer who can bring the thing under control and make it work the way it needs to. The telegraph is the key to our entire defensive plan. With instant communications—*if* the system gets regularized and properly organized—we can react instantly to any threat. It multiplies our forces without requiring a single extra man or gun, simply by eliminating confusion and wasted effort."

He took Calopodius by the shoulders and began leading him the rest of the way off the pier himself.

"I can't tell you how delighted I am to see you here. I don't think there's a better man for the job."

Calopodius' lips quirked in that wry smile which Belisarius remembered. The sight lifted at least some of the weight from his heart.

"Well, there's this much," said the young officer. "I got excellent marks in grammar and rhetoric, as I believe I mentioned once. So at the very least I'm sure I can improve the quality of the messages."

By the end of the following day, Belisarius had withdrawn his entire army behind the inner lines of fortification. The final shape of the Iron Triangle—the term was now in uniform use throughout the army, and even most of the Punjabis were picking it up—was in place.

The Iron Triangle measured approximately three miles in width, across the narrow neck between the Indus and the Chenab. The other two legs of the triangle, formed by the meandering rivers, were much longer. But those legs were guarded by the two Roman warships, which made them impervious to Malwa assault by water. The *Justinian*, a faster ship than the *Victrix*, guarded the wide Indus. The *Victrix*, whose paddles made the risk of sandbars less of a menace, patrolled the narrower Chenab.

In the week that followed, the Malwa launched two mass assaults on the fortifications across the neck of the Triangle. But the assaults were driven back with heavy casualties. Belisarius had not been boasting, when he told Calopodius about the strength of those fortifications. In the world which would have been, the Dutch earthworks which Belisarius and Agathius and Gregory had used for their model would hold off the mighty Spaniards for almost a century. So long as his supplies held out, and epidemic could be averted by the rigorous sanitation regimen which the Romans were maintaining, Belisarius was certain he could withstand the Malwa as long as he needed to.

And, every night, as he gazed down on the map in his command bunker and listened to Calopodius' calm and cultured voice passing on to him the finest military intelligence any general had possessed thus far in history, the shape of that Roman-controlled portion of the map filled Belisarius with fierce satisfaction.

It was only a small part of the Punjab, true enough. And so what? An arrowhead is small, too. But, lodged in an enemy's heart, it will prove fatal nonetheless.

After the second assault, the Roman gunpowder supplies were running very low. Belisarius ordered a change in tactics. The big twenty-four pounders which Menander had brought would no longer be used. The great guns went through powder as quickly as they slaughtered attackers with canister and grapeshot. The three-pounders would only be used in case of absolute necessity.

Henceforth, the defense would rely entirely on the mitrailleuse and the old-fashioned methods of sword and ax atop the ramparts. Roman casualties would mount quickly, of course, depending so much on hand-to-hand methods. But Belisarius was sure he could fight off at least three more assaults before the decline in his numbers posed a real threat. Calopodius was doing as good a job as Belisarius had hoped. With the clear and precise intelligence Belisarius was now getting, he was able to maximize the position of his troops, using just as many as he needed exactly where they were needed.

The third mass assault never came. The Malwa began to prepare it, sure enough, but one morning Belisarius looked across the no-man's-land which had been the deathground of untold thousands of Malwa soldiers and saw that the enemy was pulling back. As the morning wore on, it became clearer and clearer that the tens of thousands of troops were being put to building their own great lines of fortification. As if they were now the besieged, instead of being the besieger.

Which, indeed, was the truth. And Belisarius knew full well who had been able to see that truth.

"The monster is here," he announced to his subordinates at their staff meeting that evening in the bunker. "In person. Link has arrived and taken direct charge. Which means that it's ending."

Gregory frowned. "What's ending? I'd think—"

Belisarius shook his head. "Ending. Our campaign, I'm talking about. *We won*—and Link knows it. So it's not going to order any more mass assaults. Not even Malwa can afford to keep paying that butcher's bill. Finally—finally!—even that monster has to start thinking about the morale of its troops. Which is piss poor and getting worse, every time they spill an ocean of blood against our walls."

His subordinates were all frowning, now. Seeing that row of faces, Belisarius was reminded of schoolboys puzzling at a problem.

A very difficult problem in rhetoric and grammar, to boot, chimed in Aide. **Awful stuff!**

The quip caused Belisarius to chuckle softly. Then, as the reality finally began pouring through him, he raised triumphant fists over his head and began laughing aloud.

"We won, I tell you! It's finished!"

In the hours that followed, as Belisarius began sketching his plans for the *next* campaign—the one which would drive Malwa out of the Punjab altogether, the following year, and clear the road for the final

Roman advance into their Ganges heartland—the frowns faded from his subordinates' faces. But not, entirely, from their inner thoughts.

Maybe . . .

True enough, their great general wasn't given to underestimating an enemy, so . . . maybe . . .

But . . .

Then, just before dawn three days later, the telegraph began chattering again and Calopodius relayed the message to Belisarius' tent. The general had already awakened, so he was able to get himself to the pier—what Menander and his sailors were now calling Justinian's Palace—within half an hour.

Maurice had gotten there ahead of him. Within no more than fifteen minutes, all of the other commanders of the Roman army were gathered alongside Belisarius atop the platform which the Roman engineers had thrown up to protect the *Justinian* and the *Victrix*. A great, heavy thing that platform was—massive timbers covered with stone and soil, which could shrug off even the most powerful Malwa mortars which the enemy occasionally sent out in riverboats in an attempt to destroy the warships which gave Rome its iron grip on the Indus.

By then, Maurice had made certain of his count. The *Photius,* steaming toward them out of the dawn, was towing no fewer than three barges. If even only one of those barges was loaded with gunpowder, it no longer mattered whether Belisarius was gauging his enemy correctly. Even Maurice—even gloomy, pessimistic Maurice—was serenely confident that with enough gunpowder the Iron Triangle could withstand years of mass assaults.

"It's over," he pronounced. "We won."

❖   ❖   ❖

Those were the very same words pronounced by Ashot, as he came ashore.

"It's over. We won." The stubby Armenian pointed back downriver. "The Malwa lifted the siege of Sukkur five days ago. God help the poor bastards, trying to retreat back through the gorge, with Khusrau and his Persians pursuing them and no supplies worth talking about. They'll lose another twenty thousand men before they get to the Punjab, unless I miss my guess, most of them from starvation or desertion."

His enthusiasm rolled all the eager questions right under. "Bouzes and Coutzes are pressing them, too! They got to Sukkur a day after the Malwa started their retreat and just kept going, with the whole army. We've got over seventy thousand men coming through the gorge, not one of them so much as scratched by enemy action, and with nothing in their way except that single miserable damn fortress along the river."

His lip curled. "If the Malwa even *try* to hold that fortress, Coutzes swears his infantry will storm it in two hours. I wouldn't be surprised if he's right. Those men of his haven't done anything for weeks except march. By now, they're spoiling for a fight."

The pent-up enthusiasm burst like a dam. Within a minute, the officers atop Justinian's Palace were babbling a hundred new plans. Most of them, initially, involved the ins-and-outs of logistics. Keep one of the screw-powered warships on station at the Triangle at all times, using the other to tow more barges—no risk from that stinking miserable fortress once Coutzes gets his hands on it!—alternate them, of course, so all the sailors can share in the glory of hammering those wretched Malwa so-called riverboats—don't want anyone to get sulky because his mates are starting to call him a barge-handler—

From there, soon enough, the officers started

babbling about maneuvers and campaigns. Race up the Sutlej—nonsense, that's exactly where Link will build their heaviest forts!—better to sweep around using the Indus—hook up with Kungas in the Hindu Kush, you know he's gotten to the Khyber by now!

Long before it was over, Belisarius was gone. There would be time enough for plans, now; more than enough time, before the next campaign. *It's over. We won.* But today, in this new dawn, he first had a debt which needed paying. As best he could.

Calopodius, as Belisarius had known he would be, was still at his post in the command bunker. The news of the *Photius'* arrival—and all that it signified—was already racing through the Roman forces in the Iron Triangle. The advance of the news was like a tidal bore, a surge of celebration growing as it went. When it reached the soldiers guarding the outer walls, Belisarius knew, they would react by taunting the Malwa mercilessly. To his deep satisfaction, he also knew that nowhere would the celebration be more riotous and unrestrained than among the Punjabi civilians living in the city which they had come to call, in their own tongue, a word which meant "the Anvil."

But Calopodius was taking no part in the celebration. He was sitting at the same desk where he sat every day, doing his duty, dictating orders and messages to the clerk who served as his principal secretary.

Hearing his arrival—Calopodius was already developing the uncanny ear of the blind—the Greek officer raised his head. Oddly enough, there seemed to be a trace of embarrassment in his face. He whispered something hurriedly to the secretary and the man put down the pen he had been scribbling with.

Belisarius studied the young man for a moment. It was hard to read Calopodius' expression. Partly because the youth had always possessed more than his years' worth of calm self-assurance, but mostly because of the horrible damage done to the face itself. Calopodius had removed the bandages several days earlier. With the quiet defiance which Belisarius knew was his nature, the young man would present those horribly scarred and empty eye sockets to the world, along with the mutilated brow which had not been enough to shield them.

The general, again, as he had so many times since Calopodius returned, felt a wave of grief and guilt wash over him.

It's not your fault, insisted Aide.

Of course it is, replied Belisarius. *It was I—no other man—who sent that boy into harm's way. Told him to hold a position which was key to my campaign plans, knowing full well that for such a boy that order was as good as if a god had given it. I might as well have asked him to fall on his sword, knowing he would.*

Other boys will live because of it. Thousands of them in this very place—Punjabi boys as well as Roman ones.

Belisarius sighed. *That's not the point, Aide. I know that's true, which is why I gave the order in the first place. But that order—and its consequences—remain mine to bear. No one else. Nor can I trade it against other consequences, as if ruthlessness was a commodity which can be exchanged in a village market. A sin is a sin, and there's an end to it.*

Calopodius interrupted the silent exchange. Rising to his feet, he asked: "Can I be of service, General?"

Some part of Belisarius' mind was fascinated to note that the blind youth was already able to distinguish one man's footsteps from another. But that part was pushed far down, while another part—much closer to the man's soul—came to the fore.

He strode forward and swept the boy into his embrace. Then, fighting to keep his voice even and hold back the tears, whispered: "I am sorry for your eyes, Calopodius. If I could give you back your sight with my own, I would do so. I swear I would."

Awkwardly, the boy returned the embrace. Patting the general's back as if, for all the world, he was the adult comforting the child.

"Oh, I wouldn't want you to do that, sir. Really, I wouldn't. We will need your eyes more than mine, in the time to come. This war isn't over yet. Besides—"

He hesitated, then cleared his throat. "Besides, I've been thinking a lot. And, if you'd be willing, there *is* a great favor you could do for me."

Belisarius pushed himself away and held the lad by both shoulders. "You need but ask. Anything."

Calopodius gestured toward the secretary sitting at the desk. "Well, it's this. I got to thinking that Homer was said to be blind, too. And who ever got as much fame and glory as he did? He'll be remembered as long as Achilles, after all. Maybe even longer."

Before Belisarius could respond, Calopodius was waving his hands in a little gesture of denial. "Not me, of course! I tried my hand at poetry once, but the results were awful. Still, I *am* good at rhetoric and grammar, and I think my prose is pretty good. So—"

Calopodius took a deep breath, as a boy does before announcing a grandiose ambition to a skeptical world. "So I decided to become an historian. Polybius is just as famous as the men he wrote about, really. Even if he's not as famous as Homer. And by the time it's over—even now!—your war against Malwa will be the stuff of legend."

Belisarius moved his eyes from the ruined face and looked at the sheet held limply in the secretary's hand. Now that he was closer, he could see that the writing covered the entire page—nothing like the terse messages which were transmitted to and fro on the telegraph.

"You've already started," he declared. "And you want to be able to question me about some details."

Calopodius nodded. The gesture was painfully shy.

Aide's voice came like a clear stream. **And what could make a finer—and a cleaner—irony? In the world that would have been, your life and work would be recounted by a snake named Procopius.**

Belisarius clapped Calopodius on the shoulder. "I can do much better than that, lad! You'll have to do it in your spare time, of course—I can't possibly spare you from the command bunker—but as of this moment you are my official historian."

He led Calopodius back to his chair and drew another up to the desk for himself. Then spoke in as cheerful a tone of voice as he had used in weeks. "The last historian I had—ah—proved quite unequal to the task."

Chapter 43

Khusrau arrived at the Iron Triangle a week later. He came, along with two thousand of his Immortals, in a fleet of war galleys rowing their stately way up the Indus. The fact that he came in those galleys was enough, in itself, to tell Belisarius that Coutzes had made good his boast to storm the Malwa fortress in the gorge. No Persian emperor would have risked himself against those huge guns in a cockleshell galley, not even one so bold as Khusrau.

Khusrau confirmed the fact as soon as he stepped ashore. That, and many others, as Belisarius led him to the command bunker.

The Malwa were in desperate retreat through the Sukkur gorge, trying to reach the relative safety of the Punjab before they were overtaken by Khusrau's dehgans or simply starved to death.

Thousands—at least fifteen thousand—had either been captured or surrendered on their own initiative. Khusrau estimated that as large a number were simply deserting Malwa altogether and seeking refuge in the plains or mountains.

Sukkur was secure, and the entire Roman army under Bouzes and Coutzes would reach the Iron Triangle within two weeks. No Malwa force could possibly prevent the reunion of the Roman army. Once they arrived, Belisarius would have an army numbering almost a hundred thousand under his command.

Couriers had arrived from Kungas, announcing that the Kushans had cleared the Khyber Pass and held the northwest entrance to the Punjab in their hands. The Malwa were now facing the prospect of a war on two fronts.

Also—very mysterious, this message, but Khusrau asked no questions—another small party of Kushans passed through Sukkur on their way to the Hindu Kush. They asked the Persian emperor to tell Belisarius that all was going well with a certain problem in grammatical usage. Whatever that might mean.

The emperor looked around the command bunker. "This will continue to serve well enough as a headquarters. But you'll need to plan for major encampments along the Indus south of the fork. No possible way you could fit your entire huge army in this— what did you call it?—oh, yes, the Iron Triangle. An excellent name, that."

Khusrau accepted the chair being offered to him by Gregory. Needless to say, the artillery officer had chosen the best one in the bunker, but . . . that wasn't saying much.

Khusrau did not seem disgruntled by the modesty of the chair. It was a bit hard for Belisarius to tell, however, because ever since he'd arrived the Persian's face had been stiff and severe. Quite unlike his usual self, which—certainly by the standards of Aryan royalty—was rather relaxed and expressive.

The Roman general was certain he knew the source of that stiffness. He had deduced Khusrau's purpose the moment he first realized that the Aryan emperor himself had chosen to come to the Triangle. And saw no reason to postpone the issue.

Nor, apparently, did Khusrau. After seating himself, the emperor addressed all the officers in the bunker—Roman and Persian alike—in a tone of voice which was courteous enough, but unmistakably regal.

"Belisarius and I need to speak in private," he said. "I would much appreciate it if you would all comply with my wishes."

The Persian officers left immediately. The Roman ones paused just long enough to see Belisarius' quick little nod. Calopodius, moving in the slower manner which his blindness required, was the last to exit.

As soon as everyone had left, Belisarius went straight to the issue at hand.

"You want the lower Punjab turned over to Aryan sovereignty. Including the Iron Triangle. I will agree to that on the following two conditions:

"First, Persian territory will extend no farther north than Multan—after we take it next year—and will remain on the western bank of the Sutlej. I want to *end* this war, someday, not find myself caught in a new one between the Aryans and the Rajputs. And the biggest inducement the Rajputs will have to agree to a lasting peace is possession of the Punjab and its agricultural wealth. The more so since Rajputana is an arid country."

Khusrau began to speak, but Belisarius held up his hand. "Please. Let me finish. That will still leave you in control of the outlet to the Sind, along with a fair share of Punjab's riches."

Again, Khusrau began to speak; again, Belisarius held up his hand. "The second condition. The Punjabis who have placed themselves under Roman care must be treated well, and respectfully. No parceling out of their land to greedy and hard-fisted dehgans. Do as you will in the Sind, Khusrau Anushirvan, but *here* you must agree to rule directly. These lands must be imperial domain, governed by your chosen officials. And, though I obviously cannot make this part of the conditions, I do urge you to choose those officials wisely."

Finally, Khusrau was able to get in a word. The first of which was a mere snort of amusement. Then: "Have no fear, Belisarius. I have no more desire than you to get into an endless war with Rajputana. Nor—I can assure you of this!—do I intend to allow my dehgans to aggrandize themselves at imperial expense."

The emperor's momentary levity was replaced by his former sternness. "I have already made clear to the dehgans that the conditions of rule in my new provinces will be *imperial* ones. Those of them willing to accept positions as *imperial* servants will be welcome to do so. Those who insist on retaining their ancient rights will be invited to return to the barren lands they came from."

He waved his hand majestically. "Very few of them seem inclined to argue the point. Fewer still, now that I have expanded the ranks of the Immortals to include a full third of the dehgans themselves."

He fell silent, his face as stiff as ever. Belisarius began to feel a small terror growing in his belly. He realized, suddenly, that Khusrau's unusual solemnity had nothing to do with diplomacy. Not, at least, in the sense of that term used by empires instead of . . . friends.

Perhaps Khusrau sensed that growing terror. A bit hurriedly, he drew a scroll from within his imperial robes and handed it to Belisarius.

"This is from Antonina herself, General. She is quite well, I assure you." He hesitated. "Well, not from *herself*, exactly. It is a transcription which one of your scribes made of a message she sent from Barbaricum by way of the telegraph line to Sukkur."

Belisarius took the scroll and began untying the silk

ribbon which held it close. "From Barbaricum? She is not coming up the river herself? I assume—"

Khusrau cut him off. "Best you read the message, General. Antonina *cannot* come up the river. The expedition was a great success. A tremendous success, rather—the Malwa fleet at Chowpatty destroyed, and Chowpatty itself taken; the fleet at Bharakuccha destroyed likewise, and its harbor wrecked if not taken. But she could not linger at Barbaricum, much less take the time to travel upriver. She is, as you will see, needed immediately in Axum. By now, I imagine, she will be almost there."

The small terror, receding as Khusrau began to speak, surged back like a monster. If Antonina herself was well—why an immediate presence in Axum?—it could only be . . .

Finally, the stiffness left Khusrau's face, replaced by simple sadness. "There is bad news also."

Once the scroll had been read, and read again, and then again, and the tears were pouring freely down Belisarius' cheeks, the Emperor of Iran and non-Iran sighed heavily and rose. He came over to Belisarius and laid a hand on the Roman general's shoulder. "I am sorry," he said softly. "Truly I am. I did not know the young king well myself, but I know you were close. You have been a good friend, to me as well as my subjects, and it distresses me to see you in such pain."

Belisarius managed to regain enough composure to place his own hand over the imperial hand gripping his shoulder. It was a rare moment of intimacy, between two of the most powerful men in the world.

"I thank you for that, Khusrau of the Immortal Soul. And now, if you would, I would like to be alone. I need to spend some time with my own."

❖   ❖   ❖

There he remained for the rest of the day, never moving once from his chair. Noon come and gone, his officers began defying his request to be left alone. One by one, beginning with Maurice, they came into the bunker. Not to speak with their grieving general, but simply to place that same hand of comfort on his shoulder. Each hand he covered with his own, though he said nothing in response to their murmured phrases of sympathy and regret.

The only words he spoke, until sundown, were to Aide. And those were not words so much as inner shrieks of pain and sorrow. Words which Aide returned in his own manner.

What Antonina had wondered, Belisarius came to know. Indeed, a crystal could weep, and weep, and weep. But Belisarius never spoke of it to her in the years which came after, not once, except to acknowledge the fact itself. The manner of that weeping remained his secret alone, because it was a wound he would neither reopen for himself nor inflict on his beloved wife.

After evening came, Belisarius rose from the chair and went to the entrance of the bunker. Speaking softly to the sentry standing some feet away, he passed on a request for Calopodius and his secretary.

When the young officer and his scribe entered the bunker, stepping forward somewhat timidly, they found Belisarius sitting at Calopodius' desk, in the same chair he always used when reciting his history. Only by the redness of his eyes and the hoarseness in his voice could the two men, each in his own way, discern any sign that the general had spent the day mired in sorrow.

After Calopodius and the scribe had taken their seats, Belisarius began to speak.

"Every great war, I suppose, requires its own

Achilles. Perhaps that is God's way of reminding us that the glory of youth carries a price worthy of it. I like to think so, at least. It makes the loss bearable, in a way nothing else could. So I will now tell you of this war's Achilles, whence he came and how he came to be what he was."

Calopodius leaned forward, intent, enraptured. The scribe, likewise.

"We must begin with his name. His true name, not the many titles which came after. *Eon bisi Dakuen. A man of his regiment.* Record my words, historian, and record them true and well."

EPILOGUE
An artisan and his officers

"I can't believe he's doing this. Theodora is going to have my *head*."

Stop muttering, said Aide. **You're setting a bad example for your officers.**

Guiltily, Belisarius glanced to his right and left. Sure enough, at least half of his commanding officers looked to be muttering under their breath. Belisarius wasn't the only Roman military leader standing on the docks who, at the moment, was far less concerned with the danger from the enemy than Empress Regent Theodora's headsman's ax.

He turned his eyes back to the man being helped off the steamship which had towed the newly-arrived flotilla to the Iron Triangle. The *Justinian*, that was.

Appropriately enough.

Belisarius gritted his teeth. *I am* not *in the mood for jests.*

Who's jesting? Oh, look what they're starting to unload from the first barge!

Puzzled, Belisarius tried to figure out what Aide was getting so excited about. The cargo being offloaded by one of the simple cranes alongside the dock was a large wicker basket full of . . . *wheels*?

Wheelbarrow wheels, if I'm not mistaken. We can assemble the rest of the gadgets easily enough, with what we have available here—*if* we have the wheels. They'll probably triple the work rate on the fortifications.

The mood lurking beneath Aide's thoughts was insufferably smug. **I *did* suggest wheelbarrows to you, you might recall. But did you pay any attention? No, no. I'm glad to see *someone* isn't blind. If you'll pardon the expression.**

By now, Menander had guided Justinian off the dock and into the protected shed where Belisarius and his officers were waiting. As soon as he sensed that he was in their presence, by whatever means a blind man senses these things, Justinian grinned from ear to ear.

Belisarius was almost stunned by the expression. When Justinian had been Emperor of Rome, Belisarius could recall precious few occasions where the man had so much as smiled. Fewer still, when Justinian became the Chief Justiciar.

"I thought you'd have forgotten about the wheelbarrows," said Justinian cheerfully. "First thing I asked Menander when he showed up at Barbaricum. He was surprised to see me. Still more surprised when I told him it was time to start transferring the shipbuilding design team to the Iron Triangle."

Justinian swiveled his head, turning eyeless sockets to Menander's apprehensive face. Then, swiveled it slowly to face all the officers in the shed.

"Oh, stop scowling," he said, more cheerfully still. "By the time Theodora finds out you let me come to the front lines, erupts in a fury, and sends off a headsman to execute the lot of you, months will have gone by. We'll either all be dead by then, anyway, or we'll be marching triumphantly on Kausambi. In which case I'll have the headsman executed for interfering with imperial military affairs. I can do that, you know. Since I'm still the Chief Justiciar—first one ever, too—I can do pretty much whatever I want."

Belisarius managed not to sigh. Barely. "Welcome to the Iron Triangle, Justinian."

"Thank you." The blind man, who had been many things in his life, but none he seemed to enjoy so much as being an artisan, cocked his head quizzically. "Tell me something, Belisarius. Are you glad to see me?"

Belisarius thought about it, for a moment. His thought processes were helped along by Aide.

Don't be a complete idiot.

"Yes," he said. "I am delighted to see you here. We're going to need you badly, I suspect, before this is all over."

An emperor and his realm

"The actual shipyard, of course, will be moved to Barbaricum," explained Justinian. He leaned back in his chair and placed the drained cup on a nearby table, moving in the slightly deliberate manner of a blind man. "Your local beer's not bad, if you ask me. No worse than what you get in Egypt or Axum."

Belisarius frowned. "To Barbaricum? Why not keep it in Adulis?" He started to make a waving motion with his hand, until he remembered the gesture wouldn't be seen. "I can understand the advantages of having it closer, but—moving all those artisans and ship-builders, most of them Ethiopian—"

"Oh, stop fussing at me!" snapped Justinian. "By now, I do believe I know a lot more about this than you do. The disruption will only be temporary, and after that we'll save a *lot* more time by having much closer contact with the shipyard. Instantaneous contact, once the telegraph lines are laid all the way through."

The former emperor leaned forward, gesticulating with energy. "You *do* understand, don't you, that the Malwa will already have started building ironclad riverboats? Ha! Wait till they see what *I'm* planning to build to counter them!"

Belisarius was still frowning. "That's going to cause some trouble with Khusrau . . ."

"*Trouble*?" demanded Justinian. "Say better—an imperial tempest. The Ethiopians are going to demand that Barbaricum be made an Axumite enclave. Ethiopian territory, pure and simple—just like Chowpatty."

Makes sense, said Aide. **Between Barbaricum and Chowpatty—they'll probably want a piece of Gujarat, too, before this is all over—the Axumites will have—"**

"Impossible!" proclaimed Belisarius.

"Oh, nonsense," replied Justinian airily. "The Axumites can certainly claim to be entitled to it, after all they've sacrificed for Persia."

Yes, they can. Greedy damned Persians! Wanting everybody to rescue them and then trying to grab everything at the same time. The *least* they can do for Axum is give them Barbaricum. Of course—

Belisarius could feel a diplomatic pit opening beneath him. The fury of the Aryan emperor—naturally, *he* would have to be the one to negotiate with Khusrau—

—I can see why Khusrau will be a mite testy. The Persians are a trading nation, unlike the Indians, and so they won't like the fact that between Chowpatty and Barbaricum—Gujarat, too, you watch—the Ethiopians will have

something of a lock on trade in the Erythrean Sea.

Justinian reached into his robes—still imperial purple, whatever else might have changed—and pulled out a bound scroll. "Besides, you don't have a lot of choice. Antonina was just arriving in Adulis when I was about to leave. Once we had a chance to talk—my plans for a closer shipyard, her plans for a stable transition in Axum—she wrote this for you. Lays out everything, as neatly as you could ask for."

Normally, Belisarius would have been delighted to receive a letter from Antonina. But this one . . . He reached for it gingerly.

"She's quite firm in her opinion, needless to say."

She was, indeed. Gloomily, as he read Antonina's letter, Belisarius could foresee furious times ahead of him. Negotiations with his Persian allies which would be almost—not quite—as ferocious as his battles with the Malwa.

Somewhere in the middle of his reading, a part of his mind noticed that Menander and Eusebius had come charging into his headquarters. (Which was still a pavilion. Permanent construction was taking place all over the Iron Triangle, but it was devoted to the necessities of war, not the creature comfort of officers. Although the Persians were starting to make noise about requiring a "suitable residence" for Khusrau, when he came to visit.) But Belisarius paid no attention to their eager words, or the way they were waving around the design sketches Justinian had brought with him. Not until Aide jolted him out of his misery.

You really *might* want to pay attention to this, you know. Persians are Persians. The war goes on. And I personally think you need to squelch any idea about a submarine before it even gets started—hopeless, that is—but Justinian's ideas

**about spar torpedoes strike me as having some
promise. Let the Malwa fuss around with those
clumsy ironclads! We can circumvent them
entirely, the way Justinian's thinking runs.** With
great satisfaction: **Smart man, now that he's not bur-
dened with all that imperial crap.**

Startled, Belisarius looked up. To his surprise, he
saw that Justinian was grinning at him again.

"So, my favorite General. Are you *still* glad to see
me?"

This time, Belisarius didn't even have to think about
it.

"Yes, I am."

An empress and her grief

By the time Rukaiya was finally able to speak,
Antonina felt her ribs might be on the verge of breaking. The sobbing Queen of Axum had been clutching
her like a drowning kitten.

"Thank you," Rukaiya whispered, wiping away her
tears. "I have been so terrified since the news
came—more for Wahsi than myself—that I was not
even able to grieve properly. I was afraid that if
anyone saw even a sign of weakness . . . Horrible
enough that Eon is dead. To have his son murdered
also . . ."

Antonina stroked the girl's hair, nestling her head
in her shoulder. "It won't happen, Rukaiya. I promise. Between me and Ousanas and Ezana, you have
nothing to fear. Wahsi is the negusa nagast, and there's
an end to it. There will be no struggle over the succession. No Ethiopian version of the Diadochi."

Again, the young queen burst into tears. "I loved him so! I can't believe he's gone."

Rukaiya said nothing further for quite a while. Antonina was glad of it, despite the additional stress on her ribcage. No widow that young should be faced with anything in such a time, other than her own grief. Just . . .

Weep, and weep, and weep.

A ruler and her decrees

"As long as she needs," said Antonina firmly. "Weeks, months, whatever it takes. Grieving must be done properly."

Seated on the imperial throne elevated on its great dais, she stared down at the crowd of notables assembled in the audience chamber. The large room was packed with such men, Ethiopian and Arab alike. Officials, military leaders, merchant princes—all of Axum's elite was gathered there.

"As long as she needs," Antonina repeated. She scanned the crowd with cold eyes, daring anyone to challenge her.

The crowd was mute. Clearly enough, from their expressions, any number of the notables would have liked to utter a protest. Of some kind. *Trade will be disrupted! Decrees must be made! Legal disputes must be settled! Promotions to the officer ranks— now more than ever, with all the losses—must be made!*

"I will rule in her stead," decreed Antonina. "Until the queen is able to resume her responsibilities. Her *new* responsibilities, as the regent until the negusa nagast is old enough to rule on his own."

She stared down the crowd, *daring* them to challenge her. That they wanted to, she didn't doubt for a moment. But—

Ousanas was there, standing at her right. Ethiopia's aqabe tsentsen. With the fly whisk of his office in one hand, as was normal during imperial sessions. Ousanas was grinning. Which, in itself, was also normal enough. But there was not a trace of humor in the thing. It was a great cat's grin, a lion's grin, contemplating its prey.

And, on her left, stood Garmat. The old half-Arab, half-Ethiopian adviser to two kings, Kaleb and Eon both, was famous throughout Axum for his sagacity and wisdom. Since Eon's death, and until Antonina's arrival, he had been keeping the kingdom from collapsing into turmoil. Providing his teenage queen, at a time when being queen was the last thing she wanted to think about, with his invaluable counsel and steady support. In its own way, Garmat's solemn forehead was as much of a caution as Ousanas' predator grin, to anyone who might harbor thoughts of contesting the succession.

It was a fearsome triumvirate, between the seated woman and the men standing on either side of her. In the end, however, whatever hesitations any of the notables still retained were dispelled by someone else. A man who, at that moment, reminded them of the ultimate nature of all power.

Ezana, standing at the rear of the chamber, slammed the iron ferrule of his spearbutt onto the stone floor. The harsh sound caused at least half of the notables to jump a bit.

"The Roman woman Antonina was appointed by Eon the Great to oversee the transition of power in Axum," he announced. His loud voice was as harsh as the spearbutt. "I was there, as he lay dying, and bear witness. *Does any man challenge me?*"

Again, the ringing spearbutt on the floor. *"Any man?"*

He allowed the silence to last for a full five minutes. Then:

"It is done. Until the queen is ready to resume her responsibilities—which will take as long as she needs—Antonina rules Axum. Do not doubt it. Any of you. Do not doubt it for an instant."

Again, the spearbutt. "My name is Ezana, and I am the commander of the Dakuen sarwe. The regiment of the negusa nagast, which will serve the baby Wahsi for his fist. Should he need it. Pray to whatever God you pray to, o ye notables, that he does not. Pray fervently."

A queen and her weddings

"And here I thought the *Christian* ceremony took forever," whispered Kungas. "At least they managed it in one day."

"Be quiet," hissed Irene. "You're supposed to be silent for the next hour or two. Even whispering, people can see your lips move."

"You've been whispering too," he hissed back.

"Doesn't count for me," replied Irene smugly. "*I'm* wearing a veil."

In actual fact, the Buddhist wedding did not take more than a day—although it did consume that one in its entirety. But the fault lay not with the religion so much as the circumstances. Irene could have easily chosen a simpler and shorter ceremony, which Kungas would have much preferred. But she told him, in no uncertain terms, not to be an idiot.

"You want to drag half your kingdom to see the

glorious stupa you're having rebuilt on the ruins of the old one? Which just—so conveniently!—happens to be within eyesight of the great new fortifications you're building in the Khyber Pass? And then keep it *short*? Not a chance."

"You'll have to wear a veil all day," whined Kungas, grasping for any hope. "You hate wearing veils."

Irene began stroking her horse-tail. By now, she had become as accustomed to that mannerism as she had ever been to brushing back her Greek-style hair. And found even more pleasure and comfort in the deed. Her old habit had been that of a spymaster; the new one, that of a queen. The horse-tail was a daily reminder that the same insignia flew under the banners of her army.

"I said I *personally* detested wearing a veil, Kungas. But I have to tell you that the day men invented the silly things was the day they sealed their own downfall." The horse-tail stroking became smug, smug. "Take it from me, as a professional intriguer. Best aide to diplomacy ever invented!"

The day after the ceremony, Irene introduced Kungas to the Pathan chiefs. The meeting went quite well, she told him afterward.

"How can you tell?" he demanded, a bit crossly. "They spent most of their time glowering at you, even though you didn't say a single word after the introductions."

Then: "And take off that damned veil! We're in our own private chambers now, and I'm handicapped as it is. Besides"—much less crossly—"I love the sight of your face."

When the veil came off, Irene was grinning. "The reason they're glowering is because I made sure they found out, beforehand, that I'm planning to bring my female bodyguard with me to the pagan wedding ceremony we're having in their hills next month."

Kungas groaned. "Wonderful. Now they'll be *certain* I am the most effeminate ruler in the history of the Hindu Kush."

Irene's grin never wavered. "Oh, stop whining. You're just grouchy at the thought of another wedding, that's all. You know perfectly well that the reason they're unhappy is because they'd *like* to think that—but can't. Not standing in the shadow of that great fortress you're building in the Khyber, watching thousands of Malwa prisoners do the work for you. Those sour old chiefs would give anything to have a set of balls like yours. 'Manly'—ha! Bunch of goat-stealers."

Irene cocked her head slightly. Kungas, by now, was well accustomed to that mannerism also. Again, he groaned. "There's something else."

"Well . . . yes," admitted Irene. "The other reason they're irked with me is because I also made sure they found out, ahead of time, that three Pathan girls recently came into Begram and volunteered for my bodyguard unit. And were cheerfully accepted."

Her horse-tail stroking almost exuded *smugness*. "It seems—who would have guessed?—that the old Sarmatians have *lots* of descendants in the region. And who am I to defy ancient customs, even newfound ones?"

Kungas scowled. For him, the expression was almost overt. The man had found, as his power grew—based in no small part on the diplomatic skills of his wife—that he no longer needed to keep the mask in place at all times. And he was finding that old habit surprisingly easy to relinquish.

The more so under Irene's constant encouragement. She was firmly convinced that people preferred their kings to be open-hearted, open-handed, and—most of all—open-faced. *Let them blame their miseries on the scheming queen and the faceless officials. No harm in it, since they won't forget that the king still has his army, and the fortresses it took for him.*

"You're going to start a feud with those damned tribesmen," he warned. "They find a point of honor in the way one of their women is looked at by a stupid goat. Pathan girls in the queen's bodyguard!"

"Nonsense. I told them I wouldn't *meddle*. Which I'm not. I didn't *recruit* those girls, Kungas. They came into Begram on their own, after having—much to their surprise—discovered that they really weren't Pathan at all. Who can object if Sarmatian girls follow their ancient customs?"

Kungas tried to maintain his scowl, but found the effort too difficult. He rose from his chair and went over to the window. The "palace" they were residing in was nothing more than a partially-built portion of the great new fortress being erected in the Khyber. Atop one of the hills, not in the pass itself. Kungas had grasped the logic of modern artillery very quickly, and wanted the high ground.

He also enjoyed the view it gave him, partly for its own scenic splendor but mostly because it was a visible reminder of his own power. Let anyone think what they would, but the fact remained—Kungas, King of the Kushans, owned the Khyber Pass. And, with it, held all of the Hindu Kush in his grasp. A grasp which was open-handed, but could be easily closed into a fist should he choose to do so.

He made a fist out of his right hand and gently pounded the stone ledge of the window. "Sarmatians," he chuckled. "Well, why not? Every dynasty needs an ancient pedigree, after all."

Irene cleared her throat. Kungas, without turning around to see her face, smiled down at the Khyber

Pass. "Let me guess. You've had that gaggle of Buddhist monks who follow you around every day investigate the historical records. It turns out—who would have guessed?—that Kungas, King of the Kushans, is descended from Sarmatian rulers."

"On your mother's side," Irene specified. "In your paternal ancestry—"

Again, she cleared her throat. Rather more noisily. Kungas' eyes widened. "Don't tell me!"

"What can I say? It's true, according to the historical records. Well, that's what my monks claim, anyway, and since they're the only ones who can decipher those ancient fragments who's going to argue with them?"

Kungas burst into laughter.

"It's true!" insisted Irene. "It seems that when Alexander the Great passed through the area . . ."

A peshwa and his family

In her own palace, except for public occasions, Shakuntala was not given to formality. So, even though some of her courtiers thought the practice was a bit scandalous, she was in the habit of visiting her peshwa in his own quarters rather than summoning him to hers. And, as often as not, bringing Rao along with her.

There were a variety of reasons that she chose to do so. Mainly, two.

First, she was energetic by nature. Remaining in her own quarters at all times would have driven her half-insane. Not so much because of physical inactivity—since she and Rao had married, Shakuntala had resumed training in the martial arts under his rigorous regimen—but simply because of pure boredom.

The second reason was less ethereal. Downright mundane, in fact.

"Ha!" exclaimed Rao, as they neared the entrance to Dadaji Holkar's quarters. He turned his head and cast a skeptical eye upon the baby being borne behind them by his nurse. "You dote on that child, true enough. But you haven't the patience for proper mothering."

Shakuntala swept through the wide entrance leading to her peshwa's portion of the palace. "That's what grandmothers are for," she pronounced, as imperiously as she made all her pronouncements.

And, indeed, Gautami was ready and willing to take care of Namadev. The more so since the baby was not that much younger than her own actual grandchild.

As he watched his wife and the two infants, the peshwa Dadaji Holkar—as was his habit—fell into philosophical musing.

"It's odd, really, the way these things work. I am more and more convinced, by the day, that God intends us to understand that all things of the flesh are ultimately an illusion." He pointed to the two children. "Consider, first, my grandson."

Shakuntala and Rao studied the infant in question, the older of the two boys being played with by Gautami. The boy, along with his mother, had been turned over to a unit of Rao's Maratha guerrillas by a detachment sent by Lord Damodara after his men had overrun the rebel forces led by Dadaji's son.

"That the child's lineage is mine, as a matter of flesh, cannot be doubted. At his age, my son looked just the same. But as for the spirit—it remains to be seen."

Rao frowned. "You are worried about the mother's influence? Dadaji, given the circumstances, the fact that the poor woman's wits are still a bit addled is hardly surprising. The boy seems cheerful enough."

"That's not what I meant," replied Holkar, shaking his head. "Are we really so tightly bound to the flesh at all?"

He fell silent, for a moment. Then, gave Rao a keen glance. "I'm sure you heard the report of your men. The Ye-tai officer who brought my son's wife and child told them, quite bluntly, that he had killed my son himself. Yet, with Damodara's permission, was turning the family over to our safekeeping. An odd thing to do, for a Malwa."

Rao shrugged. "Damodara is a subtle man. No doubt he thinks—"

"Not Damodara," interrupted Holkar. "It's the *Ye-tai* who interests me. It must have been him—not Damodara—who spared the mother and child after slaying my son. Why did he do so?"

"Men are not always beasts. Not even Ye-tai."

"Indeed so. But why did God choose *that* vessel to remind us, Rao? As well send a tiger into a burning hut to bring out a child to safety."

There was no answer. After a moment, Holkar spoke again. "When the war is over, certainly if my daughters are returned to me safely, I will no longer be able to function as your peshwa. I have been thinking about it a great deal, lately, and have decided I no longer accept the basic premises of our Hindu system. Not as it stands, at any rate. There is a possibility—some glimpses which I got in conversations with Belisarius, and, through him, with what the Christians call the Talisman of God but I think—"

"He is Kalkin, the tenth avatar who was promised," stated Rao firmly. "Belisarius himself said as much, in a letter he once sent me."

Holkar nodded. "So I believe also. In any event,

there will be—would have been—a version of our faith called Vedanta. I intend to explore it, after the war, but the effort will make it impossible—"

"Oh, nonsense!" snapped Shakuntala. "My peshwa you are, my peshwa you will remain. Philosophize at your leisure. You'll have plenty of it, after the war. But I will hear of nothing else."

Dadaji hesitated. "My daughters—after all that has happened, they will be unsuitable for a peshwa." His kindly face hardened. "And I will not set them aside. Under no circumstances. Therefore—"

"Nonsense, I said!" The imperial voice, as always, rang with certainty. So might the Himalayas speak, if they had a tongue. "Do not concern yourself with such trifles as your daughter's status. That is merely a problem. Problems can be solved."

Still, Holkar hesitated. "There will be much talk, Empress. Vicious talk."

"And there won't be, if you become some kind of silly monk?" demanded the empress. "Talk is talk, no more than that." She waved her hand, as if brushing aside an insect. "Problems can be solved, certainly the problem of gossip. If nothing else, by my executioners."

An emperor and his executioners

"If it happens again, I *will* have that man executed," declared Photius firmly. He sat upright at the head of the enormous imperial bed, doing his best to look imperial while in his nightclothes. "I *told* him Irene was to have the very first copy."

Tahmina, lying prone on the bed with her head propped up on her hands, giggled in a manner which did not bode well for the emperor's dignity. "You're just angry because you had a bad day with the tutors. Take it out on them, instead of some poor book dealer. Besides, Irene won't really care if she gets the second copy."

Photius' face was as stiff as any boy's can be, at his age. "Still!" he insisted.

"Oh, stop it. Do something useful. Give me a back rub."

Some time later, Tahmina sighed happily. "You're getting awfully good at this."

Photius, astraddle his wife, leaned over and kissed the back of her head. The motion was easy, relaxed. "I love touching you," he whispered. "I'm almost eleven, now."

"I know," she sighed, very happily. "Soon."

A lord and his men

Lord Damodara watched Rana Sanga carefully, as the Rajput king strode back and forth in the chamber which Damodara used for his military headquarters. Sanga was giving his opinion on the progress being made incorporating the garrison of Bharakuccha into the ranks of the regular army.

Damodara was not ignoring Sanga's words, exactly. But he was far more interested in what he could determine of the Rajput's mood than he was of the item actually under discussion. Sanga was given to pacing, and his pacing always reminded Damodara of a tiger's movement. But he was struck by the absence of any sense of fury. He found that absence . . . surprising. And, given what it might imply, more than a little unsettling.

Finished with his report, Sanga came to a halt. As it happened, he stopped his pacing in that corner of the room which held the most peculiar item of furniture in it.

Sanga stared down at the chair, with its gruesome modification. The old bloodstains were still visible. They were brown now, not red, and flies had long since lost any interest in it.

"Why don't you get rid of this damned thing?" he demanded.

"I find it a helpful reminder," replied Damodara. The chuckle which accompanied the words held not a trace of humor. "Of the consequences of misjudgement."

Sanga turned his head and examined his commander. Over the years, he had come to have as good an understanding of the man as Damodara had of him.

"Something is troubling you," he stated.

Damodara shrugged. "It's hard to explain. I am ... a bit puzzled that you do not seem as enraged as I would have thought. You were devoted to your family."

The Rajput looked away, his expression stony. After a brief silence, he said: "I take comfort in philosophy, Lord. In the end, this is all the veil of illusion."

Damodara swiveled his head toward another corner and brought the other two occupants of the room under his scrutiny. Narses, as usual, was sitting in a chair. Toramana, also as usual, was standing.

"Do you also find comfort in philosophy?" he asked. The question seemed addressed at either or both of them.

"I have precious little faith in *any* philosophy," replied Narses, almost snarling. "On the other hand, I believe quite firmly in illusion. More than that, I'm not prepared to express any opinion."

The Ye-tai crossed his arms over his chest. "When I was a boy, my father and brothers taught me to ride a horse and use weapons. They neglected any instruction in philosophy. I never saw any reason since to make good the lack. It's as dangerous to think too much as too little."

This time, Damodara's chuckle did hold some humor. Very wry humor. "I suppose," he said quietly, studying the instrument of Venandakatra's execution, "delving into philosophical waters can be more dangerous than anything."

"Indeed so," agreed Narses. The old eunuch gazed upon Damodara as a statue might gaze upon its beholder. Blank, unreadable. "Especially for a lord. Best to leave such questions unasked. And therefore unanswerable, should someone ever ask you the same."

Damodara returned Narses' gaze for a moment, then looked at Sanga and Toramana. The three men who had become his principal subordinates, over the past two years. The three men who, each in their own way, held his fate in their hands.

That done, he studied the chair in the corner. And concluded, as he did each day when he examined the thing, that there were some experiences best left unknown.

A man and an infant

The two sisters knew of the arrival of the odd party of merchants, almost as soon as it happened. Not because they had seen them arrive, however. As always, such low caste traders and tinkers were taken in through the rear entrance of the palace, far from the wing where Lady Damodara and her maids lived. But the majordomo brought word to his mistress immediately and she, in turn, gave instructions to her maids.

The instructions were clear and simple. Once she was done, her maids were more confused than ever. And not at all happy.

"They will be staying with *us?*" asked the younger sister, Lata. "But—"

"We don't have enough room," said Dhruva, the older. Her tone was respectful, but insistent. "Our chamber is much too small."

"You will be getting new chambers," said Lady Damodara. "Several of them, connected together—and quite isolated from the rest of the palace. It's a suite of sorts, which I think was originally designed for the poor relatives of the palace's original owners. Comfortable, and spacious—I've inspected the rooms myself—though not as fancy as these quarters."

She hesitated a moment. Then: "It's down on the lowest floor. Just above the basement, to which it's connected by a staircase."

Lata grimaced. It no longer even occurred to her to disguise her emotions from Lady Damodara. Their mistress was a friendly woman, and not one she and her sister feared. With many Indian nobles—especially Malwa—such an open expression of sentiment on the part of a servant would have been dangerous.

Seeing her face, Lady Damodara laughed. "You are worried about being pestered by the men who work down there?"

The presence of a large party of workmen down in the basement was by now known to many of the palace's inhabitants. Their presence had been explained by the majordomo as being due to Lady Damodara's desire to expand the basement and, in the process, shore up the palace's foundations. The explanation was accepted by everyone, almost without any thought at all. The palace, for all its luxurious and elaborate design, was an ancient one. Over the centuries, it had suffered considerable decay.

Lata nodded. "There's no way to stop the rumors about our history. You know how men will act toward us."

Her older sister Dhruva added: "Some of them are Ye-tai, I think. They'll be the worst."

The majordomo appeared in the doorway, ready to lead the sisters to their new quarters. Lady Damodara considered him for a moment, and then shook her head.

"I think I'll guide Dhruva and Lata there myself," she announced. "They can return for their belongings later."

The first person the sisters noticed in their new quarters was the hawk-faced man. Ajatasutra, his name was, according to Lady Damodara. They were so relieved to see him that they paid almost no attention to the rest of her introductions. Although, once Lady Damodara had left and Ajatasutra informed them that he would soon be leaving the palace himself—and not returning for an indefinite time—their concerns returned.

"Oh, stop worrying," he chuckled. "I can assure you that being 'pestered' by workmen is the least of your problems."

The gray-haired woman sitting on a nearby settee—a Rajput, by her accent, somewhere in early middle age—laughed cheerfully. The laugh was a rich and warm thing, which matched the woman's face. The sisters felt at least half of their concern drain away. There was an unmistakable *confidence* in the woman's laugh; and, as always, being in the presence of an older woman sure of herself brought confidence to younger ones.

"The *least* of your worries," the Rajput woman chortled. "Trust me, girls. The least."

There were three children in the room, also. The Rajput woman's, presumably. The oldest of them, a boy approximately twelve years of age, stepped forward and bowed stiffly.

"You are under the protection of my family," he announced proudly. "I myself, being the oldest male of the family present, will see to it."

Again, the Rajput woman laughed. "The least of your worries!" She wagged a finger at her son. "Enough of this, Rajiv! You'll cause more trouble with your damned honor than anything else. The girls will be quite safe."

Then, serenely: "Our retainers will see to it." She bestowed an approving gaze upon the two men who were sitting on a settee across the room. Also Rajputs, the sisters suspected, judging from their appearance.

That same appearance, both sisters thought, was a bit at odds with the woman's confidence. One of the men was quite elderly. The other, though young, had an arm in a sling. The signs of long-suffered pain were quite evident in his drawn face, which led the sisters to suspect that his arm was essentially not functional.

Which, finally—reluctantly—brought their attention to the last two men in the room. Who, very obviously, were quite functional.

Hesitantly, the sisters stared at them. Barbarians from somewhere in the west. So much was obvious from their faces. That alone would have made them a bit frightening. The fact that one was a giant—obvious, even while the man was sitting—and the other was perhaps the most vicious looking man either sister had ever seen . . .

The tension was broken by the infant in Dhruva's arms. For whatever odd reason, something about the vicious-looking man had drawn little Baji's attention. He began gurgling happily and waving his arms.

"Look, Valentinian—he likes you!" exclaimed the Rajput woman, smiling. She transferred the cheerful smile to Dhruva and motioned with her head. "Hand the child to him. It's good for him. And he has to get accustomed to children anyway." With a deep, rich chuckle: "Given his new duties."

The man Valentinian did not seem pleased at the prospect. Nor was Dhruva pleased herself, at the idea. But there was something about the Rajput woman which exuded authority, and so she obeyed.

The man Valentinian accepted the child with even greater reluctance than Dhruva handed him over. From the awkward way he held the infant, it was obvious he had no experience with the task. Despite her misgivings, Dhruva found herself smiling. There was something comical about the combination of such a wicked-looking man and a gurgling infant.

In the course of groping as babies do, Baji seized one of Valentinian's fingers in a little fist. Oddly enough, that seemed to bring a certain relief to the man. As if he were finally being presented with a familiar challenge.

"The kid's got a good grip," he announced. Dhruva was surprised by the ease with which he spoke Hindi. A bit of an accent, but much less than she would have expected.

"I guess he's too young to hold a knife," the man mused. "But I can probably start him with something."

Dhruva was startled. "He's not kshatriya!" she protested.

Valentinian's face creased in a cold, evil-looking smile. "Neither am I, girl, neither am I. You think I give a damn about any of that Indian foolishness?"

He looked up at her. And, for the first time, Dhruva

got a good look at his eyes. Very dark, they were, and very grim. But she decided they weren't actually evil, after all. Just . . .

"I don't give a damn about much of anything," he added.

The statement was callous. Oddly, Dhruva found herself relaxing. He was still the most vicious looking man she had ever seen. But Baji was gurgling happily, and tugging at the finger, and grinning in the innocent way that infants do. Perhaps her infant, she decided, had the right of it.

A man who didn't give a damn about much of anything, when she thought about it, probably wouldn't go out of his way to imagine slights and difficulties and problems, either. The statement was callous, looked at from one angle. Yet, from another, it was simply . . . relaxed.

She had known few relaxed men in her life. After all that had happened since she and her sister were led into captivity, she found that prospect rather refreshing.

"I'll bet he could hold a breadstick," the man muttered. "You got any breadsticks in India?"

A general and an historian

"Let's quit for the day," said Belisarius. "Tomorrow we can start with the campaign into Mesopotamia. But I've got to get ready for the staff conference. Can't forget, after all, that I'm waging a campaign *now*. Or will be, soon enough."

Obediently, Calopodius leaned back in his chair, leaving unspoken the next question he had been about to ask. The scribe began putting away the writing equipment.

"How soon, do you think?" Technically, of course, an historian had no business asking such a question. But from their days of close association, Calopodius had become much bolder in the kind of questions he would ask his general.

"Too soon to tell," replied Belisarius, shrugging. "As always, it depends mostly on logistics. Which is complicated enough on paper, much less in the real world. At a guess? Not more than a few weeks."

He gestured with a thumb toward the north, where the sound of distant cannon fire was more or less constant, day and night. "I see no reason at all to give the Malwa any more of a breathing space than I absolutely must. Time is something which is entirely on that monster's side, not mine."

Calopodius hesitated. Then, boldly: "And what, would you say, is the factor which is most on *your* side?"

Belisarius stared at the young historian. Calopodius was so acute that Belisarius tended to forget about his blindness. But now, remembering, he let his crooked smile spread across his face in a manner so exaggerated that it would have brought down instant derision and sarcasm from Maurice and Sittas. Who, happily, were not present.

So he indulged himself in the smile. And indulged himself, as well, by speaking the plain and simple truth.

"The biggest factor in my favor is that I'm just a lot better at this than the monster is. Way better. War is an art, not a science. And for all that monster's superhuman intelligence, it's got about as much of an artistic streak as a carrot."

He rose to his feet and stretched his arms, working out the stiffness of a two hour session sitting in a chair, recounting his history.

"There are times," he said softly, "when I wish I could have been a blacksmith. But then there are other times when I'm glad I couldn't. This time and place more than any other in my life. War is also an honorable trade, after all—or can be, at least. And I suspect I'm a lot better at it than I ever would have been as a blacksmith."

He cocked his head a little, listening to the gunfire. "Soon, Calopodius. Soon I'll put paid to that monster. And teach it, and its masters, that a professional craftsman at the top of his trade can't possibly be matched by any know-it-all cocksure *dilettante*."

Cast of Characters

From the future

Aide: A representative of a crystalline race from the far distant future, allied with Belisarius. Originally developed as an artificial intelligence by the Great Ones to combat the "DNA plague," the crystals became instrumental in the formation of the Great Ones themselves. Aide is sent back in time to counter the efforts of the "new gods" to change the course of human history.

Great Ones: Originating out of humanity, the Great Ones are a completely transformed type of human life. They no longer bear any physical resemblance to their human ancestors. Indeed, they are not even based on protoplasmic biological principles.

Link: An artificial intelligence created by the "new gods" of the future and sent back in time to change the course of human history. It exists in the form of a cybernetic organism, transferring its mental capacity from one human host to another as each host dies.

New gods: A quasi-religious cult from the far future which is determined to prevent the various mutations and transformations which humanity has undergone during the millions of years of its spread through the galaxy. There being no way to overturn that present reality, the new gods decide to stop the process early in human history. They send Link back in time to create a world empire based in northern India, organized along rigid caste principles, which will serve as the basis for a eugenics program to create a race of "perfect" humans.

Romans

Agathius: Commander of the Constantinople Greek cataphracts who were led by Belisarius in the opening campaign against the Malwa in Mesopotamia.

Anastasius: One of Belisarius' bodyguards.

Anthony (Cassian): Bishop of Aleppo. He brought Aide and Michael to Belisarius.

Antonina: Wife of Belisarius.

Ashot: An Armenian and one of Belisarius' bucellarii, his personal household troops. He becomes one of the top officers in the Roman army during the war against the Malwa.

Belisarius: Roman general.

Bouzes and Coutzes: Twin brothers commanding the Army of Lebanon, later top officers in Belisarius' forces.

Calopodius: A young Greek nobleman who serves as an officer in Belisarius' Indus campaign. Later becomes Belisarius' historian.

Cyril: Commander of Constantinople Greek troops.

Eusebius: A young artisan employed by John of Rhodes in creating the Roman armaments project. Later an officer in the Roman navy.

Felix (Chalcenterus): A young Syrian soldier promoted by Belisarius. Eventually becomes an officer, commanding musketeers.

Gregory: One of Belisarius' commanders; specializes in artillery.

Hermogenes: Roman infantry commander.

Hypatia: Photius' nanny; later married to Julian.

Irene (Macrembolitissa): Head of the Roman spy network.

John of Rhodes: Former Roman naval officer, in charge of Belisarius' weapons project.

Julian: Head of Photius' bodyguard.

Justinian: Roman emperor.

Koutina: Antonina's maid.

Mark of Edessa: Another young officer promoted by Belisarius.

Maurice: Belisarius' chief military lieutenant.

Menander: A young Roman soldier; later a naval officer.

Michael of Macedonia: A monk who first encountered Aide.

Photius: Antonina's son and Belisarius' stepson.

Procopius of Caesaria: Antonina's original secretary.

Sittas: An old friend of Belisarius and one of the Roman empire's generals.

Theodora: Justinian's wife and the Empress of Rome.

Valentinian: One of Belisarius' bodyguards.

Ethiopians

Eon: Kaleb's son.

Ezana: Eon's bodyguard; later commander of the royal regiment.

Garmat: A top Axumite royal counselor.

Kaleb: The negusa nagast (King of Kings) of Axum.

Ousanas: Eon's dawazz; later, aqabe tsentsen.

Rukaiya: Arab princess, bride of Eon.

Wahsi: Eon's bodyguard; later a top military commander.

Persians

Baresmanas: a Persian nobleman (sahrdaran), of the Suren family.

Khusrau Anushirvan: King of Kings of Iran and non-Iran.

Kurush: Baresmanas' nephew; a top Persian military leader.

Tahmina: Baresmanas' daughter; Photius' bride.

Malwa

Ajutasutra: Malwa spy and assassin; Narses' right-hand man.

Balban: Malwa spymaster in Constantinople during Nika revolt.

Damodara: Malwa military commander.

Holi: "Great Lady." Skandagupta's aunt; vessel for Link.

Nanda Lal: Head of Malwa spy network.

Narses: Roman traitor; Damodara's spymaster.

Rana Sanga: Rajput king; Damodara's chief lieutenant.

Sati: "Great Lady." Vessel for Link.

Skandagupta: Emperor of Malwa.

Toramana: A Ye-tai general; subordinate to Damodara.

Venandakatra: "The Vile One." Powerful Malwa official.

Marathas and Andhrans

Dadaji Holkar: Malwa slave freed by Belisarius; later peshwa of Andhra.

Dhruva: Dadaji's oldest daughter; Malwa slave.

Gautami: Dadaji's wife.

Lata: Dadaji's youngest daughter; Malwa slave.

Maloji: Rao's friend and chief military lieutenant.

Raghunath Rao: Maratha chieftain, leader of the Maratha

rebellion. "The Panther of Majarashtra." "The Wind of the Great Country." Shakuntala's mentor, later her husband.

Shakuntala: Last survivor of the Satavahana dynasty; later Empress of reborn Andhra; "The Black-Eyed Pearl of the Satavahanas."

Kushans

Kungas: Commander of the Kushans guarding Shakuntala; later king of the reborn Kushan kingdom.

Kanishka: Kungas' troop leader.

Kujulo: Kungas' troop leader.

Vasudeva: Commander of the Kushans captured by Belisarius at Anatha.

GLOSSARY

A note on terminological usage. Throughout the series, the terms "Roman" and "Greek" are used in a way which is perhaps confusing to readers who are not very familiar with the historical setting. So a brief explanation may be helpful.

By the sixth century A.D., the only part of the Roman Empire still in existence was what is usually called by modern historians the *Eastern* Roman Empire, whose capital was in Constantinople. The western lands in which the Roman Empire originated—including Rome itself and all of Italy—had long since fallen under the control of barbarian tribes like the Ostrogoths.

The so-called "eastern" Roman Empire, however, never applied that name to itself. It considered itself—and did so until its final destruction at the hands of the Ottoman Turks in 1453 A.D.—as *the* Roman Empire. And thus, when referring to themselves in a political sense, they continued to call themselves "Romans."

Ethnically speaking, of course, there was very little Latin or Roman presence left in the Roman Empire. In terms of what you might call its "social" content, the Roman Empire had become a Greek empire in all but name. In Justinian's day, Latin was still the official language of the Roman Empire, but it would not be long before Greek became, even in imperial decrees and political documents, the formal as well as de facto language of the Empire. Hence the frequency with which the same people, throughout the course of the series, might be referred to (depending on the context) as either "Roman" or "Greek."

Loosely, in short, the term "Roman" is a political term; the term "Greek" a social, ethnic or linguistic one—and that is how the terms are used in the series.

Places

Adulis: a city on the western coast of the Red Sea; the kingdom of Axum's major port; later, the capital city of the Ethiopians.

Ajmer: the major city of Rajputana.

Alexandria: the major city of Roman Egypt, located on one of the mouths of the Nile.

Amaravati: the former capital of the Empire of Andhra, located on the Krishna river in south India; sacked by the Malwa; Shakuntala taken into captivity after her family is massacred.

Anatha: an imperial villa in Mesopotamia; site of the first major battle between Belisarius and the Malwa.

Axum: the name refers both to the capital city in the highlands and the kingdom of the Ethiopians.

Babylon: ancient city in Mesopotamia, located on the Euphrates; site of a major siege of the Persians by the Malwa.

Barbaricum: the major port in the Indus delta; located near present day Karachi.

Begram: the major city of the Kushans.

Bharakuccha: the major port of western India under

Malwa control; located at the mouth of the Narmada river.

Charax: Persian seaport on the Persian Gulf.

Chowpatty: Malwa naval base on the west coast of India; located at the site of present day Mumbai (Bombay).

Constantinople: capital of the Roman Empire; located on the Bosporus.

Ctesiphon: capital of the Persian empire; located on the Tigris river in Mesopotamia.

Deccan: southern India.

Deogiri: a fortified city in central Majarashtra; established by Shakuntala as the new capital of Andhra.

Gwalior: location of Venandakatra's palace in north India where Shakuntala was held captive.

Hindu Kush: the mountains northwest of the Punjab. Site of the Khyber Pass.

Kausambi: capital of the Malwa empire; located in north India, at the junction of the Ganges and Jamuna rivers.

Majarashtra: literally, "the Great Country." Land of the Marathas, one of India's major nationalities.

Marv: an oasis city in Central Asia; located in present day Turkmenistan.

Mindouos: a battlefield in Mesopotamia where Belisarius fought the Persians.

Muziris: the major port of the kingdom of Kerala in southeastern India.

Nehar Malka: the ancient canal connecting the Euphrates and Tigris rivers; scene of a battle between Belisarius and the Malwa.

The Pass: a pass in the Zagros mountains separating Mesopotamia from the Persian plateau; site of a battle between Belisarius and Damodara; called The Battle of the Mongoose by the Rajputs.

Peshawar: located in the Vale of Peshawar, between the Punjab and the Khyber Pass.

Punjab: the upper Indus river valley.

Rajputana: the land of the Rajputs, one of India's major nationalities.

Sind: the lower Indus river valley.

Sukkur: a major city on the Indus; north of the city is the "Sukkur gorge" which marks the boundary between Sind and the Punjab.

Suppara: a port city on India's west coast, to the north of Chowpatty.

Tamraparni: the island of Ceylon; modern day Sri Lanka.

Vindhyas: the mountain range which marks the traditional boundary between northern India and southern India.

Terms

Anvaya-prapta sachivya: members of the Malwa royal clan.

Aqabe tsentsen: literally, "keeper of the fly-whisks." The highest ranked official in the Axumite government.

Azadan: literally, "men of noble birth." Refers to a class of people in the Persian empire roughly analogous to medieval European knights.

Cataphract: the heavily armed and armored mounted archer and lancer who formed the heart of the Roman army. Developed by the Romans as a copy of the dehgan.

Dawazz: a slave assigned as adviser to Ethiopian princes, specifically for the purpose of deflating royal self-aggrandizement.

Dehgan: the Persian equivalent of a cataphract.

Dromon: a Roman war galley.

Kushans: originating as a barbarian tribe from the steppes, the Kushans became civilized after conquering Central Asia and were the principal support for

Buddhism in the early centuries of the Christian Era; later subjugated by the Malwa.

Negusa nagast: "King of Kings." Ruler of Axum, the kingdom of the Ethiopians.

Nika: the name of the insurrection against Justinian and Theodora engineered by the Malwa.

Peshwa: roughly translates as "vizier." Top civilian official of the Empire of Andhra.

Sahrdaran: the highest ranked nobility in the Persian empire, next in status to the emperor. Traditionally consisted of seven families, of which the "first among equals" were the Suren.

Sarwe: a regiment of the Axumite army. The plural is "sarawit." Individual soldiers are called "sarwen."

Spatha: the standard sword used by Roman soldiers; similar to the ancient Roman short sword called the *gladius*, except the blade is six inches longer.

Vurzurgan: "grandees" of the Persian empire. Noblemen ranked between the azadan and the sahrdaran.

Ye-tai: a barbarian tribe from central Asia incorporated into the Malwa governing structure. Also known as "Ephthalites" or "White Huns."

DAVID DRAKE RULES!

Hammer's Slammers:

The Tank Lords	87794-1 ◆ $6.99	☐
Caught in the Crossfire	87882-4 ◆ $6.99	☐
The Butcher's Bill	57773-5 ◆ $6.99	☐
The Sharp End	87632-5 ◆ $7.99	☐
Cross the Stars	57821-9 ◆ $6.99	☐
Paying the Piper (HC)	7434-3547-8 ◆$24.00	☐

RCN series:

With the Lightnings	57818-9 ◆ $6.99	☐
Lt. Leary, Commanding (HC)	57875-8 ◆ $24.00	☐
Lt. Leary, Commanding (PB)	31992-2 ◆ $7.99	☐

The Belisarius series with Eric Flint:

An Oblique Approach	87865-4 ◆ $6.99	☐
In the Heart of Darkness	87885-9 ◆ $6.99	☐
Destiny's Shield	57872-3 ◆ $6.99	☐
Fortune's Stroke (HC)	57871-5 ◆$24.00	☐
The Tide of Victory (HC)	31996-5 ◆$22.00	☐
The Tide of Victory (PB)	7434-3565-6 ◆ $7.99	☐

The General series with S.M. Stirling:

The Forge	72037-6 ◆ $5.99	☐
The Chosen	87724-0 ◆ $6.99	☐
The Reformer	57860-X ◆ $6.99	☐

Independent Novels and Collections:

The Dragon Lord (fantasy)	87890-5 ◆ $6.99	☐
Birds of Prey	57790-5 ◆ $6.99	☐
Northworld Trilogy	57787-5 ◆ $6.99	☐

MORE DAVID DRAKE!

Independent Novels and Collections: